I0659536

Dark Days, Rough Roads

3rd edition

By Matthew D. Mark

This is a work of fiction. All of the characters, businesses, organizations, and events contained in this work are a product of the author's imagination or are used fictitiously.

Dark Days, Rough Roads

Copyright © 2013 by Matthew D. Mark

Library of Congress Control Number : TXu-1-851-428

All rights reserved.

46600 Vineyard
Shelby Township MI 48317

ISBN Info:
Hard Cover: 978-0-9890045-2-7
Soft Cover 3rd Edition: 978-0-9890045-3-4
E-Book: 978-0-9890045-0-3

My inspiration was born on December 4, 1992 at 7:48 a.m. Without her this story would never exist. Since that moment in time she has been my inspiration for life and for everything that I do. This is for you, Kayla.

Love, Daddy

Acknowledgements:

In fiction there is always a small bit of truth. Without my life experiences and the people I know and love, I would not have been able to create this story. I do not claim to be anything more than a former soldier, a man who loves his country, a man who loves his family and friends, and most importantly, a father who loves his daughter.

My parents Richard and Beverly have taught me that nothing in life is easy. They taught me that life will deal you the hardest hand that it can. It was through watching their hardships and their struggles and how they overcame them that they taught me life's lessons and how you can survive anything with hard work, perseverance and love. I love you both.

Each and every family member has played a pivotal role in my life one way or another. We've shared the best of times and we have shared the worst but we have always been there together. My brothers and sister, thank you all. Families are the last great institution that America has; never fail them and protect them always.

My girlfriend has been by my side the past several years and has supported me through everything I have done. Without her I could not have completed this project. Just being by my side has meant a lot to me. Love you, sweetheart.

I wish to thank my ex-wife Candy. She and I brought our daughter into the world. Thank you for giving me such a wonderful child. After you and Mike read the story, please don't tear out the walls. Thank you for watching her while she's at school.

To all of those who I served with, all of the stupid things we did and all of the brotherhood we have shared. I would not trade it for anything in the world. I am privileged to have served with all of you. If you judge a man by the company he has kept, then I am judged among the best that there is.

Michelle, thank you for the horse information and contributions you made by letting me include you and your family in the story. It helped a great deal and I appreciate your friendship. Stay safe. Each and every person whom I have met touched my life in one aspect or another. I always take away something from everyone I meet. Of course, I can't forget my cat, Romeo, and Max, the mutant dog.

My sincere thank you to Kathleen K. and Michelle K. for the second editing, WWO for the third, and to Lacey O'Connor for the cover design.

Preface:

An alarm clock wakes you up in the morning; your coffee is brewed in an electric coffee pot. You use a computer or television to check your morning news. Your smart phone contains your daily, weekly, or monthly schedule along with the contact information for everyone you know, and it connects you to the world. You rely on an automobile to take you to work, to school, to the store or someplace else. This auto is more computer than it is car.

The food you eat and the products you use are brought in by truck and rail, rolling computers as well. Its cargo is stocked and inventory is electronically controlled. You pay by cash or most likely using a plastic card with a magnetically encoded stripe on it connected to your bank. Almost everything you do daily is affected in one way or another by technology.

This technology is run by electricity—a single spark to start it all. But we have to ask ourselves, without that spark, without that technology, how would we live? How different would life be? Could we still thrive? More importantly, if it changed today or tomorrow, could we survive?

Mother Nature's coronal mass ejections, sun activity, nuclear weapons, electronic weaponry, and more can take that spark away in an instant. Most are manmade; however, we must look at the changing world around us and wonder. Out of seven billion people, how many does it take? It takes only one. Millions of lives can be changed by only one. Yes, one person with an agenda, a grudge or a hatred for a nation.

The premise of the event in this book as illustrated above is made simple. What we cannot simplify offers just as much opportunity to bring a nation and its people to their knees. Financial collapse as seen in Greece, Russia, Romania, Bulgaria, and more show how fragile economics are. The U.S. has spun out of control with our national debt and our own economy.

Each year as we stand in lines for flu shots, the experts are trying to predict which strain will affect us most. Although the eradication of many of the world's most devastating diseases has occurred, there still exist the samples, which are easily propagated. Naturally-evolving strains of disease develop quicker than scientists can name them. Add biological warfare and nerve agents and it becomes incredibly concerning.

Natural disasters are frequent. People are still living in tents months after Hurricane Sandy. They lived in shacks or trailers for years after Katrina. Rising rivers, floods, earthquakes, tsunamis, droughts, and snowstorms all affect our lives from days, to months, and sometimes years. You must be able to survive. How many people can the government rescue at once? These disasters have shown us that the answer is very few. These disasters can take the people away who control that same spark.

A simple job loss and lack of income can affect you. The saying is "Stockpile beans and bullets." If you look around, if you pay attention to world events and our own country and what has transpired in our short history, doesn't it make sense to take some simple measures to protect you and your family?

You'd be surprised how affordable it is to survive. I'd rather have it and not use it than need it and not have it.

Table Of Contents

Chapter 1

The weather outside was pleasant and the temperature was 70 degrees. The sky was partly cloudy and a nice, bright sun poked through. It was not too hot or too chilly outside, and with this kind of weather Roger Haliday did not expect any problems when the helicopter landed. It would be another routine med flight, if indeed there was a routine flight for these guys.

Haliday had been out circling the hospital campus in the patrol vehicle when dispatch had called and told him the med flight was due to arrive in 10 minutes. This was one of his typical duties as a hospital Public Safety Officer. Haliday shot over to the helipad, where he unlocked the gate and took the cover off the 150-pound beast of a fire extinguisher they called Purple K, named after the aviation fuel fire suppression chemical it contained.

Not wanting to get wind whipped by the rotor blades, or the small debris being kicked up, Haliday retreated into the patrol vehicle and awaited the arrival of the bird. Hearing the telltale *thump-thump-thump* of the main blades, he watched closely as he had dozens of times before. Across the way, a few cars had stopped on the nearby side street to watch.

He reached down and turned off the vehicle's strobe lights and then the vehicle itself. They usually kept the strobes on until they spotted the aircraft, but then turned them off as soon as they suspected the pilot had the helipad located. There was no sense in blinding the pilot with blinking lights while he was landing.

It was always cool to watch this sleek aircraft seemingly just land for no reason in the middle of a neighborhood. This, of course, was not the case now. Stroke victim, burn patient, car accident or what not, someone needed extreme care and quickly. Still, it always drew curious onlookers.

He looked over at a large house that backed up to the helipad. Some genius had built six brand new houses right next to it. This put them up against a helipad and parking lot and was not worth the money the people had spent for the homes they lived in. The homes also bordered Pontiac, which was a less than desirable area.

Once a resident had called and complained about a med flight coming in at 0700 hours on a Sunday morning. Haliday had taken the call and said, "Hey genius, in case you didn't know, emergency medical flights generally aren't scheduled." The man just called him a smartass and hung up on him.

A few weeks later, karma played a role when the man who'd called in was hosting a picnic as another helicopter landed. Haliday still had to laugh about the flying plates, cups, and napkins whenever he thought about it.

Watching the landing before him now, Haliday called in to dispatch to have them mark the time and say the bird, this one a Eurocopter, had almost landed. They marked arrival and departure times in case the FAA audited their records. There wasn't a response from dispatch, which wasn't unusual due to the fact that dispatch was usually tied up with more important things. These were mostly caused because the campus was in the middle of a small city outside of Detroit; it was, however, just as bad.

Haliday was taking a sip of his pop when he noticed the problem. As he tilted his head back to drink, he saw the Eurocopter wobbling violently as it spun toward the ground. Haliday ducked down, using the engine compartment of the truck as a shield just as the helo struck the ground and exploded, sending pieces in every direction. A small piece of the tail rotor shot through the windshield of the vehicle, causing chunks of glass to fill the interior of the Tahoe.

Haliday slowly lifted his head and saw a wall of flames and a pile of machinery. Nobody was coming out of that wreckage alive. He grabbed the radio mic again and called for dispatch to contact the fire department. Again there was no response, so he took it upon himself to use his cell phone. A quick push of the power button revealed there was nothing but a dark screen.

He ran over to the beast called "Purple K" and charged the extinguisher system while holding the hose. He dumped every ounce of extinguisher agent on the flames, but it was useless. Looking toward the people who stopped to watch the landing, he could see them trying the same exact thing with their cell phones. This is when he realized what had happened.

Life had changed drastically in a matter of seconds.

Haliday knew it for what it was. He also knew what it would mean for the city and its unprepared inhabitants. An EMP, or electromagnetic pulse had struck. It was that, or a Coronal Mass Ejection, commonly known as a sun flare.

As he walked past the folks, someone said, "Why aren't you helping?"

Haliday said, "Unfortunately, there's nothing I can do. You all need to hurry home. An EMP has hit us and life as we know it has changed." They had no understanding of what he really meant and just looked at him with puzzlement.

Haliday continued to walk back toward the hospital in what was now a very quiet neighborhood that lacked any noise save for the slight, dull roar of flames from the burning wreckage. They were the only sounds anyone could hear. There was no music, no cars, no hum from the electric lines, no noise from anything at all.

He walked past the ER and saw staff running around like chickens with their heads cut off. It was almost as if they thought they would be able to do something about what was going on. It would have been comical if it wasn't for the fact that they really had no clue what would be transpiring in just a matter of a few short hours.

As he approached the dispatch office, he ignored those who were asking him questions. The dispatch officer was standing at the open door as a handful of people asked her questions—questions she could not answer.

"What happened?"

"Is it a power outage?"

"Will the generators come on?"

"Why aren't they?"

"How come the phones don't work?"

And many more.

The dispatch officer shrugged her shoulders and said, "I don't know. I don't have any answers myself."

Haliday looked her in the eyes and said, "Dawn, You need to leave."

She looked concerned, but not frightened. It was at this time, by telling her to leave, that he confirmed what she thought had happened. Thanks to Haliday, she was ready for the event. She grabbed her personal items and left the dispatch area. Haliday did the same and left as well, passing by the people who could not believe the campus public safety officers were leaving them at a time like this.

Haliday walked into a bathroom. It was dark, so he hit the SureFire flashlight on his belt to light it up a bit and was slightly startled when he heard a voice from a stall.

"Hey man, what's going on in here? I came in to drop a deuce and the power went out. Everything okay out there?"

Haliday told him, "Don't worry; everything will come out okay."

The guy missed the joke. Haliday told him about the EMP.

Haliday went back to doing his own thing. He commenced to quickly change from his uniform into regular old gray man camo. He put on jeans, a shirt, and a ball cap, knowing it would be stupid to look like any type of police officer, soldier or government agency robot. That would just cause issues so he had decided long ago to just blend in. He knew elsewhere that the Dawn had either already done the same thing or was doing the same thing at the moment.

Quickly stripping the gear off his duty belt and taking what he needed, Haliday then left the bathroom. He had his pack, which was dark maroon in color to help blend in, and started toward an exit door located near the administrative hallway.

A voice called out from a small conference room and Haliday walked down the darkened hall to talk to the public safety supervisor who had been helping set up the hospital's incident command center. It was just a small conference room, limited to a dry erase board and easel with paper.

The supervisor asked him where he was going.

Haliday looked around in the room to see the administration staff with various managers and staff from other departments milling around. Haliday looked at the supervisor and said, "You have no idea what just happened and what's going to happen around here do you?"

With a puzzled look, the supervisor asked, "What do you mean? It's a power outage; we get them now and again."

Haliday chuckled and said, "Not like this."

One of the managers heard the chuckle and took it upon herself to ask what was so funny. "This is no laughing matter," she said. "There will be a lot of inconvenienced people who will be upset."

None of these people had a clue even now. Haliday coughed loudly, in a very exaggerated manner, and asked for everyone's attention. Most everyone stopped what they were doing and looked at him.

"What you people fail to understand here is the fact that this is no regular power outage. This was an EMP – an electromagnetic pulse – from who knows where," Haliday said.

Immediately, the maintenance director interjected and said it was irresponsible to even mention an EMP, that it was simply a power outage. Haliday looked him in the eye and told him he could only hope. He briefly explained what an EMP was, and then began to explain how he knew this was what it was. The explanations were simple enough, but by the looks on the faces of the others, you would have thought he was trying to explain rocket science.

First off he explained the lack of power and the fact that none of the emergency lights had come on. Next were the generators, which were sitting quietly. After that he explained the lack of landlines and the lack of cell phones having power, let alone a signal. Even the most basic of all types of items were dead. As soon as he explained the helicopter crash, which they hadn't even heard about yet, their jaws dropped.

More people started coming into the room, and also gathered in the hallway to either listen to or add to the confusion. They started complaining about the fact that *this* didn't work, *that* didn't work, the staff needs *this*, and the staff needs *that*, the maintenance crew isn't fixing anything, et cetera. Haliday could see they had no idea how far up the creek they were without the proverbial paddle.

The CEO asked the maintenance director when power would be back on and everyone awaited the answer. The CEO stood silent, then repeated the question, which had an answer nobody wanted to hear. The maintenance director simply said that he honestly believed it was now indeed an EMP and there would be no power any time in the near future. He said there was simply nothing that could be done and then he turned and walked away. People were still dumbfounded and did not know what to do, and so they just sat there.

One lady spoke up. "Things cannot be that bad."

Haliday moved toward the front of the room and everyone focused on him. He looked around, saw the infectious control officer, and asked her how long the rooms and patient equipment could last without being cleaned. She responded by saying that in some of the isolation rooms it would have adverse effects within a day; within two days, about a fourth of the hospital would have undesirable consequences, and by the end of the week it would be a pure hellhole filled with far too many infectious diseases to even start naming them right now. This did not include waste handling, lack of water for toilets and sinks, and linen exchanges that would not happen.

He looked over at the housekeeping director and asked him how long before the trash cans were full, how long before the outside dumpsters would overflow, and how long until rodent control would lapse.

"Two days. That's all," the head of housekeeping said.

Haliday said, "You could add that to the infectious disease issues and realize things will be getting far worse much faster than anyone could expect."

The food services department piped in and said the spoiling of fresh food would start within days; the freezer would stay cold a few days and the fridge maybe two, he estimated.

Haliday informed him the food would be gone in a matter of two to three days anyway with as many people as there would be looking to eat. Even less as people would start to show up thinking a hospital was a safe haven. There wouldn't be any food deliveries each day like they normally had either.

He looked around once more and told them that these were basic issues that people took for granted. "Look around," he said. "Look how dependent we are on technology. IV pumps no longer working, pain med pumps not giving people morphine and other drugs, no blood pressure monitors, no pulse oximeters, no telemetry, no nothing." Haliday continued, "What you now have is a lot of people who need to leave before a lot of people start a slow, painful death."

It wouldn't be a good place to be and he started heading for the door. "I surely won't be here more than the time it takes me to get my personal gear out of my truck and leave, myself," he added, looking back at them. "That brings up another point: good luck starting your cars and making it home."

He knew some of the people in that room commuted 30 to 50 miles one way. He paused only briefly to look around at the folks who still didn't get it, although a couple of them had excused themselves already for one reason or another, most likely on their way out the door as well.

Haliday left the room.

In the meantime, during this little meeting, all hell was breaking loose around the facility. The surgical center and outpatient procedures center were trying desperately to wrap things up and stabilize patients. Unfortunately for one, there was no hope. As soon as the equipment stopped, there was no suction for clearing the surgical sites. There were no blood pressure monitors to alert anyone of low blood pressure and old fashioned cuffs were a thing of the past due to their mercury content. Most of the OR equipment was electronically controlled, so it had failed. It was a fast crash and thankfully the patient had not woken up from the anesthetic.

Up on one of the long-term care floors, they had six people on ventilators. The nurses and patient care associates were all trying to manually vent these patients, but the staff was tiring very quickly. Screams for more staff to come and help fell on deaf ears. There were simply too many patients to care for in a situation like the power failure of this magnitude. The staff was rapidly growing exhausted.

Too many patients needed care and too little staff was in the facility. Someone needed to triage and make a determination of who would live and who they would have to let go. The grand idea of saving everyone was just that—a grand idea. If they knew what the next few days would be like, they would have walked away at that moment. It was a noble idea to try and wait things out, to help the patients, but it was a risk that would be useless.

Some of the staff already started leaving. A few years back, they had had a massive power outage in the state and even with the emergency generators running and limited power, they had left in droves to go home and take care of themselves. Roughly 30 percent had left then, and even more refused to go into work.

Housekeeping, food service, maintenance, and other support staff were underpaid and would not care about working to keep the place running. Knowing it was a permanent problem, they would now care even less. The lack of these workers would impact how quickly the facility would fail.

Haliday stopped just before exiting the building as another guy shook a snack machine located by an exit near the back of the hospital. He looked at Haliday and asked him if he knew how to get a refund. Haliday pulled out his knife, which had a window punch on the end, and pressed it against the glass. The glass shattered. Haliday reached in and grabbed a few candy bars and told the guy to help himself.

Haliday walked out to his car and passed by a few others doing the same. The only difference was that he was going out to get his pack and gear and they were sitting there trying to start their cars. He heard an engine start and looked in the direction of the noise where he saw an old Ford F100. As odd as it was to see a running vehicle, it didn't surprise him.

As it slowly crawled through the parking lot, passing a few cars dead in the aisles, the driver stopped just as Haliday put his pack on and loaded his rifle which had been under the back seat of his truck. He readied himself for his walk home.

The driver was an older guy in his late 60s. He looked at Haliday and asked him where he was heading.

Haliday said, "East."

Shockingly, the driver told him he was heading that way and offered him a ride.

Haliday was not too sure about the proposal, but eyeing the passenger seat he saw a smaller bag and an empty pistol case. He noted that the pistol was strapped on the old guy's thigh. *Good company to be in possibly*, he thought. He started to refuse though.

"Hey, I'm looking for a little security until I get out of this crack hood," the old guy said, "and you seem to be one of the only ones who know what's going on, so I'm taking a chance. I saw a gal in her late 30's and in a uniform get in her car, change, and then pull a bike out of the trunk. She too had a pack. She took off before I could call out to her. I'm thinking by your squared-away looks you two were friends."

Haliday smiled and nodded yes. He then told the old guy the woman was Dawn, a dispatcher at the hospital. Haliday told the man he could stay with him about 20 miles due east and that was it. The old guy said that was fine with him. There was a different setting altogether in that direction.

Haliday was 6'2" tall and weighed 250 pounds. He was 46 years old and although he walked regularly for exercise, he was actually thankful for the ride. It would definitely save him some time as well.

The two pulled out onto the road, dodging cars here and there, and drove a bit in silence as they passed by people standing in the road and on the sidewalks. There were actually a couple other cars running, older models, but it was evident they were just old, not selected or prepped like the man's old Ford was. They talked a bit, about just a little of this and that, with no real subject, and neither brought up the EMP or the future. After about 30 minutes, Haliday said he was ready to bail and the old guy stopped the truck in a clear area of the road.

Haliday shook the man's hand, told him thank you, and wished him the best of luck.

The old guy said, "You're quite welcome and I pray you keep safe."

Haliday said, "Well sir, right now we all need to pray." Seeing the running truck, people started heading their way and Haliday told him he better get going. He waved goodbye as he started off to the shoulder of the road and toward an off ramp.

He heard the drum of the old Ford's engine dwindle away. He laughed out loud. "Yep, we all need to pray."

Chapter 2

Haliday stepped down off the shoulder of the road and looked at the surrounding suburbs. He then took a few more steps to cross over the ditch. The ground under his feet felt spongy. When he looked closer, he could see the soil was wet and since there had not been any rain in the past few days, he didn't know why. He squatted down a bit to pick up a leaf which was stuck halfway in the muck. He grabbed it by the dry stem and took a quick sniff.

It was definitely water and not sewage as he thought it might have been. At least that was a good sign; sewage would bring disease real quick and he wasn't sure how long the municipal waste system would last. He was still on well water and a septic field, so he didn't pay much attention to that information.

Slowly standing up, he looked around and saw a younger guy working under the hood of his car like it was going to do him any good. Looking past the car he saw a substation for the water system. Out here in the suburbs, he was really not far from the Detroit city limit, give or take 12 miles or so, and the water that was used was purchased from the city. It was pumped throughout Lower Michigan with pump stations scattered around the counties to help boost water pressure.

Toward the east side of the fence line there was a large pipe coming out of the ground in a sweeping elbow which reminded him of the air intakes on old ships. This one, however, was dumping water into a retention pond that had apparently overflowed a while ago. Off toward the actual substation building, he spotted another guy who appeared to be working on valves. The man was feverishly turning valves on *this* pipe, more valves on *that* pipe, and it looked like a losing battle. This interested Haliday and he started heading that way.

The young kid working on his car looked up at Haliday and then turned white. The kid started to visibly tremble at the sight.

Haliday saw his fright and had not realized it at the time, but at this particular moment the kid was looking at a guy with a .40 caliber strapped to his belt and carrying a rifle slung on his pack—just not normal for the area.

Haliday said, "Take it easy, kid; just moving on through to go check out that water plant. I'm not going to hurt anyone."

The kid got inside his car and just watched as Haliday strode by.

Coming up a little closer to the substation, Haliday saw a sign warning trespassers of an electrical fence, so he stopped. He just stood there a moment longer, watching the worker turn valves, cussing as he did so. Haliday started to wonder how the water was being pumped and doubted the extreme nature of the emergency, thinking the power loss was actually sporadic and not an entire regional or national loss. This was the reason Haliday didn't get too close to the fence.

The worker glanced up and saw him standing there. He, too, stopped dead and looked at Haliday. Again Haliday found himself telling another person not to worry. This time he got a response.

"No offense, partner, but you don't look like you're out hunting rabbit," said the worker.

Haliday said, "I guess you're right, but anyway, my name is Roger and I was just curious as to why the pump station has power when the rest of the area is out."

The guy said, "We don't have power."

Confused a bit, Haliday asked how the water was being pumped. He got a one word answer to that question.

"Gravity."

Haliday said, "I don't understand; how can that be? Could you put it in layman's terms for me? I'd appreciate it." He was always looking for this kind of information; you never know what you may need to do and how to do it.

The guy working the valves said, "It's simple. The river downtown is a lot lower than the land out here in the burbs. The pumping stations are daisy chained together to pump the water up the elevation. The pumps stopped. The back flow valves were electromechanical and they failed along with the safety valves. Therefore, all of the water pumped into the burbs is now flowing back toward the main plant and coming out of the overflows into the retention ponds located near their substations."

Haliday understood. The pond being past capacity was why the ditch was wet. The water had to go somewhere. When he thought about it, it really made sense. He asked one more question. "How much water is flowing back and what's going to happen at the main station?"

The guy paused, then said, "I don't know, but the worst that could happen is that the main plant and downtown Detroit get a few wet streets."

"No big loss," Haliday said. "As a matter of fact, that place could use a bath. Not quite the infamous Motor City with sprawling plants, bustling workers and shops that it used to be," he added thoughtfully.

He thanked the man for his time and started moving on again. He had a plan that required some very delicate adherence to time tables. He had a goal to achieve and the quicker the better.

He was only about a mile and a half away from home at this point and this early on, in what he knew would become a dire situation, he just took the sidewalks and streets. Very few people would be a threat now, but he was still acutely aware of what was going on around him. He was closer to home and cutting through a parking lot by the small local grocery store when he noticed they had the doors propped open.

Ahh, just a few steps out of my way, he told himself. He walked in.

Eddie, the store manager, spotted him and told him they were closing up.

Haliday nodded and told him, "Okay," before turning and walking out.

Eddie shouted out, "Hey, are you going bear hunting or something, Roger?"

Haliday said, "Eddie, if I were I would lock this place up tight and save the food for you and your families. Things are going to be turning to crap real fast in this country. Good luck, Eddie." He continued walking out, not saying another word.

On his way out he looked at the store front. Typical of a grocery store, it was all windows. He wondered how long these would last. Other than the back set of double doors and the one rollup loading dock door, this front entry was the only way in. Chances were that when he got back this place would be stripped clean. He didn't give it any thought; he had what he needed, but of course he always wanted more.

Hell, he thought, *I'd have been happy to walk out with a few bags of rice and beans.* That thought made him chuckle. *Beans, beans, and more beans,* he thought. *Oh boy, the butt trumpet was going to be playing a continuous melody shortly.* Simple things amused simple minds, but that was not really the case here. He was an average guy. Things like that were just plain funny.

He thought more about the market. The place would be an absolute nightmare. He didn't buy into the whole three-day food supply theory. He knew that once people realized it was their last chance, the place would be stripped in hours. *Three days my ass,* he thought. *Not in this neighborhood.*

On the other side of the strip mall, at the end, was his favorite pizza place. He found there were a few folks inside, too. It looked like all kids in their late teens. He waved at the kids who were cleaning up and getting ready to close the store. One waved him over. This kid was 6' tall, around 220 pounds with black hair.

Haliday told him he was in a hurry, and the kid, named Blake, said, "We have a couple pizzas nobody picked up. You want one?"

There was no hesitation. Haliday agreed and even offered to pay for it, but they told him not to bother. He thanked them, took the box and started to walk out. When they asked him if he knew what happened, he said, "No idea."

One kid said, "Well, sir, based on your firearms, I'd say you have a very good idea."

Haliday felt a little bad about his answer. He looked at the kids and asked them how far away they lived. A couple of miles away was the farthest any of them lived. He told them to listen carefully. He then advised them to forget about cleaning the store, forget about locking it up, and forget about anything other than getting home as soon as they could.

Gather as much food and water as you can. Out of the three kids, two left immediately. The third, Blake, who commented on his guns looked him square in the eyes and asked him just how bad it was.

"It's real bad—worse than you could ever imagine," Haliday said.

The kid grabbed the last three boxes of pizza and left in a hurry after locking the door.

Haliday opened his pizza box and took a slice out and started to eat it. It was room temperature, but he didn't care too much; it was going to be the last pizza he ate for a long time. He walked out and headed straight for the sidewalk. He saw the last kid dart down one of the nearby side streets. Haliday figured most of them were from the neighborhood.

He had almost reached the sidewalk when he looked across the street and saw the oil change shop. He made a mental note of it; although sooner or later someone would take the drums and bottles of oil, they might overlook the waste oil tank. This could be filtered and used for a variety of purposes and even burned if necessary. He started back on his way home.

As he continued to walk along the sidewalk, more and more people started looking at him. *How funny this must be to see*, he realized; *this six-foot two-inch tall, 250-pound guy with a gun strapped to his waist and a rifle slung on his backpack walking along eating a pizza like it was just another stroll in the neighborhood.*

Just 10 minutes later, he was almost home. It was a typical suburban neighborhood but with half-acre lots and the houses too close for comfort. He did not have the resources to relocate like he had wanted to thanks to the wonderful economic conditions. He had to make do with what he had and that was fine with him as long as his plans would hold.

If he could maintain a good level of security, he should be fine. He paused long enough to tuck the pistol away along with his good old rifle, which was an Armalite AR180 with a folding stock, somewhat similar to an AR15. He took his pack off, folded the stock and slung the rifle on his back and then put the pack back on.

He looked like just an average guy except for the backpack and of course the pizza box. He was not worried about his neighbors, who were out and about and talking to each other. He had maintained a great level of OPSEC—Operational Security—and seeing him with his backpack was a normal everyday event. He'd told them before it was his uniform and equipment from work and they never paid him any attention after that. They didn't this time either.

He waved as he passed the folks. He said, "Hell of a power outage, huh?"

He got a few nods in return. One neighbor said, "Sure is."

He walked the last couple of hundred yards to his house. Approaching the door, there was an electronic cipher lock which he attempted to use out of habit. No luck of course; he dug into his pocket and fished out the back up key.

As soon as he opened the door and stepped in, he breathed a sigh of relief. In one sense, it was good to be home, but in another it was bothersome because he would have to temporarily leave for a few days or more and wasn't sure what he would come home to in that amount of time. He walked around the house and made sure all of the windows and doors were locked.

He peeked out into the attached garage at his baby and said, "I'll be out there shortly. For goodness' sake," he said as an afterthought, "it's a truck. Don't talk to it. You have work to do and the quicker the better."

It was mid-October and the Michigan weather was so varied that even though one day it was sunny and 70, the next could be wet and 40. Fall was here and the impending winter would be harsh with all things considered.

The first thing he did was go over to the fuse box and turn off the main power. No sense in any lights or anything coming on by accident. Next he reached down by the floor and flipped a single switch. This completed the circuit from a minor array of deep charge batteries that ran a small series of 12-volt outlets throughout the house. Another switch actually turned them on, but until he pulled the bulbs out of their protective wrappers he didn't bother to try it.

He went into the kitchen and opened the bag that he had bought from eBay and took out a bulb. It was supposed to be like a Faraday Cage, but he thought it looked like a Mylar bag. Not even sure it would work, he screwed it into a lamp that was on the counter and went and hit the other switch. There was nothing; the light did not come on.

"Damn eBay," he cursed. He looked it all over and noticed he hadn't plugged the lamp in. One more try and there it was—light. It still worked. He turned it off, as there was enough light still outside and he could see in the house just fine. He wasn't sure how long the batteries would last anyway and he didn't want to waste them. He had a single outlet in each room and four in the garage. That was the important area of the house.

He stepped out into the garage, walked over to the back wall and removed a sheet. Under the sheet was a stack of plywood sheets he had prepared by custom fitting them to the windows in his house. Next to the sheets of plywood was a large roll of adhesive laminate plastic that sign printers used on big signs.

Haliday grabbed the roll of plastic and snagged a utility knife off a nearby work bench. The plastic was practically useless for anything other than protecting the signs the printers made, but he had a different idea for it. He cut off large pieces, peeled the backing off and placed it on every window in the house. This took him an hour and a half to finish.

This wouldn't do much other than to keep the glass from getting everywhere in case it was broken—simply less mess to clean up or worry about later on. It'd be nice not to get cut when it came time to clean that mess up. Might even be an insulating factor, but that wasn't the reason he did it; he was simply trying to avoid a mess.

Next was the plywood. Each segment had another piece that went with it. On the back of each one was attached a section of fairly heavy wire mesh. Pieces were marked with numbers so he knew which windows they went to. He put one section in place, secured it, and then put the other in place and not only secured it but joined the two together. He used large door hinges and hinge pins to do this.

They were anchored very securely in place. It would stop most folks, but those who really wanted to get in could do so with the right tools. As each room of the house was sealed up, he lit some candles to light the now darkening place. No way had he wanted folks to know he had any type of electricity, no matter how simple it may be.

He finished up the patio door leading to the deck on the back of the house and this left the front door and the garage door. Those would be last, as they required something a little different, not to mention he would still have to get the truck out. It was late evening now and he was anxious to get started very early in the morning, so he locked the front door and secured the garage.

He had drilled several holes along the garage door rail and placed six padlocks, three on each side, so the door would not roll up. The wheels would stop because of the padlocks. Before he left he would be able to secure it further, but that had to wait.

Haliday spent the rest of the evening prepping his gear and loading the truck for the next day.

Chapter 3

Time was going much faster than Haliday thought. He looked over at the entertainment center at an old wind up alarm clock he had kept for years. It was a small reminder of a family vacation home they had just across the border in Canada on Lake Erie. It was only about an hour's drive away, but it was still a totally different world over there. It was almost a different culture and in some aspects it was.

It was little streets scattered about the beaches along the lake, surrounded by farms. He wondered if they got hit by the EMP as well, but after a little thought he figured they must have since they were so close to the U.S. With all the farms and very few major congregations of people, they should be better off than most other larger population areas. They would be able to avoid the mass gangs and riots. Haliday almost wished it was his destination, but that was not the case.

He pulled out another Faraday baggie as he had come to call them and inside was an Alinco ham radio. He had talked to quite a few people and explained what his intentions were; he needed a radio powerful enough to adequately reach 300 linear miles. He wasn't concerned with getting his technician's license or anything like that. He was not concerned about anything except the fact that it would work and reach to the other radio he had ready.

He took it outside along with a single, deep charge battery. He went to the back of his lot. There he ducked behind his old shed, where he reached up and grabbed the end of an antenna he had set up in the trees a couple years prior. He had done this under the guise of trimming the branches hanging over his fence. Since it was a simple wire antenna and nothing fancy, it blended perfectly. He had tested it monthly and so far it held up just fine.

Looking around he could see candles flickering in the windows of the nearby homes. He even heard a generator that sounded like it was on its last leg. Haliday wasn't surprised by it; a lot of old generators were probably able to run in an event like this, and if the owner was prepared, there was no telling what measures he had taken to make sure it ran.

Of course, the noise would draw a lot of attention and that wasn't the smartest thing to do. Give it a few more days and it would be downright dangerous. People wanting access to power would seek him out. The noise was welcome though; it would help drown out the noise he would be making.

Seconds seemed like hours as he waited. The designated time was nine p.m. He clicked on the radio about 15 minutes before that and it came on with no problem. It made noise, but not what he wanted. He was tuned into an emergency frequency to make sure he received transmissions okay. He played with the antenna connection, but no luck. Starting to panic a bit, he tried to think of what to do.

He grabbed the wire and yanked on it a bit. After a few good tugs he was able to get a signal. He cursed himself for not using a better antenna, because obviously now there was a short in it, or more accurately, a break in the wire. He held the radio as still as he could. There was no time to try and run a new wire. Besides, that would surely attract the neighbor's attention.

Haliday, when he had purchased the gear, had said screw the licensing, screw the government, screw the hams with their etiquette—this was serious business and he didn't care who was going to say what. The crucial time was very near and he keyed the mic. "Kaybear, are you there?"

He waited. This was the nickname they had given his daughter practically at birth. Kayla was her name, but he thought she was cuddly like a little stuffed teddy bear, so thus the nickname. This was his only child and she meant everything in the world to him.

After graduating from high school she had relocated to a small town in Illinois where her mother lived so she could attend college there. Not a decision Haliday liked, but he had to accept that she was growing up and had choices to make by herself. He hadn't been on the greatest terms with his ex, but they grew to understand and respect each other more than when they were married, so it worked out.

They were better friends now and she accepted the fact, along with her new husband, that Haliday was a tad strange in his ideas of being ready for who knows what. He was sure she had a whole new respect for that opinion now. Right at this moment her ridicule would mostly turn into admiration for his foresight.

There was no answer and his heart dropped. He keyed the mic once more and repeated himself. "Kaybear, are you there, kiddo?"

Again there was no answer. His eyes actually started to well with tears. They had gone over this time and time again and she knew what to do when the SHTF, shit hit the fan. Like any parent, he was scared and thinking the worst. Far too many other scenarios ran across his mind.

He reached up and dabbed his eyes with his sleeve and went to key the mic one more time when he heard her voice.

"Sorry, Dad, I hate this thing; I told you that before."

Now his tears were streaming down his face, but this time with joy. He hadn't felt this happy in a long time, and knowing his little girl was okay for the moment, he couldn't be happier.

Haliday told her to hang on one second. He breathed deeply and said, "I love you, kiddo, and I'm glad you're okay. How about your mom and Mike?" he asked.

She replied that her mom was okay, but Mike hadn't made it home from work yet. They were worried about him.

Haliday said, "Give it time. It's fifteen miles from the house to his work. It may take a bit to get home."

He asked her how the trip from school to home was. Kayla replied like a typical teenager and just said fine. School was only about three miles away and she always kept her bike and get-home bag in the back of her car. She knew immediately what she had to do and did it. He couldn't have been prouder.

Haliday asked her if she had any packages ready and the answer was yes. He had visited a few times and during the course of those visits he had made some small preparations there. Not much, but just what he thought would be enough to get her through until he got there to retrieve her—up to about a month's worth actually. This was his planned trip.

First and foremost after making sure he could lock his house down, he was going to get his daughter and bring her home. There was no way he could leave her there and at least not make an attempt. He would rather die trying than live and wonder what was going on with her. He couldn't torture himself like that.

He had some typical prepper foods and water in place, and even though it was Illinois, he had made sure she was equipped with pepper spray, a small stun gun, a knife, and an AR15 he had built for her along with a small 9mm. While he was there one visit, he had torn a hole in the drywall, placed the rifle along with the small 9mm inside, complete with some rounds and magazines, and then sealed it up—mudding, sanding, and then painting the whole room so it all matched.

Helping her remodel her bedroom to her liking was the ruse they had pulled to hide the firearms and justify the work. No one was the wiser. Being ex-army, he had always had a love for guns and had taught her how to handle them. She was a hell of a shot in all reality. They would visit the range often so she could learn new techniques and practice.

He keyed the mic again and said he would be on at four a.m., and to make sure someone answered. Whether it was her, her mom or Mike, he didn't care. He would explain his plans then. Before she said okay, she said her mom wanted to talk to him. He knew what was coming, so he told her he had a lot of work to do and that he would talk to her either in the morning or when he got there.

They said their goodbyes and he disconnected the radio and headed back toward the house. He looked around as he walked and saw that no one had noticed him out there. That was just fine by him. He could still hear the generator running off in the distance.

He said, "Go ahead and waste all of your gas, bad move."

A couple of hours a day to keep the fridge or freezer cold or maybe charge a few batteries was plenty, but non-stop was going to run the gas out, and the noise would draw too many curious people.

As soon as he walked into the house Haliday went into the kitchen pantry and grabbed two five-gallon buckets and a cardboard box and put them in the truck. He went back inside and grabbed another AR15 and a can each of magazines and ammo and placed them in there, too. He had a feeling he would need to give these to his ex and her husband, Mike. He knew the questions were going to be *what about them* and *can they go* with him and Kayla.

He had thought about it, and there were some pros and cons, but right now the cons were outweighing any good that could come of it. The box and two buckets had enough food supplies like rice, beans, and basics inside to feed them for a couple months if they stretched it out, and the gun would help keep them safe. How safe he didn't know, but this was the best he could do for the moment.

It was close to 10:00 p.m. and he was beat. He double-checked the front door and garage door and then hit the sack. Haliday couldn't even think for a moment; he was out like a light immediately.

The alarm went off at three a.m. and Haliday slowly got up out of bed. He wandered into the kitchen and pulled out a small butane stove and boiled some water.

A cup of instant coffee, some instant grits, and then he used the rest of the water to make more coffee, which he put in a thermos for the trip. He quickly boiled additional water and put it in another thermos to use later. He tossed the thermoses into the truck that was in the garage and then went back into the bedroom to change.

After changing, he did a quick look around and then a double check. He grabbed the ham radio and ran back to the shed again. It was four a.m. He turned it on, had no issues with the connection this time, and said good morning into the mic. His ex came on and said good morning. He asked if everyone was okay and she said no, Mike was still gone. He asked where Kayla was and she said their daughter was still sleeping.

Haliday told her that he was heading out and would call back in two hours. He also told her they would talk when he got there and to give Mike more time; he was probably playing it safe. She said okay. He turned the radio off and ran back to the house. It was time to get moving and he had a lot of ground to cover.

He stepped into the garage and placed the radio in the truck and connected it to the antenna and power. He went over to the side of the garage and opened up a big oblong box that was sealed up and grabbed what was inside. This was quickly attached to the truck with magnets and then tested. It worked like a champ. It would prove to be very useful on the trip and he was banking on it to make a difference when he needed it. A few more minor details and he would be ready to go.

Next he slowly opened the garage door. He had oiled the wheels and chain very well and made sure they were as quiet as he could make them. He didn't start the truck, but placed it in neutral and pushed it out into the driveway. Thank goodness it was downhill and easy to roll.

He didn't want to alert anyone of his leaving the home and didn't want to let others know what he had. He was taking a big risk as it was. He dropped the truck into park, left the door slightly ajar, and stepped back in the garage. He slowly lowered the garage door and then placed the padlocks in place that would keep the door from rolling up.

The next step was to take some steel grid wall and set it up over the garage door as well. This was two-by-two inch-square steel grid that stores used to hang merchandise on. He had picked it up at one of the many liquidation sales that he attended for stores going out of business. This was locked in place over the door and added that extra level of security.

He stepped back into the house and then placed four locks into hasps on the metal exterior door to secure it. It would be hard to get through. Anyone wanting to get in would have to work hard at it; the windows would be easier if they were smart enough. He left through the front door and stood on the porch. He turned to the closed door and there again were four more hasps on which he placed locks. These locks were the round style meant for storage units and harder to cut into.

That was it for now.

He went over to the truck, raised the antenna mast, and placed the gear shifter in neutral and rolled the vehicle into the street. Looking around, he didn't see any candles or lights and was fairly confident he had not been seen. Now when he started the truck up, if anyone woke up or looked out, it would appear that the truck was simply driving down the street and they wouldn't know from where it had come.

It was a lot of work for something he expected he would only have in his possession for a couple days max, until it was discovered and taken away. Surely Martial Law had been declared already if the government was still around. That was the $64,000 question. He had taken extreme care in keeping the truck out of sight until needed. Even in the garage it sat under a tarp.

Haliday had no idea why there had been an EMP. The possibilities were endless. Nuclear war, direct EMP attack, coronal mass ejection, whatever—he didn't care at the moment. He turned the key – the magical moment of truth – and the truck started. He threw it in drive and took off down the road.

The truck would appear to be an official government vehicle driving down the road.

It was incredibly easy to pull it off, as far as the looks were concerned; the mechanics of it were the hard part. That had taken some doing.

Haliday had purchased a used Tahoe from an auction of government vehicles. It was white and had formerly been a border patrol truck. The officials had stripped the decals off from it, removed the light bars and interior equipment, and put it on the auction block. It was your typical government SUV and all Haliday had to do was put it back together with a slightly different design in mind.

He had waited until all of the mechanical work had been done first, however. He'd be sitting in prison at the moment if he had been caught. With the right amount of money, it was surprising what you could buy. Doing what he had planned required a lot of under-the-radar purchases.

Staging it in a friend's pole barn, they had taken out the engine and transmission and left it as nothing but a roller. A new transmission was installed with another engine that was as basic as you could get. Practically no electronics, direct linkage to shift, a carbureted engine, and wearing a distributor cap and plugs. It was as EMP proof as you could get. No radio, no air conditioning, no heat, no engine sensors, no emission control— nothing.

Anything with wires was shielded, grounded, shielded again, and the whole chassis was grounded inside the garage through a hole in the cement floor and a 12-foot grounding rod. He had been assured this would work the way he had it set up and luckily it did. Haliday's buddy had helped build it out so it would run. He had no idea what else Haliday was adding to it, however.

On the exterior, Haliday had put back on the big blue stripe, the Federal Protective Service lettering, and the big blue police lettering under that. On the fenders the words "Homeland Security" were present along with the DHS seal. He even added "Supervisor" to the rear quarter panel. On top was the magnetic LED light bar. From a distance you couldn't tell the difference, and up close you couldn't either; until you looked inside and saw the modifications.

The choice of grabbing the border patrol truck versus another government SUV was an easy decision for that very reason. The windows were tinted darker than normal due to the southwest climate and blazing sun. On the back hitch was mounted a motorcycle carrier and Haliday tucked a KLR650 into the carrier; the bike was painted white with matching logos and lettering. He had to admit, the bike was a stretch, and a big stretch at that.

What he planned might not be that easy to pull off, but 24-30 hours was all he needed. Taking this kind of risk was almost as stupid as it was brilliant. If he failed, he would surely be imprisoned or shot, but with the time table he was projecting, he was confident he could do it. The risk was worth it.

The idea came to him years ago. At the hospital, a distraught patient had been discharged. He had walked outside, climbed into an ambulance in the ambulance loading bay, and drove away with the lights and siren blaring. This guy had not only made it into Detroit, but actually crossed the Ambassador Bridge into Canada.

Customs even opened the gates for him, thinking he was heading to the hospital with a patient. This had all been prior to 9/11 and the times had changed, but Haliday's route wouldn't take him through any major cities for the most part or put him in those positions. That's what he counted on during his travel—avoiding big populations.

He was driving and thinking about how much of a fool he was for not thinking of another plan. He started doubting himself and his ability to make it. Here he was in a fake DHS Tahoe, with black BDUs and DHS patches bought from eBay for that matter; and about to drive 450 miles one way and then 450 back within an hour of getting there.

It was crazy, but then again, if you knew Haliday, it was as sane as sane would get. One more stop on the way to make and then the journey would begin.

It would become more difficult than the journey he was counting on. Things would take some very unexpected turns.

Chapter 4

Heading south, Haliday passed by another hospital. This one was actually much closer than the one where he worked, but the opportunities there were very limited, so he had chosen his present facility. Dodging stalled cars scattered on the streets was time consuming and he had underestimated travel time. Driving slower, he had time to check out the hospital.

Dawn was a little more than an hour away. Still being dark outside, the only thing he could make out was the occasional beam from a flashlight in the windows of the hospital. He couldn't believe people were still there. What could they possibly do? Delay the inevitable? For some it was likely the only thing that came to mind. Good little sheeple staying in their barnyard.

The worst part was that he saw people working their way to the hospital. Normally a safe haven of sorts, it was the last place he would go. Of course having worked at one for quite a few years, he knew what it would turn into. It had given him the opportunity to gain some valuable skills, though.

Right out of high school, Haliday had pulled a stint of active duty in the army as an MP and then pulled some reserve duty. He had put in seven years at a smalltime police department with a whopping 178 homes on a private lake with people too rich for their own good. Everyone in that department was part-time so he had picked up the job at the hospital for benefits and a steady check.

Even though he had attended a fair amount of decent schools in the service and taken a few courses here and there for the small police department, the hospital had given him the chance to excel more than the other places. He worked his way into becoming the training officer and picked up certifications to teach.

TASER, chemical deterrent—which was just pepper spray—and management of aggressive behavior, including pressure point control techniques, were some of the courses he'd taken. He was by no means a walking badass and didn't portray himself as anything other than a regular old schmuck. He simply learned to be a teacher, and thought *what better way to keep your skills honed?*

That wasn't the clincher though. Training all the new hires and making sure they had uniforms and equipment gave him the chance to purchase items under the radar. Of course he paid for them, but it was easier to have items shipped directly to the hospital under his name than to try and explain the personal purchases.

He even volunteered to take care of the vehicle maintenance. Ordering an LED light bar with red and blue lights, TASERS or pepper spray, and other equipment to a home address would have raised red flags big time. He got what he wanted, no questions asked, and no worrying about what popped up on the doorstep or who would inquire about it.

Haliday was mostly riding the center turn lanes with the occasional zigzag when he had to suddenly slam on the brakes. A couple had run into the street in front of him waving their arms for him to stop. "Oh great," he said to himself.

He hit them with the side-mounted spotlight and quickly got out of the vehicle, ordering them to stop as they approached. He wasn't taking any chances and had drawn the .40 and took a bead on the guy. His eyes darted back and forth, sweeping the area for other movement. *Why the hell didn't I wait until daylight?* he thought to himself.

The couple had stopped dead in their tracks at his command and could see his profile with the gun drawn on them. "Hey mister, we ain't criminals, we just need help. You are supposed to help us; you're the police."

Haliday had analyzed them from the very first second. Early 30s, both white, ragged jeans, and t-shirts, light jackets; maybe not outstanding citizens, but not troublemakers either.

"What's going on? What is it you folks need?" he asked.

39

"We could use a ride home. We've been walking all night since we left our friend's apartment in Rochester Hills. We only live in Warren." the woman said.

They'd walked about 12 to 15 miles and had maybe six to go. Haliday said, "Sorry, folks. I've got a job to do and playing taxi right now is not on the top of my list. Now please move aside."

The couple got upset and the woman said, "It's not like there are cars to pull over or anything. What could be so important?"

Haliday was ready for just this type of smartass attitude. "Look, folks, the side of the truck says Federal Protective Service. If we don't make sure we secure all of the social security buildings, veteran's clinics, and federal buildings and property, we could be in a world of hurt. Hell, we don't even know what happened yet.

"I'd like to explain the importance of securing the information in these buildings, but I gotta go." He then holstered his pistol and waited a moment.

The couple started to move away and all he heard was mumbling. He jumped back in the truck, killed the spotlight and took off again. His heart was beating a mile a minute and he could feel the adrenaline rush. He took nice and slow concentrated breaths to bring his heartbeat down and respirations back to normal.

Although he wanted to help the couple, he could not risk it. They would see everything inside the Tahoe and know he was up to something else. It could put his safety and mission in jeopardy.

He pulled off the main road onto a side street and he slowed down and killed the lights on the truck. He knew the area very well since his parents had lived there since '89. He crept along slowly, avoiding any cars stalled in the street. He didn't use the lights so as not to draw attention to his parents' house.

When he was three houses away, he pulled up to the curb and turned the truck off. Anyone spotting it may tie it to the house he was parked in front of. Just a little deception. Glancing around, he didn't see any lights or anyone moving. He grabbed his rifle, jumped out, locked the truck, and bolted for their front door.

Reaching the porch he stood to the side of the door and tapped lightly on it and waited. If there were any shots coming through the door he would be off to the side. He tapped a little harder and waited. At 75- and 73-years-old, they moved a little slow and their hearing was not what it used to be. They both had grey hair and slim builds.

He remembered, as a teen in high school, talking to friends in the front yard of his childhood home about buying beer for a party for that night. When he walked around the back he had found his dad sitting on the back porch. He had looked at Roger and said, "I think you're staying home tonight."

He never figured out how his dad had heard that.

Now a muffled voice came through the door. "Who's out there?"

Haliday said, "Mom, it's me, Roger."

"I don't know any Roger," was the response.

Haliday answered back again. "But you know Ruger, right?" It was a little code they had worked out to make sure she knew it was him. It was her favorite new prep item. He heard a couple of locks being opened and the door swung open wide. He stepped inside and gave her a hug and then asked how his dad was doing.

She called out, "Hey, Rich, Roger's here!"

"Okay, Bev, I'll be there in a minute."

Bev asked him what he thought happened.

"I have no idea, Mom, not a clue. All I can say is it's definitely hit the fan."

His dad came out and he gave him a quick hug as well.

Haliday looked around and saw some candles burning in the kitchen and in the living room. It reminded him that he had mentioned to them to make sure they didn't run the generator more than two hours a day, to stop running it after the third day until they could feel out the atmosphere of the neighborhood. He suggested they keep the doors and windows locked, and not to let anyone in. They had placed a few boards over the windows to stop intruders, but nothing as elaborate as he had done.

Next was making sure they were locked and loaded. His dad had an old H&R, Harrington & Richardson .22 revolver he had gotten during the riots in Detroit in 1967. His mom had a Ruger LC9 pistol and S&W, Smith & Wesson .40 pistol. He also worked them up a lightweight AR15. Everything was loaded and good to go. Plenty of magazines were at the ready. Enough lead down range and they should be able to hit whatever they pointed the guns at.

There was no time for a lot of chitchat; he told them he was heading out to get Kayla and would try to swing back by on his way home. He told them to turn their ham radio on at eight a.m. and listen. Not to talk, but listen, and answer only if he asked a question or unless it was very important. OPSEC was important here as well.

This would keep them updated on his progress and he on their current situation. Every two hours was the designated contact time and would help save on their batteries. His rig was powering his radio so he was not worried too much about leaving his on. Of course he would have to make sure he kept his truck battery charged; there wouldn't be any AAA service calls.

Haliday explained that if any of his siblings showed up to make sure it was just them and their families. He couldn't insist on this enough; it wasn't a Holiday Inn he told them. They had sorted through his mom's preps and calculated five months for the 14 family members who may show up. They had started in early '99 for Y2K and then over time added items they needed. Over the past years they managed to add quite a bit.

One of his brothers had actually worked at a survival store back then and sold everyone who came in the store on the idea. Unfortunately, these days the brother fell into line with the rest of the sheeple and dropped the whole idea. Just this past Father's Day, his brother was saying that he thought having two weeks of basics was enough for most anything. That disappointed Haliday.

He never talked to his brothers and sister about his readiness. Nothing but ridicule would ensue and he it was tired of it. His mom was different and she would welcome the family into the house to make the best of it.

———

A niece and nephew were welcome as well. They'd come in handy for labor, security, and whatever else needed to be done. The trade-off was food supply. However, strength in numbers was one of the popular sayings in readiness. Hopefully whoever showed up would bring what they could.

A quick set of goodbyes and Haliday was out the door. Heading toward the truck, he had walked straight out to the street and then toward the truck with his rifle in a low ready position. It was fairly light outside now and he could see a couple of people down the street come out of their house. They were surprised to see him there, so he kept up the act.

A young boy with them came running up and said, "Mister, my dad wants to talk to you."

Haliday rolled his eyes, mumbled a bit and said, "Fine."

He stood there as the guy walked toward him. *Oh yeah, dress like the DHS, good idea genius*, he thought to himself. People would expect some sort of aid from him if they thought he was with the Department of Homeland Security. He carefully watched the man approach.

"Excuse me sir, what's going on?" the man said.

"So far as we can tell, it's a regional terrorist attack and we've tracked some people into this neighborhood," Haliday said, "so I suggest you go home, lock your doors, and wait it out. You probably need to load up on food and water first. We'll be trying to send more agents and support in a few days, so hold out as long as you can. Power will be out for months."

Haliday hoped the guy bought into the story. It would be fewer people out in the chaos that was closing in fast. He got back in the truck and took off through the neighborhood. He passed an old lady who just waved as he drove by. She was putting an envelope in her mail box and raised the flag on the side of the mail box.

He started laughing out loud. *Oh boy, that's going to be one for the story books. Lady, there isn't enough postage to get that delivered right now.* In a few days, she'd probably try to call the postmaster and complain about how it wasn't picked up.

He pulled back onto the main road and headed west. Over in a nearby strip mall there was a small Middle Eastern fruit market with a lot of goods under a tent outside. People were lining up already. Mostly they were older Middle Eastern folks, with a few others as well, and Haliday could hear who he thought was the owner yelling at them all.

"Stand in line! I am taking only money! No credit cards! Do not buy it if you don't have cash!"

Haliday shook his head. Cash was about as good as toilet paper right now, but nobody knew it yet. How could they not know? Nothing worked. Nothing. Did they think the power was going to magically just come back on or something? Haliday was amazed how many people did not know about EMP's.

He looked at the 7-11 store and saw that it was closed. He ran it down in his mind.. He figured there was about a year's worth of junk food. Candy bars, potato chips, gum, a few bags of jerky, and some overpriced canned food—that was it. Too bad the owner didn't have the sense to hide it all. Maybe they did.

He continued his trek westward. Same thing again and again, zigzagging through the streets and dodging cars and the odd person walking the streets or sidewalk. It was still early and he didn't really expect to see many people out anyway. It was a Wednesday and even though they should be working, no one except a few people would be going anywhere. He figured only stores where the owners lived close by would be open. No power, no communications, no work.

He turned the ham on to see if he could hear any information about what had gone down. There seemed to be a lot of theories, but nothing official as far as he could tell. He reached over and grabbed a large binder from the passenger seat and flipped it open. Inside was his map set for the route he was taking.

He had printed and laminated each sheet and made notes about possible areas to stop, areas to avoid, alternates to bypass trouble when – not if – he ran into it, water holes, and more.

As he progressed, he flipped to the next page and continued doing that until he got where he needed to be. He would reverse the pages for the trip home. He had made the trip four times before to get all of the info logged.

Wading through the suburban sprawl was time consuming. It was still early enough and he hadn't had any troubles other than the interested parties seeking info from "the police." He still doubted this plan, but so far he was pulling off the scam. Reaching the more rural area just outside of the congested suburbs, he popped up onto a small state highway running east and west and was able to pick up some speed.

Even with the area littered with the cars, Haliday could maintain almost 45 mph, but the 70 mph limit would have been nicer. He looked down at the gas gauge to see it was just under a quarter of a tank. He glanced at his binder and found what he wanted. He had a few spots picked out where he could stop.

No doubt he would make it there, but he was not sure what to expect when he arrived. About 10 minutes later, he saw the sign: Ride Share 1 Mile. It was a parking lot where folks parked and carpooled in state-owned vans to go to work. It was cheaper to pay the weekly fee than to pay for gas and pay for parking in the congested downtown Lansing area.

Haliday wasn't going there though; he would split off and head south long before getting near the state capitol.

He pulled into the Ride Share lot and estimated about 45 to 50 cars parked there. He staged the truck toward the center of the lot, angled toward the exit. He didn't want to get caught in the lot or become blocked in and not be able to get the vehicle out. He hadn't seen anyone there or even nearby.

He figured anyone near the lot had probably walked the couple of miles to the little nearby town to seek help. He placed the transmission in park and looked at the time. Eight-ten a.m., real good—he was late. He hadn't heard them broadcast, which meant they were listening to his instructions.

Keying the mic, he spit out a quick sentence. "Kaybear and Bobily, alls good, on track, and safe," he said, using his mom's nickname from her grandfather. "Reply please."

———

He heard Kayla respond "Yes," and his mom respond "Yes."

Next he said two words only. "Anything bad?"

He received two "No's" in response.

There would be no extensive chatter, as this would deter anyone listening from trying to piece together their plan or any other info. No designated route info given, no locations of anyone, no time schedules to figure out or anything like that. Haliday thought this was the safest way to go.

He climbed out of the driver's seat and opened the rear passenger door. Off of the floorboard he grabbed a small plastic bag and a six-gallon gas can generally used for boating. He walked up to a pickup truck in the parking lot and placed the gas can close underneath. He unscrewed the can's top and set it aside. Out of the plastic bag he pulled out a strange looking contraption he had made just for this purpose.

Haliday had taken one inch galvanized pipe and installed a ball valve faucet in the middle. He used that to attach a hose. One end of the pipe was ground down at an angle and to a point. The other end was capped off. This was a quick and effective method to pierce the tanks.

Haliday put the open end of the hose in the gas can and then placed the spike up against the gas tank of the pickup truck. Using a small five-pound hand sledge, a quick rap on the cap and it had pierced the tank. He pulled out another plain spike and popped a hole in the pickup's tank near the top of the tank. The air hole allowed the gas to flow smoothly after opening the ball valve and in about two minutes the gas can was full.

The height of the pickup's tank and the low profile of the gas can let gravity do the work perfectly. He pulled the spike out and crammed a cork in the hole. He carried the gas can over to his truck, attached a nozzle, and dumped it in. Everything took about six minute's total.

He had full gas cans stored in the back of the Tahoe and they would be enough to get him there, but he wanted to save those for the time when he might not have the luxury of draining someone else's tank.

———

Was it stealing? Absolutely. Did he care? No. He doubted anyone would be coming back for their vehicles, and by the time they did, the gas would most likely be bad anyway.

It was not like he was taking food from someone. He wouldn't do that. That was his justification. He moved on and tapped another. He needed two more to fill the Tahoe. He hadn't changed the tank to a higher capacity because he didn't want to modify anything under the vehicle body. He regretted this now.

One last tank left to drain. It had been about 20 minutes when he approached the last vehicle, a full-size conversion van. He was about 20 feet away when the door popped open and a guy in his late 30s jumped out. Haliday dropped everything and drew down, ready to fire if he had to.

The guy didn't seem phased a bit and instead yelled at him. "Who the hell are you? Wait a minute, you're a damn Fed. What in the hell are you doing?"

Haliday told him to take it easy and keep his hands visible. The guy looked a little rough around the edges and Haliday expected trouble.

"If I don't, what are you going to do, shoot me?"

Haliday just looked at him.

"Hey moron, I asked you what you were going to do about it?"

Haliday's response was monotone and to the point. "Yes sir, I'm going to shoot you. It'll be twice in your chest and then once in the head. I'm just trying to decide if I'm going to place your body in your van or let the animals eat your carcass." He leveled the pistol at his chest, center mass.

"Damn, man, relax, okay." The guy raised his hands up slightly and asked, "What do you want me to do?"

Haliday kept his bead on the guy and reached into his left cargo pocket and pulled out a pair of heavy duty zip ties. These worked just like Flex Cuffs. In the military, they used to keep them coiled up in the top of their BDU caps while on road duty. Not that they needed them, that much, but it helped keep the caps in form during guard mount inspection.

He tossed them over and told the guy to put one around his right wrist and cinch it down. He told him to loop the other one through and then loop it around his door handle. The guy started to complain and Haliday told him to knock it off, he was doing him a favor. After the guy had attached himself to the door handle, Haliday looked him over and everything looked OK.

He holstered the pistol and walked over to the guy to make sure they were tight. The guy turned toward Haliday, slipped his hand out of the cuff and reached out and grabbed him. Haliday arm-locked the guy and bent his wrist violently downwards in a gooseneck, almost breaking it.

As the man yelled out in pain, Haliday put him on the ground and into a prone position then wrenched his arm behind his back and pulled tight. He then drew his pistol and placed it on the man's throat against his jugular. "Keep it up idiot and your jugular and esophagus become pink slime."

He told him to place his other arm behind his back and the guy complied. Haliday looped another zip tie around his wrist and this time he cinched it down himself. He helped the man off the ground and then zip-tied him back to the door handle. "Get stupid and you'll lose more than a few IQ points. You'll lose that gray matter you think is your brain."

Haliday filled the gas can again, dumped it in his truck and put everything away. He walked back over to guy who had started bellyaching about how he was desperate and wanted to get home.

"So am I," Haliday said. "You're lucky I didn't shoot your sorry ass. The next guy might have to pay for your mistake because now I can't take anymore chances being a nice guy."

"Are you just going to leave me like this?" he man asked.

48

Haliday said, "Of course. Work the door handle hard enough and it'll come off. Then go find yourself something to cut the zip ties off. By that time I'll be far enough away and won't need to worry about you." He climbed back in his Tahoe, started it and left. This was getting far too serious quicker than he thought it would.

Chapter 5

With a full tank now, Haliday calculated mileage and determined he would need better fuel efficiency. He was on a course heading south in order to avoid Lansing. This would take him only six miles west of Ann Arbor, but since Ann Arbor was home to the University of Michigan and loaded with college kids and their tree-hugging, bleeding heart, liberal staffers, he wasn't worried.

They were probably still sitting around smoking dope or hugging each other while waiting for FEMA to come rescue them. He was highly doubtful many of them were ready for this kind of situation. It saddened him that so many kids were easily influenced by people they would see only a few hours a week.

Cruising at almost 70 MPH he was glad to see the road was not too cluttered with broken-down vehicles; that meant fewer people to run into. This of course was most likely due to the fact that the area was rural farmland with small towns located between the bigger cities and most people relying on the interstates for travel. He remembered coming through the area year after year when he attended the NASCAR races at Michigan International Speedway. He was always looking for new local attractions to make the weekend more interesting.

Keeping a closer eye on the time, he noted it was close to 10 a.m. He had turned down the volume of the radio because of the same thing playing on every frequency. "What happened? What's going on? Where can we get help? Anyone have power?" It got boring real quick. The occasional conspiracy theory arose, but he couldn't stomach it. They needed to be taking care of business, not guessing what may have happened.

Time was close enough, so he keyed the mic once again. "Kaybear and Bobily, on track, all safe, reply please."

One "yes" came from Kayla and then there was nothing but silence.

Haliday repeated himself. "Bobily?" He almost laughed whenever he heard that nickname. Her grandfather was an immigrant and his English broken. He could not pronounce Beverly and it came out Bobily. It was that simple. A third try. "Bobily?"

His dad answered. "She's in the bathroom."

Haliday just chuckled.

Next was his mom's voice. "Sorry, I was in the bathroom. Dad wasn't sure he should answer."

Haliday was thinking that if anyone was listening, they were probably laughing about now. "Anything happening?" he asked.

His mom said "No."

Kayla said, "Yes."

"SITREP?" He had briefed them all on some basic acronyms and jargon to make things easier. SITREP was short for Situation Report.

Kayla answered quickly. "Mike is home, but beaten badly."

Haliday thought *Great*; he knew it would be hard to just get in and go without assuring her that her mom and Mike would be okay. "I'll check it out when I get in. I'm out."

He was trying to think of how to handle things when he got there, but couldn't come up with a plan yet. He looked down at the radio and was changing frequencies when he heard a loud horn. He shot straight upright and then swerved back into his lane. He had barely missed hitting an old tractor pulling a large flatbed cart behind it heading the opposite direction he was.

"Damn," he said. It was later in the morning and he didn't count on any moving vehicles for the most part. This old John Deere wasn't what he expected. He looked in the rearview mirror and saw the flatbed had about a dozen people on it.

He passed by an old motel and started to laugh again. The old B-rated horror movie *Motel Hell* crossed his mind. Maybe the farmer had a new crop he'd harvested. Then he stopped smiling and thought, *Man, that would suck*. He hoped people wouldn't resort to that. Cannibalism was just wrong in too many ways.

———

51

He knew that hungry people got desperate and there were going to be a lot of desperate people in a matter of weeks. Eventually some would snap and cross the boundary. He didn't want to think about it. He glanced at his binder, flipped the page and noticed he'd crossed into Ohio. Soon he would start a westward course. It would still be pretty much the same terrain and land.

The next major obstacle was a small city named Bryan. Population was under 9,000 and its major business was Dum Dum suckers and candy canes, along with Etch-A-Sketch. *There's one that will make a comeback*, he thought. *Hey kids, can't get that X-Box working? Well, don't you worry; the old-fashioned Etch-A-Sketch is back and it's bad.* About another five miles would put him smack dab outside of the downtown area.

He slowed down and brought the vehicle to a stop. After the Ride Share escapade, he wasn't taking chances. He stepped out and swiped a pair of binoculars out of the console. He eyeballed the road ahead and thought he saw a roadblock. He grabbed his thermos and poured a quick cup of coffee. Drinking it, he kept peering down the road. After finishing the coffee, he stepped over to the shoulder of the road and took a quick leak.

Finished with his business, he got back in the truck and slowly moved forward at about 20 miles an hour. The closer he got, the more it looked like a roadblock ahead. *Here we go again*, he thought. He got a little closer and realized it was a train stopped on the tracks and not a roadblock. That was just fine with him; he would actually be running along a small county road parallel to his side of the tracks anyway.

He was just about there when a couple of figures popped up from the top of a boxcar and one of the boxcar doors slid open, revealing two more people.

Haliday slammed on the brakes and turned the LED light bar on. One of the figures in the boxcar looked at him.

Haliday quickly looked around. He had his foot on the brake with the truck in reverse, ready to gun it. He couldn't hear what the guys were saying, but one kept motioning toward him as he talked with another guy.

He sized up the figures on the boxcar and noticed that some of them had on RealTree camo and that one wore old gray-tones urban camo.

First thought was that they were some sort of militia, but then Haliday noticed a patch on one guy's shoulder that identified him as a police officer. Haliday looked in all directions, scanning for anyone coming up from behind him or from the sides. As he looked to his left, he saw a slight reflection now and again about 300 yards away.

He knew he was screwed at the moment and he knew these guys meant business; likely someone had a rifle aimed at his head right then, too. He assumed whomever it was probably was a good shot or they wouldn't be out that far. Either that or he was a chicken shit. The guy with the patch ordered him out of the truck.

Haliday just sat there.

Another shout to get out of the truck came once again.

Still he didn't move. He heard a round whiz by and the report of the rifle.

The third command started with the guy yelling that he meant business and to get the hell out of the truck.

It was time for Haliday to start responding. He put the truck in park and slowly opened the door. After getting out, he closed the door so as not to expose the interior to the sniper hiding to his left. Standing outside of the vehicle and looking to the left, he was now able to make out the man. Haliday shook his head. *A ghillie suit*, he thought. *You have to be kidding me.*

Haliday was almost embarrassed that he didn't spot it sooner, but then again, his sitting position and angle didn't really allow it. The cop approached and Haliday took a few steps forward himself before he was ordered to stop. He obeyed the command, but crossed his arms and canted his head to the right. As soon as the cop got about 10 feet away, he told the cop to stop.

The guy did, but looked at Haliday with a puzzled expression.

53

Haliday saw he was about 25- to 28-years-old. In a raised tone of voice he said, "What the hell are you doing firing on a federal officer?" He had to get the upper-hand here. "What's your name, officer?"

"Uh, um, I'm Williams, sir."

"Is this how you treat fellow law enforcement officers?"

Williams replied, "No sir, but you have to understand we ain't ever been in a situation like this and our chief said he saw programs on TV about this kind of stuff—"

Haliday cut him off. "On TV, son?" Being 46 years old, he figured he was safe to go this route by using "son."

"Well, I mean, he went to some seminars and events too."

"Look, son," Haliday said, "yes, things are screwed up right now, yes it sucks, and we are all trying to figure out what the hell happened; but in the meantime, there are things that need to be done and I gotta make sure they get done quickly."

One of the other guys started to walk toward them and Haliday told Williams to have him stop.

Williams asked, "Why?"

"I don't know you from my ass and you could be some nut job playing cop, getting ready to cap my ass, and I'm not ready for that," Haliday responded.

Williams actually apologized and assured him he was the real thing.

Haliday said, "That's fine, but if you don't mind, I need to get over to the Social Security Office and make sure it's locked up and the safe inside is secure as well."

Williams offered to take him there.

Haliday said, "No thank you. I think you need to stay here." He looked past Williams and between the railroad cars and saw what looked like a side-by-side four-wheeler. "You have running vehicles?"

"A bunch of ATVs and about a dozen old cars," Williams answered.

"How about gas?"

"Plenty of that."

Haliday asked him how long the train was and Williams said, "About a half-mile each way. We got lucky it died here. Makes a good roadblock."

One of the other guys shouted over and asked Williams to come back for a minute.

Haliday watched Williams walk up to the railcar and then noticed him talking on a radio. That wasn't a good sign.

Williams walked back over and told Haliday their chief wanted to talk to him. He also asked if Haliday could drive over to the station.

Not good at all, definitely not good at all, Haliday thought. He had to think quickly. *How the hell am I going to get out of this?*

"I'll tell you what I'll do," he said. "Have someone meet me at the end of the train and then I'll go check the Social Security Office, and then they can take me over there."

Williams waved the guys off and said, "Okay."

Haliday walked back to the truck, climbed in, and started the drive toward the end of the train. He glanced between the cars and saw the four-wheeler keeping up pace. He reached the end of the train a moment later.

As he had driven along, he noticed most of the cars had been opened. This town or group of people knew enough to check for supplies and equipment. Seeing they were this organized heightened his fear quite a bit more; a close inspection would reveal his ruse for sure.

He crept over the tracks and stopped by the four-wheeler. One of the guys in real tree camo was sitting there. The kid was young, maybe he was 18 years old at the most. "You ready to go?" he asked Haliday.

"Not yet," Haliday told him. "I'm low on gas. Can you spare that can in the back of that four-wheeler?"

"Sure. I'll just refill it back at the police station. You can fill up there too."

Haliday got out, and walked over. He grabbed the can and started dumping it in his tank. He was just about done when the kid walked over and commented on the KLR on the back of his truck.

"Yeah, they give us some pretty cool toys when we travel through BFE, Bum F' Egypt. What do you have there?"

"Oh, it's a rhino we were able to get running."

The next comment started a shit storm.

The kid looked at him and put his hand in his coat pocket. "Why do you have a government plate on the truck, but a Michigan plate on the bike?"

The kid pulled his hand out of his pocket and Haliday saw the Glock. He dropped the gas can and grabbed the kid's wrist before he could raise it.

A shot rang out and they began to struggle. Both went down to the ground. The kid was small and wiry, but strong. Haliday pinned the kid down and looked up to see two more guys running their way. He brought his fist down hard in the kids face and knocked the kid out. He was careful not to kill the kid.

Haliday jumped up and ran over to the Tahoe. He grabbed his AR180 and fired close to a full magazine at the guys running toward him. They ducked for cover under the train cars and tried to fire back, but the shots went wild as they tried to stay covered.

Haliday slid behind the wheel, started the truck, and jammed it in gear, closing the door as he sped off.

He bounced over the tracks and floored it. The wheels were spinning like crazy as they tried to get a decent grip in the gravel along the rails. Finally making it to the asphalt, he gunned it some more. He kept looking back and saw the two guys had made it to the four-wheeler. They picked the kid up and sat him down as he held his face.

They jumped on the four-wheeler and started off after the Tahoe.

Haliday cussed to himself as he tried to control the Tahoe. The road wasn't straight and he was taking the turn a bit too fast, so he slowed enough to gain control. As soon as the road straightened up a bit, he floored it again. The guys behind him were actually trying to catch him. He saw another hard turn up ahead on the road and as soon as he reached it, he slammed on the brakes. He jumped out with his rifle and dropped to his knee.

When he saw the four-wheeler just hitting the curve he fired three shots at the passenger front tire. The four-wheeler lurched down and tumbled over a couple times.

Haliday didn't see any bodies flying out, he hoped they were ok, but he could not stay to make sure. He didn't want to kill these people, but he didn't want to get delayed or locked up either. He jumped back in the Tahoe, shoved it into drive, and floored it again. As far as he could tell, there was no one else following.

Chapter 6

Dawn had started her own journey immediately after the EMP. Haliday had suggested she leave right away. She had left the parking lot where she had retrieved her get-home bag and mountain bike. She had gone through her CPL course and then had purchased a couple of pistols.

She always carried them with her in her truck after following the concerns Haliday had expressed and reading a couple of books about various TEOTWAWKI scenarios—The End of the World as We Know It. She was an above-average shot and had taken tips from Haliday at the range on a monthly basis to hone her skills.

Just a few days earlier, they had tried a new outdoor range north of her, where she had commented about needing to get a rifle, too. Haliday had been unloading his 12 gauge from its case and she asked to fire it. He loaded up one round and gave her a quick demo on how to operate it. She was a little miffed, feeling almost as if he was treating her like a little kid. He had said shotguns were easy; one round is all you needed to appreciate it.

She had held it to her shoulder, squeezed the trigger, and practically fell backwards when it fired. Haliday had burst out laughing and she'd simply called him an ass. At 5'7" and 135 pounds, she could have handled it okay; it was just the sheer surprise of the recoil and loud report that caught her off-guard. Her hat had fallen off and she had to tuck her shoulder length blonde hair back up under it.

He pulled out a .22 and told her it was more her style.

She'd said, "That looks cute."

"Cute" was not quite how Haliday ever referred to firearms. He'd given her a rundown on that, loaded a magazine, and let her fire away. She'd really liked the model. She told him she wanted to buy one.

He'd said, "Next gun show."

As she was riding toward her house now where she lived with her twin sister and mother, she rubbed the bruise on her shoulder as it started to ache a bit. She cursed Haliday under her breath. She had ridden about five miles when she turned onto an access road that led to the county municipal complex, where she was greeted by a sheriff's deputy who stopped her.

"Where are you going?" he asked.

She responded that she was going to meet up with her mother in one of the parking lots so they could go home together. The deputy asked a few questions and was satisfied with her answers and told her to be careful. Seeing her pistol, he also told her to cover it while on the grounds of the complex for safety's sake. She pulled her windbreaker down over it and took off.

She rode into the parking lot and spotted her mother, Karen, and rode up to her. At 6' tall, 155 pounds, blonde and grey hair, she was easy to spot. There was a bunch of people standing around talking to each other nearby. Her mom had been standing there talking to an elderly female friend.

This friend looked at Dawn and said, "See, I told you guys to store food and gear. I hope you have guns." The lady looked like she was about 80. She showed Dawn a Glock and said, "I have mine."

Dawn said, "Good for you. You go, girl."

Dawn then said hello to her mother. At this time, Karen started to change her shoes and put on a pair of tennis shoes. There was a quick goodbye to the elderly lady and then Dawn and her mom left. They had about eight miles to go before they made it to their house. Dawn slung her mom's get-home bag over the bike frame and they walked along.

She looked around at all of the people just standing around in the parking lots. Every once in a while she spotted a deputy who looked to be standing guard. She asked her mom what everyone was talking about.

Karen said, "Most people think it's just a big power outage, but some left. It looked like they were ready for this event, too."

The deputies were telling everyone it would be okay, that they suspected it was just an industrial accident at one of the nearby electronics manufacturers that did defense work. If any of them would have taken a walk to the rooftop of the highest building there and looked around, they wouldn't be saying that. They'd see trouble for miles.

The area was known as Automation Alley. The obvious belief was that something one of the manufacturers did must have caused a small interference with the electronics. That, of course, was just wishful thinking. Shockingly, the deputies had some old radios that worked that had been stored in a sub-basement long ago by the county's emergency management department. This almost bolstered what the deputies had said. Dawn and her mother shrugged their shoulders and took off.

The walk was slow, but Dawn and her mom moved along at a steady pace. They had to stop every mile for a quick break as Karen wasn't used to walking at all. She'd merely tolerated Dawn's preparedness, but didn't suspect it would amount to anything. She kept the gear in her car only at Dawn's insistence.

There was no way at age 70 she was riding a bike, she had told Dawn. The pace was a very slow—two miles an hour. After five hours they headed into the entrance to Chrysler's world HQ's, a mammoth spot now swarming with people, where they met up with Dawn's sister, Diana. She had ridden her bike there herself from about five miles away and had been sitting waiting.

The parking lot was much the same as the county complex. People were either standing around in bunches and talking or sitting wherever they could find a seat and talking about what was going on. There were people who kept trying to turn their phones on every few minutes. The site was surreal. The complex sprawled over 500 acres and had over 10,000 employees.

There were thousands of them just standing around like cattle waiting for feeding time. The mentality of the majority of the people was shocking, Dawn noticed. Just who did they think was coming to help them? And when did they think this would happen? She, along with her mother and sister, all wondered what the mass of people would do when it was totally dark outside.

Dawn glanced toward the sky and thought about how clear the stars would be at night. No bright haze from parking lots, billboards, and buildings scattered across the country. It would be pure darkness, except for moonlight or starlight.

"Time to get going," she said to Diana and Karen. They got up and started their trek.

Only about four more miles or so and they should be able to make it home by about midnight. All three had pistols, all three could at least point and pull the trigger, and they felt safe. As they walked along they just shared some small talk, took an occasional drink from their water bottles, and nibbled on some granola bars to quell their hunger.

They were walking along the four lane roadway as there wasn't any real way to reach their street easily and they didn't want to cut through the metro park next to their neighborhood. They had passed a couple of other folks heading the same way, but didn't say anything to them. One lady had asked them if they had any water.

Diana pulled out a small eight-ounce bottle of water and handed it to her. She also gave her a granola bar and then just turned away and continued walking without saying anything or even responding to the thank you she received. They were just shy individuals, not necessarily rude.

About a quarter of a mile up, the three women paused to rest again. It was quite dark out now. Very few stars were out in the night sky.

While taking a quick moment to stretch, a guy walked out from behind some bushes where he had been hiding. He had seen them coming and wanted their bike. He approached Diana and grabbed at her bike and pushed her away.

Karen stepped over and said, "Stop that!"

The guy pushed her hard, causing her to fall to the ground. He flicked open a large-sized pocket knife, exposing the blade.

Dawn yelled at the guy.

He turned to look at her, stepped forward, then saw nothing but muzzle flash. It was a single shot clean through his heart.

Diana helped their mom up and they all stood there motionless, staring at the fallen man. They didn't know what to say, each still gripped in the sudden fear of surprise and near-assault. Dawn looked down at the motionless man as her nerves edged and she threw up all over him. She gagged a bit on her vomit and tried to spit it out, but just puked some more. She walked a few feet away, opened her water bottle and rinsed her mouth out. She was still dry heaving a bit and they all moved a bit further away from the body.

Finally she cleared her mouth and said, "We need to go."

Diana looked at her. "You shot the guy to death."

"Well," she said, "it was him or us. Didn't you see his knife? Let's go."

They started walking again and no one said anything. Dawn kept thinking that they should have just let him take the bike. They didn't know if he would actually use the knife or not. He had pushed them around, though, and that was enough she decided. She would not let harm come to her family, and all she knew was her instinct at the moment led her to squeeze the trigger.

The three women kept walking the rest of the way, which was another mile and a half home. Once there, they opened the garage and put their gear and bikes inside and then went into the house. They lit up some candles and went to work. Although tired from the walk, they were also exhausted from the encounter they had just an hour ago.

They placed some large wooden dowels in the tracks of the windows and door wall, made sure everything was locked, and closed the shades. And then they all just fell asleep right there in the living room. They decided they would get up in the morning and finish what needed to be done then. None of the three really slept well that night.

Right around seven in the morning, a racket began outside the house. Dawn jumped off the couch and ran to the front window and looked outside to see the cause. Her neighbor across the street had an old Chevy Nova II that he used to take out on weekends, which used to really make her mad.

His routine was to start it, gun it a couple dozen times, then leave it running for almost half an hour before he would leave. He had it straight-piped for no reason other than the sound, so there were no mufflers to keep it quieted down.

On her weekends off, Dawn had preferred to sleep in, but was always woken up early by this rude noise. Now she watched for a few minutes and noticed the guy and his wife were loading up the old Chevy with suitcases and boxes. She remembered Haliday telling her that if they were going to bug-out, to have everything ready beforehand. If they had decided to take extra clothes, use good old army surplus laundry bags.

The reason behind using the surplus laundry bags was that they were cloth, thus they were flexible, and with the odd shapes of trunks they could be mashed into the tighter spaces to save room. The shapes of suitcases and boxes didn't really make good use of trunk and cargo spaces; too much wasted room in his opinion. She wasn't about to tell the neighbor that, though. *Screw him*, she thought. He probably didn't have them anyway, but trash bags would work.

All those weekends waking up at six in the morning were for nothing Dawn thought. The neighbors looked like they were finished and he closed their garage door and got in the old Chevy. Halfway down the driveway it stalled out. He tried to start it again, but no luck. After a couple of minutes, he got out and opened the hood. He wiggled a few wires, checked some connections on the spark plugs, got back in and tried again, but no luck.

He got back out, now visibly upset, and glanced toward Dawn, whom he now saw standing in the window. She had the biggest smirk on her face and obviously he saw it.

"Oh, is this amusing you?" he yelled.

Dawn raised her hand, flipped him the bird and then went back into the living room.

That actually felt good, she thought to herself. She couldn't recall ever giving anyone the bird and used to scowl at Haliday for doing so, which happened quite regularly because he suffered some of the worst road rage you could imagine. On their trips to the ranges, inevitably someone driving along pissed him off. He was quick to salute anyone he thought deserving enough. A quick toot on the horn made sure he had their attention.

When she walked back into the living room, her mother and sister were sitting there. They just stared at her a bit.

"What?" asked Dawn.

They just looked at her some more and she glanced down to see what the problem was. She saw dried blood droplets all over her clothing from her shot to the man with the knife, and the previous night's events rushed back to her.

She ran to the bathroom and threw up again. She grabbed a towel and wiped her face off. She knew this was a natural reaction. She knew it would haunt her for some time, until she learned how to handle it. Haliday relayed a story about what to expect.

—

Years ago in the mid-80s, when Haliday had been stationed down at Fort Stewart, Georgia, in the 24th MP Co., he had been involved in his first shooting. There was a grunt, or infantryman that had gotten in trouble financially and decided he was going to get out of it by robbing the post credit union.

The man walked in one morning with a nylon stocking over his head and carrying a shotgun. A cashier spotted him as soon as he walked in and hit the silent alarm which went directly to the Provost Marshalls Office where they monitored the alarms. Units were dispatched before the guy even made it to the counter.

The road patrol supervisor had been the first to arrive and he started approaching the door to glance inside. He didn't really know any better. He was a freshly promoted sergeant, E-5, and had little experience. His original MOS, or Military Occupational Specialty, was communications.

He had just finished changing his MOS and graduated from the MP academy three months earlier. Just two months before that he had gotten his promotion. To top it all off, his English was hard to understand because he was from Puerto Rico. But, being the army, there was no rhyme or reason, so there he was in a position he didn't need to be in.

In the meantime, two patrol units showed up toward the back of the credit union and one more up front by the road patrol supervisor. The grunt inside saw the reflection of the blue lights and got scared. He started toward the front door and the road patrol supervisor literally lost it and took off running toward the back of the building.

The grunt exited the building and headed the same way. The unit up front hadn't even gotten out of the car yet and was in awe at what was happening. The units in back were standing ready when the sergeant came running around the back yelling in Puerto Rican.

Haliday's senior partner, who was also from Puerto Rico, was the only one who knew what was being said. He yelled, "Watch out!" and motioned toward the side of the building. No sooner had the road patrol supervisor passed them by when the grunt came around the side as well.

The four MPs at the back were yelling for him to stop. The grunt almost fell over trying to stop so quickly.

"Drop it! Drop it now!" It was in chorus from all four of them.

The grunt shifted his stance and raised the shotgun. The sounds of the 1911's .45 caliber pistols firing was a deafening sound. The grunt was jerking violently around and then dropped to the ground in a large mass of flesh and blood.

Haliday and his partner approached the grunt's body slowly after a quick magazine change. One MP from the other car stood watch while the fourth called the matter in to dispatch. Dispatch acknowledged and said they were sending an ambulance; wouldn't do any good for the grunt, but the road patrol supervisor could use it. He was standing there in shock.

This was his worst day as an MP and this would also be his last day as an MP. Looking down at the poor guy, they realized he never had a chance. Between the four MP's, 32 shots of .45 had been fired. They only hit the guy 11 times, but with a .45 it was enough to turn him into hamburger. Haliday had never seen anything like that in his life.

He had told Dawn the story and of some of the emotions she could expect if she ever had to do something like this. There would be shame because you took a life, but you could justify it with the "It was them or us" thought process. There would be anger because the person made you do it and you didn't want to. There would also be sadness that you could not associate with anything at all. Sleepless nights would occur at first, but you would eventually get past it. You would get physically sick and probably throw up. But after time, you would learn to live with it. You would never forget it, but you would learn to live with it.

Dawn snapped back from remembering the story Haliday had told her. She grabbed a trash bag out of the kitchen and went upstairs to her room, where she took her clothes off and put them in the trash bag. She put on fresh clothes and went downstairs and she tossed the bag in the laundry room. She wasn't sure if she should wash or burn them. She told her mom and sister to either go change and get ready for some breakfast or just head to the kitchen. They needed to get a lot done and get it done as soon as they could.

Moments later, everyone was sitting at the table. They boiled up some water and made instant oatmeal and sat there eating. Her sister asked her what they had to do next. Dawn went to the living room and grabbed her notebook. She had a list—she had lists for everything. She always wanted to know what to do and what she needed to have. She didn't quite have everything they needed, but at least they were ahead of the curve.

She liked the name *sheeple* she had read about and heard on occasion. The sheeple were going to be in big trouble. It was the sheeple she was preparing for. They were also going to be a big problem for those who had taken the time, energy, and money to prepare for whatever event would change their lives forever.

"Time to get to work," she said. "First things first." She hated that saying. Wouldn't first things always be first? Just like *It is what it is*—another one she hated. She thought the degradation of the English language was a big part of why the country was turning out the way it was. She remembered stores and gas stations being closed on holidays, people attending church and not just on the holidays, and TV being clean and fun.

Her favorite show was *Leave it to Beaver.* Haliday said he watched it as a kid and she had remarked, "It's good isn't it?" He burst her bubble by saying he and his friends only watched it because of the pointy bras and boobs like June Cleaver used to have. That drove Dawn nuts. Haliday drove her nuts. He always had something to say. *The good old days*, she thought. She outlined what needed to be done and she and Karen and Diana set about getting it done.

Dawn tried to keep herself busy by thinking of other things, like Haliday and good TV, but soon enough the work around the house replaced those thoughts. She opened the garage door and grabbed some plywood. Haliday had helped her make the window covers like the ones he used.

Now she, her sister, and mom got busy putting these on the windows of the lower level of the house. It took two of them and sometimes all three, especially with the door wall to the patio, to fit the protective wood into place. The lower level was finally finished. They took a quick break then readied themselves for more.

The upstairs windows were hard to get to. Only the two smaller bedrooms had an eave under them, with the rest being out of reach. They added a couple more dowels to keep these secured and then retrieved some fire extinguishers from the basement to place by each upper window.

The two windows over the eave could be access points, so these they handled differently. Since they actually provided a very good line of sight for the front of the house, they used quarter-inch thick Plexiglas, which was secured in a frame with a couple boards across the middle for strength.

The eave itself would have a few surprises. During preparations, Haliday had taken some two-and-a-half-inch nails and painted them black. He then took some heavy duty tar paper and pushed the nails up through them. The pieces of tar paper were trimmed down enough to slide up under the shingles. There were 60 of these ready to go. The eave was a mere 20 feet wide and only four feet deep, so there were plenty of foot and knee pokers, should the need arise.

As Haliday told her, "Kind of like punji sticks, like they used in Vietnam."

Dawn went outside with a ladder from the garage and then put the nail-blankets of tar paper in place and went back inside when she was done. She locked the garage door down along the rails but did not have a grid wall like Haliday did. Instead she had four two-by-six boards which, when placed vertical, spread across the garage door. They were connected at the top with five long screws into the door header.

The bottoms had taken a bit more finesse. There was a base plate attached for strength and then a large hole drilled through. This was attached to the eye bolts they had secured in the concrete floor. If someone wanted to push through the door, it wouldn't be that easy as they would meet a good amount of resistance.

The windows and doors were now locked down and secured. The three women took another break and decided to go over the list that Dawn had made. She got up from the living room couch, walked over to a nearby shelf and flipped on her ham radio there. They had strung a wire antenna in the trees next to her house and ran it into the house, next to the fireplace where the ham was plugged into a 12-volt source.

She only had a couple of outlets running on a few batteries. It was nothing like Haliday's setup. She would wait a bit and then try to reach him. She had been asked by Haliday to wait for 24 hours, enough time to get home, secure the place, and take care of any little things. To travel 12 to 15 miles in one day was more than acceptable the first couple of days of an event such as the EMP.

She looked down at the fireplace, which was natural gas. She saw the pilot flame flickering. It was great news. She knew that Haliday's mom and dad had watched a video online about fuel sources and what to expect in SHTF scenarios. They had told him that natural gas was a constant source and would continue to provide fuel at a constant pressure unless it was turned off.

Haliday had done a little more research and had passed the information on to Dawn. Through him, she learned that in Michigan they had a lot of natural gas wells and it was possible they could have natural gas flow for four to six weeks, if not longer. Of course, there were a lot of factors that could change that, but they could use it as long as they were able.

She turned up the volume on the radio and listened. She double-checked the frequency list she had made and found it was set correctly. She waited. The voice she heard was definitely his.

"Kaybear and Bobily, on track, all safe, reply please."

The replies came: "Yes," "Yes."

And then Dawn added a, "Me, too."

Haliday asked, "Who is this?"

"It's Munch." He called her munch, short for munchkin, and she hated it. He was just like that big brother that made life hell.

"Anything bad going on?" he asked. There was silence. Dawn was thinking about how she had killed a man. "Anything bad?" he asked again.

Dawn finally said, "We are fine, but we had a problem."

"Okay, if you are fine then you need to move on," came his response. "Stay busy and worry about the problem later. Work will take you're your mind off things a bit. With everyone here now, I'll revert to more normal talk on the ham, but refer to my instruction sheet on keeping security on the net tight."

Of course everyone except Dawn wondered what had happened.

Chapter 7

While Haliday was on his way to Illinois, Rich and Bev had been going over things all day long. They were also checking the radio every couple of hours to make sure they had things ready and secure. Bev had gotten serious about prepping again about six months ago. Although she still had stock from her Y2K preps, she always wanted to build upon that.

Over the years, she kept a large quantity of canned foods on hand and constantly rotated through them. She had also kept large supplies of toilet paper, paper towels, soap, deodorant, and more like items on hand. You could go over there and shop in a pinch and be able to take home enough food or supplies to get you by until payday if you had to.

Rich just went along with the program. He was not into being ready like Bev, but he was a good supporter of the cause and helped when he could. He would run out to the store to catch the sales, hit the gas station to fill up gas cans, and help stock and inventory things. They had sectioned off a small part of their basement and dedicated it to preps. His reward was a trip to the casino every couple of weeks, which he enjoyed a lot.

Often times, Haliday joined them for a little fun at the casino. Next to smoking, gambling was Rich's only vice. He never really thought anything would happen to the electrical grid, and now that it had, he found himself appreciating the readiness of the household.

They had continued to stock enough food and were fully prepared to take in some immediate family members if they were able to make it to them. At last count, there were a dozen more mouths to feed and they calculated they had enough food for about five months or maybe seven if they were careful on portion control. There were even pudding packs they'd bought at a warehouse club once they found out that the dairy cups lasted almost two years.

These would be treats for the kids. Rich was fond of making sure these were sufficiently rotated. Bev had canned a couple hundred pounds of meats just in the three months before the incident because, as she said, she had that *feeling*. Rich kept telling her not to waste her "feeling" on the end of the world—instead tell him what the winning lottery numbers would be.

They were checking on their water supply, which was not the best. They had two 55-gallon drums ready and a couple cases of bottled water. They also had the hot water heater, but would be saving that for bathing and cleaning over the next couple days.

They knew the water wouldn't be hot, but warm enough to clean up without having to boil any water. They heard a knock on the door. They both went upstairs from the basement. Haliday had told them never to answer the door alone; someone should always be at the ready, out of view, in case they needed to fire on an unwelcomed intruder.

When they got upstairs to the door, Bev asked who it was and heard the reply. It was her granddaughter, Sarah, with her three-year-old great-granddaughter Elizabeth. They went through a little word game so Bev knew it was safe to open the door. She opened the door and let them in. They gave each other a quick hug and closed the door.

Bev asked where Sarah's husband was and she said he had not made it home, so that morning she had packed up and they walked there. They had been walking all day, but mostly Sarah pulled Elizabeth in a little wagon. It had only taken them about four hours to make the 10-mile trip from their trailer park.

Sarah said she was worried about her husband, Erik, but Bev told her Erik knew where the house was and should know to meet them there. That didn't seem to satisfy Sarah, though, because Erik had only been about 15 miles from home when everything went down. She thought he should have been home by the time she left.

*****

———

Little did she know that Erik was stuck in an elevator and didn't know how to get out. He had been the only one in it when it stopped and he didn't have any idea how to get the doors opened and he couldn't reach the access hatch on the top of it.

He had been moving some cleaning equipment from one floor to another in a very small three-story office building that was under construction when the elevator he was in suddenly stopped. As far as he knew, it was just a power failure. His phone was out in his car charging and when he had yelled for help, all he heard was another guy tell him the power was out, but he would try and get help. There had been only around 20 people in the building working on it and most of them had left.

Erik sat there waiting in the stalled elevator, shouting for help every once in a while.

*****

Sarah got settled in at Bev's place and asked if she could rest for a bit. Bev was understanding, and Sarah and Elizabeth went into the guest bedroom and lay down on the bed to take a nap. Rich and Bev let her sleep because it was obvious she was up most of the night worrying, and the walk had taken all of the energy she had left.

As Sarah laid there trying to think about where her husband could be, she drifted off to sleep. She wouldn't wake up for another four hours.

Elizabeth slept for only two hours. When she got up, she left the room and chased the cats around the house and played with them. Then she asked if she could watch TV. Bev said it was broken. Elizabeth said it was broken at her house, too. Bev gave her some paper and crayons and she drew pictures. Bev had made sure there were things around to occupy their time instead of just sitting around.

Rich came in from the garage where he had been looking for a water filter. "I found it, Bev," he said. "I'll try it and see if it works." He noticed Elizabeth was awake and now coloring. "That's a nice cow you have there," Rich said.

Elizabeth frowned, "It's a pony Great-grandpa."

He climbed down the stairs to the basement and went over to the sump pump. He dropped the end of a hose in the sump and pumped the handle of the water filter until water came out. He filled a plastic cup and set it aside.

Next he put a small float in the sump and then measured how far down it was and made a note of the time and depth. They were not too sure how much water would seep into the sump, but they knew it would have to be monitored so the basement did not flood.

He took the cup upstairs and placed it on the kitchen table. "Here you go, Bev."

Bev walked over and looked at it, holding it as though it was a lab sample of some sort. She handed it to Rich and said, "Try it."

Rich said, "I'm not trying it. I'm not going to be your guinea pig." He was very insistent that he would not be trying it.

"Oh, come on now," she argued. "Roger said that filter could clean pee so it was good enough to drink."

"Well, let Roger drink it when he gets back," he quipped. "I'll use it for flushing the toilet, but I'm not drinking that stuff." He paused, wondering how long the toilets would be able to be flushed. The running water was gone for sure, but he didn't know how long it would be before the sewer system was shot.

Sitting around the kitchen table, Bev made a quick lunch. It was late in the afternoon, but they had been busy and had not eaten yet. She simply warmed up a big can of ravioli and pulled out some bread and butter. Bev, Rich, and Elizabeth sat and ate lunch. They saved some for Sarah who was still sleeping. When she got up, surely she would be hungry.

Elizabeth asked for dessert and Bev handed her a pudding. Rich teased her a little bit and acted like he was going to steal it from her.

Elizabeth squealed in protest.

He smiled at her and acted miffed. "How about you just give me a little bite?"

74

"Great-grandpa, you can lick the top," she said.

He laughed and said, "Okay, that's a deal."

She handed him the foil lid and ran off with her treat.

Bev walked over to the radio and turned it on. A call was received and she was starting to feel better about the trip Roger was making. She figured that he would be the one who could get the job done as fast as possible and as safe as possible. Her only concern was how Linda, her ex daughter-in-law, and Linda's new husband would react to him taking Kayla out of their home. Although she knew if it became an issue, Roger would be able to get something worked out.

Sarah had gotten up and walked into the kitchen and kissed Elizabeth, who had returned with an empty pudding cup. Sarah sat down and Rich warmed up her ravioli and put the plate down in front of her. He buttered up a piece of bread and set it on a napkin, along with a glass of tea next to her plate.

She slowly ate, and they could see she was still deep in thought.

She finally just said it aloud. "I hope Erik is okay. I'm praying nothing bad happened. I thought he would have been home or have been here by now."

Elizabeth said, "Mommy, where is Daddy?"

"On his way here," she said. On his way here, she hoped.

*****

Erik was still in the elevator and was literally going crazy at the moment. He had no idea how long he had been trapped there. He had taken several short naps, and was thirsty and hungry. His voice was weak from yelling for help, and he had resorted to urinating and defecating in a corner of the elevator.

What in the hell is going on out there? he thought. *Why the hell hasn't anyone rescued me?* He had flipped the service cart, also trapped with him on its side, and stood on it to try and find a hatch in the ceiling. He found it, but it wouldn't open. As time passed, he thought about nuclear war, a tornado, power outage, or some other disaster, but wasn't sure what had happened.

75

He paid attention to sports and had watched a lot of horror movies, but he too was really just a sheeple who didn't mock the preparedness society, but saw it as a waste. He'd never gotten into doomsday movies. He didn't really know what an EMP was and he sure as hell didn't know the effect one was going to have on him.

The darkness of the car alone was really bearing heavy on his mind. He kept thinking he felt something touch him and would jerk away. The slightest sounds were amplified and he would scream for help, believing the noises he heard were from rescuers. The air inside the elevator car was stale and the odor from the urine and feces was overwhelming.

*****

The evening was approaching and soon it would be time to light some candles. Sarah had stayed at the table and played a few games of dice with Rich and Bev. Elizabeth either ran around chasing the cats or played with a few toys kept around the house for the great-grandkids. They were waiting for six o'clock, which should be the next time that Roger checked in. In a normal world, he would have been there already, but that was taking highways and cutting through major cities, all of which would be very dangerous now.

Bev asked Rich to run the generator for a couple hours. He went into the attached garage, opened the garage door a crack and started the generator. He wasn't going to screw around with back fed circuits, so he had had a transfer switch installed. He switched it over. The door from the garage to the house was well sealed, but he still had a fan by the muffler to act as an exhaust to vent as much as he could outside. He stood there for a bit and smoked a cigarette. He went back inside and heard the ham.

*****

Erik had finally managed to get the handle off the floor buffer that was also with him in the elevator. He used it to try to pry open the doors of the elevator, but they wouldn't budge. Next he started jabbing at the ceiling where he had finally found the hatch and actually managed to get it to pop open. He got up on the service cart and tried to lift himself up.

———

It took him quite a few attempts, but he managed to get up on top of the car. He rested there; the task was too much for him and he needed a break. The one thing he noticed was the air seemed quite a bit better now with enough flow to help overcome the rankness he'd left on the elevator floor. He had covered it with rags, but that didn't help keep the odor down much.

After resting and thinking about his family and what may have happened, he lifted himself up and felt around on the door mechanism. He had been on the third floor when he got on the elevator and was only halfway down to the second when it stopped. He tried to pry the doors open that led to the hallway, but these, too, did not give very much. He could catch a glimpse of daylight when he did this. He wasn't sure how long he had been in here. He thought it might have been only hours, but couldn't tell for certain. All he knew was that he was hungry, very thirsty, and starting to get cold.

And, he was going crazy in all literal senses.

*****

Haliday had checked in with Bev and Rich and told them everything was going okay. He told his listeners quickly of his encounter and said he might be delayed in checking in every couple of hours, so they should wait until 15 minutes past the hour before turning the ham off. He didn't want anybody's radio overheating. They were too valuable and the handhelds they had for back up didn't have the range for clear enough communication's at that distance. This was going to have to work for now and he assured them he would be okay.

After the call, Rich returned to his games. He liked playing dice games. He had put his time in for the "Big Three" of the auto industry in skilled trades, and usually on breaks or during down time in his working years, he and the workers would play dice, dominoes, or some cards. This would amount to hours sometimes as he would program his machine and let it run its cycle. He now occupied himself with these games and crossword puzzles. After a few more games, he excused himself from the table to go turn off the generator and use the bathroom.

Sarah and Bev sat at the table alone. Bev told her not to worry just yet, that there was a lot going on out there, and that things were not that easy to do these days. She reminded her granddaughter that she was still waiting for her own children to make it in. Bev had six total, five boys and one girl, and what a handful they were. One son and the daughter lived out of state. Another son had forsaken the family and the family had forsaken him for reasons they never really talked about. That left Roger, a younger brother David, and an older brother Alan in the state.

Bev had worked in a variety of jobs as a waitress, at packing boxes in a warehouse, and had ultimately put herself through school and became a substance abuse counselor. She had the ability to help people think clearly through problems and this experience came in handy at the moment with Sarah. She was able to keep her calm during the long wait.

*****

Erik got up one more time to see about prying the doors open. He was shouldering one of the doors when it started to slide open. Encouraged, he moved his feet to brace himself for leverage and stepped into the open hatch, causing him to tumble down into the car. He landed hard and snapped his leg just above the ankle.

Pain flooded him. There was no way possible he was going to get out of this by himself now. He sat there in agony and straightened his leg out a bit. His pant leg was damp and he knew he was bleeding despite the darkness. He grabbed the service cart, latched onto some rags, and tied them around his leg.

All the while he was thinking about Sarah and Elizabeth and hoping they made it to her grandma's house. Despite the pain, he thought about how cute Elizabeth was during her ballet recitals and how good of a cook Sarah had become. He reminisced about all of the good times they had had over the years. Now tired, he drifted off to sleep with these thoughts on his mind.

Erik would never wake up.

Chapter 8

When Haliday checked in again he pretty much figured that everyone would be okay. With just about a day and a half since the country had gone dark, things would still be fairly civil. In another couple of days, the people would start to panic.

This was when things would start to go Wild West as he used to say. Rule of law would become rule of gun. He wanted to be as close to home as he could be at that point. He would prefer to be back in Michigan, period.

He was well clear of Bryan and now into Indiana, heading west, just about 15 miles above Fort Wayne. He would soon start to head south and run through another small town called Warsaw. Hopefully there wouldn't be any problems. He had noticed a lot of old tractors and ATVs on the road, but very few cars.

What cars he did see you would expect to see in a museum or better yet, the Woodward Dream Cruise—Detroit's only saving grace in recent years, the one day dedicated to cruising Woodward Avenue with vintage autos. One thing he did not see yet was any sign of military vehicles. Of course he was trying to avoid any military installation of any kind. There would be far too much explaining to do if he got caught.

With dusk setting in he flipped on the headlights and continued his trek. He was making pretty good time. A lot of the vehicles on the road had been pushed out of the way, making travel easier.

It was much different than up in the Detroit area. People up there had no respect for anything and just left cars where they were. They did that when one broke down in normal times. Civilization in the Detroit area had turned for the worse years ago and just kept turning even worse as far as he was concerned.

Staying off the highways and sticking to smaller county roads, Haliday encountered very few people. When he did, he simply flipped the light bar on and honked the horn to clear them out of the way. He learned quickly that if he didn't bother to slow down they got out of the way much faster. He heard plenty of shouts as he passed by but he didn't listen. Most of them were yelling "pig," "useless feds," and some more colorful choices. He kept the windows up and paid no attention. No distractions; he had had enough of them already and it wasn't fun.

Through his years of military service, working as a police officer and in private security, he had given up a lot of his life. He had made many sacrifices for a lot of people. It was now his turn which is why he concentrated solely on his task at hand.

He skipped through some frequencies on the ham and stopped at one in particular. The guy sounded like he was reading from a script. He was telling everyone in the armed services, National Guard, reserves, and all branches to make their way to their installations as soon as they could. He told all hams to pass the message along as best they could, to post messages in communities, word of mouth, any way they could.

Was this guy crazy? Haliday wondered. *How many of these guys were going to leave their families?* There was no telling. A lot of the troops would have figured out by now how dire the situation was. He wasn't too sure they would respond as requested.

The distance he was covering now was great. He was pretty much in the middle of nowhere and didn't see any houses or people close by, so he pulled over and turned the lights off. He grabbed a small bag and one of the thermoses from the truck and walked around to the hood so he could keep watch and stretch.

He opened the thermos and a small bag of instant soup and dumped it in. He closed up the thermos and shook it violently to mix the soup. Cheddar broccoli, not his favorite, but it would do. He opened the thermos and drank it down. It was just barely warm, but he hadn't really had anything yet and needed to eat.

He grabbed a bottle of water, dumped a tube of powdered Tang in it, and drank this down quickly, too. He had bought some plastic tubes used for making candy art at school carnivals and filled them with pre-measured amounts of Tang so it would be easier to mix. He got another bottle of water and swished a little of it in the thermos and dumped it out. He stopped what he was doing. He looked toward the direction he was heading and heard a noise.

Clop-clop-clop-clop.

He went over to the passenger side door and opened it so he could grab his rifle. He left the door open and took cover behind it and then watched as a figure came into view. It was a teenage girl riding along on a horse.

She stopped and looked at him. "You okay, mister?"

He said, "Yeah, I'm fine. What are you doing out this late?"

"I'm going home; I was visiting my friends down the road."

He slid the rifle back into the truck and walked around the front of the Tahoe.

"Your truck die, mister?"

"Not at all," he said. "I stopped to grab a quick bite to eat and something to drink."

She asked him how it was possible that his truck was running when most of the cars around there weren't.

Haliday cursed himself under his breath and began thinking that dressing as Charles Manson might have actually been a better idea; more risk of getting shot right away, but fewer bothersome questions time after time.

"The government has a fleet of hardened vehicles in case of problems just like this. The EMP that went off did not affect the fleet and the vehicles can be used in the recovery of the nation," he explained. "How far down the road do you live?"

She said, "About another mile or so."

He remembered seeing a smaller farmhouse with a large barn.

"Well, you better get going, and let me give you some advice," he said. "You never want to get caught out here in the dark, and you never want to get caught out here alone. Times are different, young lady. You have no idea what type of people you'll start to encounter out here."

She said thank you and that it was time for her to get going. She started riding off, and as she did, he walked around to the road and watched her. Her right hand holstered a pistol of some sort, but he couldn't tell what kind. She had drawn it and kept it out of view before she got to him, but he could tell by her one-handed control of the horse and by her keeping her right hand down by the saddle that she was hiding something.

"Damn," he said. "Some of these people just might do okay."

He looked around as sounds of the horse got quieter with distance. He went to the truck and reached in and grabbed a roll of toilet paper and bottle of baby powder. He walked over to the ditch and took a squat. Before he pulled his pants back up, he used a little baby powder. The BDUs were rubbing him raw and he needed a little comfort.

"Ahh, big difference," he told himself. He walked back to the truck, climbed in, and took off.

He made up some of the lost time, but was still short of his goal. He turned a flashlight on and looked down at his binder on the passenger seat. He had made it through Warsaw okay and a few smaller towns as well. He was now about 150 miles out from his destination. His radio checks hadn't revealed any problems or any new info. Things were going good right now. He looked down at his dashboard and noticed he needed gas soon. He would have to start looking for some.

It was close to midnight by now. He had been driving for almost 18 hours total. Six and half hours—that was his record back in the days when they used to travel to see Linda's folks who lived there. Her folks had since moved to Florida when they retired, but after the divorce she had moved back to where family was. They had no plans to move because Mike had just gotten settled in a new job.

Just past a little town called Monticello, Haliday stopped by a big old Ford dually stalled out on the side of the small two lane road. Haliday figured it to be a diesel and so he went and checked the fender. He had turned the headlights and Tahoe off, so he used a red-lens flashlight to look at the big truck.

F350; no symbol other than that.

He walked around to the other side where he saw the same thing. "Are you kidding me?" he said out loud.

He checked to see if it was unlocked, but no luck. He peered inside on the dashboard. There it was—Unleaded Fuel Only.

He grabbed his gas can and gear and went to work draining the tank. He hit a homerun with this one; he was able to fill the Tahoe completely from this one truck.

From there Haliday had about 20 miles until he hit the left-hand turn that would put him south until he headed west again to Decatur. He made another check on the radio and told them he was about three hours out. He continued running through the small towns he encountered with the light bar on.

Only a couple times did he have a close encounter with hitting a stalled car or truck. He was in the home stretch now. Thank goodness it was nighttime. Everyone seemed to be hunkered down at home and asleep. It wasn't until he was just a few miles away from where he wanted to be that he ran into more trouble.

It was 2:30 in the morning and he was looking forward to a few hours' sleep. It wasn't such a bad thing that he was rolling in at night. He was in the home stretch. He stopped just two miles from where he needed to be and killed the lights immediately and watched in disbelief.

Haliday could not believe what he saw. It appeared that the whole intersection ahead of him was ablaze. *What in the hell is going on down there?*

He got out and tried to look with his binoculars but couldn't make out anything specific through the smoke or the flames. He reached in and grabbed the ham. "Kaybear, are you there? Kaybear, are you there, kiddo? Kaybear, talk to me."

"Hey, Roger, this is Mike," said a man's voice. "I've got them hiding in a closet. All hell is breaking loose around here. It's bad. I've never seen anything like it."

Haliday could hear an occasional gunshot in the background.

"What the hell is happening, Mike?"

"You ain't gonna believe this," Mike said.

"Come on, Mike, I need a SITREP."

There came no answer.

"Mike, you copy?" Haliday asked urgently. "Mike, you copy?"

Mike replied, "Okay, I had to ask Kayla what a SITREP was. Situation Report right?"

Haliday grew impatient. He was concerned about their well being. "Yes, Mike, now what the hell is going on?" He strained to see what was going on through the binoculars and kept hearing the sporadic reports of what sounded like an AR15 and a shotgun. "Mike, tell me what you know."

Mike came back and said, "Damn, I think we need to get the hell out of here."

"Bullshit," Haliday told him. "You don't know what the hell you are walking into; you better sit put and try to figure this out. You put a gun in everybody's hands right now; I don't care if it's a damn flintlock." He hated that damn FOID Illinois residents had to have. You could barely look at ammo without having a congressional inquiry. His adrenaline was pumping strong and he had to fight the urge to storm down there. "Mike, you have any idea what's going on?"

"Roger, this is all I know and I heard it from a neighbor. The jail unlocked when this all happened lots of prisoners took off. The deputies were able to contain some, then one by one they started to leave. Soon there were more prisoners than guards and they rushed them," Mike said. "A few of them that were waiting for transport to the state prison for murder convictions rallied a couple more guys together and they took off toward the strip mall. They ran across a police car stalled in the intersection. It had a Gator 4X4 used to patrol parks on an attached trailer.

"They managed to shoot the cop guarding it and take the shotgun and rifle and then they torched the vehicles. Now they're just shooting blindly at anything. Some of the houses have been hit. The escapees have been sitting around for a couple hours now drinking, smoking, and eating everything out of a party store."

"How do you know this, Mike?" he asked.

"My neighbor is a sheriff's deputy at the jail. He took off before it got too bad."

Haliday looked at the side of the Tahoe that read "Police." *Real good* he thought.

The ham lit up; Mike was trying to talk, Haliday's mom and dad were trying to talk, and Dawn was trying to talk. It was mass confusion.

Haliday managed to get a few words in. "Stop the racket and listen. What's going on is out of my control right now. I can't get the info I need if you're all interrupting me. Now stop so I can talk to Mike," he told them all. "Mike, go get me your neighbor. You have to do this or it isn't going to work."

Mike agreed and returned a few minutes later to the ham and Haliday took notes as he asked questions. There was only one way into the neighborhood and that was going through that intersection. The alternative was crossing a river and that meant trying to walk in and out. *This has to work*, he kept telling himself.

After the call, Haliday backed the Tahoe up slowly onto a side street so he was out of sight. Police vehicles had installed toggle switches so they could disrupt power to the brake lights for just such a circumstance. He looked around to see if anything else was going to be a problem. This seemed like a decent spot.

He looked at a nearby house that had a "For Sale" sign in the yard. There were no blinds or anything on the windows, so he got out and took a quick peek inside. It was empty. He went back to the Tahoe and backed into the driveway and started going over his notes.

He'd have to wait until dawn. If he went through with his plan now, there were far too many risks. He kept going over the map of the area. No other route to get in and out easily. It was the river and a walk or the neighborhood and fences and houses to go over and cut through. Kayla only had a small bit of luggage, but even scaling it as far down as possible was still too risky. Taking her through the neighborhood was far too risky, too. Especially with convicts on the loose.

It had once been the premier housing for the area's two biggest companies which processed corn and soy into the many products commonly used. As the companies grew bigger and the economy grew bigger as well, the execs moved into larger homes. They had done this a few times and now they were spread out in the more rural suburbs on large lots with mini-mansions. This area was now blue collar with the slums not that far away.

It was time to get ready. Haliday keyed the mic on the ham and said "I'm going in now. You'll have time, and this is what I need you to do." He gave some simple instructions to Mike.

He then grabbed the gear he would need and locked up the Tahoe.

Haliday took the side streets of the subdivision as far as he could go. He cut back out toward the street and looked around a bit and spotted the perfect place. It was a large group of mailboxes with a bunch of trash cans next to it and the mouth of a cul-de-sac. He slid in behind the cans and opened his bag and placed a small foam mat down on the ground. He opened up the cans and pulled out a piece of cardboard and few other pieces of trash. Next he moved one of the cans aside slightly to create a small gap.

He unlatched his case and pulled out his rifle. He made ready by covering himself with as much of the trash as he could. The sun would be rising behind him so there shouldn't be any glare off his scope. He had made sure he kept this rifle zeroed and always checked it each month. He had taken out a loan against his 401K to buy it from an older man who had bought too much gun for his ability. Haliday loved the thing and never thought he would own something like it.

He and a couple of other guys from his platoon had excelled in almost all of their duties and rated near perfect on an IG, Inspectors General inspection and were rewarded with a trip to Ft. Benning. They wanted the full-blown sniper school, but had to settle for a one-week designated marksmanship course which had still taught them more than they could have imagined. The skill set they learned was incredible and Haliday never lost it.

He reflected on that time and the times that followed during his active and reserve duty when he had to rely on that skill set.

When he'd spotted the Remington M24 system on Migunowners.org, Michigan's local gun forum, he had called immediately. The price was only $3,000 and the guy selling it said he had barely put 40 rounds through it. The Leupold made it a nice combination and it was a steal. Normally five grand, Haliday couldn't pass it up. He borrowed against his retirement fund and paid himself back. Well worth the cost—not to mention he wouldn't have to repay the rest of that loan any time soon.

The sun was coming up and he looked down the street. There were guys hanging around the burned out vehicles where they had dragged whatever would burn closer and tossed it into the trunk of the cruiser to keep a smaller fire going. Trash littered the entire area.

Haliday could see they were still drinking and smoking and sitting around doing nothing but wandering around the intersection. Had to be better places for them to go, he knew, but then again they didn't look like geniuses. Probably trying to stake out a claim or stock up on whatever they could steal from people passing by.

The sun was fully cresting the horizon now. Haliday peered through the scope and watched as an old man pushing a shopping cart walked by. The dirt bags started in on him and began pushing him around, taunting him.

Haliday couldn't make out any of the conversation, but knew well enough that the old man was in over his head. One of the guys threw a quick jab into the old man's stomach and the old man went down. The others gathered around and kicked him, then dumped beer and liquor all over him.

———

The old man was pleading for his life by the looks of it. His tormenters stopped and stood there for a moment. The man reached into his pocket and pulled out a small bag, which one of the tormenters grabbed and opened. Haliday could barely hear the guy call out to another man.

This other man came walking over from the fire and looked down at the old man. After talking to him a minute he kicked him. Evidently he was convinced the old man was hiding something more. He knelt down next to the old man and pulled out a knife, waving it at the petrified old man.

Haliday sat there watching through the scope. He had made his adjustments long ago. The guy loitering over the old man looked up and Haliday saw a typical piece of crap felon. The guy had a black Mohawk, tattoos all over his neck, a bushy mustache and goatee and looked exactly as the deputy Haliday had spoken to had described. Haliday already had his breathing under control, so he exhaled, felt his heart fall between beats and squeezed the trigger. It was only 600 yards out but the round still reached the target before the report did. The old man on the ground went limp.

It was obvious that the old man had no idea what the hell had happened, but knew better than to get up. The worst thing he had to endure right then was the blood and tissue that had peppered him as the ringleader's head came apart above him. Almost instantaneously there came another report from the opposite side of the intersection somewhere down the street.

Haliday had instructed Mike not to take aim; he merely wanted the shot to be heard to confuse the band of prisoners. From his brief description to Haliday, Mike had gotten beaten pretty good, and with swollen eyes Haliday knew it would be a wasted shot, so there was no sense in exposing himself.

The plan worked like a charm. The scum bags didn't know which way to run for cover. They ran and hid on both sides of the debris. A couple of the men took off running down the northern side street. Haliday took these guys to be the lightweights, most likely serving a year or less for crap like breaking and entering or assault, but nothing major.

The few guys still on the scene were more hardcore. These were the felons waiting to go do some serious time in a state or federal pen, or guys easily lured into a life of promised crime and ruling the city through fear. You always had guys who could not think for themselves and liked to be told what to do all the time.

As this group started looking around, Haliday just waited. Even with the sun over his back he wasn't giving up his position just yet. No sooner had they looked the other way toward Mike's direction than Haliday squeezed off another round. He had miscalculated his breathing and this one dropped a little low, striking the next guy in the base of the neck.

With half of the man's neck gone, his body just slumped down with a small spurt of blood from his jugular every couple of seconds from a heart that just had a few beats left.

Mike's rifle report came just as quick. This time, however, he hit the frame of the Gator. The hiding felons all moved over to Haliday's side of the wreckage.

They looked up and down the street trying to find Haliday. Another guy took the opportunity to take off and headed out at a full sprint. Of the two men left, one guy leveled a shotgun and dropped the deserter with a shot spread to his lower back. The man tumbled forward and then squirmed on the ground.

The other man looked up the street again toward Haliday, and started shooting at what he thought might be a good hiding place. The assault rifle he had wasn't going to reach out at 600 yards accurately, but a wild shot would ruin the day just as easily. Haliday was not sure how many rounds they had at their disposal.

Haliday tried to count the number of rounds fired at him. A bullet hit the mailboxes and that was a bit too close for comfort. He just laid there waiting. The idiot with the shotgun was pumping round after round into the chamber and firing it up the street as well. *What the hell does he think he's going to hit?* Haliday thought. The shotgun was out of rounds real quick. He knew by the pause that the gun was empty and when it didn't fire again, he knew it was out of ammo. *One gun down, one to go,* Haliday thought.

Haliday's eyes darted left and right quickly. He could see people peeking out their windows from homes nearby. *Why don't you people just come on outside and watch the show?* he thought. *I could use the distraction.* He couldn't believe people would risk getting hit, just to see what was going on. The AR was still blindly searching for him. Mike had fired a few more shots toward them and the guys had spun in the direction of the shots, but couldn't spot Mike.

Haliday knew Mike was hiding behind some bushes and blended well, and he stayed hidden until he saw Mike's muzzle flash. He saw the man with the AR come up and take aim at Mike's position and fire four quick shots. Haliday quickly readjusted himself and squeezed off one more shot. This one was dead center to the back of the man's head.

The AR dropped to the ground and Haliday instantly took aim on it and put his fourth and final round of the fight through the receiver, rendering the rifle useless. He sat and watched for about 15 minutes as the last guy of the felon group sat there, shaking in his hiding spot.

Mike had stopped firing and Haliday wasn't sure if he was still alive. He wouldn't be going to check soon either. Whether Mike was alive or not would be answered soon enough.

Haliday scoped the area and didn't see anything other than the last felon sitting there, and the man who'd taken the shotgun blast squirming around on the ground. He also saw the old man who was now trying to get up. Haliday was about to get up when he saw yet another man come out from behind the party store and approach the old man with a revolver in his hand.

"Damn it," he breathed. He was readying the shot when he saw the guy reach down and extend a hand to the old man and helped him up.

Haliday controlled his breathing and heart rate again and kept careful aim. The old guy steadied himself on his shopping cart. The guy with the pistol then walked over to the prisoner sitting there shaking and pointed the pistol at him. Haliday watched through the scope as the man executed the felon with either little or no remorse.

He then watched the man walk over to the squirming figure on the ground and do the same. He reached down and grabbed the bag the guy had been holding. Turning back around, he helped the old man with the shopping cart get back to the sidewalk and gave him the bag back. It explained why his buddy shot him, Haliday decided. No honor amongst thieves or something like that. The guy was running away with the loot.

Haliday waited another 15 minutes or so, and then satisfied he was safe, rose and packed up his rifle and rolled up his mat. He looked down at the trash. He wasn't about to pick it up. He looked toward a couple of the houses and at the people sneaking peeks between the curtains.

He looked at one guy and gave him a thumbs-up sign; the guy returned it with a thumbs-up.

Haliday walked back toward the Tahoe. It had been an intense morning. Looking down at his watch, it had actually only been a total of about 10 minutes from the time the first shot was fired until the last was fired, if even that long.

Reaching the Tahoe, he opened it up, looked around, and saw more people looking at him through half-open doors and parted curtains. He threw his gear in, climbed behind the wheel, started the Tahoe, and turned the ham on.

"You there, Mike?" he asked.

Linda came on and said he was at the table having a drink. She asked Haliday if he was okay.

'Oh yeah, an absolutely run-of-the-mill morning,' is what he wanted to say, but he was too tired. He just said, "Yes. See you guys in a few minutes. Have the garage door open."

Five minutes later he was backing up into the garage. He walked inside to the kitchen, gave Kayla a huge hug, and told her he loved her. Kayla had not changed much since high school. She had long, dishwater blonde hair, pink ends, 5'1 and only 100 pounds.

She was in tears and he was, too. He nodded toward Linda, then wiped his face, walked over to Mike, and said "Good job, old man; can you spare one of those?"

Mike poured Haliday a couple fingers of Jack. Haliday drank it quickly and put the empty glass on the table.

Mike looked up at him, speechless. He hadn't expected anything like what he had just seen. He finally told Haliday that when he saw that AR pointing at him, he rolled over a few times and laid there and prayed he wouldn't die. He had wanted to just run at that point. It was one thing to fire at guys to scare them, but another to actually kill them.

He asked Haliday "How come this doesn't bother you?"

Look, Mike," he said. "I don't have time for it. Suffice it to say that my daughter – hell, you guys, too – all needed me. I did what I had to; not for me, but for you guys." He looked at Linda and then Mike again. "I guess we have some business to talk about now."

Chapter 9

Haliday's parents had heard the exchange that morning over the ham and waited it out while drinking coffee and smoking cigarettes, not knowing what was transpiring, or even sure they wanted to know. Dawn had listened in as well, but had a better idea of what had most likely taken place. All of them were glad when they heard his voice and knew that he was okay. They also decided to leave him alone until he called them.

As for Haliday, he was still looking at Mike after the altercation. "Wait a minute," he said, nodding to the bruising on Mike's face from his earlier beating. "Before we talk, what the hell happened to you?"

Mike told him that the higher-ups had made everyone stay at the plant for almost four hours until they realized the power wasn't coming on any time soon. When they all started to leave, Mike cleaned out his locker. He started the walk home and made his way, going well around the hood. But it turned out he hadn't gone far enough away from it.

He ran into a group of four punks that were shaking people down for drug money. Pickings were good with everyone walking to wherever they needed to go. He told them he didn't have much and tossed whatever cash he did have down on the ground.

One crack head said, "What, we ain't good enough for you to put it in our hands?"

"That's all I have," Mike had told him. "No offense, but I don't want any trouble."

The punks had circled him and started making threats. Mike tried to push his way through, thinking they were bluffing, but they weren't. They quickly jumped him and started throwing punches. He'd dropped to the ground and they started kicking at him. He managed to grab one's leg and pull him off balance, and get to his feet.

They threw more punches and Mike had fought them off the best he could before managing to get away and make a run for it. He ran through a hole in a fence and into an old tire factory. He managed to hide himself and sat there while they searched for him. He'd been certain they would have killed him if they found him.

"We're going to kick your ass when we find you!" one of them had yelled.

They searched for almost an hour, but didn't find him. Mike stayed hidden for hours though. Eventually he finally ventured out. Once out, he got as far away as he could and finished the walk home. It was slow going; he was sore as hell and had bruises everywhere. His face was a mess and he had lost a of couple teeth in the fight.

Haliday shook his head at him. "That sucks Mike." Getting back to business, he put it as plain as he could. "I brought some food that will get you by for a little while." He got up and walked around, looking in their kitchen cupboards.

They had quite a bit of food. Linda was a food hoarder of sorts, always stocking up on sales, but not prepping.

"With all the corn around these parts and this extra food, you should be able to make it until spring," he told them. "Whether you can find a FEMA camp or not before then – if they even exist – is up to you. I don't trust them. I can leave you an AR and about five hundred rounds. You have Mike's bows and you can hunt enough to help. But game will become scarce very quickly with everyone hunting. Flat lands and cornfields won't yield many animals."

Kayla started to tear up. Mike and Linda just kind of hung their heads low. Haliday said if he had any way of supporting them he would take them back, but there was no way they could make it adding two more adults to the mix.

He walked over and opened the freezer and saw it stacked with meat. He grabbed a package and read the label; it was venison. "Where did you bag this deer, Mike?"

Mike said he got it on his friend Bill's farm.

94

"In Michigan, right?" Haliday remarked.

Mike said, "Yes; couple months ago when we were in to visit."

Kayla said, "Dad, please, can't they come with us? Mike and Mom helped get you here." That was partly true, especially about half an hour ago. She was crying steadily now. "Dad, please, can they stay with us?"

Haliday sat down and motioned for her to come over to him. "I don't have room and food, sweetie." He looked at Mike and Linda who were almost in tears as well. "I'll tell you what, though. I'll take them back to Michigan and get them to their friend Bill's farm if they know for sure he'll take them in."

Mike said he was positive Bill would take them in. He'd offered many times before that they could come and stay if they ever wanted to return to Michigan. Mike was even more convinced his friend could use their help with the farm considering the current situation. They were sure of it and Haliday was convinced as well.

Linda gave him a quick hug and said thank you. Kayla gave him a bigger hug. Mike told him anything he needed him to do, let him know.

Haliday said, "Good, because there is a lot to be done. Grab some paper and write this down."

Linda grabbed a notebook and took notes. Haliday left them very specific instructions on what to do. He told them what to pack, no more, no less, what to do with the food in the house and the rest of what he wanted them to grab.

Mike said, "We'll put it all in the truck."

Haliday said, "No, put it next to the truck. When I get up we are going to repack the load in the Tahoe." He went over to Kayla's ham radio on the counter and told Dawn and his folks he would be off the net for a few hours.

"I'm going to go get some sleep. Wake me in three hours and we'll finish getting ready," he told Linda. "You have the list. Get it all done and make sure someone stands guard. Don't let anyone in, including your neighbor the deputy."

Haliday went into the living room and lay down on the couch. Just before he passed out, he thought it would be nice to have the extra guns on the trip home, but questioned if they could do what it might take if it came down to it.

He didn't even remember falling asleep.

"What the hell?" Haliday said as he jumped up. Something was licking his hand as it dangled off the couch. He looked down at the floor at the mutant dog standing there. He couldn't figure out if it was supposed be: a Chihuahua, Border Collie, Pomeranian or what.

Kayla saw his startlement and said, "Good morning, Dad."

"Kayla, what the hell is that?" he asked, looking at the dog.

"That's Max."

Haliday thought, *Great, by the time I get out of here that damn Tahoe is going to look like something out of the 'Beverly Hillbillies.'* "Kayla, you expect to take him or can you leave him with the neighbors?"

And here came the argument. "Did you give Romeo to the neighbor?"

Haliday thought about that a minute. Romeo was his male Siamese cat that he had had for over 12 years and he was 16-years-old now. Romeo, however, could be left for days on end and could fend for himself. He had a two gallon watering dish and a gravity feeder that held enough food for a month.

"Okay," Haliday said, "but if it comes down to it, Max is BBQ."

Kayla threw a shoe at it him for saying that.

Haliday grabbed a bottle of water, went into the bathroom, took care of business, and then gave himself a quick wash down, covering the vital areas. He walked out to the kitchen where everyone was sitting. He was livid. "Who the hell is watching the place?" he yelled.

96

No one said anything.

Linda said, "I thought since we were all up—"

"Listen," Haliday interrupted her, "let someone get in here, and then you have to go look for a gun. It's over if that happens. We do as I say and that's final. Let's go see what we have."

Kayla grabbed her AR and said, "I got it covered."

She stood watch while they went over everything in the garage. Haliday told them to pull everything out of the truck, which they did, and then they repacked it. He asked them if they had every ounce of jewelry and everything of value out of the house that was small and might be worth trading. They did. Linda had also grabbed a couple of photo albums and Kayla grabbed a small box full of pictures.

Haliday told Mike to grab the two gas cans he had seen in the garage and then meet him outside. They drained the gas from their cars and filled the Tahoe and the gas cans. Haliday wedged the gas cans between the KLR and the Tahoe. Room was tight.

"Last thing on the agenda," he said, "go put on black clothing. I don't care what it is, but make sure it's black, plain black, no bedazzled or sequined anything either. Look around, say goodbye to the house and what it has meant to you and meet me by the truck."

They went and changed and then met him back in the garage. They had been crying again. Haliday knew it was like saying goodbye to your whole life. Taking very few possessions was hard, but leaving the security of their home was harder.

"Mike, you get the door," he said. "Linda, jump in the back seat. Kayla, you keep guard and I'll pull the truck out."

There was a small yapping sound and Haliday looked down at Max and then at Kayla.

"Knock it off, Dad," she said. "I know what you're thinking."

He clenched his teeth. Max was then loaded up.

Mike opened the door and Haliday pulled the truck out of the garage. Kayla walked out behind it and then Mike closed the garage door.

Kayla was standing there with her rifle at low ready when they heard the neighbor, Tom—the deputy. He cut through the bushes and asked Mike what was going on.

Haliday got out of the Tahoe and answered immediately. "We are leaving."

Tom looked at him and said, "I recognize you; you're Kayla's dad. What are you doing with this truck?"

"Mind your own business. We're leaving."

Tom had his duty belt on over his jeans and put his hand on his pistol.

Kayla raised her rifle and said, "Mr. Tom, not a good decision."

Tom looked gravely at them all. "You guys are breaking the law. You're stealing government property."

Haliday sent him an impassive look, drew his pistol out and aimed at him. Tom had thoroughly pissed him off now. "Kayla, get in the truck. Mike, head down the street about a hundred yards and then someone get out and cover me." His attention was still on Tom as he told him to unbuckle his duty belt, drop it, and then kick it over to him.

Tom said, "You won't shoot me; I'm a sheriff's deputy."

"Look, jackass," Haliday said dryly, "I spent the morning cleaning up the mess you and your fellow deputies left at the intersection down the street. Now if you really want to try my patience, please don't."

Mike said, "Tom, you're going to want to do what he says; trust me on this."

Tom unbuckled his belt and let it drop before he kicked it over to Haliday.

Mike got in the truck and drove it down the street just a ways.

Haliday picked up the duty belt. He pulled the pistol. He took about 15 steps backwards and turned his head quickly to see Kayla covering him. Haliday jacked the slide back on the pistol but no round came out. He looked at Tom.

"Tom," he said, "are you that frigging stupid that you carry a pistol without one in the chamber?" Tom's lips parted and Haliday interjected, "Don't answer. Here's the deal, Tom. I'm going to walk back to the truck and I'm getting in and leaving. I'm going to leave your pistol on the sidewalk about halfway there. As soon we leave, I suggest you go get it, put one in the chamber, and keep it that way. Forget you're a cop, take care of your wife, and leave it at that. Put together as much food and water as you can and safeguard it like gold. Good luck."

Haliday walked backwards for about 50 feet.. He turned and jogged back toward the truck and dropped the pistol on the grass next to the sidewalk as he ran. He had noticed a few more neighbors outside looking around.

Indicating Haliday, one said, "Hey, buddy, thank you for this morning. The party store owner was robbed and beaten, and after that, those hoodlums raped his wife." He turned to the other neighbors. "The store owner is the one who cleaned up the last two guys this morning."

That had explained a lot. Haliday simply nodded and jumped in the truck and they sped off.

Haliday grabbed the mic and told Dawn and his parents they were on the way back. He asked if they had heard anything. Bev said she heard the big cities were really becoming a mess with a lot of looting and small riots. She heard that the government was having a hard time responding anywhere because a lot of equipment was unusable. Haliday asked them if anyone else made it in and she told him no. *Damn*, he thought. He was certain that at least his brother David and David's son, Bobby, would have made it there.

"Okay, folks, here's the situation," he said. "I have extra company for now. I can't give you a timeline and I can't guarantee regular check-ins. Just make sure you guys double-check your security and keep someone awake at all times. Take turns; three-hour shifts will you give enough of a break in between watches so you can catch some sleep. Keep a pistol on you at all times, too. I have a hell of a trip to make trying to get back. Hopefully I'll see you guys soon."

*****

Meanwhile, Dawn had everyone meet back in the kitchen. "Look," she said, "it's getting really bad out there right now and we need to make sure the house is secured. I'm not sure it's safe to go out yet and there's no telling how long we will have to stay here."

Diana asked her what Haliday thought.

"Well," Dawn said, "he's quite busy right now and said to stay put and run tight security. Everyone is going to have to take a turn watching the house."

Karen asked her how long.

"Three hours at a time is good," Dawn said.

Karen didn't seem to like that.

"We don't have a choice," Dawn said. "So we have to get used to it. Let's check the house."

The three of them started to double-check the windows and doors when Dawn heard Haliday on the ham.

"Dawn, can you read me?"

She answered yes.

"Listen," he said, "go to A2."

This was an alternative frequency set up just for them. He did this in case he needed to relay information that he didn't want anyone else on their net to hear. He did this for his mom and dad's house, too. He had something to say he didn't want Rich and Bev to hear.

"Roger, I'm here," Dawn said on the radio.

Haliday responded, "Look, my folks only have Sarah and her baby there. I'm not sure if they are going to be able to hold down the fort long. They are closer to the city than any of us and if the animals start taking to the streets and moving into the suburbs quicker than I thought, then there are going to be some real problems there."

Haliday added, "You might have to alter your plans, so get things ready. If I call and tell you to get moving, then move out. You need to monitor the radio to keep in touch with what's going on out there. There will be a lot of exaggeration and panic, but a lot of good info as well. Just pay attention to what happens close to you and give me a SITREP when I call."

"Got it," she said. She flipped back to the other frequency and so did Haliday.

Bev's voice came over the ham. "You guys there?"

Haliday said, "Yes, is there a problem?"

"What were you guys talking about?" she asked.

He figured her curiosity would be killing her. "Dawn sometimes doesn't like to share information; she likes her privacy, and I was making sure she didn't need to tell me anything."

"Oh, because I changed frequency as well and didn't hear anything," his mother said.

Haliday said, "That's right. That's why I gave you guys different frequency lists. Security purposes," he told her.

She didn't seem too happy with that.

Dawn and Diana finished double-checking the doors and windows while Karen kept watch. They went into the basement and came up with boards loaded with nails. The boards were one-by-sixes with three-inch nails hammered through. They set these with the nails pointing up by the windows and doors in case someone managed to get in. Anyone who did make it in would impale themselves. While it might not stop them, it would surely slow them down.

Dawn went out into the garage and started the generator for a couple of hours. She had a custom muffler made and had installed so that it extended through the wall of the garage and vented the exhaust outside. They had always lost power six or seven times a year minimum, and they got tired of restocking the refrigerator all the time.

Her neighbors were used to the noise, even though it was fairly quiet. She used this noise as a cover for her next check. She walked over to the Polaris inside the garage and tried to start it. It fired right up. Good, she thought. It was a good four-by-four vehicle with a front and back seat, and had a small trailer. It was completely stock except the mods to make sure it ran, and the tires.

She went back inside and told Diana they had to load up. A knock came to the door and everyone looked at each other. Dawn ran upstairs and looked down at the porch where she saw her next door neighbor. She went downstairs to the door, but didn't open it.

"What do you want?" she asked.

The neighbor said he heard her generator and asked if he could plug in an extension cord.

Dawn said, "Remember the window your son broke playing catch with his friend, the one that you never paid for? Go screw yourself."

"You bitches!" he replied. He left, mumbling under his breath as he walked away.

*****

As Bev took a nap, Elizabeth sat with Sarah. "I want to see Daddy," she said.

Sarah told her, "Maybe later, honey. Daddy might be busy and still trying to make sure he gets here."

Rich was listening in and asked Elizabeth if she wanted to play a game. She gave him an eager yes. They were still playing when she asked him if he thought her other grandma had TV.

Rich told her he didn't know.

"Can we call her?" she asked.

"Not right now. The phone is broken too."

"Everything is broken," she said with a pout. "It's not fun."

Rich was thinking about Susan, his only daughter, who had moved to Texas a couple years ago. He was wondering how her and her family were doing. He thought of his son Greg in Missouri as well. He was the oldest of all the boys. Alan lived about an hour's drive away with his family. His other son, David, lived about half an hour away with his grandson, Bobby.

Rich and Bev had expected all of their kids in the state to make it there, plus Sarah with her husband and another couple of nephews who lived in Michigan to make it in as well. Up until two weeks ago one the nephews had lived with them, but moved out for what he called "more freedom." Rich and Bev didn't know how hard it would be for them to travel without vehicles.

Sarah was just sitting there numb with worry. It had been a full two days now and she couldn't help thinking the worst. She could understand maybe half of a day, even a full day, but not two. Her hopes had dwindled and she resigned herself that she could remain hopeful, but had to expect nothing. This put her into a state of depression.

Bev woke up and seeing Sarah's mood, asked her to cook some dinner. Sarah obliged.

Bev thought, *Good; I will have to keep Sarah busy to help her get through this.*

Rich and Bev knew enough to know Erik was gone.

There came a loud crashing sound from outside in the backyard. Rich and Bev both grabbed their pistols and Bev peeked quickly out the window. Over by the wood pile, she spotted two people. She wanted to open the door and shoo them away because she thought they were stealing their wood. She also wanted to tell them she would shoot them if they didn't leave.

Rich said, "Wait a minute, Ma, that's Kevin and Randy."

Bev immediately realized who they were – their two grandsons, Sarah's brothers.

Kevin and Randy ran toward the door and yelled to be let in.

Rich opened the patio door wall and the two young men stuffed their bags through the wood planks installed across the opening and then squeezed themselves through. They fell onto the floor of the dining room huffing and puffing, trying to catch their breath. Rich asked them what happened and they each raised a finger signaling him to wait a minute. They rested a few minutes and caught their breath. Sarah had run over and asked if they were okay and they nodded yes.

Randy said, "They wanted to kill us."

Kevin said, "No, they just wanted your shotgun."

Randy had purchased a Mossberg 500. He made it all tacti-cool as a birthday present to himself one year. He'd had it for almost two years, but had never even fired it. He had just a few big boxes of ammo for it, maybe 100 rounds total. It was a mix of everything from 00-buck to small game loads because he never really knew what to buy. He wasn't really the outdoors type or a gun nut. But, it was a Mossy and it was cool.

Kevin told them they had been sitting around and decided the power wasn't coming back on, so they left early that morning to come there. They had a fairly uneventful trip until almost the last half of a mile. They were passing by a grocery store where people were basically stripping it clean. Some guy spotted them and yelled at them to drop their gun. He called them punks and said he wanted it. The man called a friend over and they walked toward Kevin and Randy. At this point, Kevin and Randy started running and the guy and his friend chased them.

Kevin was 22 years old, 5'11 and weighed 165 pounds. He had short brown hair and an athletic build. Randy was 23, 5'10" and only 150 pounds. He sported collar length blonde hair.

They cut through the neighborhood, going over the fences, and didn't stop until they got to Rich and Bev's. They were scared and just ran for their lives. They had no idea what the guys would do to them. They just didn't want any trouble and didn't want to get shot with their own gun. Randy said when they went over the fence in the backyard, they'd forgotten about the wood pile. They landed on it, sending it crashing down to the ground.

Randy said, "Grandma, you should have seen the grocery store. It was chaos. I think as soon as they opened this morning everyone was getting what they could. Money or not, it became a riot and people were fighting each other for anything they could get their hands on. I don't think anything's left. They were knocking people down in the parking lot and taking other people's thing's. People were hurt and bleeding all over the place. A lot of them were running with their arms full to the apartments across the street." He then asked for some water.

Rich said, "Hold on a minute, it's downstairs." He left and brought them up a pitcher of water filtered and filled from the sump pump. He had been getting about 15 gallons a day out of it, but was only filtering a few gallons. He'd used a rotary pump to drain the rest.

Haliday had installed a separate check valve on the sump pump's discharge pipe and Rich attached the hose from the rotary pump to that. Now Rich had found himself some guinea pigs. Kevin and Randy drank the whole pitcher down and didn't complain. Rich guessed it was safe to drink, which was a good thing. Water would be plentiful as long as the groundwater kept up at a decent level.

Sarah gave them a big hug. She was happy to see her brothers. Kevin asked where Eric was.

The room fell silent.

Sarah began to tear up and said, "I don't know. I don't think he's going to make it here."

"Don't worry, sis," Randy said and hugged her some more. "There's still hope."

Elizabeth, who had been watching, said, "I want hugs, too." She ran over and got her share of hugs.

Having Randy and Kevin there would be a great help. It would make bringing things up from the basement a lot easier and pulling security easier as well. Bev went over to the ham and called Haliday ; she told him what had happened.

Haliday said, "Okay, you copy, Dawn?"

She replied yes.

Haliday said, "Okay, everyone, keep up the good work, and talk to you later."

In transit from Linda's house, Haliday was relieved there were more people at his folk's house now. "Dawn," he said into the ham mic, "A2 again."

He waited while she switched frequencies before he spoke. "Okay. I want you to hold tight right now. When I call you I want you to go ahead with the first plan you have in your notebook. Any questions?"

Dawn asked if he had an ETA.

Haliday said, "Hell, Dawn, I'm not sure we'll even make it. If we don't get back in the next twenty-four hours, the rate this country is falling apart will make it impossible. It's going to be hard. No doubt about that. Switch back and talk to you later."

Haliday was just about to tell everyone he was going to check back in a couple hours when he looked down the road and noticed something different. "That wasn't there when I came through earlier," he said to himself.

He brought the truck to a stop and Mike asked him what the problem was. Haliday handed him a pair of binoculars.

Mike glanced ahead of the Tahoe and said, "Oh shit."

There were four Humvees sitting there with about eight men as far as Mike could tell.

Haliday said, "This could be real bad. Give me a hand, Mike."

He got out of the truck with Mike following and they walked around to the back. "Help me unload this thing."

They unloaded the KLR and Haliday opened the hatch and searched for some gear.

"They gotta be wondering what we're up to right now, Mike. We're not too far from Danville. I'm not sure, but my guess is it's a National Guard unit, most likely the Thirty-Eighth MP CO. Not sure what their mission is right now," Haliday said, "but I'm about to find out.

You keep that ham tuned in and you listen to me. If you hear me say 'Aww shit, you got us fellas,' you get the hell out of here as fast as you can. I'll try to buy you some time if I can, but don't expect much. There are maps in the binder; find an alternate route. Right now they have us spotted and if we outright take off, someone is going to follow."

Mike nodded, a little overwhelmed.

"Here's my plan, let's hope it works." Haliday told Mike what he was going to do. He put a helmet on, placed an AR15 instead of his old Armalite 180 into the sheath on the bike, buckled on an equipment belt with thigh holster and mag pouches, slipped into a tactical vest loaded with more gear, and then more importantly, attached a handheld ham. "I'm Gecko Forty-Five," he said with a laugh.

Gecko45 was the name of the notorious mall ninja known across the internet for his ability to save the shoppers and keep the peace while dressed like an entire swat team. Haliday attached an earpiece and push-to-talk mic to his vest and the ham. He started the bike and rode toward the road block.

Haliday slowed down as he approached the roadblock. He looked at the stenciling on the vehicles and the lights mounted under the windshield. "38th MP CO."

He turned the bike off and one of the MPs approached him. He noticed the guy didn't actually have a unit patch on his right shoulder, which meant no combat assignment. He quickly glanced around and there was about a 50-50 split; the two on the Humvees' guns were combat proven— a MK19 automatic grenade launcher and a M240 G/B machine gun. Both not weapons to mess with, but only the 240 could reach the Tahoe.

The MP was an E3, a PFC, Private First Class. He approached Haliday and asked him for ID.

Haliday reached into a pocket on his vest and pulled out a black nylon ID holder. It was dirty, looked well-used, and the vinyl window was fogged over. The ID inside was visible, but it would be hard to identify any detail without taking it out because of the fogged over window. Haliday had actually stitched the opening closed a bit to make it harder, just in case. The PFC looked at it and handed it back to him.

Haliday wanted to grin. You can do wonders using a laser printer, and hobbyist sand paper could nicely wear down the clear vinyl to make it look worn. He asked, "Private, who's in charge here?"

The PFC said, "Specialist Benson is, sir."

Haliday said, "I'm prior Army and was an NCO and worked for a living; please don't call me *sir.*"

The PFC waved the specialist over. "This here is DHS officer Haliday."

Benson looked at Haliday. "What brings you around here, Mr. Haliday?"

Haliday responded, "What are you guys up to? You have a checkpoint out here close to nowhere. In my day we would have said we were getting the big green weenie."

The PFC looked at the specialist and said, "He's prior service."

Benson just looked Haliday over.

Haliday said, "Easy guys." He reached into his pocket and pulled out a large decorative coin. One side had the Department of Army Seal and the other side had the crossed pistols of the Military Police. He handed it to the specialist.

Benson looked it over and handed it back to Haliday. It was a challenge coin. "Any other day, Mr. Haliday, and I'd be buying you a beer."

"Call me Roger," Haliday said.

"Okay, Roger, but back to business. What brings you around these parts and who is down there in the truck?"

"That, Specialist, is my partner with a special couple of folks that Governor Anders asked us to bring back from the University of Illinois for some of his staff members. As you can guess, it's rough traveling out there and I am not taking any chances of running into rogue groups or militias of any kind.

If you've been listening to anything on the com net, you know why. I'm guessing that's why you guys are out here, correct? Unless, by chance, I'm in the middle of a well-executed ambush." Flattery can get you a lot, Haliday hoped. Throwing the governor's name around helped, too.

"We reported to the armory, but not many of us made it there," Benson said. "We were told to wait for orders and haven't gotten them yet. Well, the town manager asked us to help out until they could get a volunteer force together. We only have two groups out here and we secured the two county road entrances into the city. The rest is just farmlands. We have a few more guys making reliefs at the checkpoints. We'll stay until we get orders or the town manager gets some guys together."

"That's a smart move for Mr. Watts," Haliday said, [indicating the town manager].

Benson looked at him. "You know Watts?"

"No, not personally, but since I've been assigned to Indiana the past couple of years, it's been my job to get to know the leaders of cities where there are assets like the Danville armory. And his name is easy to remember—Watts as in electricity."

"Makes sense to me," Benson said. Another side note he made on the clipboard he held; he updated the info constantly.

Haliday asked if it was okay to move on and if there was anything else Benson needed.

"Just your name on the log sheet if you don't mind," Benson answered.

"Sure thing, Specialist Benson." Haliday wrote his info down and handed the clipboard back to him. "Anything else?"

"Sir, do you know what happened by any chance?"

Haliday remarked, "I wish I knew. All I do know is an EMP or something took out most of everything. I'm surprised your vehicles are running. We don't know who, we don't know why; all we know is it's FUBAR, F'd Up Beyond All Recognition. I got my orders through the radio and was assigned to the governor's contingency. I wish I knew. I honestly do. Can I expect the same thing going through the other side?"

"I'll call them and tell them you will be coming through."

Haliday said, "Thank you. If you don't mind, Specialist, I'll wait here for my partner to drive through. Not that I don't trust you, but better safe than sorry. I gotta get those people home."

The specialist ordered the Humvees to open the roadway.

Haliday called Mike and told him to bring the Tahoe through. "Quickly, Mike, go forty-five to fifty mph."

Haliday started the bike and waited. The Tahoe came through and with the dark-tinted windows and speed it was hard to discern who was inside. Just a few figures was all it looked like.

Haliday took off behind the Tahoe. He waved goodbye to Benson and then sped ahead of the Tahoe. He signaled Mike to follow him.

They slowed a bit and worked their way through town. They approached the second roadblock, and as soon as they started nearing, the Humvees moved aside and waved them through.

They drove for about 15 minutes and then Haliday pulled over and stopped. Mike pulled over as well. Haliday got off the bike and took the gear off. He was sweating like crazy.

Mike said, "You're not that hot, are you?"

"Mike, go in that toolbox and get me a Phillips head please."

Mike just looked at him and then went and got the screwdriver. "You got a screw loose?" he quipped.

Haliday said, "Worse than that, I have two on tight."

He walked to the back of the bike and unscrewed the Michigan license plate there. He told Mike to put it in the toolbox.

Mike said, "Wow, that was pure luck."

"No, it was stupidity; it almost got me killed on the way here and I should have fixed it then. I could explain not having a plate on it, but it would be too hard to explain why there's a civilian plate on it." He then grabbed some dirt and tossed it on the bare spot where the plate had been.

Mike asked him how he got a government plate for the Tahoe.

"Well, Mike, military recruiters are all over the place and all it took was a minute to unscrew it with an electric screwdriver. Right now there's no LEIN, Law Enforcement Information Network machines or MDCs, Mobile Data Computers to run plates, so I'm not worried about it showing up stolen. I kept it hidden until now."

He told everyone to grab a drink of water and stretch. After about 15 minutes of checking for anything else he might have missed, they loaded up the bike. Max yapped and they let him out to pee. Everyone loaded back into the truck and they started off again.

"Hey, Mike, flip that binder open," Haliday said as he drove. "I can't afford any more military checkpoints. Time to change the route. I'm not sure I could do that again and get away with it."

They were just west of Indianapolis, a major city with plenty of problems.

Chapter 10

Haliday and his group would be coming up on a small town called Avon soon, but would head north just before they got there. This was still too close to Indy for comfort. They would work their way up to State Road 32, which was east of a small town called Gadsen, and then move east from there. These small towns provided much more comfort than the big cities. Once back in the Detroit area, it would be a nightmare. So far everything was okay.

They made a quick stop and dumped the two cans of gas wedged between the KLR and Tahoe into the truck's tank. Getting more gas was a priority. Haliday figured Gadsen would be the ideal place to do so. They'd be there in just about another half an hour. They'd break for lunch, grab some gas and get back on the road.

It was late afternoon as they pulled into Gadsen, or at least what Haliday thought was Gadsen. There was a sign and that was about it.

Mike said, "What the hell is this?"

Linda asked him what he meant.

He said, "There isn't anything here."

Kayla said, "No kidding. Is this what you mean by BFE, Dad?"

Haliday said, "This is worse."

They just kept cruising through. Haliday spotted a sign up ahead for an airport. It was just a regional airport, but worth checking out. The next city was another 15 minutes down the road; he wanted to fuel up by then.

They pulled into an open gate of the airport and took a look around. Up by the main building there were a few BMWs, Mercedes, Lexus, and other expensive cars, maybe a couple dozen vehicles total.

Throughout the property they saw some service trucks, a couple tractors, and of course a few planes. It was the Indy executive airport catering to the rich who could afford private planes and the place to keep them. Midway down the runway they saw what was what was left of a small Gulfstream scattered about.

"Guess he picked a bad time to land," Haliday said. Everyone just looked around.

It was like a ghost town.

Haliday drove down between the hangars. There was an open hangar door and he paused and looked inside. He drove the Tahoe into it and turned it around so it was facing the door. He got out and went over to see if the door would close manually, and after disengaging a chain drive he was able to lower it.

"Okay," he said, "Mike and Kayla, you guys keep watch and I'll make some food real quickly. Make sure you guys pay attention."

He pulled out a butane stove from the back of the Tahoe and a can of butane. Within seconds it was lit and ready. He grabbed a pouch of dehydrated veggies and opened it up, and dumped the contents into a small pan with some water. He let it sit there a few minutes to rehydrate a bit. Next he added a pouch of powdered egg and mixed it thoroughly.

As this started to cook up, he grabbed a vacuum-packed pouch of cooked bacon crumbles and opened it up. "Ah, bacon," he said. "Gotta love bacon."

Next he tossed in some powdered cheese and just scrambled it all. He walked over to the truck and pulled out some flour tortillas he had grabbed off his counter at home to take on the trip. He whipped up some big breakfast burritos, and although it was late afternoon, they did the job just fine. Quite tasty, too.

He threw some Gatorade mix in some water. Kayla didn't want any.

"You don't have a choice," he said. "You need the electrolytes to keep your system balanced. It's important that we all do."

She reluctantly drank it. So did everyone else.

"Okay, this is for the road," he said. He grabbed a thermos, heated up some more water, and filled it with instant coffee. A small luxury right then, but since everyone was out in their own little world, it might help them to stay focused. He grabbed a chunk of beef jerky and tossed it to the dog. "Don't get used to that, mutt."

After the stove cooled and he wiped out the pan, they packed everything up. They were ready to get on the road. He asked anyone if they needed to use the bathroom before they went to look for gas. They took turns watching out while everyone went to go do their thing.

Haliday peeked out the hangar door and ducked back in real quickly. He told everyone to grab their guns and find cover. Haliday hid in a small office near the front of the hangar.

Linda hid behind a large tool cart in the rear corner of the hangar. Mike was behind a starting cart toward the middle of the back wall and Kayla was behind a toolbox near a small Cessna.

Three guys were coming down the road between the hangars.

Haliday told everyone to just hang tight. It dawned on him that he hadn't given Linda a weapon. "Just stay low," he said. They weren't sure what to expect.

He heard the newcomers as they approached. It seemed that they were looking in every hangar as they went down the row. He could hear them forcing doors open and anywhere from five to ten minutes later they would move to the next hangar. As far as Haliday could tell, they had only one more before they got to his.

Everyone just stood near their hiding places. Haliday was standing in the office doorway. He held his finger to his mouth to tell everyone to keep quiet. He placed his hand out and motioned for them to get down. He ducked into the office.

The hangar door opened and one of the guys peeked in; he whistled and Haliday could hear the other guys come over and start talking to their friend.

"God damn, how the hell did that get here?" one said.

"Hell if I know, but if it runs, it's ours."

They walked into the hangar and started looking around.

"You smell bacon?" Haliday heard one say.

"Hell yeah. Someone has been in here hiding or something."

One of them walked over to the Tahoe and peeked inside.

"Holy shit, we got a gold mine."

Linda shifted slightly and a small can on the floor near her feet fell over.

One of the men raised a rifle up and said, "Who's there?"

There was no answer.

"I said who's there, damn it?"

Another one of the men took a pistol out and started looking around as well.

Haliday peeked out of the office doorway and tried to watch them through a reflection in the glass of the truck. He saw one person had a rifle and one had a pistol, but he didn't have any idea if the third one was armed, and if so, what he had. By the looks of the crew, it was a man in his late 40s and two younger guys in their 20s. He was thinking father and sons.

The older man who had the rifle spoke up. "Listen, you're gonna wanna show yourself, and if ya ain't alone, you're gonna wanna both come out."

Linda shifted a bit more and the can now rolled out from behind the toolbox she was hiding behind.

"I see you," the man said. "You better get up."

Linda panicked and stood up and put her hands in the air.

"Don't you move. Who else you got in here. lady?"

"Just my husband," she said.

"He some kinda cop or something?" the man asked.

"No, we just found the truck," Linda answered.

"Aww, bullshit, we saw what's in there. We ain't stupid, you tell him to come out now," the man said. "We ain't gonna hurt anyone."

"How do I know that?" Linda asked.

One of the younger guys yelled out. "Listen, bitch, you'll know what we want you to. Now do what the hell he said and tell that asshole husband of yours to get out here now before we change our mind."

Haliday could catch a peek now and then, but nothing to formulate a plan or see what was going on. He looked over toward the door that the men had come in and saw a small duffle bag lying there. He thought about this for a minute. They were looting. They were going hangar to hangar and probably through every car and plane, taking anything they thought was valuable.

Haliday tried to think it through. *Why the hell didn't I get radios and headsets?* he wondered. On the other hand, he had two passengers he hadn't counted on, either. How much gear could he afford, or even carry? *Wouldn't do much good having just two sets now, but then again,* he told himself, *that would have been two coordinated people. That would have been better than this cluster.*

"Damn it!" the older guy yelled. "Get a move on, bitch!"

Max, who had just been laying there, stood up and started yapping.

"Damn mutt, shoot it," the man said.

One of the younger ones replied, "I ain't shooting it; you shoot it."

The older man said, "I'm watching this dumb bitch. Shoot it or give your brother the gun."

That was exactly what Haliday needed to know. The odds were better, but still not good. He was about ready to crawl over to the doorway when he heard the man speak again.

"That's it, bitch, I warned you."

Mike stood up and said, "Wait! Wait, don't shoot!"

Haliday saw the man place his finger on the trigger of his rifle and say, "Too late." Haliday bolted over to the doorway and started firing toward the group. They returned fire in his direction and he dove back into the office and to the office floor.

Linda dropped to the ground and lay there, paralyzed with fear.

Mike ducked down and was trying to flip the safety off his rifle. He heard a few rounds strike nearby. He was afraid to stand up again and get shot.

Haliday heard an AR fire; he didn't know who it was. Rounds started flying everywhere. No one could get a good shot on anybody, good or bad.

Haliday was laying there when the window above him shattered and he covered his neck as the glass fell. His hands were cut and bleeding. There was a lot of screaming going on at each other in the hangar. He popped up and aimed at the man with the rifle and fired, then ducked down again.

The guy dropped. More rounds came his way.

Mike looked around the side of the starting cart and fired off almost a full magazine in the invading men's direction.

Kayla took aim at the older guy, who was still firing from the ground; he had been hit, but not mortally. She fired three shots toward him and the man stopped moving at that point. She didn't have any more lines of sight and made sure she was. The toolbox in front of her rattled with pistol fire from the kid who had been shooting it. Soon enough there was a click from his gun.

"Cease fire!" Haliday yelled. "Cease fire!"

There were a few minutes of silence.

Haliday crawled over to the doorway and took a quick peek into the hangar. All he saw was haze from the gunpowder and the men now huddled near the Tahoe. He got up and peeked around the corner again. It was now or never. He reeled around the door frame and aimed at the group. One of the younger men was holding the oldest man in his arms. The other younger man was laying there next to him, holding his leg and chest.

Haliday drew down on them and approached slowly. He kicked the rifle aside that they had been using. It was an older AK variant. He told Mike to come out and get the rifle and check it.

Mike came out, grabbed the rifle, and checked the chamber. It was empty.

"Hold onto it." Haliday called out to Linda and Kayla, "You guys okay?"

Linda said, "Yes."

Kayla also said, "Yes."

"Okay," Haliday said. "Come on out, but be careful."

He was still watching the men. The youngest was crying as he held his father. The other kid was no longer holding his leg and Haliday noticed his shirt was full of blood. The kid was foaming at the mouth with a frothy pink spume. Haliday figured he must have been hit in a lung. He was about to walk up and check him when the kid flipped his arm around.

Haliday squeezed off a round out of his .40 the same time the kid fired at his chest. The kid had hidden a small snub-nose. The kid didn't have a chance to fire another round; the .40 struck him center mass.

Haliday stumbled backwards and fell to the ground. He laid there trying to get his legs to move and get his feet up under him. He wasn't able to get up.

Kayla ran over and started yelling. "Daddy! Daddy! Are you okay?"

Haliday couldn't speak right then, either. No words would come to his mouth and his breathing wasn't normal.

The younger kid looked over at him and said, "That's what you get, you bastard. You can rot in hell!"

Mike whipped the kid with the AK's butt stock, knocking him out.

Linda went over to Haliday and knelt down. Kayla was holding his hand, crying. She noticed it was blood-covered.

Haliday spoke, but he managed only a few words. "I love you, kiddo."

"I love you too, Daddy," she said.

Max came over from cowering under an oil can rack and sniffed at Haliday and whimpered. Haliday's eyes blurred and then started to go black. He closed them and tried to take as deep a breath as he could and then exhaled. Kayla spoke to him, but there was no response.

Max walked around in a few circles and whimpered some more. Linda was shaking Haliday, but there was no movement. Mike had been keeping an eye on the youngest kid who was the only one left alive, but he now came around to where the others were. He kept his eyes on the kid, waiting for him to wake up.

Kayla ran over to the Tahoe and grabbed a first aid kit. She ran back over to Haliday's body and knelt down next to his head. She opened the box and pulled a small capsule out and snapped it in the middle, then waved it under Haliday's nose. Haliday opened his eyes and whipped his head to side. The ammonia capsule did the trick.

Kayla asked him how he was doing. His breathing was still a little off.

"Damn, I feel like someone dropped a brick wall on me. I'm pretty sure my ribs are broken." Haliday had managed to catch the round from the .38 snub-nose with his body armor. The impact had knocked the wind out of him and forced him down. Kayla had thought he was hit because of the blood on his hands, but then noticed his shirt didn't have any blood on it.

She remembered he still had his vest from when he worked as a police officer and used to tell her he would make contact with people first because he had a little protection. It was only a Level II vest, but would stop most handgun rounds. He'd sacrificed safety for comfort—a dumb thing to do. There was no doubt a Level III would have been better in the situation.

Haliday looked at everyone and said, "From now on we make sure everyone is dead."

Linda asked him how they would do that.

"With a head shot," he replied.

Mike, in an unsure tone of voice, asked him if he wanted him to shoot the last kid.

Haliday looked over at the kid, who was now staring at him. "No, just tie his ass up, and then come over here and help me get up."

He laid there for a few minutes while they tied up their prisoner. The kid never said a word. Mike then came over and they all helped Haliday get on his feet.

Haliday took his shirt off and ripped open the Velcro side flaps holding the vest in place. He took it off, wincing as he did. He had a large welt growing on his right side. It would be a massive bruise soon. He pushed in and felt his ribs. "Might not be broken clean, but hairline fractured for sure," he said. "A good two or three of them. This hurts like hell."

He asked Kayla to grab his bag. She brought it over and he dug out a t-shirt that was part cotton and Lycra and changed his shirt. It was a size too small. He hoped the compression would help a bit. He called it his "Ahh-nuld" shirt. He'd put it on, used his best Swarzenegger accent, and tried to look super buff. Kayla used to laugh at him and make him change it.

He kept it to help keep his "12-pack" as he called it, from bouncing around during training. Next he wrapped it with an ace bandage. He looked at the vest and was amazed. Best investment he ever made at this point. He put the vest back on and then his shirt. *The hole in the shirt would be hard to explain*, he thought.

Next he looked around and went over to the small office. Broken glass crunched under his feet. He opened a refrigerator that was inside, complete with a couple bullet holes.

Linda followed and said, "You aren't going to eat that stuff in there are you?"

"Nope," he said. He held up some Fiji water. "Gotta love snobs and their quest for quality. I'm going to wash my hands off." He grabbed a couple of clean rags from one of the Box-O-Rags dispensers nearby. Kayla brought over some antiseptic rinse. As he wiped his hands, he asked her how she was doing.

She said, "I'm okay, Dad."

He said, "Come here, sweetie."

She walked over and he hugged her. "It's going to be okay," he told her. "We had to do this. If we didn't, there's no telling what might have happened."

She teared up a little bit. He had spent a lot of time with her, training her in marksmanship and weapons handling, but never expected one day she would need it. She was a natural at it, just like her old man was.

They walked back over to the truck. It wasn't a pretty sight at all. There were quite a few holes in the body and a couple in the side window glass. The kicker was a flat tire. A quick check of the KLR showed it to be okay except for one hole in the front fender. Unfortunately the bike wouldn't hold them all. Haliday looked down at the ground, thinking. There was Max, looking at him, wagging his tail. "Max the mutant," he said aloud.

"Hey, I heard that," Kayla said.

Mike said, "I have an idea. I'll take a quick look around at the vehicles here and see if I can find a match. If anything has the same bolt pattern and rim size, we can put one on."

"The spare tire is full size and will work if it's not flat," Haliday said.

Mike said, "Yeah, that might be fine, but then we're out of a spare tire in case we get another flat. I'll go look and see. You guys wait here."

Haliday thought that was a good idea. "Hey, Linda, grab a rifle and go with him. I'm going to have Kayla keep an eye on me while I rest a bit." He lay down and did not get up until almost two hours later.

Linda stood there watching Haliday. Kayla had lain down as soon as she and Mike got back. Mike was working on the truck.

Haliday got up, still sore, and moving a little slow. "How's it going, Mike?" he asked.

Mike looked up from the wheel and said, "Almost done. I found a Chevy pickup around the back of the hangars; they must use it for plowing. I took the best two tires off it and put them on the back here. That'll give us a matched pair in the back and we still keep our spare."

"Thank you," Haliday said. He looked around the hangar and saw that Mike had dragged the bodies over to the side and covered them with a tarp. "Thank you again."

Kayla got up now and stretched. The event had taken a toll on her. You can never fully prepare for this kind of thing. She walked over to the truck, reached in, and grabbed the thermos with the coffee.

"What are you doing with that?" Haliday asked her.

"What, I can't have any?" she asked.

"Not unless you share," he said.

She poured out four cups, one for each of them. They drank it down and looked around. It was now late evening and dark out. Haliday walked over to the kid still sitting there tied up.

The kid just looked up at him and told him to go to hell. "You're going to pay for this," he added.

Haliday said, "Look, kid, we were just minding our own business, trying to get home. Nothing here is stolen. You were walking through this place like it was your personal shopping mall. None of those goods in that bag over there belongs to you.

They went through it and checked. How do you explain that, smartass? Not quite the exemplary citizen, are you? Then you're going to go pointing guns at people, and bitch and moan about getting shot at?" Haliday was getting angry now.

Kayla walked up and touched his arm. "Dad, relax," she said. "His gene pool is probably a little shallow." She was a smartass like Haliday in this regard.

He turned and walked away.

122

Kayla looked at the kid. He was her age, 20 maybe 21. "You can't blame us," she said. "You can only blame yourself. You caused this to happen. No one has the right to steal anything, regardless of what's going on."

"You clueless little bitch," he said. "People out there are taking what they want; police can't stop them. What's the big deal anyway? They can afford it."

She looked at him. "If the lights came back on right now, how would you justify what you've done?"

The kid said, "Ask yourself the same question, bitch."

"I did," she answered. "I helped save my life and my family's life from you."

While Kayla tried to speak with the surviving young man, Haliday covered the holes in the Tahoe's back windows with some hundred mile an hour tape. Most people just called it duct tape, but in the army he came to know it as hundred mile an hour tape. Legend had it that during WWII, people said it was so strong it'd hold a Jeep together going a hundred miles an hour. He chuckled at that. *Yeah, try and find a Jeep that could do a hundred,* he thought. He found a small whisk broom and they cleaned out what glass they could of the Tahoe, but it wasn't much.

"What are we going to do with him?" Mike asked, motioning to the kid.

"We are going to walk him out to the gate and we are going to cut him loose and drive away," Haliday answered. "He can do whatever the hell he wants after that."

Mike reached down and he and Linda pulled the kid up. They opened the hangar door and Haliday slowly drove the truck out to the gate without the lights on, and then they walked the kid to that point. They cut the kid loose and everyone jumped in the truck.

As they were pulling away, the kid just stood there. He started walking back toward the hangars.

Haliday could figure one of two things: he was either going to bury his father and brother or most likely he went back for the bag of loot they were stealing. Haliday couldn't help but wonder what the hell people were thinking.

It had been two-and-a-half-days and they were pulling this crap already. He got to thinking about what Kayla said to the kid. She got it. It was a hard lesson, but she got it and did what had to be done. He felt bad; this is not a lesson he thought any kid should have to learn. Unfortunately in the new society, it would happen again and again across the country.

He looked over at Mike as he drove along and said, "Take a breather. I'll keep a look out for some gas."

Mike said, "I did that already."

Haliday looked down and saw that the tank was full.

Mike added that he filled the two empty cans as well. He reclined the seat and took a nap.

Haliday did a quick calculation. Twenty-six gallons in the tank, 10 in the cans wedged between the bike and tailgate, 25 more in the back. With 61 gallons total and about an average of maybe eight miles a gallon with the crude engine, they would have a range of almost 500 miles. They might be able to make it without having to stop for anything but rest breaks.

That was if things held out okay. That was a big *if*.

It was late and he looked down and turned the ham on. He spoke into the mic. "It's Roger. Anybody on the net?" He just waited. "Hey, it's Roger; is anybody on the net?"

While he waited, he popped open a small bottle of Tylenol and sucked some down. He took four of them, hoping to take the edge off the throbbing pain of his ribs. He had some heavier meds, but hated taking them. Besides that, he needed to be fully aware at the moment. Everyone else had fallen asleep. He really wanted to join them, but wanted to be back in Michigan more.

"Anybody out there?" he repeated. He heard a voice.

"I am."

"Who is 'I am'?" he asked.

"It's Karen, Dawn's mom."

"Oh, okay, must be your turn to watch the house." He was tired and didn't recognize the voice at first. She just said yes. "Where is Dawn? Is she available?"

Karen told him they were sleeping. "Diana is next to pull security and then Dawn after that."

"Okay, have Dawn call me when she gets up. Anything going on over there?"

She told him that they heard the grocery stores were stripped and so were a lot of other stores where people were taking generators and all kinds of other supplies. "No real trouble yet," she said.

He said, "Okay, take care, and talk to you later. Bev, Rich, how about you guys, you there?"

Kevin came on and said they, too, were all sleeping.

"Okay, anything new on your end?" Haliday asked.

"Hold on, Grandma is here now."

"Hi, Roger. We haven't heard from you in a long time. What's going on? Is everything okay? You almost home?" she wanted to know.

Roger didn't know where to begin. He didn't want Karen, Dawn or Diana to hear. They were very new to this and might get panicky if they knew how bad it was. "Switch to A2," he told her.

He waited and then she came on. "Are you there Roger?"

"Yes, I am, Mom. Listen, we hit a major snag and it tied us up for hours. We weren't sure we were getting out of it alive; I'll explain it when I get there. Anyway, we are going to be a while longer. A few things have happened that are going to make it harder to get back so you might have to move a little quicker than expected. Is there anything major going on?"

She told him that other than a few people wandering around door to door asking to borrow food there hadn't been anything unusual.

"Okay, well, just tell people to go away if they come to the door. Make sure one of the kids tell them to go away, too, so they know there are more people in the house. Switch back to the regular frequency."

Haliday told them he would check in later. She asked him what had happened, but he didn't reply.

Kayla woke up and asked where they were. He turned his light on and glanced at his binder and maps. They were making good time. They were well north of Indy and he was actually heading back toward Warsaw. His plans were to skirt it this time. If the Indiana National Guard was active, though, then they would be there as well. Other than the small infantry unit there, he didn't know what else might be waiting. No more games with them, that was for sure.

It took him a while, but he managed to skirt the city and was getting close to the Michigan border. He headed straight for Three Rivers, Michigan, but was going to avoid it like a plague. There were quite a few railroads that ran through it and he didn't want to get tied up in that mess. As for the train yards, there would be stopped trains carrying people from Detroit to Chicago and freight trains from just about anywhere. There would be a lot of people hanging around. Not the spot to be, that was for certain.

Chapter 11

It was Dawn's turn to keep watch. She did a check around the first floor of the house. Everything seemed to be okay; she walked over to the radio and called Roger.

"Yeah, go ahead," he said.

"You wanted me to call you, didn't you?" she asked him.

"Oh yeah, uh, give me a second." There was a muffled sound as he adjusted himself in his seat and had forgotten to release the mic.

She could tell by his voice that something was wrong. He asked her what the SITREP was and she said, "So far okay; nobody is really out doing anything. Roger, you okay? What happened to you?"

"Long story; don't worry about it. We're all okay, though. We are going to stop for a break, top off the tank, and then move on."

Dawn asked how far out he was.

"Well, on a normal day about two hours or more, but with the route changes we have to make, probably eight at best and twelve at the most, especially with the travel being one shit storm after another. Have you seen any other cars or trucks? Vehicles of any type out there?" he asked.

"We aren't seeing too many." She told him that there was an occasional older vehicle, a lot of ATVs, and some scooters and thing's like that.

"Any government troops or anything like that out there?"

"None that I've seen or heard."

That struck Haliday as odd. He asked her if she was ready to go and she told him yes. "Okay," he said. "No sense in taking chances. Why don't you make the first move in the morning?"

Dawn said that was a good idea. "I'll let you know when we leave and when we get there," she added.

"Okay," he said. "Stay put there until I get things organized and get everyone else on a schedule. Talk to you later."

Rich had been listening in. "Anything we need to know?" he asked.

"No, Dad, you have separate plans," Haliday said. "When the time comes, I'll have you guys go ahead with them."

"Okay, talk to you later, Roger," he replied.

After getting off the ham, Dawn double-checked everything in the garage. She had gone to disconnect the generator when she heard a noise outside. She stopped and listened for a minute to see if she could identify it. She was hoping it was one the neighborhood cats or a raccoon or something, but it sounded different somehow. As she listened she heard a hollow metallic clinking noise. She had no idea what it was. *It isn't anything good*, she thought.

Dawn ran into the living room to wake up her mom and sister. They got up groggily and Dawn told them someone was outside. They sat there trying to fully wake up and then said they didn't hear anything.

Then Karen said, "Wait a minute, I hear it out front."

Hearing the noise, they were fully awake now.

At first it sounded like the wind blowing the tree branches against the siding, but they weren't sure. Diana and Dawn ran upstairs to see what was happening. They took a quick peek outside and saw the top of an extension ladder against the gutter. It had been the leveling feet of the ladder Dawn had heard clinking around.

Diana and Dawn both looked at each other and backed away from the window. Dawn aimed her pistol toward the window. Diana saw a figure getting ready to climb on the roof and she turned on her flashlight. All they saw was the figure trying to climb on to the roof, then they heard a man yell, and then heard him tumble down into the bushes below.

Diana thought it was actually amusing, but Dawn reminded her that someone had just tried to break in. They didn't go near the window in case someone tried to shoot at them. The nails on the roof had done the job. They didn't plan on sleeping that night now; just planned on getting ready to go.

It was almost five in the morning by now and almost 72 hours since the EMP had hit. The weather had started to turn colder. That was what you got in Michigan—70 degrees on one day and 40 the next day. This close to winter, there would be far fewer warm days and they would have to prepare for that. It was almost a blessing that the event had happened now and not in the dead of winter. Traveling in snow would be very difficult.

Everything was packed and ready to go now. They triple-checked everything and did a walk-through of the. Karen stood there and cried. This had been their home since her divorce years ago and they had made it their kingdom. They had folk art, knickknacks, and reminders of their Norwegian heritage and they hated to leave it. All three of them cried and couldn't bring themselves to leave.

They went into the garage where the ATV was waiting. The sun would be rising and people would be getting up soon and the women wanted to be out of there before it became apparent that they were leaving. Diana opened the garage door and Dawn pulled the ATV out into the driveway and then backed up and connected it to the trailer that was also inside the garage.

Diana and Karen kept their eyes open for trouble. Dawn then pulled forward and they closed the garage door and put a few padlocks on it. With no one there, it was just be a target eventually anyway; no sense in trying to make it Fort Knox.

Dawn made Diana walk out by the street and check that area out. Diana protested, but Dawn just looked at her and told her to go. She walked out, looked around, and looked across the street. The guy with the old Nova that broke down had come outside and was watching them intensely.

Karen climbed into the front seat next to Dawn and they pulled out toward the street. At the end of the driveway Diana jumped into the back seat and they moved out into the road.

As they were pulling out, Dawn looked at her neighbor and flipped him the finger again. He returned the salute promptly and all three of them noticed his hands had bandages on them.

Diana said, "That prick tried to break in last night. We should have shot him. He'll be breaking in as soon as we are gone."

Karen said, "Let him; nothing left but a drum full of water in the basement." The rest were just memories that they had to take with them in place of the physical items.

As they traveled east a bit they only got a few strange looks, but they still maintained a vigil to keep themselves safe. They would have to snake through some neighborhoods to avoid the main roads and populated areas in order to end up about 18 miles north of their home in Metamora. Here they would stay until they got word to move to the next point. There weren't a lot of people where they were heading and it was harder to get to than their house where they had been. Metamora was much more rural.

What a sight the thing was. They were a double-seat Ranger towing a small five-by-eight single-axle trailer loaded to the hilt with a large amount of food and some water along with their personal items, which was not much at all except for what Diana had stored. Diana had packed like it was the end of the world. In a sense it was, but there was a lot she wouldn't need. Business attire wasn't on this year's post-apocalyptic fashion runway.

The Ranger was stock, except for the engine mods to make it run. The tires had been changed from their beefier off-road rubber to a set more suitable for pavement. They could always change them out if the need to remain off pavement arose. The trailer was just plain with added locks. In a pinch they could sleep inside if they emptied it and were stopped in a safe location.

They were on their way; Dawn called Roger and told him.

*****

About the same time over at Haliday's parents' home, they were all sleeping. Randy was supposed to be up keeping watch, but he'd fallen asleep. He was jolted awake by a pounding on the door. He went over and asked who it was. He heard a familiar voice.

"It's Uncle David. Let us in."

Randy wasn't sure what to do.

He heard his uncle say, "Hurry up, Randy. Bobby is hurt."

Randy opened the door and David, who was half way carrying his 14 year old son Bobby, rushed into the house.

"Go get Grandma," he said.

Randy just stood there looking. Bobby was bloodied and in pain.

David frowned at Randy. "Go now!"

Randy closed and locked the door and ran to get Bev.

A moment later, Bev came out into the living room to find Bobby lying on the floor bleeding from his head. David was trying to hold a t-shirt against the boy's head, but Bobby just screamed in pain. Bev told Randy to go into the basement and bring up the plastic container marked First Aid. Rich and everyone else got up at this point after hearing the screaming.

Bev grabbed a blanket and put it under Bobby's head. "What happened?" she asked.

David was shaking. He was a big guy, shaved head, 350 pounds, 5"11 and 40 years old. This was Roger's younger brother. He was not really in great shape, and the incident had taken a toll on him. He had halfway carried Bobby about a quarter of a mile as fast as he could. He was breathing heavy, frightened for his son. What he said didn't make any sense. No one could really understand him at the moment because he was so winded.

Bev moved the t-shirt and looked at Bobby's head. Most people would have fainted, but after six kids and the accidents they had growing up, it was almost normal to her. "David, don't worry, it's not as bad as it looks. He'll be okay."

She put the t-shirt back. Randy had come up from the basement with the large container. Bev looked at David and told him he would have to hold Bobby still. She told Randy and Kevin, who had joined them, to help him.

She went over to the kitchen sink and used a bottle of water to wash her hands and then took another bottle over to where Bobby was. "Put him on the coffee table," she said.

They put him on the coffee table and she pulled up a kitchen chair next to his head. She put on a pair of latex gloves. "Okay, hold him down." She removed the t-shirt again and took a flap of skin the size of an orange peel that was loose from Bobby's head and lifted it up. She gently poured water over it, rinsing the area well.

Bobby squirmed at the contact, but his cousins and father held him still. Rich looked on, hoping for the best.

Bev placed the skin back and held it there, speaking softly to the boy. "Rich, go wash your hands and come back and put some gloves on."

Rich did as instructed and came over.

"Hold this in place," she said.

He held the flap of skin down, but didn't watch what was going on.

Bev pulled out a suture kit and stitched the flap back in place. "It's not going to win awards, but it'll have to do." She covered it with a clean dressing. From the kit, she dug out some antibiotics they had bought on the internet. "He'll need to take these just in case of an infection. Now what happened?" she wanted to know.

David had caught his breath and began to tell them how he had made it home and waited to see if his girlfriend Sheila would show up. Bobby had actually said she would probably just go to Grandma's house because it was closer. It made sense, so they set out for Rich and Bev's house. They had stopped in the evening behind an abandoned shop and took a nap and rested. When they woke up they started out again. They ran across a woman walking down the railroad tracks about a quarter-mile away from their destination.

The woman looked like she had been through the ringer. She was maybe in her 50s, with a thin build, oversized clothes on, missing some teeth, ragged hair.

When they encountered her, Bobby had said, "Look, Dad, I think she's a bum."

The woman had started walking up to him, screaming and yelling about being called a bum and David told her to back off. He wasn't armed and had no way to defend them. He tried to walk away, but she kept telling them, "You ain't no better than me now! You gonna learn life's hard knocks now!"

Bobby, being a typical 14-year-old kid, said "Shut up, bum. You're a bum and always will be." He left David's side and walked right up on her.

David had tried to call him back, but he didn't listen.

"Bum, bum, bum, bum!" Bobby had taunted.

She'd swung her walking stick at him like a golf club and it glanced off his forehead at just the right angle, splitting it open. Being a facial wound, it bled like crazy.

Bev thought how odd it was that head wounds would bleed like crazy, but aren't that bad.

David had picked up rocks and started throwing them at the woman and chased her away. He had then grabbed Bobby and rushed to the Haliday's.

And that was what put them there now, with Bobby bleeding and Bev bandaging.

*****

Haliday had never been happier to see the Michigan border as he drove through. They were coming up on US12, aptly named Michigan Avenue. You could actually take it from downtown Detroit to downtown Chicago. No one really did that though, unless they wanted a sightseeing tour. Too many small towns and stops in between.

It was night out and he looked for a place to pull off. He couldn't continue driving much longer and with the amount of time left, the break would do him good. He looked over at Mike, who was hovering between sleep and consciousness. Haliday asked him to look in the binder and see if there were any notes regarding the area. Mike looked and said something about races.

Ah yes, Haliday thought. The year Earnhardt senior had taken a fatal right turn during a race, Haliday and the family had just become weekend rednecks. They started following NASCAR very consistently. Rather than haul their camper to the track itself, they went about half an hour further to enjoy a small out the way campground. After his divorce, Haliday and Kayla continued the tradition each year up until she left for college.

He still knew the area very well. Since it was closed for the season, it might make a great place to stop for a while. He glanced down at the binder and got his bearings. He told Mike what the plan was. Mike offered to drive, but Haliday told him he needed to get out of the truck for a while and give his ribs some rest.

"Besides," he said, "the rest will do us all some good."

They passed farm after farm of crops that had been cleared weeks ago. Corn and soy beans were the top crops. Over in Hillsdale, not far off, there used to be a Pillsbury plant that had closed a few years back. It just reminded him of what he took for granted. Pop the can open, biscuits in the oven, enjoy. Nope, homemade from now on, and who knows for how long.

He turned the lights off and approached the small dirt road that led to the campground. The main gate was about 200 yards off the main road. He told Mike to wait there for 20 minutes, then drive around the main gate and then the secondary gate and stop about 25 yards from the camp store. He told Kayla to come with him. They set off on foot toward the wood line.

Mike waited and then did as he had been instructed to do. When he got there, he placed the Tahoe in park and noticed there was smoke coming from the stovepipe in the roof of the little store. He saw a regular house trailer was attached to it.

He and Linda waited. He was going to make sure he thanked Haliday for using them as bait.

Just about five minutes later he heard a male voice command them to exit the vehicle and put their hands up. Mike looked at Linda and they climbed out. A spotlight turned on and illuminated them.

"Walk to the front of your truck and face the hood!"

They complied. Max jumped down out of the truck and sat and watched the activity.

A man in his mid to late 40s approached them. "Don't get any bright ideas and try anything stupid," he told them. "What's your business here?"

Mike looked at Linda.

She said, "We used to stay here...well, I did, years ago during the races. We are trying to get home and needed a place to stop. My ex-husband thought this would be a good place."

The guy looked at her. "What do you mean your ex?" he asked "Where is he?"

"I don't honestly know exactly where he is, but I would assume he's watching us right now."

The guy looked around and then back at them. "Well, I have a few guys out there myself. Not sure he could handle them."

Linda was thinking the opposite. "Listen, we don't want any trouble," she said. "We just wanted a place to stay for a bit while we rested. It's been a rough few days and we are beat."

The guy said, "How do I know you're telling the truth?"

"Are you the owner?" she asked

"Close enough," was the reply.

Linda went on to explain a few things. "You still have the old Ms. Pacman in the arcade? Your boat rentals are actually across the main road by the dock. You keep a cinderblock on top of the dumpster to keep the raccoons out and a chain on it so the cinderblock doesn't go missing. The pump out station has a sign that says 'This here honey hole ain't sweet, wash your hands before leaving'."

The guy said, "Okay, sounds legitimate, but what we have here is quite a pickle. I'll tell you what; you call your ex-husband in and we'll go from there."

Linda said, "Okay, but you call your guys in after that."

"Deal," he said.

Linda called out, "Roger, you hear that?"

Roger appeared a couple minutes later. As he approached he watched a red dot dance across his body. He looked over and saw another spot off Mike.

He walked up, looked at the guy and said, "Hey, George, thought you'd be gone by now."

George recognized him; he had seen him for five years in a row every August. George had taken over running the campground from his dad who had retired. That explained him not knowing Linda.

"Well, we were planning on it, but we still hadn't finished the season. We extended it this year to host a Halloween weekend. Thought we would make a few extra bucks." George whistled and two guys came walking up from down the drive, one with a handheld spotlight.

These were George's two sons who helped him run the campground before they closed up each year and then all headed to Florida for the winter. Max walked over and inspected them, then walked back to Haliday and looked at him as if to acknowledge his approval of the guys.

"Want a dog?" Roger asked.

Linda said, "Kayla will be mad—keep it up."

Haliday asked him if he knew what was going on.

George told him that he listened to the campers enough to know that some were preppers or survivalists or whatever they called themselves. He had taken some basic precautions himself. He figured it was serious when everything went dark. He had used the old tractor to go into town to confirm this. He said he went back as soon as possible and bought as much food as he could before people figured out there wouldn't be any soon. He shook his head. "I never figured you to be one of those folks."

Haliday said, "What kind of folks do you mean?"

George didn't really say anything, just shrugged his shoulders.

Haliday said, "Ready. I'm just ready."

George studied him. "Hey, can I ask you a question, Roger? She mentioned Kayla. Where's your daughter? Is she at school?" George was shocked by the answer.

"No sir, she's out there with a bead on you guys as we speak."

George looked around. "You can call her in."

Haliday had noticed the two lasers and knowing he only had two sons, he was comfortable calling Kayla in.

Kayla came walking in. "Dad, it's cold out here." She looked at the campground owner and said, "Hi, Mr. George."

"Hi, sweetie," he said. "Let's all go inside."

They walked inside the store. It was warm and comfortable. Kayla stood by the wood stove to warm up a bit.

Haliday glanced around the room. "George, you going to call in your third man or leave him out there?"

George laughed, went to the porch of the store and blinked his flashlight a couple times. "How did you know?" he said, returning.

Haliday said he saw smoke from three of the rental cabins. "I figured someone was out there. Two cabins, one for each son, you in the main trailer, and someone in the third cabin."

"What about you, Roger? Any more surprises?"

"No, sir. Thank you for letting us in, George."

The winter caretaker walked in and George asked him to let his wife, and the caretakers own wife know it was okay to come out. The caretaker went and retrieved the wives and they all returned from hiding behind a rental cabin in the woods.

They talked a bit about what was going on and what had transpired, but Haliday didn't share a lot of details about any of the gunplay incidents. It was the last thing they would want to hear and they might not trust them then.

"How did you know we were here, George? Your alarm system working?" Haliday asked.

"Oh, hell no. We used some fishing line and tied it across the driveway by the main road. When you tripped it, that pulled a stick out from under a can full of rocks. These rocks fell on a couple of more empty cans to make even more noise." George further explained that they had made sure they ran it across some trees to use the bark to help keep the line from sagging too much. Crude, but it worked. George looked at the caretaker. "You mind?" he said.

The caretaker said, "No problem," and then went to reset the alarm.

The lasers and spotlights were unusual as well. George explained it was a good time of year for spotlighting deer. Haliday didn't care about that. He asked them if they were set for food and everything. He didn't expect George to tell him much, but George actually filled him in on everything.

George had hit the local Sam's Club in town, where he often bought a lot of supplies for the campground. He had towed the trailer he normally used for firewood delivery behind the tractor. They managed to get a couple hundred pounds of rice, about 12 cases each of canned fruit, canned vegetables, and beans, plus some flour and other items.

They paid cash, of course, and Haliday figured George kept most of the cash from the campground to hide from the IRS, so he had enough on hand. He also had what was left in the camp store. He told the people at Sam's that it was for the last big party they were having. Not sure the people realized otherwise, as it hadn't even been 24 hours yet since the blackout had happened.

They'd make spring with no problems, so long as no one got to them here. Haliday said, "Hide it. Hide it all and not all in one place. Keep your guard up, too. In the next few weeks they'll remember who was buying what and they'll want it. But, back to the business at hand. Can we rest for about six hours?"

"Sure thing," George said. "We'll keep guard for ya."

Haliday said, "We'll help you stay awake." *No sense in waking up dead,* he thought. They slept in shifts, but they let Haliday sleep the whole six hours since he had the least amount of sleep in his group.

Chapter 12

Dawn, Diana, and Karen were continuing their own journey. They were making about five miles per hour. They were a couple of hours into their trip with only about an hour left to go. They didn't have to stop at all, which was nice. They did get a lot of questions about what they had and where they were going, and of course some people were asking for handouts. Diana was driving now with Karen in the passenger seat. Whenever they were approached by people, Dawn would stand up in the back seat, rifle at the ready.

Haliday had shown her a dual 10/22 Gatling gun monstrosity as a joke and she had actually wanted one mounted on the vehicle's roll bar. Haliday laughed it off, but she was now thinking it might not have been a bad idea. The 22lrs were not quite battle-tested, but then again, nobody liked to leak blood. It would have been like getting stung from a beehive but only worse.

Dawn was listening in on the ham when she heard Haliday call Bev's house.

"How's everything going?" he had asked.

Bev filled them in on David's event.

Haliday pretty much thought it likely. The city Haliday's parents lived in was barely north of Detroit and the auto industry was its primary job source. Over the years, it had become almost like a smaller Dearborn with a heavy Middle Eastern presence, but with a lot of Eastern European mixed in as well. It was quite a melting pot. Throw in the mass amounts of apartment complexes and it was outright dangerous right now.

Haliday said, "Okay, it's time for you guys to get moving. You need to pack up everything and get everyone going. I want you to head over to my place. I'm about six hours out now and leaving here in an hour or less. When I get there we'll get things ready for the long haul."

"What about Alan and his family? We're still waiting for them." Bev said.

"Okay," Haliday said, knowing it would be a delicate situation to handle. "Let me put it to you guys like this: So far, I've shot at about a dozen guys. I know I've dropped at least four, I've been shot at and hit, and Kayla has been shot at and had to shoot someone, Mike and Linda have been shot at and I don't even know if they dropped anyone. Things are that screwed up. Everywhere we go it looks like we will be eating lead. This country is out of control and getting worse by the minute.

"You get out now or you probably don't get out at all. Sit and wait for anyone else and you might as well start digging your graves. You will have to hope Alan and his family are doing what they need to do in order to make it right now. That's the best you can do at the moment. I hope you guys understand. It's about all of you right now, not just any one person or just part of the family. It's about those of you that are there right now."

Dawn, Diana, and Karen just looked at the radio in awe. "Holy crap," they all said. They had it made compared to what they had just heard, with the exception of Dawn's little incident. They had more ambition now to get the hell out of there. They kept moving on. They were only a couple miles away from their destination. It was totally different there and they were only 20 miles north of Haliday's house.

Bev wasn't happy one bit. In her eyes it would have been the whole family uniting and moving out. She and Rich talked a bit and then Rich called Randy, Kevin, David, and Sarah into the kitchen. He told them to get things packed up and ready to go. He handed them a list of instructions and told David to delegate the duties, but make sure it all got done. They would do what they could to help.

Rich was 75, 5'10", 165 pounds with thin grey and black hair. Bev was 73, 5'3", had gray hair and weighed only 90 pounds. Both had worked hard all their lives and were quite frail now. A lot of manual labor right now would be far too tiring. They would still help as much as they could however.

In the garage at Rich and Bev's residence was another five-by-eight-foot trailer. This one was loaded similarly to Dawn's. They also did the same thing, going through the house and triple-checking everything. Bev left a note on the top of the entertainment center. It was cryptic, but whoever was reading it would know what it meant if they were meant to read it. It gave them instructions on what to do and where to go.

David called Randy and Kevin over. "We are going to go out the back door, over to the corner of the yard, and get the Cherokee from under the tarp. I'll drive it around to the front and back it up to the garage door. Open the door when I get there. I'll back up to the trailer and connect it. You guys have to stand guard."

They proceeded with their plan.

The Cherokee was an '84 with about 120,000 miles on it. They had it reworked and kept it in good running order. They rarely drove it, just enough to keep it clean and running. The old Cherokees were almost bulletproof with the inline six cylinders, automatic tranny, and lever activated four-wheel drive. Small, but durable and dependable. Great for converting to a BOV, Bug Out Vehicle.

*****

While Rich and Bev were busy getting their group together, and Haliday was still on his way back home, Diana turned the ATV down the driveway. She looked around and saw the barn manager coming toward them. Her group had made it to their first stop.

Mandy, the barn manager, was a woman in her early 40s, blonde, thin and attractive, but weathered from the outdoor lifestyle. The tattoos didn't help much either.

She greeted them and assumed they were there for the horses. "I guess you guys are getting out of Dodge."

"That's the plan," Diana said. "Maybe later tonight or early tomorrow; we're not sure when."

Mandy said, "It looks like you have a place to go."

Dawn said they had been invited to stay at a friend's, but left it at that.

Dawn and Diana had two horses. One, a Quarter Horse mare named Trixie that was really just ridden for mere pleasure, and a Fjord they called Thor because he was a big, solid brute. He was a beefy draft horse and well-trained in a wide variety of riding styles, but more importantly, able to pull a cart. They'd be using these horses for more than riding.

They looked around the barn and pastures. The barn had 18 horses total and they were all out in the pastures at the moment. They asked Mandy what her plans were.

"Well," she answered, "if I go anywhere I'll take my two horses and cut the rest of them loose. They can wander and graze off the grasslands. I'll throw all the hay out, too. That's the best I can do; not that I have family nearby or a place to go."

Dawn asked how much feed she had left. Jerry, the barn owner, had stocked them up with enough hay for the winter and grain for about 90 days.

Dawn asked, "What about you, Mandy?"

She said she had about six weeks of stock in the house or maybe a bit more. "I know how to hunt," she added, "and maybe I'll see about taking a deer or two to stock up. Freezer in the stable help's lodge should stay cold enough with no heat in there this winter."

Dawn asked Diana and Karen to come with her and talk. They walked through one of the barns. When they returned, they proposed a deal for Mandy. "You cut the horse rations in half and that will get them to spring, but you have to watch their hay as well. We'll leave you with some additional food, you should be good for about four months. Nothing special, just basics. Cut it back and you can make it to spring as well. The chickens in the back will help you out with eggs and the goat's milk is good for you, too."

Mandy asked, "What happens in spring?"

"We can't tell you. We don't know. But we'll check in on you then," Dawn answered.

Mandy said, "What the hell, I'll do it?"

Dawn told her they were going to park by the little lodge house and would get back to her before they left. She called Haliday and let him know they had arrived okay.

*****

In the mean time, David had backed the old Cherokee up to the garage and Randy opened the garage door. He connected the trailer and pulled out of the garage. The neighbors had heard the Cherokee start and it drew a lot of curious onlookers. A few asked them what they had and where they were going.

Rich, Bev, Sarah, Elizabeth, and Bobby came out. They closed the garage door and locked it down. They started to get in but had to figure out the seating arrangements. Elizabeth, Sarah, and Bobby were the smallest and had to ride in the very back cargo area. David and Rich were up front, with Bev, Randy, and Kevin in the backseat.

As they were getting ready to leave, a few people from the crowd starting getting closer, demanding to know what they had. David told everyone in his group to get in the Cherokee.

The crowd had grown to about 35 people now. They had seen a rare vehicle running around on occasion, but with this one having a trailer, they figured it had something good in it.

They moved to block the driveway. Some lady yelled that they had to share if they had food.

Bev said, "We're not welfare; we're not sharing anything."

Randy fired a round into the ground and pointed the shotgun at the crowd. It was a little dramatic, but had the desired effect. Half ran away and the other half just moved aside.

He jumped in the Cherokee and they took off. It was about 12 miles north to Haliday's house, but a day's walk for these people.

Sarah asked if they could stop at her trailer to check for Erik. This would add about eight miles onto their trek. Rich said they needed to get to Haliday's house first and then he would send Randy and Kevin to the trailer to check it out.

"Can I go, too?" she asked.

Rich told her no. "You need to stay with Elizabeth. It'll take them a half hour tops to get there and back. That'll have to do."

He knew Erik would not be there, but couldn't dash her hopes.

*****

Haliday was prepping to get on the road as well. Haliday walked over to the Tahoe with Mike. Linda and Kayla were inside the trailer with George and his family finishing breakfast. They'd only had coffee and oatmeal with brown sugar, but it was nice to sit down and enjoy something hot and fresh. When Kayla and Linda finished, they would change into regular clothes and go help Haliday and Mike.

"What's the plan, Roger?" Mike asked.

Haliday told Mike that they were going to strip the magnetic light bar off the Tahoe and toss it in the back. They did this and next pulled the KLR off. Roger began peeling off the DHS decals on the bike.

"Mike, go ahead and slowly start peeling them off the Tahoe. Go slowly and pull it back onto itself so that the vinyl doesn't tear," Haliday instructed. "Try not to leave pieces on the truck at all. I'll help you when I'm done with these."

The Tahoe was stripped now and appeared to be just a plain old Tahoe except for the spotlight. Nothing Haliday could do about that though. He grabbed a bucket from George's storage shed and filled it with water from a hand pump. He pulled out a stiff wire bristle brush and started washing the KLR down. The white paint started coming off to reveal the original OD green.

Haliday had used half a dozen coats of washable paint and sprayed it on to get a good finish. He had then used a clear coat, which held the paint on until it was brushed off. The decals were the last to go on. The bike was OD green originally, but he needed white for the DHS look. They loaded it back on the Tahoe. The truck was now ready to go.

144

Kayla and Linda helped clean up from breakfast and then went outside to help, but found the men ready to go.

"Watch this while we change," Haliday said. He and Mike went back inside and changed. Haliday put on his Best Buy Camo—khaki pants and a blue polo shirt. They then went back outside.

George walked out as well. "Well, looks like you are ready to go; I wish you the best of luck."

"You too, George," Haliday told him.

"Roger, any advice?"

"I have a bunch, but not that much time. Here's the *Reader's Digest* version," he said, condensing the vitals. "Store as much water as you can. Hide as much of your food as you can in case you get raided. Let them take what they want. No sense in shooting anyone if you don't have to." *There was a contradiction*, he thought. "If you do have to shoot, shoot to kill; don't leave anyone alive. Hunt for food now, eat that first and save your stores for as long as you can. Beef up your security and add traps.

"I would consider moving everyone into the main trailer there, otherwise it's easy to take you out one at a time. Safety in numbers. Privacy is out the door now anyway. Don't go into town unless you absolutely have to. Bad decision either way; I mean if someone is dying, that's one thing, but otherwise stay away. No hospitals or clinics are open and if they are open they are full of disease."

"What about FEMA and other help agencies? Won't they be coming?" George asked.

Haliday told him, "It's been three days. I haven't heard of any movement to help people at all. Ran into a small group of troops in Indiana that got orders the first day, but even they had been waiting, and as far as I know, they are still waiting now. I wouldn't count on much yet, George, especially from the government. Hell, we don't even know what happened exactly."

That was the thing that really bothered him. Of all of the radio traffic on the ham he had listened to, he didn't hear anything about the government other than that one original broadcast for troops to report. He hadn't even heard that again. That was one of the reasons to go back to the civilian version of the Tahoe; too many people would be looking for government help. "George, I can't thank you enough for the hospitality. You have a twenty-two rifle?"

"I sure do. Keep it around for the small varmints."

Haliday walked to the Tahoe and returned with a brick of 22lrs. "Here ya go," he said. "Save them for small game. Good hunting and good luck, folks."

They all climbed in the Tahoe and started to pull away. Haliday quickly stopped, got out, and George asked him what he forgot.

A quick whistle and Max came running; he paused to give Haliday the evil eye before jumping into the truck. Then they left.

Haliday took the back roads like they used to do when heading to the track. They were able to avoid all of the traffic that way and he knew that other than Hillsdale, there was nothing out in that area. Hillsdale itself was easy enough to get through; just a few lights and stop signs was all. They drove along and made it through with no problems.

Since it was farm country, there were a lot of tractors on the road compared to the cities and suburbs. A lot of them were loaded up with household goods. Haliday wondered where they were going. No telling what people were doing; hopefully they were banding together. Hopefully people were figuring out they needed each other to survive.

He popped back up onto US12 and looked down the road. It really didn't seem too bad at all. He looked at Mike. "I'm going to run US12 down a ways and then head north. Ann Arbor is going to be in bad shape and we can't get that close."

They made it over to M52 and headed north. Haliday kept glancing at the binder. He was close to where he needed to head east, but also had to skirt around a lot of populated areas.

Everything considered, he was doing quite well on the travel time. At this rate, it would be just about three hours, tops. He started paying attention more closely to the homes in the areas he passed. He could tell who had fireplaces and who didn't. Just how much firewood they had would be another question. These people were used to having fires once in a while for atmosphere or romantic settings and not for heat. The homes were not designed to be heated with the fireplaces around there—just not efficient enough.

He'd always liked the idea of a fireplace, but the practicality of a wood stove for heating was better. Unfortunately he never got around to putting one in. He bought one, but it sat uninstalled in his garage. The stove was one thing, but when he went to buy the hearthstone and wall board along with pipe and roof vent, it got expensive and he'd always put it off. For three years now, actually.

He had gone as far as to even stack free wood when he got it. He had about three full cords which would have been enough for the winter. He was sure the neighbors would use it. Someone would use it for sure, but not him. It would disappear very quickly. Hungry people were one thing, but cold and hungry were another.

They pulled over so he could check the maps and come up with an alternate route. He wanted to avoid Howell and started laying out the route. "Write this down Mike." He spit out the instructions and Mike wrote them down. "You might have to call out the directions as we go, okay?"

Mike said "Okay."

The ham went off. "Roger, it's David. We have a problem."

Haliday said, "Hey, nice to hear from you, brother. Been a while. Actually, a couple of months."

That was the conversation where David had said a couple weeks' worth of supplies was plenty. *Bet he thinks differently now,* Haliday thought. "What's going on?"

David went on to explain the situation. "We got to your house without encountering any serious trouble. When we got there though, we noticed someone had worked a hole through one of the windows in back. It wasn't a very big hole, though. We checked the door wall to the deck and sure enough, it was open. We went inside to check it out. Everything is gone."

Haliday had to think about this a minute. "Damn. David, is my cat okay?"

David said, "Yes, he was under the covers on your bed. Looks like his food and water is still okay. Roger, aren't you upset?"

"Yes I am, but what am I going to do about it now?" he asked. "Is everything gone?"

David said, "Yes. Cupboards are empty, closets were searched, attic was checked. It looks like it's all gone. Not sure what you had, though. Safe in the bedroom was open and guns are all gone, too."

"I have those with me," Haliday told him. He was ticked off now that he thought about it. "Hey, David, anything else missing?"

"Wait a minute and I'll go check."

Haliday forgot David was running back and forth to the truck to use the radio.

He came back and said, "No, just looks like your food. That's all. Everything else was turned over and searched."

Haliday responded, "Okay, get the garage opened and get the trailer inside. Go get my trailer from the back of the yard and put it in the front yard backed up by Kayla's window and then put the Cherokee in the garage, too. Wait for us there. Couple more hours, I'm thinking." Roger put the mic down.

"Keep a watch out, Mike," he said. "I'm going to dump those cans of gas in. I'm running low."

Haliday threw 20 gallons in the Tahoe and left it at that. Haliday figured it was enough to get back. He realized that what he forgot to ask David was, was if the gas in the garage was gone. No sense in worrying about that either though. If it was gone, it was gone.

They got back on the road. Haliday looked at the map. They would actually be passing by the hospital where he'd worked. How different it was only 72 hours ago.

Chapter 13

At Roger's house they finished putting the vehicles away and checking the house. Randy and Kevin loaded up the shotgun and took a pistol as well. They headed off to check Sarah's trailer. Elizabeth gave them a hug and asked them to bring back her daddy. The trailer park was only four miles away and they took off to check it out.

When they got there, they found the door wide open and windows broken.

Cautiously, they walked inside and then immediately left. The whole place had been stripped—literally stripped. There wasn't any food left, dishes were scattered and broken all over the floor, the furniture was gone, clothes were tossed all over the place, even the TV and DVD player were gone, along with the stereo. It hadn't taken long at all.

On the way to the Cherokee they noticed a lot of people were watching them, which made them really nervous. They also noticed that a few of the gawkers started walking their way, so they hurried up and got back in the vehicle and took off quickly. They weren't going to hang around and answer questions or risk losing the Cherokee.

As they left the trailer park, they passed by a group of people who were sitting outside drinking beer. Randy noticed the couch they were on had been Sarah's. There was no shame. Those guys didn't care. In another couple of days, however, they would. Once food was gone, they would change their behavior drastically.

They arrived back at Roger's and parked the Cherokee in the garage. When they walked inside, Elizabeth ran up to them.

"No Daddy?" she asked.

Sarah went up to her and told her Daddy was probably very busy trying to help people and might not be home for a long time. This was her way of finally giving in to his fate.

Rich had turned on the 12-volt light system Haliday had installed. They straightened up the house a little. Next they worked out a watch schedule. It would require two people on guard at all times. With the break-in and all of Haliday's food preps gone, they were taking no chances. They suspected the looters might return.

Bev called Haliday on the radio. "I have a big favor to ask."

"Go ahead, Mom," he said.

"Is there any way you can stop by and check on Alan and the family?" Alan had a wife, Nancy, and two children, a boy, Matthew who was 12 years old and a girl of nine named Theresa.

Haliday looked at the binder as he drove. It would take him about 25 miles out of his way, away from the direction he was heading. "You guys going to be able to keep the house secure until I get there?"

"We should be able to."

"Okay, I'll drive by the house, but that's it. I can't be searching the state. I'll call when I get out of there." Haliday slammed the mic down. *Oh sure, why not a city tour looking for family and friends? Nobody took this preparedness serious!* But now of course it was his job to save them and the world. After a few minutes he settled down and knew it was the right thing to do regardless. He was just still on edge from the past few days.

Dawn called him next. "What do you want us to do?"

"How safe is it there?"

"Well, there's not much going on."

He thought about it a minute. Most of the property outside of the small town was large 25- to 50-acre lots. The populated areas were very small. "Go ahead and stay there for now if you can."

"Okay, got it."

Back at Roger's house Rich used his keys to access the garage. Rich found a large piece of plywood in the garage and he had David screw it over the hole in the window. This would seal the house back up.

While Rich was out there, he noticed a couple shelves that had some candles, matches, propane bottles, butane bottles, and a few other items as well. He was surprised these were still here. He was surprised no one had broken in to it.

He looked around and saw a camp stove and lantern. He walked over to a barrel sitting there. He opened the bung on it and closed it right back up. It was filled with gas. A smaller 15-gallon container nearby was filled with kerosene. The generator there was chained down to the floor.

Haliday had cut a large square of concrete flooring out and dug out the hole. He then laid fresh concrete with a massive eye bolt in it. He had staggered spacers and washers so there was no pulling it out. He'd figured the block of cement itself weighed about 500 pounds, so it wasn't going anywhere easily. The chain was reminiscent of something on a ship's anchor—big and heavy, lock included. It would take an immense amount of work to cut through it.

Over in a corner was a kerosene heater. Rich had David grab it and they also took a smaller can of kerosene that was next to it. David took it inside and got the heater going. It was going to be cold that evening and with Haliday's detour they didn't know when to expect him to be home. They wanted to stay warm and ready in case anything happened.

They gathered everything they could find that they thought Haliday would want to take with him. They piled it all behind the trailer in the garage. This would make it easier to load when he got here. They walked through the house, but didn't find anything else they thought they could use.

*****

Back at the barn, Dawn, Diana, and Karen moved the Ranger and trailer behind the barn so it wasn't visible. They locked the steering wheel down. Haliday had shown them how to disconnect the wires to the spark plugs, so they did this, too.

They also placed a wheel lock on the trailer and double-checked the doors to make sure they were locked. They couldn't afford to lose anything now.

They walked over to the little lodge house that was there. It was really just a large one-roomed building about 15-by-20 feet. It had a fireplace, TV, bathroom, and a queen-size bed in one corner and a small kitchen area with large refrigerator. It had been used for barn parties or for guests who stayed the night. They pulled out some books and read, waited to hear from Haliday, and took turns on guard duty.

Mandy came up and knocked on the door.

They let her in and she asked if they would be there for a while. They said it looked that way. She told them she was going to get an early start on hunting. She had seen a few deer earlier in the morning while out for a ride and was going to see about getting one. She had a bolt action 30-30 with her and held it like she knew how to use it.

Dawn asked her if she hunted a lot.

"I was born and raised in Kentucky. My dad and older brothers included me in everything they did," Mandy told them. "I was pretty much a tomboy. I moved up here chasing a boyfriend, which didn't work out, so I took the job here running the barn." She told them it wasn't great pay, but the free use of the house and utilities made it worthwhile. She earned extra money giving lessons to newer riders.

She went out to a barn and saddled up her horse and took off.

The three remaining women just looked at each other, all thinking the same thing: Yuck, deer.

They were all vegetarians to one extent or another. Karen snuck in meat once in a while at work on lunch. Dawn did the same thing, but no beef at all, and Diana was a straight up vegan. Haliday loved offering her jerky when they would all go to the range for practice. He loved torturing people like that.

It hadn't even been an hour when they heard a single rifle shot. About an hour after that Mandy came back in, dragging a buck behind the horse on a canvas deer drag bag. She paused by the lodge house and asked if they would want any steak or anything, but the women declined.

Mandy told them she would be over by the house processing it and she would be making a lot of jerky with this one.

The three women were impressed in a sense, even though she was currently making herself bambi-kabobs.

*****

David was checking Bobby's bandage. He explained to him that what he had done was wrong. Not only was rude behavior wrong at any time, but in the days to come it would get him killed and almost did. Bobby asked what the big deal was. David explained that WROL, the country was a changed place.

"WROL?"

David told him, "Without Rule of Law. It's the Wild West now. It's respect or expect."

"Expect what?"

"Expect to get killed."

Bobby just said, "Fine, Dad." The look on his face though acknowledged that the lesson had sunk in.

It was getting to be late afternoon and Randy went out in the garage and tried listening to the radio, but the reception was poor inside the garage. He asked Bev if he could open the garage door.

"No, use this and go out on the back deck." She gave him a handheld ham radio with a whip antenna. He went outside to use the ham. David looked over and thought: *where was that earlier?*

"Uncle Roger?" Randy said.

"Go ahead," Haliday said.

Randy asked him, "Anything going on? Are you almost here?"

"Negative, we are getting ready to pull into Uncle Alan's neighborhood. We'll call you back in a bit when we find out what's going on. Let Grandma know."

"Okay, I'll tell her," Randy said. "Good luck."

Rich, Bev, and David joined Randy on the deck. They all lit up a cigarette. They didn't smoke in the house; Roger didn't allow it. They knew he would sniff it out in a second. They were allowed to smoke in the garage, but after eying the drum of gas, they decided not to.

Everyone was listening for the report to come in. Dawn, Diana, and Karen gathered around their ham to listen. They were 50 miles away but still interested in how Roger's family was doing.

*****

Haliday had re-routed himself to his brother's house. The area was populated with large, 3,000 square-foot homes on postage stamp sized lots. There was literally about 20 feet of space between homes. The only benefit was a large shared common area in the back of the homes. They all looked the same with the exception of different trim colors once in a while.

He was getting ready to pull into the subdivision and hesitated. Toward the entrance it looked like a roadblock, but upon closer inspection he saw that it was a stalled car. He checked out the exit side and it was clear, so he drove down that side. Just a few scattered cars here and there. About halfway there, he noticed Nancy's Durango stalled out about three houses down from their own house. That was good news; she was close to home when it hit.

Haliday didn't see Alan's truck anywhere nearby. Alan worked for a construction company as an estimator and salesman and his job took him everywhere across the tri-county area. That was going to suck, as there was no telling where he had been at the time of the EMP. None of them bought into the preparedness realm, so Haliday knew they didn't have GHBs or anything. Not even a pistol that he could remember.

The Tahoe's occupants got a lot of looks from people as they drove up. Haliday backed into Alan's driveway. He would get used to doing it for tactical reasons. He did it in the military and they did it at work; it saved time from trying to back out of areas or parking spaces so you could get out quicker, or respond quicker without the hassle of ground guides or constantly watching your mirrors. Too many blind spots that way and it took too much valuable time to back up.

"Kayla and Linda, you guys cover the Tahoe. Keep everyone away. Fire two quick shots if you need us," Haliday said, "or if you need to take action, keep firing and we'll be here ASAP."

Haliday and Mike got out and walked around the house and noted it was all locked up. A neighbor came out of the house next door and asked them what they were doing.

"I'm looking for my brother Alan," Haliday said.

The neighbor only slightly recognized him, but more so he saw the family resemblance. Alan was Rogers older brother, looked just like Roger, but was thinner at only 220 pounds.

"Have you seen him?"

"No, haven't seen anybody, but I just got home last night."

"Thank you," Haliday said. "I'm going to go in and check it out."

They walked around to the garage and he tried the handle, but it was locked. He went to the Tahoe and grabbed a pry bar. He used it to force the garage door open.

Once inside the house he called out to see if anyone answered. There was no answer at all. He started to do a search of the house and began in the kitchen. He walked in and looked around and spotted a piece of paper on the table under a glass. He picked it up and read it. He didn't know what to make of it.

Waited for the kids to walk home from school. Then we waited as long as we could. Packed up what we had and went to Ken and Barb's. We'll stay there as long as we can. Hope you make it there. We love you.

He assumed Nancy and the kids had been there and left the note for Alan.

Haliday was glad the kids got home okay and they'd gone to stay with someone, but he had no idea where that might be. He looked around for an address book, but figured there wasn't one. Nancy most likely kept it all in her phone and on her computer like everyone else nowadays. There was nothing he could do there. If it was close, he would have picked them up, but he had no idea where they were.

He went in the garage and looked around. He spotted a five-gallon gas can that was almost full. He went and dumped it in the Tahoe. He went back in the garage and walked over to Alan and Nancy's Harleys. He pulled the fuel line from the tanks and emptied them into the gas can and dumped that in the Tahoe as well. He got about an extra 10 gallons total, which was good enough.

He loaded everyone up and looked around. Neighbor people were just standing there. To him it almost looked like the zombie apocalypse. These people looked that far out of it. Unshaven facial hair, unwashed hair, dirty clothes, dirty faces, blank stares, and that look of despair. What the hell were they waiting for?

These were upper middleclass, who thought they were immune to disaster and probably counted on a government rescue. *Wait until the lower class gets a hold of them*, he thought. Wait until they turn on each other.

He was thinking about the note saying the kids made it home from school. Since Kayla was in college he hadn't really thought about that. He wasn't worried about the junior high or high school kids. *What the hell did they do with the smaller elementary school kids? Did you turn loose a five- or six-year-old? Hell, a seven- or eight-year-old?* That was scary to even think about. In some areas they needed buses to get home.

He guessed that they might have food for a while at the schools, but eventually that would run out. What about the staff? How long were they willing to stay and watch them, if that was even the case? Would people be able to walk there, pick up their kids, and make it home? With so many people relying on two family incomes to live, he wasn't sure how many would have been close enough. He didn't really want to think about it..

Mike said, "Hey, we going to get back on the road?"

"Oh yeah," Haliday said, jerking his thoughts to the task at hand. "I was just thinking."

"Thinking about what?"

"Nothing really." There was no sense in sharing his concern with the rest of them; there was nothing they could do anyway. The thought of kids in school or abandoned haunted him a bit. It was time to continue home now though. He pulled out of the neighborhood, ready to get home. "Listen, Mike, what do you say we run the highways as far as we can go?"

Mike asked if that was risky.

"Well, it's the quickest way to get back home and there might be some issues, but look at it like this. We'll be clear of Detroit, so we are avoiding that sewage dump. I figure we have an hour and a half using the highways or four if we use the county roads and smaller streets.

"I think it's worth the risk," Haliday figured. "Too many little cities on the county roads, the gas mileage sucks, and the highways should be clear of people as they most likely found their way into the neighborhoods. I'm betting we only have to dodge cars. I'm tired, I'm sore, and I want the hell out of this damn truck."

"Do it, Dad," Kayla said.

Linda said, "Whatever Mike thinks is good with me."

And Mike said, "Yeah, let's do it."

Haliday knew the way home from there and he was ready to get there. He dreaded making this call. Everyone was still listening and waiting for the report when he came back on the air.

He had dumped the radio protocol long ago and as long as he didn't reveal last names or locations, no one knew who they were, where they were, or what their plans were. Everyone else understood this as well, so he just clicked the mic and laid it all out there.

"You guys out there?" He got the two responses. "Okay, Alan's house was empty. It appears Nancy was home and the kids made it home too. They waited and then packed up and went to a friend's house. No idea who, no idea where. There's no sign of Alan; he might have made it home and then went there later. I don't know."

Bev asked him if he checked the area.

"No, not at all. I kept an eye out for his truck around the general area as we drove in, but we are getting back on the road now."

"Can you just look around a bit more?" she asked.

"No." He left it at that.

She didn't argue the point either. She knew it would be a losing battle with Haliday.

He understood the endgame more than anyone else there. He was thinking about his brother in Missouri and sister in Texas, wondering how they were doing right then. If he could help them at all then he would have.

It was late afternoon by this time and would be dark in a couple more hours. On the highways there was the occasional vehicle, but not many. Haliday did notice a couple people looking through cars and just figured them to be looters. He kept telling himself, *Just three lousy days.*

The zoo gates had opened and the animals were set free.

He headed north on a main road called Telegraph and hung a right on Square Lake Road. This would dump him onto I75 where he would pick up M59 East back toward his house. He couldn't help himself; the hospital was too close to pass up. He could hang a left, pass by, and then head home.

He passed the hospital slowly. A big dark building lurking there as dusk set in. In another 30 to 45 minutes, it would be totally dark. He looked at all the buildings on the property and it was clear they had all been ransacked. No doubt the residents of this place they called "Ponticrack" had done a thorough job taking what they wanted.

He popped up on M59 and headed east. It was like déjà vu. He remembered all of the cars being there and the trip he'd made with the old man within just an hour of the event. He passed by the little strip mall and saw that the grocery store had the windows broken out and, just as he predicted, was completely empty.

He pulled into the parking lot and slowly drove by. Definitely empty. He drove by the pizza joint and noticed it too, was empty—nothing at all, not even the pop. He pulled out onto the road and started to head for home. Just another mile, that was it. They would be home; they would not be there long, but it was still home.

Kayla screamed out, "Stop, Dad, stop!"

Haliday hit the brakes hard. Max had taken up residence on the center console and tumbled forward. He looked up at Haliday, who just smiled down at the dog. They had a love-hate relationship—they loved to hate each other. Haliday thought, *What is it I missed?* Haliday put the Tahoe in park and started looking around.

"There," Kayla said, pointing away from the Tahoe.

"What?" Haliday said.

"Over there, Dad." She pointed out the window.

"Okay, I guess I'm blind. I'm not seeing it." Haliday said.

"It's Blake, Dad, from school." Kayla told him.

"What school?" Haliday asked.

"High school, Dad. He played football. Remember?" Kayla said with a condescending tone.

He nodded. "Okay, it's Blake. Let's get home."

"Wait, Dad. Hey Blake!" she called out the window. "Come here!"

The kid came walking up slowly from the sidewalk next to the road, then quickened his pace when he recognized her. Kayla jumped out, causing Haliday to jump out, too. He was ready to draw his pistol in case of trouble.

Kayla gave Blake a big hug. "Dad, you know Blake."

He looked at the kid recognizing him and said, "Yeah, thanks for the pizza."

"No problem, Mr. Haliday."

"Why didn't you say something the other day? I didn't recognize you. Of course, whenever I saw you it was during the football games and you had a helmet on," Haliday said. Kayla had been a cheerleader since seventh grade and then into her first year of college. After that she decided to work to help pay tuition. "It's been a couple years since then, too," he added.

Kayla asked Blake how he was doing.

"Well, I went back to the pizza shop and took the flour, canned pizza sauce, food, and took it home. I used my mom's garden cart for that. I only started at the pizzeria a couple weeks ago, so I didn't have a lot of money, but bought some thing's from the grocery store before it closed for good," he said. "I saw it get looted this morning. There was nothing left after only a couple hours."

"How's your mom?" Kayla asked.

Blake looked down at the ground. He lived with his mom who was widowed. He and Kayla were like brother and sister when Kayla had lived at home with Haliday, who was still single as well. They had a connection based on that, but that was it. She had helped him get through Spanish in high school and he helped her with her math. Then there was student council, football and all that other extra-curricular activities they both belonged to.

Blake just looked up at her, but didn't say anything.

Haliday sensed something was wrong. "Blake, is she sick or hurt? Does she need help? Take me there and I'll see what I can do."

"She's not home," he said.

"Does she work near here? Was she at work?" Haliday asked.

"No," Blake said. "She went on a cruise with my Grandma. They would have been at sea when the power went out."

Oh shit, Haliday thought. Another thing to consider. If the ship got hit by the EMP, it would just be floating around out there. He wondered what would happen. No bilge control pumps, no water desalination, no way to cook really, and thousands of people on a small floating hell ship just drifting wherever the current would take them. He shuddered at the thought.

Mike and Linda had gotten out of the truck at this point.

"Kayla, grab the Tahoe, back it into Blake's driveway and wait for us there," Haliday said. "Mike, you and Linda go with her. We'll meet you there." He recalled that Blake's driveway was only about 150 yards down the road. "I need the walk. I need to talk to Blake here as well."

They left for Blake's and to wait for Haliday and Blake to arrive there.

Haliday studied the young man. "Blake, you have any family close by?"

"No, sir."

"Where's the closest family you have?"

"My aunt is in Kentucky and my Grandpa, who didn't go on the cruise, is in Florida."

"Any close family friends around here?"

"No, sir."

They walked on, each with similar thoughts.

"What have you been doing the last few days?" Haliday asked.

"Well, sir, I boarded up the windows of the house and hid everything inside. That's about it. I looked around in the garage for thing's I could use. I found some firewood for the fireplace, but not much. I was going out to look for some to use tonight because I ran out."

Haliday and Blake reached Blake's house at this point where the Tahoe was waiting.

"Kayla," he said as they met the truck, "take Linda to the house, get Randy and Kevin and bring them back here quickly. Bring the Cherokee and bring flashlights, too. It's getting dark. Make sure they have firearms and make sure the house is secured and everyone is on high alert. We got a lot of people watching us right now."

"What are you going to do, Dad?"

"We're going to get Blake here packed up and bring him along."

Kayla started to cry a little bit.

Blake looked at Haliday. "I don't know what to say."

"Well, for starters, just say thank you, and secondly, that you will abide by the rules," Haliday told him. "And third, that you will pull your weight around the homestead. Final item, she's off limits," he said, pointing to Kayla. "Now, just so you know, we aren't staying around this area. We'll be leaving in the morning. Is that a problem?"

"No, sir, not at all, and thank you." Blake said.

Haliday did not know the boy that well, but could not leave him.

The group arrived shortly and Haliday had them back up close to the door. Next they went inside and he had Blake show them where all the food was. They piled it in the living room. He helped Blake pack clothing and some personal things. Next he told Blake to grab anything of value like jewelry or coins or anything he could use to trade. He told Blake these would be his bartering items and no one else's.

He walked the house with Blake, and then the garage as well to see if there was anything else. In the garage was an older Yamaha 250.

"Does it run, Blake?"

"Yeah, but I don't have any gas in it."

Haliday told Randy to grab some. There were a couple jerry cans on the back of the Cherokee. He grabbed one and dumped a little in the bike. They'd be taking that, too.

"What about firearms, Blake?" Haliday asked.

"I don't have any."

"You know how to use them?"

Blake shook his head no.

"Well, there'll be a crash course tonight or tomorrow morning. You'll be expected to use them if we need to," Haliday said. "Any problems with that?"

"No, sir."

"Okay, we're heading over to my house now. Anything else you need here?"

"Just one second, please."

Blake ran into his bedroom and grabbed a handful of pictures out of his nightstand drawer and a small picture frame with a picture of his mom in it.

He grabbed a black marker and wrote on the living room wall; he didn't want any notes blowing away or getting lost. *Went with Kayla and her dad. Be back…*he looked at Haliday.

"Spring, Blake, in spring."

Be back in spring, Blake wrote. *I love you, Mom.* His eyes were glossy.

Randy, Kevin, and Mike had thrown everything into the Cherokee and Randy wheeled the Yamaha out front for Blake. With a final look, Blake closed everything up in the house and then made sure the bike started. They all went back to Haliday's.

When they pulled in, they put the Yamaha and Tahoe in the garage. They pulled the Cherokee around back and locked it up tight and put a steering wheel lock on it. A good old-fashioned "The Club" came in handy now that alarms were useless. They double-checked everything and went inside.

There were lots of hugs, kisses, and tears. It had been a hell of a trip. There were a lot of questions, but not a lot of answers right yet. There'd be plenty of time to talk soon enough.

Haliday had introduced Blake to everyone as well. "He'll be treated like family," he added. "Anyone have problems with that, it's too bad. That's the way it is. Now, first off, we get security set for the night, and then we eat and sleep."

Haliday called Dawn and told her they were back. "Make sure you're ready to move out in the morning," he told her.

She said, "Glad you're back safe. Talk to you in the morning."

"See you guys soon," he said. He hoped they would all make it.

Haliday went into his bedroom and into his bathroom. He took his shirts off and looked at his abdomen. The bruise was about the size of a basketball. *Damn, that had hurt.* He left it unwrapped and baby powdered his skin, then put a shirt on. After that he went back into the living room. He saw the kerosene heater and stood by it for a minute.

Fall was here and winter was well on its way.

He just looked around and then went and checked the closets and cupboards. He shook his head from side to side.

"Is it all gone?" Bev asked.

"No, not really; a drop in the bucket, considering," he answered back. "About two month's worth of canned goods and dry goods." Still it made him angry.

He peeked in the garage, but didn't comment.

He called for a meeting. Everyone gathered around.

"Look," he said, "this hasn't gone as planned and it's probably not going to be any easier. This is what we have to accomplish in the morning and through tomorrow night."

He laid out the objectives and asked if there were any questions. No one had any. He wandered off to his bed and crashed hard.

Morning would be there soon, and then it was back on the road.

Chapter 14

Haliday got up and walked out into the living room. Everybody else was already up. He looked around and they all returned his attention. Immediately he went back into the bedroom and put on some clothes. He was used to walking around either naked or in just his underwear, and thank goodness he had his underwear on. He looked down at his cat, whom seemed to have made friends with the mutant dog.

"Romeo, you're a traitor," he said. He knew that Bev's cats could have cared less about the dog.

When he walked back out into the living room, he could see they were cooking breakfast. He could also smell fresh coffee in the percolator.

David glanced to him and said, "Nice bruise I saw there. How did that happen?"

Haliday said, "Long story. Thank goodness for body armor."

Blake was at the griddle making pancakes. There was a pitcher of Tang, too. *This kid may be alright if he stays away from Kayla*, he thought. Everyone ate and then enjoyed some coffee before getting to work.

Haliday called Dawn, but Diana answered. "You guys ready to go?" he asked.

"Pretty much, I guess," she said.

"Well, get started as soon as you can. It's going to take you guys a little bit longer to meet us at the first checkpoint. Do the same thing, use tight security. Is your mom able to drive the Ranger okay?"

She said she could with no problem.

"Okay then, let me know as soon as you guys head out," he said. He then asked David to get the Tahoe hooked up to his trailer.

David couldn't figure out why Haliday wanted it in front of Kayla's bedroom window, but figured he was just tired when he had asked or maybe it was closer for loading.

Haliday had the biggest trailer out of the group. He had a 7-by-16-foot dual-axle, with extra height and a ramp door.

"Put it right at the walkway with the ramp on the cement. That will make it easier to load," Haliday said.

David looked at him and told him there wasn't much and they could have it loaded up in 10 minutes.

"I don't think so, David. Just do me a favor and do it please."

David and Kevin went outside and got it hooked up and moved. They then backed the Cherokee up to the garage door, but didn't open it or connect the other trailer yet. They just wanted it ready.

David said, "Okay, guys, get the gear in the garage into the trailer."

"No, no, no," Haliday interjected as he came out. "There's a specific loading plan I have in mind. This way everything will fit."

Bev said, "Roger, in case you forgot, you don't have much to load."

"Yeah, that's what you think."

They all looked at him.

"Listen up," he said. "This is the drill. Linda, Kayla, you guys will stand guard on the trailer and in front of the house and door. One on each side; make sure you can see each other and up and down the street and around the sides of the house. Mom and Sarah, you do the same thing, but in back." He gave them each a plastic whistle he had bought at a novelty store for two bucks a dozen. "Whistle if ya need us. Dad, I want you up in the front of the trailer to direct the load. No heavy lifting; just observe and instruct. I don't have an AED and we can't deal with heart problems."

Rich had had stents put in years back after he had suffered a heart attack..

168

"The rest of you will form a bucket brigade, and I mean that literally," Haliday said.

David and Kevin came back in. Haliday stationed them between the front door and just inside Kayla's bedroom. Sarah's daughter just stood and watched.

Haliday walked over to Kayla's closet. It wasn't big; it was just a typical wall closet that spanned the width of the wall and was about two feet deep. He knelt down off to one side, moved a bunch of various items and grabbed the edge of the carpet and pulled up hard. Under the carpet there was a small hatch about 24-by-32 inches. He had cut a small finger hole in it when he'd built it earlier and now managed to pull it up. He reached down and hit a switch and the area below lit up.

David was in the room with him. "What the hell is all that going on down there?"

Haliday just looked at him and smiled. "Well, put all your eggs in one basket and you're screwed if you trip on your way to the market. I planned on possibly tripping, so I built this. It took time to do it without anyone knowing, but when it was done, it worked like a charm."

Haliday's house sat on a Michigan basement. It was only a little more than six feet deep and looked more like a crawl space from the road, but it was all concrete floor and cinder block walls. In the back of the house outside was a large half door to access it. You opened that door and took a couple small steps down and you were in the crawl. The furnace, hot water heater, well pump, sump pump, and water softener were down there.

When you looked around you saw a square basement— cinderblock walls, waterproofed, with one-inch foam insulation glued to the walls. It was solid all the way around. You could peel off the foam and scrape the waterproofing, but you still had cinderblock. No big deal. Why the builder had never gone another two blocks to make it a full basement though, Haliday never figured out. He was the second owner and didn't know why it was never done, except maybe the water table was too high.

Haliday's house, however, had a unique shape. When you approached it, there was an attached garage on the left that jutted out, Kayla's bedroom on the right that jutted out, and the walkway to the porch which was in the middle, giving it kind of a "U" shape. There was no crawl space under the garage for obvious reasons, but there was under Kayla's room.

Haliday had started in her room by cutting in the hatch access and reinforcing the joists. Then he'd brought cinderblocks and mortar through the garage and down the hatch where he sectioned off the area under her bedroom. After going in the main section and applying the waterproofing and insulation along with a few other small touches, it looked completely natural.

The hatch being in the closet was in a space no one walked on, so it would not have the flexing give that most floor hatches had. With Kayla being a typical high school girl, no one wanted to go near the closet anyway. Too much teenage girl stuff lying around. Haliday didn't like going near it. He never cleaned it because it reminded him of Kayla, but he would glance in there when he was missing her.

With the underground construction being completed, Haliday had a cache right at the house that was 10-by-12 and a bit over six-foot-deep. This was loaded with buckets upon buckets of food and cases of food and other supplies. He never stored water because his lot backed a small lake and he could filter it or filter water from the sump. He was still on a well rather than sewage and city water lines and he could power the well pump, too.

He had gone with square buckets to save on space. Round buckets were cheaper, easier to get, but square really saved space and made a big difference. He did have some round ones, too, but not that many. He jumped down into the crawl area and looked around. Everything was still there. This was great news.

He climbed out and David asked if everything was okay.

"Yeah, I just need one of the kids down there lifting instead of me. I won't be able to do it." He switched places with Blake who was standing nearby. "You're going to earn your keep today, Blake."

"I don't mind, Mr. Haliday."

Haliday preferred being called Roger, but wasn't going to let the kid get too comfortable too quickly. "Start with the square ones, Blake."

With a nod, Blake traded places with Haliday and started handing up bucket after bucket, which made their way to the trailer. The first row was in; 48 of them fit. Labels read basmati rice, jasmine rice, parboiled rice, lentils, red beans, navy beans, split peas, black beans, barley, sugar, flour, and on and on it went.

They got four rows in at the trailer before it became time for the round buckets; there were only two rows of these. Next were cases of #10 cans and boxes of other supplies and paper products, too.

Haliday grabbed his shirt and pulled it up on his head and started walking around with a roll of toilet paper. "I need TP for my bunghole. I need TP for my bunghole. I am Cornholio."

Nobody else got the *Beavis and Butthead* imitation though.

Haliday went into the spare bedroom he used as an office and walked over to the closet. It had a modular closet system in it. He yanked the pole down, grabbed hold of the sides and pried them loose. Next he removed the back section and revealed some small shelves and more rifles and shotguns hanging in plastic bags coated in oil with desiccant packs in the bags. These were loaded up in the trailer as well as some ammo that was in the spare room.

After all the loading was done, the gear from the garage went in as well. There was barely enough room for Blake's Yamaha, but they made it fit. Haliday told them to pull the Tahoe forward, load the bike up, and close the trailer. They put Romeo and Max in a cage and put them in the truck.

Suddenly they heard a whistle. Everyone grabbed a weapon and ran outside. There had been a crowd watching from nearby, but now they started getting really close.

"Randy, go around back and help," Haliday said. "Kevin, you watch out front. Blake, get that garage door opened up and the rest of you get the drum of gas emptied into the vehicles and into any spare gas cans. Everyone stay calm, but on alert."

Haliday walked out toward the front to see what was going on. He made a concerted effort to slap a magazine into his AR180 and jack a round into the chamber. This, of course, was for effect. He had unloaded it before he went out just so he could put on a show and let the crowd know he meant business. Besides, everyone else was locked and loaded already.

"Get all of the vehicles hitched up and ready to roll!" he hollered.

As the Haliday group was checking the vehicles and trailers to make sure they were ready to go, the crowd moved in closer yet. There were quite a few neighbors Haliday recognized, but a lot of people he didn't. They began demanding that he tell them what they had in the trailers.

Haliday shouted out, "It's none of your concern!"

They kept yelling out that they wanted to know.

Haliday slightly raised his rifle. He called the group from the back of the house to the front then and told them to watch the rear and sides from where they were. He had Kevin lock up the house.

"Go ahead and shoot us. You ain't got the balls!"

Haliday eyeballed the guy who said it and noticed he had a baseball cap on. *River Bend Apartments* was stitched on the front. Of course, a half-mile south Haliday had 10 complexes of various sizes. He had taken daily walks around the neighborhood all the time, scoping out who lived where, who had what, who might be prepared or who might be problems. He figured the apartments would be a lot of trouble.

"Look, man, we're leaving, okay? No problems need to arise. We're out of here in two minutes," Haliday told him.

The guy walked up a bit closer to the front of the crowd and said, "Bullshit; we ain't letting you leave with that shit." He turned around and took a shotgun from another guy in the crowd. He turned back to Haliday. "You look like you got plenty to share."

Haliday said, "Look, that ain't going to happen."

His next door neighbor, Phil, was standing outside now, watching. Haliday looked over at him and nodded. Phil nodded back. His kids walked out onto the porch and Haliday looked over at them. One of them was sucking on a pouch of peanut butter from an MRE. She was also holding a small doll, obviously not grasping the lethalness of the situation.

More and more people were demanding that Haliday's group share.

The guy from the apartment complex was the loudest. "We're going to give you to the count of ten. After that we're taking it, asshole."

Haliday quickly looked at his group, then scanned the other group. Most were just standing around empty-handed; a bunch had knives and a few had various guns visible.

Haliday noticed a neighbor across the street standing on his porch. He didn't really know this neighbor, but had watched him closely over time and knew enough that he, too, was prepped for SHTF. He was surprised the guy himself hadn't taken off.

The man's son lived next door and Haliday would catch them late at night unloading provisions into their small pole barn. The guy went back inside. *I don't blame you*, Haliday thought. *Keep out of it. Remain unseen and unheard. Protect your own stash.*

The loudmouth with the hat started again. "You must be deaf or dumb, you son of a bitch."

Haliday was at his wit's end. "Okay, genius, this is what we are going to do." He raised his rifle and leveled it at the man's head. "We are leaving and that's going to be good enough for everyone here. You understand?"

"Screw you, ya bastard! There are more of us than you!"

"We're all armed, numb-nuts. You aren't. You'll lose this one," Haliday told them.

He whispered to David and Mike, who then got into the vehicles and started them. He told Sarah to get in with Elizabeth. He told Bev and Rich to get in as well. "Linda and Kayla," he said, "you guys walk up the street a ways." He looked to the drivers. "When they get down a few houses, move the vehicles out. Watch your backs. Blake, close the garage and lock it. Then go with them and cover the rear."

"I told you that ain't gonna happen." The group moved a bit closer.

Haliday looked at Phil.

"You're on your own, man," Phil said. "Nothing I can do. You have to take care of business yourself. It's each man for himself."

Haliday knew Phil had a hunting rifle and plinker, but figured as much. Phil's wife was standing next to him now. *Thanks for the help, neighbor*, he thought. He heard the vehicles shift into drive. The crowd came closer yet, about 30 yards out now.

Haliday said, "Okay, I'll tell you how it's going to work. If you aren't armed, I suggest you step back now. The rest of you, well, it's going to be us against you if you want it that way. I'm going full auto, and so are these guys. You do not have enough firepower to win this." His rifle was full auto capable, but he hadn't finished modifying the others yet.

"Now, I'm ready to kill. I already have and I will again. No doubt in my mind I can do it. I prefer not to though. You hear that? If it's food you want, my house was cleaned out. Phil there has it all—a good few months' worth. He's got five cases of MREs alone. Now he broke into my house while I was gone and stripped it clean of all the food." He looked at Phil who had turned white as a ghost. He nodded at Phil again with a smirk on his face this time. *Every man for himself, right neighbor.* Haliday thought.

The group had separated a bit as some of the people backed off. The loudmouth said, "How you know that?"

"Well, the MRE peanut butter could be his, but I doubt it. He doesn't know how to spell MRE. Now the doll his kid is holding is my daughter's. It's a one of a kind custom we had made for her at a doll show years ago."

Phil's wife called him a bastard.

"Look, Heather," Haliday said, "I'd beat feet away from the house."

She grabbed her kids and ran across the street away from the crowd.

Phil looked at Haliday and pleaded. "Don't do this, Roger; I was just trying to keep my family fed. You can't do this, man."

"Look, Phil, your best bet is to walk away now. Let them take it when we leave. Breaking in to my house and stealing my food put's you in the same class as them," Haliday said as he pointed to the crowd.

The loudmouth piped in. "How you know we're going to let you leave? I keep telling you, it ain't gonna happen. Just more stuff for us."

Haliday said, "Look, guys, you can live or you can listen to this loudmouth. My guess is you want to live. Take what's in that house, split it up, and move on. Don't die like this man is going to." He still had his rifle leveled at the man in the hat.

"I've had enough!" the loudmouth yelled at him. he started to raise the shotgun up.

One, two, and the number three came in the form of a three-round burst from Haliday's gun. He quickly leveled it at the next guy and barked out orders. "Keep your weapons down! Keep your weapons down! Go, go, go!"

The vehicles moved out, leaving Haliday, Kevin, and Randy standing there.

"Kevin, you lead. Randy and I are walking backwards," Haliday said.

One of the guys in the group brought his own shotgun up quickly and fired at Randy, but luckily he missed. Randy returned fire with two rounds which seemed to miss. Haliday fired a few quick shots as well. The guy dropped to the ground in a heap.

Haliday yelled out again. "Don't do it! Don't be brave!"

He kept the rifle leveled at the group that was trying to stop him and were now standing by themselves. There were five left. Haliday and Randy started walking backwards, and as they did, the group of bystanders moved back as well. You could tell they didn't want any more of the gunplay.

"Like I said, the food is in that house," Haliday said. "Help yourself; it was mine anyway."

Phil's kids across the street were crying.

Phil just yelled at Haliday.

The armed individuals watched Haliday, but moved toward Phil's house. Haliday and Randy kept moving backwards and they saw a few more people head to Phil's house.

They were about 75 yards away when they reached the trucks. Haliday told everyone to get in. He stepped on the sidestep of the truck and held onto the window frame with one hand. He kept looking back at the mob that was now at Phil's house. They were like ants on a piece of candy.

He heard a few shots as well, but didn't see anyone firing at them. The crowd was probably arguing about who got what. He saw Phil standing there watching his house being raided from across the street. Phil's wife and kids were in tears.

Haliday smacked on the Tahoe roof when they hit the end of road and Mike stopped. He switched places with Mike behind the wheel. He pulled up next to the Cherokee and saw terror on the faces inside. He said, "Follow me," and they drove off.

Only about two miles away, he pulled off into a large parking lot of a small fabrication shop. He signaled for everyone to get out. They all stood around and he walked up to Randy. He grabbed the shotgun from him.

"I had to shoot him, Uncle Roger. I had   "

Haliday put a finger to his mouth to shut him up. He pumped the shotgun, emptying the shells onto the ground. "Pick them up," he said.

Randy picked them up and held them out.

Haliday grabbed one and looked at it. "Number nine shot. You used number nine shot? You didn't kill that guy; I doubt you even pissed him off with this crap at that distance. Go find your double-aught and load it up there Mr. Dick Cheney. Smaller the number, the better for people," Haliday said.

Randy loaded his shotgun.

"David, Kevin, Randy, and Blake come here. Basic gun course now."

Thirty minutes later they were back on the road.

Chapter 15

While Haliday was teaching his quick gun course, back in Metamora, Dawn, Diana and Karen were all set to go. They stopped by the main house to drop off a few things and the extra food for Mandy. They noticed a smoker going. She had taken care of that deer pretty quickly. They figured if she wasn't raped, beaten or killed, she might do pretty okay for herself.

In all reality, it was not a bad place to be, though. It was a good distance from a city of any size, and since there weren't a lot people around, there wouldn't be much scavenging in the area. Just have to hide from roving bands of scum.

"Thanks again," Mandy said.

"Thank you," Dawn, Diana and Karen replied. They were horse people and glad the horses would have a fighting chance. "We'll be back in the spring or maybe sooner, depending on how things progress after we find out what's going on and when everything settles down. It'll get worse before it gets better. People will be very hungry and desperate in the next few weeks."

They gave her Haliday's security speech. With a "Take care," the three women were on their way.

Karen drove the Ranger and Dawn and Diana saddled up the horses to ride. They checked out their map. They were taking as many small roads as they could. This way the horses could use the shoulders of the road and stay off the pavement. They had two legs of the trip to make. The first leg would take them to a preset cache with a few items and some gas if they needed it and a spot to rest. The next would take them to meet with Haliday.

The women enjoyed the slow pace. They checked out the various farms as they passed them. You would almost think nothing had happened out there. They listened to the ham and couldn't believe what they were hearing. Some of the rural areas were just like this, but then most urban areas, especially the largest cities, had basically crumbled overnight.

They were hearing stories of widespread looting. People had cleaned out all of the grocery stores within the first few days. They heard of people rioting in places like Sam's Club, Costco, and other big box warehouse stores. People were taking everything—electronics, clothing, whatever they could get their hands on, they took. Most of the item's were useless, but they guessed people figured it would be an easy fix to get power back.

Police everywhere started giving up. The only thing they could even attempt to do was try to keep people from killing each other. Most had left their jobs and were worrying about their own families. There were very few places where people banded together and took actions to secure their communities. Most of all, it was the small towns in rural areas that would be safer, where travel by foot was impossible due to the distances.

Over the ham, one guy up in Oregon was telling everyone to start hunting and gathering meat. He explained that hunting would be widespread. He went on to say that the animal population would be overhunted within a month. This would severely reduce the animal population and those left would be hard to find as they hid from hunters. Winter would make hunting very difficult. There were just no amenities to keep warm, move around easily, stay the night in camps, and bait the prey or anything.

It was still puzzling that the women did not hear anything about any government movements or assistance to anyone anywhere. No one could figure it out. People said that a lot of the military bases seemed locked down, but they also said they did not see the amount of troops that they normally did. Some commented that there had been a lot of desertion from all rank and files. Little to no equipment was moving and surely none of it was moving off the bases.

The women couldn't concern themselves with any of that. They would figure it out later. What they had to concern themselves with was getting where they needed to be and when they needed to be there. They had a great disadvantage right now, since there were only three of them and the pace they kept was the speed that the horses moved. They almost wondered if maybe they should have left them.

They were coming close to their first stop. They hadn't noticed anyone following them and they headed down a small dirt road. Haliday had scouted the area many times before with them. They knew it was not used more than maybe eight times a year; they couldn't even figure out why. Maybe kids getting busy after a hot date. They came across an opening in the woods and headed down that way.

Karen was having a hard time navigating the path with the Ranger. They had cut a few branches off some of the trees to make it more accessible, but had to leave enough so it did not look too obvious. They would be about a quarter-mile away from the dirt road and well enough hidden to stay the night. They managed to reach the spot without too much more trouble.

They tied the horses up and got them some water and grain. They planned to leave the saddles on in case they had to bug out quickly, but that would not be the case. They commenced setting up camp for the night and opened the trailer so they could pull out the gear they needed.

After getting everything out, they started to set up. The first thing they did was string a few booby trap simulators up around the perimeter. This would alert them to anybody sneaking in. Haliday had Dawn buy these at one of the gun shows they had frequented. They just had to hope animals wouldn't set them off, but they placed them two feet off the ground, so unless it was deer, they were good to go.

They set up a nice little four season tent. It wasn't big, but big enough for two to sleep comfortably with some gear close by. They tossed in a couple sleeping bags that were zero-degree rated, so it would be warm enough. The temperature was only going to dip down to about 35, but they wanted to keep warm in order to stay nimble and quick.

They placed a light blanket over each horse. They pulled out a small camo net and covered the trailer. After some squabbling about who would pull guard duty first, they settled in for some food. They heated up some water on the small camp stove and made soup. Afterward they opened up a can of pears and split it.

Dawn looked around. She had to use the bathroom. She grabbed a bucket with a potty lid on top and a biodegradable trash bag in it they had brought along and hauled it over behind a tree. Haliday taught them to use the blue RV chemical in it to keep the odor down and help degrade the mess. She finished her "squat" as Haliday called it and headed back to camp. She hated his crudeness at times.

They made sure the camp stove was out, no food was left out, and they hunkered down for the night. They figured on three-hour shifts, which would give everyone six hours of sleep. They looked up at the stars. Without any lights, the stars were so bright now. There were few places on earth you could experience total darkness.

The night was uneventful and the three women all laughed about camping the next morning. Years ago, camping was a motor home in the parking lot of a hotel. That was as rough as it got. Now they'd learn to appreciate nature.

They fed and watered the horses and then they whipped up some nine-grain cereal using instant soy milk and made some Tang. They took some vitamins and started to break down the camp.

The last thing was the morning bathroom break. Karen didn't mind the bucket, but Diana had a fit. Dawn explained that there was no Four Seasons resort close by, so that's what she got. After a few minutes of potty dancing, she gave up. The three of them then sat there looking at the bucket. *What do we do with it?* they each silently wondered. None of them wanted to touch it.

After a few minutes Dawn said, "You dig the hole Diana. I'll pull the bag and dump it."

They disposed of the mess and got ready to leave. Everything was taken down and they called Haliday.

"We're on our way to meet up with you," said Dawn.

Haliday said, "Sorry, I should have told you guys to leave a day earlier; we're already on the way there. We'll be there waiting. Call if you need us."

Karen started the Ranger; Dawn and Diana climbed up on the horses, and they started back toward the road. They were only about 50 feet from the camp site when Karen got the trailer stuck. They tried for an hour and a half, but could not get it free. They couldn't leave it there, so they called Haliday to let him know.

*****

Haliday had told Dawn to head out and now they themselves were on the road after the tense morning incident. He'd be seeing Dawn sooner than he thought; he just didn't know it yet. She would have a small problem he would have to deal with.

He looked around. Nobody was saying anything. They were still in shock at the early morning incident. Not only did they shoot a guy, but Haliday had left Phil and his family in quite a bind. They broke into his house, took what Haliday needed to survive, and were ready to stand there and let him get killed as well. *Screw Phil*, he thought. He didn't expect them to be there in spring when he got back.

Mike said, "Hang a right at the next road." Another mile and they would be at Bill and Linda's farm.

Two Linda's. That would be weird. He could see it now, "Hey, Linda," and both would come running. Linda said they usually answered based on who called them, so to him that made sense.

They pulled up near the gate of the farm. Haliday saw it was locked. He grabbed his binoculars and looked toward the farm's house. Smoke from the fireplace was visible; he saw some cows and a couple of horses in the pasture. He couldn't see anyone though. He wasn't about to go walking up to the door, either.

"Well Mike, it's your friend," he said. "You feel safe walking up there?"

"I'm sure we'll be okay," Mike said.

"We? There's no we, it's you, I'm not taking the chance. You go. Here, use this." Haliday went and unscrewed the antenna for the stereo. He didn't need it now anyway. He tied a white rag around the end. "Wave this as you approach."

Mike headed toward the door. He got about 50 feet from the house when the front door opened and Bill looked out.

"Hey, Bill."

"Hey, Mike," Bill said, looking at the vehicles. "Are they with you?" Bill was in his mid 50's, 6 foot tall and about 220 pounds with black hair, bald on top.

"Yes, they are," Mike said.

"Okay, here's the gate key."

Mike walked up and got it.

"Please lock the gate behind you when you come back up."

"Thanks, Bill." Mike walked down back to the trucks and opened the gate and then they all rode up to the house.

Bill had put on a percolator for coffee. He had this sitting on a wood burning stove near the kitchen. When Haliday and Mike and their group arrived, they all exchanged hellos.

"Where's Linda at?" asked Mike.

"She's taking a nap," Bill said. "She was up early tending the chickens and livestock. I heard you guys coming and kept a watch out. I thought it was you getting out of that truck, so I didn't bother to wake her. Hell of a mess we're in, huh?"

Mike said, "That's for sure. The past few days have been pure hell, Bill."

"I can see by that eye, did you win or lose?" asked Bill.

"I lost that battle, too many of them, but I'm alive."

Bill asked who was up for coffee. Everyone almost in unison accepted his offer.

"Okay, I'll empty this pot and then I'll get another one ready."

Linda woke up and came out and greeted them. She had a concerned look on her face. She was Bill's age, 5'2 and maybe 110 pounds. Graying brown hair touching her shoulders.

Haliday said, "We're not staying, just stopping by."

She looked a little relieved at that.

She said, "I'm sorry, was it that evident?"

"Don't worry, I don't blame you. These days you have to count your blessings and your beans. We understand completely. That brings me to the next question. Mike, it's your ball now."

Mike didn't get a word out of his mouth.

Bill and Linda said they could stay. "We can put you in the middle bedroom and Kayla in the end bedroom," said Linda.

"Oh, I'll be going with my dad," Kayla said. "But thank you."

"No problem, honey." Bill said.

Haliday asked them what they had heard. "Anything going on or anything worth sharing?"

Bill said he had talked to a neighbor who went into town. A few folks had set up a small blockade and seemed to be trying to control everything in town. He wasn't sure if they meant to do good or meant to do harm, but he was avoiding town at all costs. He said most people around there were just trying to ride it out.

"How are the people around here set for food?" Haliday asked.

"Well, most have soy, corn or wheat, and a lot of us have some cows and poultry, but other than that I don't know. We can get through for a while, but it won't be gourmet."

"How long is that?" Haliday asked.

"I guess we can make it until planting season with no problems. We usually stock up for winter and we can slaughter a cow and that'll give us a lot of meat. We should be okay."

"Water going to be an issue?" asked Haliday.

Bill said, "Not at all, we have an old hand pump and rain barrels."

"You got a tarp by chance?" asked Haliday.

Bill said, "I should have one around somewhere. Why?"

"I'll teach you how to make a rain catch, that way no contaminants get in it. Bird crap mainly. It rains, you unfold and secure the tarp, and it catches in the barrel," Haliday told him.

"Sounds like a plan," Bill said.

"Your tractor running?" Haliday asked.

Bill said, "It is, but we're saving the fuel for it, we only got about two hundred and fifty gallons of diesel for it."

"Okay, save it then. Firewood and everything else?" Haliday asked.

Bill said, "Plenty of that too."

"How about security?" Haliday asked.

"Well, now that we have two more, maybe we can get something set up. Hoping my son makes it here, too," Bill said.

Haliday spent the next two hours explaining how to secure the farm and house as much as possible. "Last but not least, firepower?"

Bill smiled. "Oh, I got plenty of that."

"Let me see what you have," Haliday said.

Bill led him to the den. He opened up a safe and exposed a fairly impressive collection; a 30-06, a couple of 12 gauges, a little Marlin 22, but most noticeable was the two AR15s and a couple of 9mm pistols.

Haliday said, "Nice; you got ammo?"

"I have about a thousand rounds of five-point-five-six, five hundred nine millimeter, couple thousand 22lr, and about two hundred each for the rest. Got bows, too," he added. "Mike bring his?" asked Bill.

"Yes, he did," said Haliday.

They walked back into the kitchen. "Bill, you mind if we stay in the barn tonight?" asked Haliday.

Bill answered, "I sure do; I'd prefer you to crash anywhere in here you guys can find a place."

Haliday said, "We appreciate it."

It was close to dinner time now. Haliday said dinner was on him. "Before I cook though, can we park the vehicles in the barn?"

"Sure thing," Bill said.

Haliday had everyone get what they needed for sleeping that night, had them bring in the cats and dog, and then he walked in with a bucket of groceries. He went over to the kitchen and began cooking. He cooked up a hell of a dinner. He made some chicken Alfredo, some corn, even made some naan, and for desert they had some bananas and honey. He mixed up a couple pitchers of Arnold Palmer lemonade and iced tea. There wasn't anything left when they were finished eating.

They talked a bit longer before setting the watch schedule and heading to bed. Haliday went over a few more things with Mike and Bill.

Bill, too, asked about the government.

Haliday said, "Nothing from them at all. As far as I can tell they are nonexistent."

They headed off to bed.

Haliday checked with Dawn and heard they, too, were camping for the night. It looked like they were in the home stretch.

The morning sun arose and Haliday's group all got ready to go.

"Kayla," he said, "can you load up the cats."

She nodded. "Okay, I'll grab them."

"Take your mutant dog, too."

She called Max; he came prancing by and stepped on Haliday's toes as he passed. Before he walked into the cage, he took the time to look back at Haliday. Almost as if to rub it in his face, Kayla grabbed Romeo and stuffed him in there with Max. Haliday really hated that mutt about now.

Everyone said their goodbyes. Mike and Linda hugged Kayla and told her to be careful, listen to her dad, and that they loved her. They were all relieved that right now everyone was safe.

Everyone piled into the vehicles and Mike walked down and unlocked the gate.

Haliday paused at the gate and called Mike over. "I have a gift for you." He handed him a handheld ham. "You can recharge it with the small solar panel I left back in the barn. Directions are on it; it's easy. You can flip it on every hour on the hour and if we need you, we'll call then, and we'll listen for you as well. You know the protocol—no last names and no locations. I left a couple other things in there as well. We're only going to be about thirty miles away, but these days that's a lot. Good luck, old man."

Mike locked up the gate and then went into the barn. There were some buckets and boxes of food along with the little solar panel and frequency chart. He found a few notes on how to cook the food and what proportions to use. There was a lot of soup, rice, pasta, beans, and some canned meats. This would help them get through the winter easily.

Mike looked around at some bales of hay which he moved aside and then hid everything. He went into the house and told Bill and the two Linda's what they had. They were all more relieved. He would go hunt for a deer to start them off before they got to the cows. The longer they could keep those, the better. It was the same for the chickens.

Haliday's group made it to the rendezvous point. He heard from Dawn earlier and told her they would be waiting. They had two more places that could be trouble and they would need to go through together.

He was making some instant coffee when the radio went off. "Roger, we're stuck. The trailer is stuck and we can't get it out. We've been trying for over an hour and a half."

Haliday said, "Hold tight; I'll be there in a bit." He had the guys unload the KLR and he got ready to go and help. They were about 20 miles away and he would go it alone. Everyone else would stay there and wait. They were out of sight, out of mind, and as long as they stayed that way and kept quiet, they would be fine. He kicked over the bike, turned his radio on, put his earpiece in, and rode off.

Haliday set out west to meet up with the three stranded women and see what he could do. He should have asked them to be a bit more specific about how they got stuck, but then maybe someone would try to figure out their location. No one knew if there was anyone listening in on their frequency or not. He'd see what was going on when he got there.

He was cruising down the road when he passed an older Jeep coming in the opposite direction. At his speed, it caught him by surprise. He glanced in the mirror of the bike and noticed the Jeep was turning around. As far as he could tell it had a couple of guys in it. He couldn't tell their age because they had the top off and looked like they were bundled up a bit. It was one of the coldest days yet.

He hadn't given the temperature much thought because he had slipped on some thermals under his pants and shirts, since the ride on the bike would be cool anyway. He saw them coming up closer now. There didn't seem to be any glass in the windshield which might be the reason they were bundled up. The closer they got the more detail he could see.

He slowed down and took a right-hand turn. The Jeep followed. Two guys only, wearing camo of some type and both had balaclavas on, he noted. Now he wasn't sure they were both male or not. Judging by their size, he was pretty sure they were. It was that or they were big women, but he doubted that. He wondered what happened to the glass in the windshield.

The Jeep pulled up almost right on his rear fender now. He glanced back and saw the passenger waving to him to pull over. *I don't think so*, Haliday thought. He throttled the KLR a bit more to put a space between him and the Jeep.

The Jeep started honking the horn and the passenger was waving again.

Haliday gunned it a bit more and as he increased speed, so did the Jeep. He glanced back and saw the passenger holding what looked like an AR, which was resting on what looked like a bipod on the hood.

That explained the missing glass, but why didn't they just flip the windshield down? he thought. Maybe they had broken it doing that.

188

Haliday saw an access drive for the corn field next to him; he slowed and spun the KLR into the field. The field had been cleaned of the ears of corn, but the farmer hadn't yet turned it under. The stalks hit him as he drove on and they hurt like hell. He felt like he was getting whipped across his shoulders; thank goodness for the hand guards and helmet.

The Jeep had whipped in, too. Haliday heard a couple shots and hugged the bike as low as he could. He didn't know if these were warning shots or to kill him. He slammed on the brakes, kicked the back tire around, and then cut across the rows. It was bumpy as hell and the Jeep would be bouncing like crazy. That would make it harder to target him.

He whipped back around once more and headed back to the road. He cut through the ditch and bounced up onto the pavement. The Jeep had a tougher time navigating this and Haliday increased the distance between him and the vehicle. He needed this distance. He would have to slow down a bit for a brief few seconds.

He slowed so he could handle the bike with enough control only using one hand. He reached down and opened a bag attached to the tank. He managed to open the Velcro top of it, exposing the contents. He took a handful of the contents and tossed it behind him. He did it once more. Real 007 stuff here, he hoped.

The bag had been filled with what he called star jacks. These resembled the kid's version of jacks; however, were made with large spikes that were sharpened to a point on each end. No matter how they landed there would always be a spike pointing upward. Most people called them caltrops. He learned this trick during the Detroit Newspaper Strike back in the early 90s. This was done to flatten the tires of the replacement workers vehicles.

About three dozen of them landed behind him. The Jeep didn't have time to swerve and ran over where they had landed. It just kept right on following him. Haliday cursed to himself and gunned it again. He looked in his mirror but now saw the Jeep slowing. He noticed one of the front tires going flat. He'd gotten at least one tire and that was good enough.

The Jeep came to a stop by the side of the road. The men inside had their own radio and called in to some kind of headquarters. As far as they were concerned, they were the new law around there and somebody had just disrespected them. Their group would not tolerate this behavior; they were dictatorial in nature.

Haliday looked around at himself and made sure he wasn't hit. The only thing he noticed was a small tear in his cargo pocket but that looked like it was from the cornfield. He took a few more roads and got back on route. He was wondering who the hell the men were. He was trying to remember who might be in the area.

There was no military or militia as far as he could remember. If they were militia, they were different than the typical TV yahoos and kept themselves under the radar. This could be a problem. If they had a sizable group, they could damper his own group's efforts. He made note to check this out; he didn't need any big headaches.

He came up to the dirt road and spotted horse tracks and those of the Ranger as well. He got off his bike and looked around.

"That should do the trick," he said.

He walked over to the side of the road and grabbed a bunch of smaller branches and spread them out. He pulled out some Para cord and tied them together and then tied them to the back of his bike.

He keyed his mic and told Dawn he was coming in. He got back on the bike and dragged the branches down the road behind him. While it didn't completely cover up the tracks, it did do a good job and took away that fresh track look. He would do the same on the way out to try and hide the cache site since they hadn't needed to dig it up.

He reached the path and paused long enough to cut the branches loose. There was no way he could drag those through the path. It wasn't quite what he remembered. No wonder they'd had trouble. The winter months played hell on the trees and tree limbs had dropped, blocking the path a bit more than usual.

He came up on the three women standing there waiting. They were grouped together, but at least had the brains to make sure they were ready to fire. He would have had them spread out and hidden. It could have been a trap for them. Haliday turned off the bike and dismounted. He walked over and gave Dawn a hug. He said hi to Diana and Karen and said he was glad they were all safe.

"Let's see what you have here," he said.

He walked around the Ranger and trailer and then looked underneath. He saw that a tree root near the surface had broken and came up and wedged itself between the axle and the floor of the trailer.

He tried going forward again and still no luck; it wasn't going to break free. He tried to pull it out, but he couldn't get the leverage to do this either. He lay down on the ground and worked himself under the Ranger a bit. "Dawn, can you hand me a saw out of the toolbox."

"You want a pocket chain or regular saw?"

"Pocket chain."

Haliday never thought one of those would come in handy, but this awkward position proved its worth. He worked the saw back and forth for about five minutes until the root gave way. He pulled the chunk loose and tossed it aside.

"That should do it," he said. He started the Ranger and it moved freely now.

Haliday called them all over. He thought it might not be a bad idea to tell them what happened. He explained the incident with the Jeep as best as he could.

"We're going to take a slightly different route back just in case they are still out there. The horses will need to move as quickly as they can without exhausting them."

The realization that this area was now changing, too, had hit the three of them like a ton of bricks.

Haliday said, "Welcome to the new world disorder."

Chapter 16

As soon as they reached the dirt road, Haliday hooked up his branches. "Listen," he said, "I'm going down that way about a half mile and then I'll double back and catch up to you guys. I want to try to throw anyone off the track if I can."

Dawn, Diana, and Karen took off and he did too. He doubled back quickly and caught up.

Haliday heard a low guttural roar like that from a 155mm cannon and looked around. The horses were spooked and reared a bit. There came another roar before Haliday realized this was thunder. Well, the effort he'd made hiding the cache was going to go to waste except now it'd be even better as the rain would wash the road clean of the tracks much better than his dragging did.

He signaled them to stop. "You guys have rain gear?"

They all nodded.

"Okay, put it on. Looks like we are going to get hammered." He grabbed a set out of his saddle bags and put them on. Windy, cold, wet, and exposed. This was getting to be all kinds of fun. People out and about would be heading home, but those still out in this weather would have a purpose. It was best to avoid those folks. Dark clouds started moving in and the wind picked up.

Haliday called David and asked them how they were doing. David said they were just sitting around waiting for them to get there.

"Well, with the weather change it's going to be a while. Make sure everyone gets something to eat and keep some hot liquids on hand," Haliday said. "Have everyone dress warmer. I have a feeling tonight is going to be rough."

Haliday told David they would be staying the night there, to go ahead and get things set up. "Kayla will help you. If you have any questions, let me know. Watch out for intruders, they are a high level threat. Treat them as such. Do not take any chances."

David asked him if he wanted him to set up a hide for someone using Haliday's rifle.

Haliday told him, "No offense, but nobody is to touch that rifle." He highly doubted anybody could explain mil-dot, MOA, windage, spin drift, or anything else they would need to know in order to use it. They wouldn't even know what rounds to use. He kept three basic loads for it for various conditions. They'd just load what they grabbed, not understanding the differences.

"David, just set up for the night, set a solid watch roster, and keep everyone warm and dry. Do not move out, do not send out anybody to recon the area or anything else."

David answered, "Got it, brother."

David went over to Kayla. "I need your help. Your dad says we are staying the night."

Kayla started barking out orders and got everyone moving.

She was a smart girl and although at times she thought her dad was a little crazy, she made it a point to listen to him. Now she was doing what he would be doing right then. She ordered the vehicles realigned and had them parked so that they formed a small modern day circled wagon train.

The Tahoe and trailer were parked so that the trailer was almost at a 90 degree angle to it and opposite that were the Cherokee and its trailer. This formed a mutated square, but left ample coverage for everything in the middle. They would set up a small 10-by-10 pop-up tent in the middle with some side panels and cover everything with a camo net.

They weren't worried about the aerial view, but didn't want anyone seeing them from the side. They had chosen an area with plenty of pine trees because the rest of the foliage was already down for the fall, but they still didn't want to be seen. The camo net was designed for this use in particular.

Haliday had taken numerous pictures and sent them out to a large format printing company in China and had "Nature Billboards" printed. He hated to use the Chinese company, but it was a tenth of the cost compared to the U.S. companies. He had a few for the different seasons.

They were designed to be hung on buildings and printed on a mesh so you could see through them when you were close enough, but people who saw them from a distance couldn't. Custom camo nets. He literally paid less than 75 cents a square foot for the panels. Well worth the cost.

They lit up a small propane heater. No fires and so no smoke. They pulled out a butane stove and boiled up some water for coffee and hot cocoa. They would get lunch ready, too, but Kayla had already determined it was going to be soup. This was everyone's first afternoon and night exposed to the elements. Best to stay warm.

Haliday was taking the lead now and shot up a ways to scope out the intersections ahead of Dawn, Diana, and Karen. Once they passed by, he would shoot up ahead once again and check the area. This would keep them from having to do it themselves and save a little time. If he spotted any trouble, he could tell them and they could stop and he could try to draw the trouble away from them.

Kayla called him on the radio. "We got a problem, or to be more exact, you have a problem."

"What's going on?" he asked.

"Well, I was scanning through the frequencies and it stopped on one which I listened to for a while. The signal was strong, so I figured it was close by. I wrote the frequency down. I'll give it to you in a minute. Anyway, I assume it's you they are looking for."

Haliday was trying to figure this out. "Kayla, what exactly did you hear?"

"Okay, it was hard to decipher at first because the transmissions were kind of choppy and I came across it halfway into the conversation. But here's the short story," she said.

"Some group called the Bad Axe Minute Men had some patrols out. One of those patrols came across a guy on a motorcycle. They said they tried to stop the guy, but he ran. They are calling him a fugitive. They mentioned chasing him until he flattened two of their tires with spikes. I figured it was you. Now they put out an APB to their other patrols and headquarters."

She added, "They pretty much said to just shoot on sight. They said OD green motorcycle, one man, large build, khaki cargo pants, black jacket, and full face helmet. Sounds like you, Dad. You really pissed someone off. I'm trying to listen in and gather some more intel. I'll tell you what I hear."

"Okay, kiddo, thanks for the good news."

She gave him the frequency and got off the radio.

Haliday slowed down and looked at Dawn, Diana, and Karen and shrugged his shoulders. Nothing he could do now. They were listening to the same frequency he was, they had heard the news, too. He looked down at the map on top of the tank. *Here we go again, time to change the route.*

He would head back south a bit. If the Jeep guys were indeed out of Bad Axe, then they were a good 30 miles out from the center of their operations. That meant they were only about 15 miles from his own group's destination.

Thirty miles is a long way out for a patrol, he thought. They were either very large or very dumb. He'd have to figure this out quickly. He was getting pelted with rain now. He signaled another stop and pulled over. He programmed his radio with the frequency Kayla had given him.

Dawn and Diana watered the horses quickly and then put a cover on the Ranger to help keep the rain out. It was coming straight down, but the small top would provide at least a little relief. Haliday refused to let them put the whole top on. There was not enough visibility with it on.

He checked the map once more. "Okay, here it is," he told them. "This is the route. We are about eight miles away now and we have to push it. We can't risk stopping around here for the night. They going to make it?" he asked, nodding toward the horses.

"Yeah, they'll make it," Dawn said.

Haliday said, "Okay, good. Let's go."

Diana asked him what would happen if one of those patrols found them.

"People would die. Who, I don't know, but people would die," he said.

He grabbed some hundred mile an hour tape and covered all of the lights on the bike and Ranger. He didn't want anyone spotting the lights; it was late afternoon, the sky was dark, rain was coming down and anyone would easily see the lights.

They got moving again.

Haliday flipped the radio over to the frequency Kayla had given him and listened for a while. He started taking mental notes on what he heard. There was actually quite a bit of chatter. He was glad Kayla was taking notes. This was going to be a big problem he had not expected.

He thought of contacting the new group from Bad Axe to sort it out, but that was a stupid idea as well. They would know he definitely had their frequency and they would most likely change it. This reminded him, if they stumbled across the militia frequency, they could find his. He would have the group start using the frequency list and change it often.

He needed as much intel on these guys as he could get. Five days now and militias were out hunting already. Probably more like staking out their kingdoms. He knew however, not all militias were bad guys. There were actually a lot of good ones. He just happened to come across a bad one.

After a couple more hours of slow moving, he called Kayla and told them they were coming in.

Once they got there, they got situated and went into the small tent to warm up. Bev gave them some coffee, hot cocoa, and offered them some soup as well, which they gladly accepted.

Kayla came in. "Okay, Dad, here's what we have."

Kayla had taken meticulous notes on everything she heard. She started with manpower. "They have four patrols out in designated areas with an additional patrol that seems to be a quick response unit that can backup any of the other patrols. It sounds like that unit stays either at, or close, to their headquarters. I would say two people per patrol."

That was 10 people right there.

"They pulled a shift change at 1800 hours," she continued. "When they did this though, they only had two patrols out and one for response for the night. They mentioned seeing each other in the morning, so it looks like twelve-hour shifts. So that gives them another six people. I assume one at HQ to coordinate or answer the radio. We have a definite eighteen people on external security details.

"Now, they said something about camp watch and I couldn't quite make that out, but it sounded like static posts to watch their HQ or their compound. Maybe a watchtower or who knows what. I didn't catch this during the day, so I'm not sure. But it's safe to say they have at least twenty-two to twenty-four people and most likely more." She consulted her notes. "I didn't catch anything about where the HQ or compound was though; I didn't expect to. I didn't catch how many people were currently not on patrol or watch duty. No way to really calculate their total numbers because there was no telling if wives, girlfriends, or kids were involved. I did hear some people in the background once in a while. Someone was giving out chores to be completed. If I had to guess, Dad, you have forty to fifty people total and that's minimum."

They were daunting numbers.

"Now here's where it gets interesting," she said. "They call in checks once in a while, but not sure what they are checking or who they are checking. They use code numbers for that. A21 checked and secured, B13 checked and secured, like that. Could be other family, could be caches, could be a lot of things. One more important detail is they act like there's Martial Law. They are acting like they are the combination military and police for the area.

They mentioned catching some looters and taking them somewhere, but I don't know exactly where. I missed what they said. It might have been the police department. Either way, they think they control the whole area and it sounds like they just might be doing that."

"How do you know they are the Bad Axe Minute Men?" he asked.

"I heard them call to another group in Bay City. Well, the other group didn't answer. I think they forgot to change frequencies when transmitting. I don't know, but I heard them say Bad Axe Minute Men calling Bay City Minute Men, then it went dead. They must have changed frequencies then."

"Good job, sweetie. That helps tremendously. The unfortunate thing is we are on the edge of their patrol areas and then we'll be within ten to fifteen miles away from their HQ when we move to the cabin," he said. "I don't know exactly what they are trying to do, but if it's run the Thumb Area we have problems. If they'll leave us alone then that's much better."

"What about trying to strike a deal with them, Dad?"

"I thought about that. I'm thinking we might make the next leg of the trip tomorrow and then go from there. I wish I knew more about these guys, but they kept a low profile and I had no idea they were out here. Not like I can do any research now."

"Wait a minute, Dad. Call Mike. Mr. Bill might know something; he's more of a local here."

Haliday was impressed. He hadn't thought of that. "Okay, kiddo, go for it. Tell him to change frequencies though. If that group is scanning frequencies I don't want them to hear anything about us."

Kayla got a hold of Mike and asked him how things were. Mike told her Bill and Linda's son and daughter-in-law had made it in. That was good news.

She asked if Bill was around and if she could talk to him. "He's napping right now; is it important?"

Kayla said to go wake him; it was about the militia with a wanted poster out for Dad.

A few minutes later Bill came on the radio. Kayla asked him if he knew anything about the BAMM.

There was a pause before Bill answered. "I actually know one of the guys who is a member. I assume that's the group he belongs to. He tried to recruit me a while back. He mentioned Bad Axe but not the name BAMM specifically. He did not say much at all, really. Just that he belonged to a group that would run the community if something major ever happened."

"Do you know what their mission is?"

"If it's the same group I'm thinking of, then they are out there to keep law and order. But here's the catch: While they are not quite government-friendly, they are not quite people-friendly either. I don't think they want people other than themselves enforcing any law and order or carrying firearms.

They might feel different about the police but I'm not sure. They might actually be a part of them; not many cops are in this area. Most were county sheriffs and a couple state troopers; that's all. The sheriff up there is a real ass and he's involved with them somehow. He has a real attitude and acts like his crap smells like roses."

"Anything else?" Kayla asked.

"Yeah, they don't take too kindly to outsiders. I think they mean to take over the area and run it as their own small state. If that's the case, you guys might have issues, depending on where you're going. My friend is kind of an ass, I would say the BAMM are not friendly."

Kayla said, "Thank you, sir."

"No problem. Take care. Your mom says hugs and kisses," Bill replied.

Kayla looked around. Everyone except Kevin and Blake, who were on watch, was sitting there listening in.

"How's this change things?" Bev asked.

Haliday said, "Well, we have a couple choices here. I'm not sure any of them will be acceptable to these people if they have that attitude. One, I can meet with them, see what they are up to, and if they'll let us go about our business. They might see us as a threat and say no and then tighten their security and look for us as we try to move in. They may even want payment or outright take what they want and kick us out. It could get ugly."

"Two," Haliday continued, "we can try to sneak in, take hold on our land, and then let them approach us when they discover us. We can feel them out then, show them we are just there to mind our own business, and see how that works out; but we could end up defending ourselves. The Michigan Alamo. Same results too; it could be bad.

"Third, we could hunker down somewhere, go on the hunt and try to shake up their ranks. But we're talking about guerrilla warfare. We are talking about a long, drawn-out campaign with some pretty good chances of losing some of the ranks here. I'm not really advising this. So far they just tried to kill me, if that's what it was; not really sure they are a threat to all of us. I probably appeared to be a threat to them. On the other hand, who were they to try and stop me anyway?"

He took a breath. "Fourth, I could go it alone, take out whomever I can for a while and see how that works out. There's enough supplies here to get you through for quite some time. Then we could move onto our land. Or you could head back to Bill and Linda's. The longer we wait to get to the cabin, the better the odds are that they might find something and we lose it all. This would really piss them off."

They all sat around talking about it for a while. Some different ideas were thrown out, but not much really made sense. It really came down to one thing: How could they get all their people to the house and stay there as long as possible with the least amount of trouble? That would be one hell of a trick.

They set up another 10-by-10 and joined the two together. They put the heater in the middle. It was still close quarters, but better than nothing. With any luck, it wouldn't be like this much longer. They would be at the land and in the cabin.

There were 14 of them in the group. Only 12 were able to pull watch. Elizabeth and Bobby were too young. Kayla had figured out a schedule. Two on at a time would be okay. Hour and a half shifts would help keep them awake, although the cool weather would do that, too. They had set up some traps like Haliday instructed.

Haliday had them set up some booby trap simulators to alert the group if people got too close. Those had been purchased from a surplus store. He also had them set up what he called trigger hooks. They were three-by-three foot-square fish line nets with fish hooks scattered around them. These were placed face high. Once they snagged anything, any attempt to take them off snagged things even more—clothing, hair or skin. Man's natural reaction to brush something away allowed them to work. The barbed hooks dug in deep.

It was an uneventful night; however, a few of them did not sleep. They tossed and turned, thinking about how to reach the house, what to expect the next couple of days, what had happened the past few days, but mostly what was happening to family members. They didn't have any idea what was happening to any of them. Being together tonight reminded them that there were family members who were missing.

Morning came as usual. Everyone got up and started warming up around the heater. Bev put some pots of water on for oatmeal and coffee and hot cocoa for the kids. They packed up any non-essential items and ate breakfast when it was ready. Haliday called a quick meeting.

"Time to vote," he said.

The rumbling started immediately. No one wanted to decide. They deferred the decision to Haliday.

"Okay, this is what we are going to do," he said. "Like it or not, since there was no decision, it's my ball game. We are going to pack everything up. I'll be on one bike and Blake on his. We'll be riding well in front of the Ranger, with the horses behind it, followed by the trucks. If we spot trouble we'll hit the sides of the road and take cover. The rest of you will be expected to do the same.

"The Ranger will go left, horses will go right, Cherokee left as well, and Tahoe to the right; that will even things out on both sides of the road. We'll work out vehicle assignments. Do not bunch together—stay within earshot of each other and keep your eyes open to all sides as well as front and rear. If we have to fire, make sure you do not cross fire and do not fire up by us. You will have to watch my signals." Haliday covered some brief hand signals.

"I've altered the route a bit, but it will only take us two days if everything goes smoothly. Make sure the vehicles are gassed up. We'll stop once for lunch and that's all. When we stop for dinner, we'll also make camp for the night. I'm not going to try to contact the militia at all. We are going to try to sneak in there.

"If we encounter a problem, I'll raise them on the radio and set something up as far as a meeting goes. I have a couple ideas of how to do that. In the meantime, let's get ready to move out. Blake, get your bike and bring it here. We have a quick modification to make."

Blake rolled his bike over to where Haliday was.

Haliday took a long pipe that had an elbow on the end and held it up against the fork of Blake's bike. He used a few heavy round clamps and secured it in place. Haliday walked over to his own bike and slipped a similar pipe into a sleeve he already had attached to the fork and used a big cotter pin to secure it in place.

"What's that for?" Blake asked.

"It's so we can keep our heads on. If these guys are looking for me on a bike, there's no telling whether or not they set up any traps. The most common is a wire strung between trees or poles. It catches you at neck level and it's all over. The pipe will catch the wire. It might not snap the wire, but the pressure will knock the bike down and you with it. Much better alternative. Now," he said, "here's a multi-tool."

"What for?"

"To clip the wire, Blake. Just in case, that's all, understand? We don't need wire getting caught in any wheels or anything."

Blake didn't like this idea, but he was the most experienced rider next to Haliday.

"Blake, get your head in the game. Listen to my instructions and you'll do fine."

Haliday was listening to the Minute Men frequency.

"Papa Four is out at Delta Thirteen," came over the radio.

"Almost sounds like cops." He waited about seven or eight minutes before he heard them again.

"Papa Four is back on patrol. Parties at Delta Thirteen said they haven't seen anything unusual."

Haliday figured Kayla had hit the nail on the head. These were locations of houses and they were checking them regularly.

He listened in a bit more.

"Papa Two is out at Bravo Seven."

He waved everyone off and motioned for them to sit. Kayla came by with her notebook and took notes. After about 25 more minutes they had a pattern figured out.

"Papa" was obviously a patrol number, and they noted each patrol had an area assigned to them. One was Alpha, two was Bravo, three was Charlie, and four was Delta. That made sense.

What didn't make sense was that they could not possibly have numbered every house or building in the area.

Rich said, "They have a neighborhood watch set up. They probably have people in key locations and they check in with those people. Intersections, ends of roads, wherever they have a vantage point."

"Good catch, Dad." Haliday had to figure out two things. How did they convince these extra eyes to play along? And what area were they in? Make that three things, he decided. What area were they trying to get to as well? He studied the map to see if he could figure out the areas. He noted everyone else getting anxious.

"I learned this in the army, folks. It's called hurry up and wait." Haliday studied the map some more. He had lost himself in it when he heard Kayla say bingo.

"Bingo what, Kayla?"

"Dad, you didn't hear that?"

"All I heard was cantonment." Damn, he got it. They wanted Papa 3 which was the Charlie sector, to stay in their cantonment area. He had used cantonment areas, or rather districts, down at Ft. Stewart as an MP.

Haliday divided the map up into equal sections now. They were covering roughly 40-by-40 miles. The yahoos he ran across had gone out of their area and were cautioned to stay in their area today. These would be the Papa 3 units with Charlie sector. At night he figured the two units covered north and south. Someone had military training or read a lot of field manuals.

This posed another problem. The Bay City Minute Men most likely bordered the Bad Axe areas. If they had a mutual aid pact, that increased the odds of trouble. They would definitely have more firepower. Haliday was going to have to completely rethink the situation.

He called everyone over. "Time to change the plan. We are going to make a very short move to this location here." He indicated the map. "This will put us just inside the edge of their patrol area. We'll set up camp and you'll stay there tonight and through tomorrow as well. Early the next morning you'll move out and head straight to the cabin. I'm going to head up over here and stir the pot." He jabbed a finger at the map.

He added, "I'll stir it enough to draw them away from you guys. Once you get there, you fortify the hell out of it. There are instructions, diagrams, notes, everything you will need right there in the cabin. Kayla knows how to get to everything. I'll work my way back and we'll go from there."

"What if we're spotted?" David asked.

"They have the patrols calling in the checks from their spotters, so I doubt they have a way of communicating. They'll be too busy with me to do the normal checks. Like I said, I'll buy you the time to get there. I do need a volunteer to go with me. Blake, it's your bike and you know how to ride. It's going to be you. Let's move out folks."

About two hours later they reached the campsite. Haliday and Blake made their preparations while the rest of the group set up camp, placed the booby traps out, and got settled in. They covered a few more informational items, wished each other luck, and said their goodbyes. Haliday and Blake headed out.

Chapter 17

Haliday and Blake rode out and used a lot of the back roads. They avoided the main roads, even though they seemed to be clear. The reason behind this was that Haliday figured this was where most of the spotters were located, almost like border patrol outposts. The militia would know when their little border had been breached. It was this particular reason that Haliday laid out the plan the way he had.

They were as careful as they possibly could be while in area Charlie, the area they would settle into for the long haul. Once they reached the other sector, however, they made themselves plain as day. They made it a point to be seen by who they suspected were most likely spotters. This was the beginning of the plan.

After another hour they stopped and pulled over into the woods. Haliday and Blake had the portable hams so they could keep in touch. Haliday told Blake to cut back through the woods, change over and come back through the area that they just came from.

Blake cut through the woods, stopped, and made some quick changes. He changed his outer jacket cover that Haliday had given him. He had a couple of these; they were just shells of various camo patterns and not full jackets. He also altered the looks of his bike.

He took some black hundred mile an hour tape and made some large stripes on the yellow tank and fenders. He placed one across his helmet as well. He took off and headed to where they had originally stopped.

Haliday in the meantime had taken some black and brown tape and put squares on his bike to give it a quasi-digital camo look. He simply took his helmet off and put on a boonie cap to go along with his own jacket change. The difference was good enough that most people would think it was someone else.

About half a mile before Blake reached the woods, he stopped right in the middle of the road in front of a small farmhouse on a corner lot by a small intersection. There was a lady standing there on the porch. Blake looked down the main road and raised his arm and gave a quick wave.

Haliday came up behind him and they both took off. As far as the lady on the porch knew, there had been two pairs of bikes that just went through. A multiplication of manpower through deception.

Next up, they caused a little trouble. They rode up close to a small town called Pigeon. Haliday scoped out a small gas station with only a few people near it. They rode up slowly and pulled in. A guy in his mid-20s was standing there with a pistol stuffed in a thigh rig. Blake was facing the guy and Haliday made it a point to face the direction they came in from.

A man at a gas station said, "You guys don't look too familiar. How can I help you?"

Blake looked around. Haliday looked around as well and then the ruse began.

Haliday clicked his mic and said, "There are four bodies here, all armed. Hold your twenty."

The guy looked up the street and then back at Blake.

Blake said, "Any chance we can buy some gas?"

"How much you need?" asked the station attendant.

Blake said, "We need to fill six bikes and six two-gallon cans."

"Is that all?" the attendant asked.

Blake said, "For now, but we might need to fill our trucks in a couple hours."

"That's going to be a problem for sure. Where you guys from, anyway?" the attendant asked.

Blake was good at the ploy. "Just around," he answered.

The moment was getting a little tense.

Haliday clicked the mic again. "No, hold your twenty. Doesn't look like they want to play nice with us." He glanced over at the guy who was standing there. "Well? We get gas or not?"

The guy said, "No, we're under orders not to sell it to anybody that doesn't have a gas card."

"Where do we get a gas card?" Haliday asked.

"You can't; the militia gave them out," the attendant said.

"You mean the military gave them out?" Haliday asked.

"No, the militia," The attendant said.

Haliday looked at the guy. "So let me understand this. You guys are taking orders from a group of yahoos who think they run the country now? You guys have a say in that decision of how they would distribute what's yours?"

The guy didn't answer.

Haliday said, "Let's go. These people are suffering HUA."

The guy asked Haliday what HUA meant.

"Head up ass." Haliday clicked his mic once more. "We're coming back out. Have Dave in truck five fill up a couple gas cans for the bikes and meet us at…" He then stopped, looked at the guy, and said into the mic, "I'll call you back with that info. Thanks for nothing, partner," he told the man. "We'll go find our gas elsewhere."

They high tailed it out of that area quickly.

Of course there hadn't been any transmissions or any truck number five, but appearances counted now, not the facts. Haliday and Blake found themselves a little place to hide behind some small stores. They sat it out for about two hours, trying to listen to see what was going on. Haliday grinned when he heard the first message pertaining to them.

"Papa One is out at Alpha Ten with information. Stand by."

A few minutes passed.

"Alpha Ten reports that there were at least four men on motorcycles who passed by a couple hours ago. They report there might have been more, but definitely saw four. We have a direction and will head out and see what other info we can find."

About half an hour later came another transmission. "Papa One is out at Foxtrot Delta Three."

Haliday thought about that one. Okay, fuel depot, these guys really wanted to play army. Good for them. He openly laughed at the next transmission.

"Papa One to HQ. We have reports that confirm six motorcycles and possible trucks in the area. Maybe up to five or more, but makes and models are unknown. There are an unknown number of hostiles. Seems they wanted gas and were denied. We understand the guys were some sort of wannabe Special Forces jerks with attitudes based on the way they acted."

Haliday got a kick out of this. "Oh boy, these people are hilarious."

They pushed their bikes further into the woods and covered them up. Haliday broke out a small camp stove and some water. "Mac and cheese this evening, Blake. Is that okay with you?"

"Sounds okay to me."

"You want coffee or cocoa?"

"Uh, can I have something else?"

"Water, Kool-Aid, Arnold Palmer or Tang?"

"I'll have some Kool-Aid."

They finished their quick dinner and then checked in with his group. "Everything is going fine," Haliday said. "Tonight can you monitor the militia freq and take notes. Do not worry about what you hear about us. I want you to concentrate on what they are doing. Have a couple people listen in to make sure you get as much info as possible." He turned to his partner. "Okay, Blake, you ready to go?"

"Yes, sir."

"All right, then let's get busy."

Haliday double-checked to make sure the lights on the bikes were taped off. He rigged up the headlights so that you could pull a strip of tape off and it would uncover the light in case they needed to see. The moon was fairly bright and provided enough light to see at the speeds they were moving. They moved slowly using back woods trails.

They came up on a small road and turned the bikes off. They walked up to a stalled car there and punctured the tank and filled their smaller gas cans. They went back and filled the bikes and then went back and topped off the gas cans. Haliday let the gas flow out of the tank though instead of plugging it like he had the other tanks.

He grabbed a cigarette out of a pack in his pocket; he didn't smoke, just used them for projects. He grabbed a wooden match and poked it through the cigarette near the filter. He bent a paperclip into shape and placed this down by the gas on the ground. Looked like a little cannon pointing toward the sky. The cigarette would burn down, ignite the match, which was close enough to the gas, and that would set it all ablaze.

This would buy them time to get out of the area. They walked back into the woods and took off. They were well enough away from the area when the gas ignited and the car became engulfed in flames. This drew the attention of the nearby homes as the people came out to look at what was burning. This would be reported if it wasn't seen by a patrol.

Haliday and Blake hit another spot about four miles away and further north. Haliday showed Blake how to do it.

"We don't need the gas, but we need the diversion," Haliday said.

Blake looked at the car they'd found. "Oh man, Mr. Haliday, it's a Camaro."

"What's wrong with that? They don't burn? Blake, the car is useless. If it makes you feel any better, I'll write the owner a check. Let's move."

Blake set the makeshift fuse and they took off again.

"Last but not least, the grand finale for the night. This third car is where it gets risky. This is what we'll do." Haliday explained the plan to Blake and they got ready to go. "If we get separated, you meet me back here at this intersection. Let's go."

They cut the engines on the bikes and rolled down a hill about an eighth of a mile. Along the side of the road they stopped by a third car. Haliday went and punctured the tank. No gas, though. He walked over to another one and there was no gas in it either. This wasn't going to work out that well. There were no other cars far enough away from the homes.

He looked around and saw an older store by itself with a dirt parking lot that looked empty. He checked it out and it appeared to have been empty for probably 10 years or more. The people in the Thumb Area had it made. Nice rural areas, but they still had that American dream—they'd open a business; it would fail and then sit empty. Simply not enough people around to support it.

He found an old bottle and poured a little gas inside with a piece of rag to make a Molotov cocktail. He lit it, then grabbed a rock and tossed it through a window of the store. He tossed the flaming bottle in next.

Blake and he started yelling and fired a few shots from their rifles and also Haliday's .40. They got on the bikes and took off. There were plenty of flashlights and candles now glowing in the neighborhood.

They were heading down the road when they spotted a pair of headlights coming their way and a spotlight sweeping the road. Haliday peeled off the tape from his headlight and shot into the woods. Blake followed him. They got about 150 yards in and killed the bikes, laid them down, and took cover. Haliday grabbed a camo jacket shell and tossed it over his bike. Blake grabbed one and did the same thing.

Haliday liked this kid. Blake learned quickly. They threw some small deadfall branches on them as well. There was not a lot of wooded area there and they'd be easy to spot if they tried to make a run for it. Staying put was the only option next to abandoning the bikes. They couldn't afford to do that.

211

The vehicle that was approaching stopped about a mile down the road from the burning store. It was moving slowly toward the store and sweeping its spotlight into the fields and woods searching for them. The vehicle occupants must have misjudged distance because they did this for almost half a mile past the store. They weren't sure where their targets were hiding. With the spotlight, Haliday knew they weren't using NVGs or any type of thermal unit.

As they sat and waited, another vehicle came screaming by. It didn't stop until it got near the store. Haliday looked through his binoculars the best he could. Once again he wished he had NVGs. Looked like an older Jeep and older pickup. Four guys were standing near them, talking and waving toward Blake and Haliday's general area.

"Mr. Haliday, I'm a little scared."

"Look, Blake, just stay down; do not move or do anything. Listen to what I tell you. We'll be OK."

Two of the guys got back in the truck and then the truck made another sweep down the road with the spotlight.

Haliday covered the binoculars up and looked at Blake. "Don't worry, kid. Just put your head down and don't think about it. I'll tell you what they're doing and then tell you if you need to do anything if that helps." Blake looked down and remained still.

"Okay, Blake, they are still spotlighting the road and the whole area. If they had spotted us they would be coming at us already. They are heading back toward the store. The Jeep is taking off now. It's heading in the direction of the second car fire. The guys in the truck are still looking around. Looks like they plan to stay a while because they just opened up a cooler and it looks like it's meal time.

"Blake, carefully low crawl over to your bike and grab that wool blanket out of your pack. Cover yourself up with it. We're going to be here a while." Haliday followed suit and grabbed one out of his saddle bags. The nice thing about the KLR bags was that they were more like small suit cases. They had a lot of cargo room for all the gear Haliday kept in them.

They laid there for a while watching the guys stand by the burning store.

Haliday asked Blake about football, why he didn't go to college, anything to help keep the kid calm. Haliday had waited like this before, hours upon hours; it didn't bother him.

Blake had pretty much settled down and now it was almost 2:30 in the morning.

The guys got in their truck and took one last look around before they left.

Blake asked, "Can we go now?"

"Absolutely not. Watch, you'll see what I mean."

They still laid there. About half an hour later the truck drove back by.

"That's why we waited, Blake; they were still looking for us."

After another hour they got up and shook off the cold. Haliday grabbed a map and hid under Blake's blanket with a red lens flashlight to read it. After a while he turned out the light and flipped the blanket off. "That was something else, huh Blake?"

"Oh yeah; ranks up there in my top ten list of favorite things."

"Get used to it. It ain't combat, but you are fighting for your life. Remember that. Any time you feel giddy enough you can head to the cabin if you want to."

"No way, Mr. Haliday. I just never thought I'd see stuff like this happen in America and I don't like those guys for some reason. I don't trust them."

"Tape your headlight up again and let's get going."

They worked their way to another farm area. Haliday spotted a rundown barn with a "For Sale" sign just off the road. He could see a house. He walked up to the "For Sale" sign and pulled a piece of paper out of a plastic box that was on the side of the sign post. The paper bore a description of the property.

He grabbed his flashlight and blanket again and read the paper. "Fifty acres, good for sugar beets, blah blah blah, old barn can be repaired, mobile home removed from property, but foundation left in place. Good, abandoned."

They worked their way to the barn, pushing the bikes, just in case. They went inside and except for a few rusted old hulks of farm implements, it was empty.

"We'll stay here for a bit, Blake. Go ahead and make yourself comfortable and grab a couple hours of sleep. I'll wake you up later and we'll switch off."

Haliday went to his bike and grabbed a few granola bars and turned to offer Blake one, but Blake was already out like a light with his sleeping bag just draped over him.

Haliday munched on the treat and took a look around the barn and land. *This wouldn't have been a bad place to build,* he thought.

He changed the frequency and gave his group a quick radio hello.

"Hey, Uncle Roger, it's Randy," came the response.

"Hey, Randy, everything okay with you guys there at the camp?"

"Well, we could all use a drink." Randy said.

"Why, what's going on?" Haliday asked.

"You guys have definitely stirred the pot. There are a whole lot of people wanting to skin you guys alive. They are super pissed off. It was quite intense to listen to." Randy told him.

"Well, that's our plan," Haliday said, pleased. "You guys learn anything good?"

Randy said, "Kayla and Dawn took notes and then after it all settled down, Grandma and Grandpa took notes, too."

"Okay, I'll call again in a few hours; we're getting some rest right now. Tell everyone we are okay and talk to you soon." Roger then put the radio away.

Haliday walked around a bit more after touching base with his camp and then went over and woke Blake up. The sun was starting to rise and Blake should be able to stay awake now. Haliday doubted he would have been able to take the first watch.

"Before I crash, you want any coffee or anything?"

Blake said, "I'm a little hungry."

"Here, start with this." Haliday tossed him a Snickers bar. "After that go ahead and crack open an MRE. Eat it all, Blake. You'll need the calories and energy."

Haliday dropped his sleeping bag to the ground, unzipped it, and climbed in. He wanted to zip it up, but also didn't want to get stuck in it if something happened. He looked over at Blake struggling with the MRE.

Blake glanced over and saw him watching.

"Blake, the directions are on the side. Use the red-lens flashlight." The kid would need a couple more hours of sleep before they moved out so he was more aware of what was going on.

Blake nudged him awake. Haliday opened his eyes. Blake was telling him to be quiet.

Haliday slowly got out of his bag. "What's going on?"

Blake whispered to him that someone else was there already.

"What the hell, where are they?" Haliday walked over to a window and Blake pointed them out.

About 50 feet from where the concrete pad of the mobile home had been was a door sticking up in the air. There was a man and a woman standing there talking. Haliday and Blake had walked their bikes right by it when they'd come in last night. It was an old tornado shelter and it looked like it had been used last night.

Haliday looked around inside the barn and saw that the bikes and gear were all there. At least they hadn't been discovered yet.

He motioned for Blake to check his weapon and make sure it was ready to go. He checked his own as well and then signaled Blake to go to the other end of the barn. Haliday found a hole in the side of the barn and watched them for a few minutes. They were just standing there talking. A third figure appeared out of the shelter.

This was a young child, maybe eight or nine years old. It looked like a boy, but with some of the hairstyles kids wore those days Haliday didn't make judgment just yet. The kid turned around; definitely a boy. The parents stretched a bit and the kid kicked around a rock. He came close to the barn a couple of times, which made Haliday and Blake nervous.

For a minute, the boy eyeballed the barn and started walking toward the door.

"Timmy, don't go in there! It's dangerous!" the mother called out.

The boy turned around and walked back toward her.

"We need to get moving again. We have a long way to go," she said.

They went down into the shelter and the father came out with a bicycle. He went down again and came back out with another one. One more trip and they all three had their bikes.

He went down once again and brought up a small two-wheeled cart like those you tow behind bikes with your dog in it. They retrieved some packs and things, then started getting everything loaded up.

Haliday said, "Looks like they just stayed for the night."

The three were about to pedal away when they heard a vehicle coming down the road.

A truck pulled in and right up to the family. A man and woman climbed out and walked up to them. It looked like they were wearing some kind of Russian camo pattern.

The man from the family spoke first. "Who are you guys?"

The camo wearing man said, "We're members of the Bad Axe Minute Men. Who are you?"

"My name is Steven and this is my wife, Jill, and son, Tim."

The Minute Man spoke, "You guys from the area?"

"Yes we are. We're from Port Austin." The father said.

The woman from the truck walked around the three of them and looked down the steps of the shelter. "Anyone else down there?"

"No, we were just staying the night and getting ready to leave."

The woman went down into the shelter and re-emerged. "No one else down there." She went and stood back next to the other guy.

Haliday was shocked at how much risk they took.

"What about the barn?" she said.

"We looked in it last night, but it's empty. We chose the tornado shelter because it had the old cots down there. There was too much rusty equipment to get hurt on in there and my son is curious," the mother said.

The militia woman said, "Where you guys heading?"

"Imlay City, to my parents' house. We left yesterday and stopped here for the night. We hope to make it there some time in the next couple days before it gets much colder, the father said.

The militia man walked around and looked at their bikes and packs. "You have any weapons?" he asked.

The father said, "No."

"Mind if I check?" asked the militia man.

The father replied, "Yes I do. You're not a cop. You don't have the right."

"Look, bud, times are different. This area is under control of the Bad Axe Minute Men now. What we say goes. We have a no weapons policy for travelers." The militia man told the father.

The father insisted, "You don't have any right to search us."

217

The militia woman walked up and grabbed the guy's pack; he struggled, but then got hit by the militia man. The wife yelled at him to stop it and the little boy began crying and yelling for them to stop. The Minute Man laid one more punch in the guy's face and knocked him down.

Inside the barn, Haliday was fighting the urge to fire. Blake just had a WTF look on his face, but Haliday signaled him to stay down.

The Minute Man picked up the bags and dumped everything out. He picked up a small pistol.

"No guns, huh?" He kicked the guy while he was down. "You answer with the truth when asked a question. We'll be keeping this. You're damn lucky we ain't taking your food, too. Now get the hell out of here."

They were about to get in the truck when they heard a noise by the barn and stopped.

Everyone looked over at the barn.

Haliday was ready. A big raccoon went scurrying out from one of the windows down the side of the barn and across the field. The Minute Men lowered their rifles and got back in their truck. They told the family to get going and then took off down the road.

Haliday heard them call on the radio and report the check. That was a close one.

Blake said, "Let's go see if they need help."

Haliday said, "No, we can't. If they get stopped again and they are afraid, they'll rat us out in a heartbeat. It'll take them two days tops to get to Imlay City, maybe three, but they'll make it. You go hit the sack for a little bit more and I'll keep watch again; it'll be a while before it's safe to go."

He watched the family gather themselves and head out. What the hell kind of militia was this? These guys should be helping these people, not beating them and disarming them, especially when they were on the road. That was total BS in Haliday's mind. *Were these guys rogue from their own militia group?* Haliday thought.

He kept wondering about them. He should have shot them and given the truck to the family, but that would have opened up a whole different can of worms. Especially if they were caught with it.

After the family left and was well on their way, Haliday called his group. "Hey, listen, if you are approached by a group of militia or members of the militia, be careful. They seem to have designated a Russian camo as their uniform, which looks like the old U.S. woodland BDU pattern, only with finer detail and the colors are not as contrasting.

Shoot the bastards on sight. Don't mess around with them." He relayed to them the story of the family. It was obvious this militia was a bad one.

He then woke Blake up. "You feeling better?" Haliday asked.

"Yeah, I'll be ready to go," Blake answered back.

"Good. Now tonight is going to be tense as well. I'm going to cover a few more basics on the rifle with you. We can't live-fire or we'll attract attention, but you'll do fine," Roger told him.

He spent about an hour covering a few marksmanship skills and safety points with him.

He then called back to camp. "This is Roger. You there, Kaybear?"

"Yeah, Dad, I've been waiting," Kayla answered.

"Okay, let me know what the latest news is," Roger said.

"Okay, you ready Dad?" she replied.

"I'm going on memory, Kayla; I don't have the time for notes."

"Ahh, all righty then. How's Blake?" she asked.

"Kayla, he's fine. If you want him to stay that way, spit it out." *It's starting already,* he thought.

"Okay, they talked on the net about contacting the Bay City group and how Bay City themselves had big trouble and could not send help. It sounds like they are running the four patrols and two response units twenty-four hours a day now. I did notice they seemed to be concentrating on the northern areas a bit more. That's the plan, right?"

"Yes, it is, kiddo. Anything else?"

"Oh yeah, lots more. They have been talking about people traveling and how they have been disarming them. They even mentioned seizing a truck. Sounds like their own version of Martial Law. They also said they were posting signs: Looters would be shot on sight. They set out signs for curfew as well. No one is to be out from dusk until dawn. Now, here's the information on you.

"They think there are six motorcycles and about a half-dozen trucks. They said your manpower would be at least twenty-four to thirty or more. They figure you guys to be operating in the northern sector somewhere. They are trying to find your base camp. One last thing, Dad; they'll shoot you first before they try to stop and ask you questions. Be careful. Love you, Dad."

"Love you, too, kiddo."

"Roger, you want us to stay on schedule?" It was David now.

"Yes I do. Promptly. You'll have to get the horses moving quickly. If it becomes an issue, they are going to have to leave them. Be firm about it. You might want to give them an hour head start, actually. You only have about twelve miles to go. Get them there, okay, Brother?" Roger instructed him.

"Okay, be safe." David said.

"You, too." Roger said, and then put his radio away.

Chapter 18

Haliday and Blake were getting ready to go. It was noon and they wanted to be in place by dusk. They wanted the BAMM to be tired and pissed off. If they started around 1800 hours, that would put the fresh shift on duty. The off going shift would not be in bed yet.

Chances were they would all want to play cowboy and show up for the festivities. When morning came, around half would still be tired from the night before and the other half ready to go home.

Haliday and Blake took off and followed a small river toward Oliver Township. They crept along in order to avoid loud engine noises. Haliday remembered people always talking about what vehicle you should have for something like *this*, what you should have for *that*, and it drove him nuts.

Pretty much anything running was a gem these days. What really drove him crazy were the guys who swore by two-stroke engines. Way too loud—way too easy to find.

It seemed like it took forever. Once they reached a secure location just outside of town, they got off the bikes. They dug into a couple MREs before they got going again. They would be walking for the next couple of miles, so they camouflaged the bikes and took some mental notes of the surrounding woods.

Haliday pulled out some small reflectors and pushed them up high onto some trees. With any luck the moon would catch them and make it easier to find the bikes in a hurry. He explained this to Blake, adding, "If anything happens to me, get the hell out of here."

By now Blake had studied the maps and would know where to go.

Haliday set to work on the distractions. He pulled out four small wind-up travel clocks and wound them up, then set the times on each so they were all set to the same time. He had ripped off the plastic face covers and attached some metal connectors to the minute and hour hands. These would set off a small igniter which would then light a piece of fuse.

He packed these into some small containers along with gun powder inside so it that would create a small explosion. Next to these he would place a few bags of various chemicals mixed together, including liquid drain cleaner, diesel, and Styrofoam pellets which would ignite and stick to surrounding objects. He'd read up on this on the internet.

These he would locate next to some old abandoned buildings or vehicles. He placed another igniter system nearby to ignite the gel. The explosion, mostly just noise, and the accompanying fire would make a great distraction. The gel was to make sure the fire spread rapidly throughout the area.

They were set to go off about 15 minutes apart and should draw quite a crowd. He had used up valuable space in his cargo bags and hoped they would work.

They waited until it was nice and dark out. The clouds were covering the moonlight as they passed through the sky now, so Haliday told Blake how important it was to remember where the bikes were. It would, however, help provide better cover for them. They were well camouflaged, Rambo face paint included.

They took off for their destination. First up was a small sugar beet storage plant. They approached from the side and didn't see anyone. They went up to a small maintenance shed which they found unlocked. It looked like it hadn't been used in quite a while. Haliday placed the box on the work bench. They left and followed some train tracks down to a golf course.

Here they found the storage barn for the golf carts, but the small vehicles were all gone; so were the charging stations and parts for them. Someone had these now and Haliday's guess was confiscation by the militia. He set up the device and they moved on.

They were close to the center of town now and he looked for another target. Haliday heard a vehicle approach and they ducked behind an old trailer. The vehicle passed by, but Haliday couldn't see inside well enough to make out who it was.

They waited a few minutes and then they came across a few cars and an old tow truck parked in an auto shop. Blake placed a device on the back of the tow truck. He said, "One left, Mr. Haliday."

"Call me Roger, okay, Blake?"

"Um, okay. Roger." It sounded odd to Blake.

They looked down the street; too many candles glowing in windows, which meant too many people down there.

Haliday looked around.

Blake said, "Look," and pointed across the street.

There outside another auto repair garage were six golf carts.

Haliday said, "Go over there and put it on one of the carts."

Blake looked around and then darted across the street. He had just placed the box on the back of one of the carts when another vehicle, an old Blazer, approached. Blake ducked down low.

The Blazer pulled into the lot. The occupants swept the area with a spotlight.

Haliday got his rifle ready. Someone jumped out from the Blazer. Haliday was praying Blake was well hidden. The guy who jumped out walked up to the door and peered inside. He then walked back to the Blazer and climbed in and sat there for a minute.

Haliday kept watch, but reached down and hit a button on his ham and changed frequencies. All he heard was the end of a sentence.

"...It's all secured at this time."

He changed the frequency back. The Blazer pulled out of the lot and took off.

Haliday called on the ham and told Blake to wait a few minutes.

"You expect them to come back?"

"No," Haliday said. "I want the aroma to clear out from you crapping your pants."

Blake waited just a couple minutes, then bolted back across the street to join Haliday. "No, I didn't crap my pants; almost, but I didn't."

"Let's get the hell out of here now." Roger said.

They worked their way back toward the river. Once they got there, they started the trek back to the bikes. It was almost nine now. They took another half an hour to make it back to the bikes.

Haliday and Blake were still about 50 yards away when they saw a flashlight. They dropped down low immediately. The light came nearer and nearer and they heard voices.

"We're going to be in trouble," one voice said.

"No, we're not, only if they catch us," a second countered.

"It's way past curfew, and plus Mom will be mad." Said the first.

"We had to go; she won't mind." The voices went back and forth.

"They aren't the police anyway. I don't know who put them in charge."

"Well they are in charge and whether we like it or not, that's how it is. If they catch us with food they'll shoot us."

"We didn't steal it; we left a note. It's our aunt's house and they aren't home. I don't think they would care."

The kids sounded like they were maybe 14 or 15, and sounded like two brothers. They walked right by Blake and Haliday, but didn't see them.

After about another 15 minutes Haliday and Blake got up and finished heading back to the bikes. Blake asked if he thought the militia would really shoot those kids.

"I don't doubt it a bit. I hope they make it home. They have about twenty minutes before the fireworks start."

They sat down and waited. They heard a decent explosion.

Now it had started.

They got up and secured their gear and got on the bikes. They pushed them to the riverbank and waited again. The second device exploded and they started the bikes and headed along the river toward town. They put the bikes down and watched the activity. They saw two vehicles near the fires and a third coming down the road.

The third device detonated and now it looked like the Keystone Kops were in action. These guys didn't know what to do. They were running around their vehicles and talking into their radios. Haliday couldn't make sense of what they were saying. Everyone was trying to talk at once.

The guys were pointing in every direction and barking orders at each other. The fourth device detonated and two vehicles shot toward the noise. A fourth truck showed up and went down to the garage where the golf carts were. The guys tried to use fire extinguishers, but it didn't help.

The ham was blaring away. "These pricks blew up the repair garage! The golf carts are all on fire! We can't put them out! We saw some of them head north! We're going to send a couple patrols after them!"

Haliday was amused. *Who the hell saw what?* he thought. But then again the moonlight, flames, and the dark night made for some great optical illusions. If they thought they saw something, more power to them.

All of a sudden everyone ran away from the repair shop. In just a matter of about two more minutes, there was a big explosion and flames everywhere. One of their trucks had caught fire from this explosion as well.

Blake and Haliday just looked at each other and wondered what the hell happened. Blake hadn't noticed the 100-gallon portable gas tank sitting there.

"Those sons of bitches blew up a fuel tank! Damn near blew up all of our trucks too!" came over the radio. "Looks like Jim's Blazer is toast. We need to find these sons of bitches now! I'll be damned if they think they're going to run around in my region and pull this terrorist shit on us! Don't let me find out people are helping them or I'll shoot them, too!"

Haliday looked at Blake; they hit the road and took off.

Coincidentally they were heading to Port Austin, where the family from the tornado shelter was from. Haliday had a few fond memories of the area. He had taken Kayla camping there a couple times as a small girl—old-fashioned tent, hotdogs, sitting around the fire eating smores.

Another time David, Rich, and one of David's friends and he had chartered a fishing boat and spent the day catching Lake Trout. The water had been rough, but they insisted on going out and had a great day on the lake. Those were good times. *Life was simple then,* he thought. Before he knew it they were there.

They pulled in behind a large billboard. Haliday climbed up to the platform, which actually wasn't very high, and pulled out a roll of hundred mile an hour tape. He wished he had spray paint for this but it was never really on his list of preps, except for some basic colors of Rustoleum to keep at the cabin. It took him about 15 minutes, but he finished it and it would have to do.

After climbing down he looked at Blake. "You get the next one."

Blake grinned. "That hard of a climb, old man?"

Haliday figured it was time to shake him up a bit and keep him focused. "No, too easy of a target being up there."

Blake's smirk disappeared instantly.

They went down the road about half a mile. Haliday found a stalled out car. It was an old Chevy station wagon. He was surprised it was still on the road, so he didn't feel bad about what he was going to do.

Haliday opened the fuel door. He dropped a model rocket engine down inside about six inches. The igniter was attached to one of his last two alarm clocks, complete with nine-volt battery. The alarm would hit, the rocket would shoot down into the tank, and another nice little fire would occur. They took off and found another billboard.

Blake grabbed the tape and asked Haliday what he wanted him to put up there.

Haliday chuckled. He was thinking of *Red Dawn*. "Put 'Wolverines' up there," he said. "That ought to make their day."

"Okay," Blake said. He climbed up and went to work.

As soon as he was done, they moved a little ways down the road and found another stalled out vehicle. This one was a conversion van and the thing would burn like a champ with all the plywood and upholstery inside. Haliday opened one of the back doors to make sure the flames reached inside and rigged this one up, too.

He went over to his bike and opened a saddle bag. He reached in and pulled out a small bag and walked around and tossed some trash the ground. This was all done to add to the illusion. Keep up the appearance of more than two guys doing this. "Now it's time to get the hell out of Dodge."

They followed the shoreline road along the east side of the thumb. Just past a little town called White Rock, they went into a wooded area. They hadn't seen anyone up this far and they were hoping most of the militia was over by Oliver and checking out that area.

Haliday was beyond tired. He'd eat and get some rest. "You hungry, Blake?"

"Yeah, I am, but I have, um, uh, well, Mr. Haliday," he said hesitantly, "I have to, uh, well...I can't *go* and I need to."

"Oh, the poop pipe is plugged?" Roger quipped.

"Uh...yeah." Blake said.

He dug into his pack and tossed Blake some constipation medicine. "It's the MREs. Take that and you'll be set to go, no pun intended. I'm going to take the first rest break; you keep watch and wake me in two hours. Blake, hope everything comes out okay." Haliday cracked himself up.

Blake woke up Haliday later and they switched places.

Haliday called the group on the radio. "We're doing okay and ready to get the hell out of here later on. We're going to stay here until we know you guys made it okay. Once you're there, we'll make our way over as soon as we can. Move out at 0630; that's when it should be the safest for you guys. Get Diana and Dawn out earlier on the horses, but tell them to be careful."

Rich came on. "Okay, we'll keep you updated."

"No, don't call unless you run into some serious trouble or until you make it there. This is the point when we need to make sure it runs like clockwork," Haliday said. "We have the last little surprises to set and that will give you all the time you need to get there. Anything else going on?"

"Well, your 'band of terrorists' has really shaken them up. They don't seem to have the people to double up patrols, or don't want to, and have been arguing about using their camp sentries to assist in finding you.

But, they think it's a trick so you can invade their camp. As far as we can tell, they are concentrating most of their troops on their camp and the northern areas where you've been busy. I think half are assigned to security and the rest run the camp. It's too hard to really tell what their logistics are. They are pretty organized though."

"That's good news for you guys. Tell everyone we're fine. Wish you guys the best of luck."

After the call, Haliday heated himself up an MRE and made sure he took some fiber pills himself after eating. *Those things really do a number on you, that's for sure.* He didn't eat the cheese spread; that usually hit him for days. He tossed it back in his saddle bag.

It was 6:30 right on the nose. The first car caught fire and the flames overtook the entire car. It was fully ablaze in about 10 minutes. Haliday was listening to the militia frequency but didn't hear any response yet. About another 10 minutes went by when he heard a patrol call in that they saw smoke and were going to check it out. It was about this time that the second fire started. The conversion van went up a lot more quickly.

The ham went crazy, "Papa Two to HQ; we have two fires going on. We need help over here! These bastards are at it again. They gotta be close. Send us help!"

"HQ to Papa Two; we have units on the way. We're sending Papa One and Papa Four to your location. Papa Three, we need you to head north and cover Papa Two's area. We have the response units moving into that area and the camp on alert."

The whole northeast portion of the thumb was crawling with militia now. When they reached the conversion van, Haliday heard more chatter.

"HQ, we think they have four or more guys running around here. We found all kinds of MRE garbage on the ground. They might have stayed somewhere around here last night. They must be close. Everyone check the marinas and the parks."

Blake was up now and listening to the radio as well. "We heading out now?" he asked.

"No, we have to stay in this area to make sure the group gets in safely, just in case we need to keep the militia in the area." Haliday listened to the ham some more. The guys were seriously pissed off at them. The next transmissions almost made Haliday piss his pants.

"Papa Two to HQ. Those bastards wrote graffiti on a billboard."

"What does it say?"

"One says 'Wolverines'. Those smartasses."

"What do you mean *one*?"

"There's another one, too. Papa Four saw it."

"Well, what's it say?"

229

"It says 'BAMM sucks dick'."

"Tear that shit down! You hear me? Tear me that shit down now! I will not have the people of my community think I'm a dick-sucker!"

Haliday was almost in tears. This must be their commandant, Oh-Fearless-Leader with a Napoleon complex or something. But, those words the man had said: "his community"?

This guy was on a power trip and this early in the game that was dangerous. This guy would get out of control and if someone didn't put him in check, there was no telling what would happen around there. It would affect Haliday's group and the cabin.

Haliday and Blake waited at their camp. The next transmission alarmed them.

"Papa Two to HQ, we got 'em , we got 'em! We have their location. We found fresh tracks and we are moving in on them."

Haliday looked at Blake and grabbed his rifle. He dropped down prone behind his bike and pulled out some extra mags. Blake was 7 feet away from Haliday and dropped down, too. He piled up his mags next to him.

"Papa Two to HQ. We have Papa One and Four with us along with response unit one. We are moving in slowly. We are about one hundred yards out, copy."

"HQ to Papa Two, we copy. Proceed with caution. Repeat, proceed with caution. If possible, keep one alive for interrogation, you copy?"

"Papa Two copies; we are now seventy-five yards out."

Haliday looked at Blake; he pointed to the selector level to make sure he had it on fire.

"We are now fifty yards out," the radio relayed.

Haliday and Blake scanned the woods for movement.

"Papa Two to HQ. We have two in custody. We will be bringing them in to HQ."

"HQ copies; good job, guys. Any casualties?"

"That's a negative. We didn't even have to fire; we overwhelmed them, shouted commands, and they just gave up. We have one motorcycle we will be bringing back and two hostiles. We have one male and one female."

Haliday looked at Blake and Blake looked back at him.

"What the hell are they talking about?" Haliday low crawled over to Blake. "Listen, they nabbed someone else and must think they are part of our group. I have no idea who they are or where they were. I'm not sure what they were doing, but they are in for a rude awakening."

Blake asked him what he thought would happen to the mistaken captives.

"I don't know. I really don't. I'm sure they'll be beaten and interrogated and after that, who knows. These BAMM guys are dumb enough to think whoever they caught is part of our group. Hopefully they figure out the truth and let them go."

It wasn't sitting that good with Haliday. These people were out there minding their own business and got caught up in the trouble he had created. They were probably just trying to get the hell out of here or get to their own location. They could have a cabin nearby, a boat, or who knows what. He was determined to find out though.

"Blake, I want you to head out and go meet the group at the cabin." He looked at the time. "It's almost eight now and you should get there about the same time the group does. I have to go find out what's going on with these guys and what they are doing with the couple they grabbed. After that I'll head to the cabin myself. You just be careful and head straight there."

"Mr. Haliday, uh, I mean Roger, I'd rather stick it out with you. You might need some help and I would rather do that than leave you out here alone. Isn't that the way it works, never leave a man behind?"

"Yeah, that's it, Blake, but *I'd* rather you get going and help out at the cabin."

"Roger, I can't do that. I'd be starving in my old home in another couple of weeks or so if it wasn't for you. I'll stay."

"Good enough; thank you, Blake." Haliday studied him and said, "We need to get some more sleep."

They spent a little more time camouflaging their area and setting up a couple booby-trap simulators. Blake laid down a piece of plastic and then a wool blanket folded over. He laid out his sleeping bag on top of that and climbed in. Haliday boiled some hot water and made hot cocoa. He flipped back and forth from his frequency to the militia frequency.

He flipped back to his frequency and heard the call from Kayla. "Go ahead, kiddo."

"How you guys doing?" she asked.

"We're fine, just resting, but we have some minor problems to handle." Roger told her.

"Okay, well, we got here. We all made it just fine. We have the trucks and trailers parked in the pole barn. The horses are in the stalls. We got into the house and everything is okay. What do you want us to do?" said Kayla.

"Go ahead and set up a security watch," Haliday said. "The rest of you guys can take a break or whatever you want to do. Today you guys need to empty those trailers and trucks out into the cache. Don't leave anything out there if you don't have to. Make sure the vehicles are immobilized as well. Keep them out of sight in the pole barn. Make sure the pole barn is completely secured. My old Jeep okay?" Roger said.

"Yeah, it's fine. Uncle David started it and ran it for a few minutes." Kayla answered.

"Okay, great. Make sure that all gets done today." Roger said.

"You guys coming in soon?" Kayla asked.

"No, we can't." Roger told her.

"Why?" she asked. "What's wrong?"

Roger responded, "It's hard to explain. We stirred up some crap and need to see it through. In a nutshell," he said, "a couple people got caught up in our crap and may end up taking the blame for it. I need to see what the BAMM bums plan to do with them and Blake volunteered to stay and help."

232

"Can't you guys just leave them alone?" Kayla said.

"I wish we could, but burning down some old stores and abandoned cars is different than letting these people possibly die. I just can't do that. I have to find out what's going on with these militia guys. All we're going to do is head in and take a peek. That's all," Haliday insisted. "I need you guys to set up two hams; one for us and one on the militia freq. If you can, set up a third and scan it for traffic. Find out what the hell the government is doing or if anyone else is in the area."

"Okay, Dad. Call us with any more info."

Haliday woke up Blake and briefed him on what was going on with the group. He asked him if he was sure he wanted to stay and Blake again said yes. Haliday inventoried their food and found they had enough for two more days, three if they ate lightly. Water wasn't an issue, as they had purification tabs and filter straws. Most of the food was kept in Blake's saddle bags.

They each took another turn sleeping. Haliday inventoried everything else now as well. He wouldn't be setting up any diversions; he had used everything he had. He didn't expect this little problem to arise. He did a quick ammo check. That might play an important role sooner or later.

They each had seven magazines for the rifles—five 30 rounders and two 20 rounders, and all were full. The 20 rounder's made it easier for prone fighting positions. In addition to that they had some bandoliers filled with stripper clips. All in all, they had roughly 500 rounds each. He had about 100 for his .40 left. No way could they launch an offensive with that. It would be suicide. He had to figure out a plan and he had to find out where the militia HQ was.

Bad Axe was the biggest town in the Thumb and it made sense that the group would name themselves after it, but they had to have another reason. There had to be another tie somehow. Haliday just had to figure out how. These guys would need a large area, one that would support their operation, give them ample storage, enough land to farm, water, a central location now. Where the hell were these guys staying?

They had responded pretty damn quick last night. They definitely had a good layout of the land. They also felt comfortable enough wherever they were to pull the extra manpower out of their camp for the hunt. It'd be too risky to approach the locals and ask. They might not even know and if they were afraid of these guys, they would definitely be talking to them.

Haliday pored over the map. He searched his memory. He kept picturing the vehicles and the people, listening to their transmissions over and over again in his head. He concentrated on the family near the tornado shelter and the two militant types who had shown up there. He got his answer.

The Huron County Memorial Airport.

The guy had been wearing wings and Haliday had thought the guy was reliving his airborne, days but he was actually sporting aviator wings—a military-issued insignia designating him as a pilot. At the distance Haliday had seen him from, it was an acceptable mistake. If they had aircraft, they would have used it by now. This was probably something they didn't count on, losing electronics entirely.

"Oh man, you've got to be kidding me," he said aloud.

Blake asked him what he was talking about. Haliday laid it all out there for him.

"So that makes it real hard, huh?" Blake asked.

"Well, based on my last airport experience – and I'm not talking about being groped by the TSA – I don't want anything to do with it." Roger said.

"What are we going to do then?" Blake asked.

"We're going to think about it carefully," Haliday said. "Blake, these railroad tracks will take us right through what I think is their HQ," He added. Haliday pointed at the map. "The airport on the right and this land on the left with the big pond is probably theirs. The airport gives them an advantage on three sides as far as visibility; it's all open. The front can be covered easily with manpower, especially if they are using the main building as their admin area."

"What I propose we do is take these tracks up as far as we can. We head into the woods to the east of the airport and then walk up as far as we can go. We'll listen in to their traffic and watch for a while and take some notes. See what we can learn. We might have to stay a couple days. After that, we play it by ear. No rescues, no diversions, just recon.

"I'm going to call the group and let them know what's going on," he told Blake. "I want them to get a couple guys together and keep them on alert in case we need some help. It wouldn't hurt to have some extra firepower in case it gets hairy and we need help getting out. If that happens, we'll shoot straight for the cabin and say our prayers along the way."

Haliday and Blake took off. All of the radio traffic they had heard recently pointed to the militia patrols still concentrating on the northern areas. They used this advantage to creep up into position. They settled into the wooded area directly east of the airport. They covered up the bikes, grabbed their gear, and started the short hike toward the airport.

Chapter 19

Haliday and Blake were close to the perimeter, but still hidden in the woods. They laid down their wool blankets on the cold ground and concentrated on concealing themselves.

This might have been a good time for a ghillie suit, Haliday thought, *but how much could he actually carry on the bikes?* Blake's didn't have stock saddlebags. He had to use some extra canvas packs that Haliday had and with the rest of the gear, it was tight. That was the main reason Haliday had left his M24 at camp.

He did take his spotting scope and was using it. He had Blake cover himself up with a smaller blanket and use his flashlight to take notes. Haliday's maps had aerial photos of the Huron County Memorial Airport and he used these as a guide to jot down a rough sketch of the area and number the buildings. They were ready.

"Okay, Blake, I definitely see activity. I think this is the place." Haliday slowly worked the scope around as he looked over the airport. "Building One, definitely their HQ." Through the scope he could see how the BAMM had altered the small but once modestly active airport for their needs.

"They have stalled cars in place around the entire front and the sides of it for protection. Concertina wire inside the fence, too. Looks like they also have some fighting positions fortified in a few locations amidst the cars. Everyone seems to be going in and out of this building.

"It looks like they pushed the planes out of the hangars and are using Buildings Two and Three as some sort of motor pool. I can see the door open on one and some vehicles inside, but the other one just has a vehicle parked in front of it."

Sounds of a small vehicle reached them and Haliday covered the scope and ducked down again.

The vehicle was running along the fence line and spotlighting it as it drove along. The closer it got, the more Haliday could make out. It was another side-by-side four-wheeler of some sort with two people in it. One was driving as the other spotlighted the perimeter. Both were wearing the same Russian camo and were armed. They continued on with their check.

"Blake, it's 2200 hours; write that check down."

Haliday waited and listened. As soon as the four-wheeler stopped by the admin building, the occupants went inside. They weren't calling in these checks, so Haliday figured they must be reporting when they went inside that everything is okay. He wondered what they would do if they came across a problem. Probably best not to find out.

He scanned the other buildings as well. "Blake, Building Four has activity, but I can't tell what. I can only see the back of it. Looks like they are taking parts into it, but I'm not sure what kind. They might be trying to get a plane working. The other two buildings look big enough for their motor pool. I doubt they need a third. We'll have to keep checking on this one."

Eleven p.m. rolled around and the four-wheeler made another circuit around the fence line, only this time they went the opposite direction. Midnight would reveal their pattern. *Hopefully it's not every hour on the hour and just alternating direction*, Haliday thought. Security 101—do not create a pattern. Change it up every time. Same with the time; you do not do it on the hour, half hour, etc.; you had to make it seem random. *Someone must have OCD or something*, he thought.

He waited and then scoped the area once again. He saw the hangar door of the third building open. "Yep, definitely part of their motor pool. They have a couple deuce and a halves in there."

"Deuce what?" Blake asked.

"Big trucks. Blake, think of the movie *Good Morning, Vietnam* when they were all sitting around in the trucks waiting to move out."

"I didn't see that movie, but I understand now." Blake responded.

"They have something else in the back, but I can't quite see it." Haliday saw a few guys leave Building Four and turn the lights off. "How did I miss that?" He looked around and found it. "Okay, got it. Building Six looks like it's a power house or generator building. I can see the exhaust. They must have power to the whole complex, but selective on what they are running. I wonder how much fuel they have. No telling though. It looks like an underground fuel tank."

He eyeballed the rest of the buildings over the next hour. Nothing he could really see going on. Midnight came along and the security check was just like the first.

"Unbelievable," he said. "They are too routine for their own good. They have half of it right, but then make some dumb mistakes. They make it too easy for someone to plan something."

He heard a loud truck in the area. He watched the airport entrance closely and saw an old army surplus fuel truck pull in. Two guys were at the main gate checking vehicles that were entering and exiting. He watched the fuel truck as it pulled up near the generator building. "Looks like they are siphoning fuel from the gas stations and then filling these tanks."

After the truck emptied its load, it went and parked near the motor pool. Shortly afterwards the whole complex went almost dark. They had either turned the generator off or killed most of the power to everything except what was critical, Haliday decided. Maybe just the admin building was still powered up.

"You need to stretch or anything, Blake?"

"No, I'm okay for a bit," Blake said.

"Okay, but rotate your ankles. Stiffen your legs, then bend your knees, and rock from side to side to keep your blood flowing and legs warm. Do not let them fall asleep. If you have to get up and run, you'll be in a world of hurt. If you need to go to the bathroom, then get up and go; don't get plugged up again or risk an infection from not wizzing." He told Blake.

Other than the security patrols of the compound, nothing else really happened all night. Haliday did notice a lot of checks around Building Seven though. He hadn't picked up on this earlier. Maybe it was due to the activity during the day and none at night. Might be that he simply noticed the flashlight more in the dark.

Right around 0530 the activity started to pick up. There were people coming out of what he called Buildings Eight and Nine. These looked like they may be the housing for the complex. They probably had sleeping quarters set up in there; easier to keep everyone warm that way without heating too many buildings.

Haliday waited until the 0600 patrol made its round and then called Mike as he continued to watch. "Hey, Mike, put Bill on for me, will you please?"

"Okay, here he is," Mike obliged.

"Roger, it's Bill," the man's voice came over the radio. "How can I help you?"

"What can you tell me about the Bad Axe airport?"

"The Memorial Airport?"

"Whatever they call it I guess. What do you know?"

"It's very small, mostly all private planes, smaller aircraft, and a couple of helicopters, I think."

"What about the buildings?" Haliday asked. "What about the main building?"

"Oh, it's their offices. Actually when you go in there it's pretty nice; they have a small little snack bar, and you can rent out a large conference room, too. Nice big lobby. That's all I know."

Haliday committed this to memory. "Okay, that helps. Thanks."

"What's going on there?" Bill asked.

"It's the militia HQ now." Haliday responded.

"My buddy is a pilot, the one who wanted to recruit me. So are a couple of his friends." Bill added.

"Is he a big guy, black hair, mustache, bad attitude?" Haliday asked. He thought maybe it was the militia man from the tornado shelter.

"No, my buddy is a smaller, gray-haired guy." Bill told him.

"OK Bill, thanks." Roger said as he ended the conversation.

Haliday was trying to figure out who the leader of this group was. During the conversation he noticed that the patrols had changed shifts. The day shift headed out and within 10 minutes the night crew came in. After putting their vehicles away, the new guards went into the HQ. People continued to filter out of Eight and Nine and head to the HQ. Haliday figured they used the snack bar to cook and the conference room to eat and hold meetings.

He turned to the young man beside him. "You ready to go, Blake?"

"I sure am." Blake said.

They were about to get up when Blake said, "Look, Roger."

Haliday looked and saw three people heading toward Building Seven pushing a cart. Two were heavily armed. They opened a couple locks on the door and pushed the cart inside and took what looked to be a partially empty one out. People locked in a building meant captives. It was chow time for their captives. This was where they were holding them, whoever *they* may be. No telling how many of them there were either, Haliday realized. Enough to need a cart for their food.

The small group went back to the HQ.

"Okay, Blake, we need rest. Let's go get some."

They packed up, messed up their area to hide their presence of being there, and went back to where the bikes were.

It was a quick meal and radio call, then some rest. They'd make sure they got some decent sleep over the next eight hours. Haliday was analyzing the info he'd just acquired as he laid there.

"You sleeping yet, Roger?" Blake asked.

"No, what's up?"

"Why are you so worried about these people and what they are doing?" Blake asked.

"You mean the militia?" Haliday said.

"Yeah, them."

"Well Blake, here's the way I see it. Here in this country we have our Constitution," Haliday told him. "Now it's been crapped on time and time again the past few years, more so than any other time period. Slowly but surely, its meaning is being eroded and the Supreme Court is – rather, *was* – trying to rewrite it from the bench.

The country is in a position now where we need to make sure we live up to the meaning of the document in its purest form. We are practically back to that period in time when it was written. Oh, we have modern housing, some conveniences and such to an extent, but the next few years will be very different than they were a week ago, but very similar to a couple hundred years ago.

"Within the Bill of Rights are some very basic rights we can't take for granted. The right to bear arms, the right to freedom of speech, the protection from unlawful search and seizure, no cruel or unusual punishment, and the right to a fair trial. You follow me so far?"

"Yes sir, I do." Blake answered.

"Okay, good. Now here is what I see now. This group has declared this area to be theirs. They are taking what they want, when they want, and from whom they want; not for the good of the people, but for their own good. I don't see them sharing anything with anyone. You think they paid for anything they brought in there? I doubt they paid for that tanker full of fuel. I doubt they paid for this airport or anything else they have acquired most recently.

"A traditional militia is about their own community, but they also support those around them. They may not take them under their wing or into their shelters, but they certainly don't steal from anybody or pull the BS these guys are pulling here. They really don't make sense to me. To me, they are an enemy."

Haliday brought it home a little for Blake. "They took that family's gun at the tornado shelter. That man had a right to bear arms and carry that gun—more so today than ever. This group has people down there being held prisoner for who knows what reasons. You think they had the right to due process? You think they are getting trials? Who knows how they are even being treated, especially the ones caught while they were looking for us. They are forcing their will upon the people around here and I would say they're doing it with fear and with force.

"I don't see these guys as a typical militia. I see them as nothing but a bunch of hoodlums who have strayed far from their original goal, if they even had one. I see a force of people no better than a lot of war criminals or Third World warlords. Years ago I took an oath. In that oath it stated enemies both foreign *and* domestic. These are enemies, Blake. I know that now.

"I'm not in the service now, but I will maintain and uphold that oath," Haliday said solemnly. "I will not stand by and let these people hinder the freedoms of other Americans for their own personal gain. I don't know what I can do, but I have to do something. Sooner or later I will have to show my hand. I hope it's good enough to win. I want to get on with life as much as the next guy, but when they come knocking on our door, what do we do then? And is it too late at that point?"

"I hear ya, Mr. Haliday. I had that same feeling. I just don't have the experience you do."

"You don't have to, Blake. You just have to have the willpower to want to help and to want to make a difference. That's all. I'm glad you're here. Now, we have some more recon to do, so let's get that rest," he said with finality. "I'll call the group and check in; let them know we are okay."

The sleep was very welcome. Both were weary and the past few days had taken a toll on them. After tonight they would head to the house and get all the rest they needed. One last night of recon would give Haliday enough info on the compound. He still didn't know what he would do with it though.

They moved out, heading to a new area when they awoke.

"Why not the spot we used last night?" Blake asked as they left.

"It was a great spot, but there are a couple things to consider," Haliday told him. "You visit enough times and you leave telltale signs that you were there. You start to alter the soil and the vegetation, and it makes it easier to see that someone is hiding and, or, watching you. Secondly, we need another vantage point so we can see what else is going on in there."

They went out of their way to avoid some houses along the way and ultimately ended up northeast of the airport, across the street. It was a great spot for watching the militia. It gave Haliday and Blake a completely different viewing angle. They did the same thing as the night before and laid-up for the night.

Haliday looked over into Building Four and indeed the BAMM had two small planes in there. Piper Cubs, ancient, simple, parts everywhere, but still not running. *Not sure what they could do with them*, Haliday thought with a frown, *other than some aerial recon, which would be nice*. Maybe they could arm them somehow, he guessed. By the looks of it though, they had a long way to go.

Haliday started thinking, *Damn, should have brought the M203.* Well, it wasn't really a M203, but rather a 37mm grenade launcher. Too many questions would arise with a true M203 40mm launcher, not to mention the registration for it with the BATFE.

Those planes wouldn't be running for at least a couple of days. He looked around some more. He saw the same routine with the security again. Every hour on the hour a perimeter check. Looked like checks of the prison building, but that view was now somewhat blocked. Nothing really different had happened yet. It actually kind of reminded him of the old football game that when you plugged it in and the men just vibrated across the field in random directions with no sense of purpose.

At the HQ building he saw a few guys get into a four-wheeler and head over to the prisoner building. The next view he had of them was when he spotted them at what Haliday called Building 12. They had a man with them that they took inside.

Haliday didn't see them for almost an hour. After that he watched them drag the guy from the doorway and back to the prisoner building. It looked as if they must have beaten him something fierce.

Haliday's blood was boiling. He told Blake, "Mark down that they torture people."

He watched again as they took a woman inside the same building. He waited again and noted the time. Barely half an hour passed before they brought her out and dragged her back to the building. "Damn it," he said.

He had an idea who these people were. The couple captured along with their motorcycle. He was ready to go down there, guns blazing. Evidently he had been speaking aloud and mumbling because Blake had poked his head out from under the blanket again.

"Roger, do you think that's who they thought we were?"

"Yes I do, and I'm f-ing beyond pissed off right now. I'm half tempted to go down there, but that would be the end of me for sure. I'll get even with these pricks, mark my word. I'll get even with these pricks."

Blake had put his head back under the blanket.

"Blake, you only need to poke your head under when I tell you info to write down; you don't have to stay under there all the time."

"It's warmer this way."

"It's that or you like Dutch ovens."

Blake frowned. "You're a sick man, Mr. Haliday."

No one else had been taken out of the building and interrogated that Haliday had seen. It was late in the night and the men started to close up most of the buildings. They seemed to still be working around the motor pool, though, as if they had some kind of project they wanted finished; Haliday just didn't know what. He hadn't gotten a close enough to look inside that building to see.

He was watching this building when he saw a man walk out of one of the motor pool hangars. Haliday watched him and following his motions said, "Oh my god, you've got to be kidding me." He told Blake to stop taking notes and look.

Blake poked his head out of the blanket.

"It's a guy waving his arms like at the airports."

"No Blake, it's a ground guide. Watch."

They could hear the rumbling of an engine, and soon a track vehicle appeared.

Blake murmured, "Holy shit."

"Yeah, that's what I say," Haliday breathed, gaze locked on the vehicle, "I can't believe it."

It looked like an M113 armored personnel carrier but slightly different. It had to be some kind of variation or prototype that had made its way into civilian hands.

Haliday still couldn't believe it.

The ground guide walked it out to an empty area between the hangars and one of the runways. Once there the driver ran it around in circles, spun in place a few times, shot up and down along the runway, and then eased it back toward the motor pool hangar. Quite a crowd of militia had gathered around and was cheering. They walked it back into the hangar.

Blake looked at Haliday. "That's pretty bad ass. I wish we had one."

"Oh yeah. Hell, I wish we had several. Some Bradley's, a few M1s. Hell, why stop there? Couple Cobras and Apaches, a Blackhawk or two." Haliday was rambling now. He stopped himself and looked at Blake. "No problem at all, Blake. It won't do them a damn bit of good."

"Why is that?"

"Let's get going back to camp. I've seen enough for now and I'll explain it on the way."

"Okay, Blake, let me explain a few things about tracked vehicles," Haliday said as they walked. "They can't really operate continually on paved roads. It tears up the track pads on the tracks and sooner or later they fall off. They start to fall off and expose the tracks, making them more prone to damage. There's a reason they get trucked everywhere; so unless they get a truck and trailer going, I don't think they'll be running around the area with that thing."

"What about cutting through all of the farms?" Blake asked.

"They could do that, sure, but it's a large area with a lot of varied terrain. Eventually their luck is going to run out and they'll throw a track or something else. I just don't think they have the parts to really utilize it the way they hope to, or to make repairs in the field if something goes wrong. Maybe they hope to use it to defend their compound and that's it. That's what I would do.

"It has two firing ports on each side for rifles and whatever they wanted to use that upper turret for," Haliday continued. "Actually it's not a turret, but really just a half-armored turret. The gunner would still be exposed from the sides and the back. I doubt they have any light or heavy machine guns to mount. That would have cost them nearly as much as the track. At least, I hope they don't.

"Either way, whatever they plan to use it for, if we take it out of action, it's a done deal. I'd rather worry more about them getting those planes in the air. Yet another thing to worry about. They can spot us easily if they can do that. We'd be restricted to moving at night, and at night only, and that still wouldn't guarantee anything. Airpower is supreme." He added wistfully, "I'd settle for a paraglider about now."

"You're full of all kinds of good news, huh?"

"No, it's just better that we understand what we are up against. With education we can make educated decisions. Now we have to quiet down because we have to cross through the residential area here." He heard some chatter on the radio and they stopped to listen.

"HQ this is Papa Two," came over the radio. "We went by the Grindstone marina like the couple said. We found their boat and checked it out. It was exactly where they said it would be. We boarded it and searched it. We found food and weapons on board, a pistol and an AK47 with about one thousand rounds total. The food looks like it's about a couple of months' worth. The boat does start and run, so we locked it down and seized it. The cradle it's in can be lowered manually to put it in the water."

"Did you confiscate the food and equipment?" came another voice.

"Roger that; we loaded up everything worthwhile and will be bringing it back to HQ. They had some charts, too. Looks like they were heading somewhere offshore, maybe a cabin on one of the islands. We can check that out tomorrow when it's daylight if the weather is OK. See what they have out there."

"Good job guys; not sure if they are with the hostiles or not. We'll keep pushing them for info, but at least we have a new toy."

Haliday was fuming now. "You see, Blake, I told you. I told you. I told you. These people were trying to get to their boat and get to their own camp and now these dickheads have beaten them, seized their food and firearms, and plan to do who knows what to them now. They are going to go to their cabin and take what's left? I don't think so." What started as a reconnaissance mission and bug-out ended up being much more for Haliday.

As soon as they got back, they called in to talk to the group.

David said, "Everything is okay here. We had a patrol come by but they didn't pull in. You still want us to shoot on sight?"

"I do, but only if you are certain they did not call in a location for the stop. If they didn't, hide the vehicle, bury or burn the bodies, whatever, just get rid of them. We have a field operation to conduct in the morning so we won't be coming in yet. I'll call you guys later," Haliday answered.

The sporadic radio calls were wearing on the group. They couldn't handle the suspense. But, they did what they were asked.

David and Kevin were at the ready to respond if they needed to. Kayla wanted to be involved, but she knew more about the cabin than anyone else and would need to stay behind.

Hopefully they would not have to respond. The group at the cabin hated listening in though, and hated never knowing what to expect.

Chapter 20

Haliday and Blake went as far as they dared and then pulled over to wait until 0530. Haliday had his group switch to using military time to keep an accurate schedule. This would eliminate any confusion of whether or not someone meant AM or PM.

They filled the bikes tanks and knew they would need to get some more gas soon. They had about 100 miles of operating distance left now and about 15 miles to make it to the marina. When 0530 rolled around, they took off.

They turned in at the marina when they reached it and Haliday looked around. It wasn't a very big place, but he had to move quickly. He searched up and down near the boat hoists. There it was.

A small cruiser, maybe 30 feet in length. Older, but it looked like it was well cared for. The winterizing plastic had been ripped open and a ladder had been left near by it, too. This was the right boat.

He looked around and found a place to hide the bikes and then prepped Blake as well as he could. He gave him a couple Snickers bars.

"Eat them fast; you'll need the sugar rush. If you can't hang, just drop your weapon and hit the ground and lay there. Use the radio and tell the group what happened and what's going on," Haliday said. "Make sure you flip to the right freq first. Just push that button right there." He indicated the button on the radio.

"I'll be here, Mr. Haliday, don't worry."

Haliday had his doubts. The kid just learned to shoot a few days ago and hadn't pulled the trigger yet, not even to practice. He just hoped the kid didn't get himself killed.

They found some hiding spots and Haliday briefed him on fields of fire. "You start firing as soon as you hear the first shot or if they are pointing a gun at me and ready to shoot. You make sure they are dead. If they go down, you put a bullet in their head. You hesitate, you die. One more thing, Blake. See how I'm dressed?"

"Yes."

"Remember that when you pull the trigger. They have the Commie camo on."

Haliday heard the noise then; the militia had brought one of the deuce and a halves. He bolted for his cover as quick as he could. The good thing about a deuce was that you heard it a long time before you saw it. His adrenaline was coursing through his veins.

The deuce pulled in and paused, the driver was looking at a piece of paper that must have been a hand-drawn map. He put the deuce back in gear and pulled up close to the hoist.

Two guys from the back jumped out and stood there as the deuce backed in as close as they could get. It would make it easier to unload the boat when they got back. Haliday noted they had either taken the cargo top off or didn't have one. It didn't matter, but it did allow him to count the number of militia.

The driver and passenger got out and walked around to the back as well. They had pistols strapped on but no rifles and the guys from the back had the standard ARs the group had been carrying. One handheld ham, one ham mounted on the truck.

Haliday knew who his first target would be if it came down to that.

The group walked over to the boat and opened a lock and chain around a wheel gear and started cranking it to lower the boat into the water. When it was in the water they started to take the plastic winterizing completely off.

Haliday raised himself up slowly, aimed, and called out, "Halt or I shoot!"

The two riflemen spun in his direction and started to raise their rifles. The driver reached down for his ham.

Haliday fired once and the bullet shredded the driver's hand and his radio.

Haliday spun toward one of the riflemen and fired a quick burst toward his chest before he dove back for cover. He heard a splash in the water. Blake hadn't fired yet.

Damn it, he froze, Haliday thought. He heard the radio guy screaming in pain and then some pistol shots and rounds hitting near him. He was behind a metal dock box filled with rubber bumpers and ropes and saw holes punch through the metal. He hugged the ground as low as he could get.

He looked under the dock box; head canted sideways; because he only had about four inches of clearance. He fired at the feet of the only guy he could see. One round hit its mark and the guy dropped to his knees. Haliday could hear more rounds hit the dock box. He saw the knee of the guy and fired another round. He watched the guy's kneecap explode out the side of his pants, causing the man to fall prone.

The guy then fired randomly at Haliday.

Haliday couldn't get a good line of sight on the guy and kept his head low. The shots from the rifle kept him down as they tried to hold their own cover. Haliday tried to keep near the bottom and edge where the metal was thicker. He heard the pistol shots, but didn't hear the rounds strike the box; just items close by. The AR went silent and he could hear the injured guy moaning in pain. He also heard him struggling with what sounded like a magazine change.

An AR cycled through a couple more rounds and then stopped. Haliday grabbed a quick peek; the injured man had managed to sit up. He cleared his rifle and fired at Haliday again. His rifle stopped firing, jamming again. He struggled to clear it.

Haliday couldn't risk exposing himself for the shot yet. He looked around to see if he could crawl somewhere else, but was stuck where he was.

It jammed on you, Haliday thought. *Good for you, you f-ing prick.* He grabbed a quick peek and jerked his head back when he heard the AR fire.

He then heard more shots.

Damn, I gotta get this guy. He peeked again. *Hell yeah,* he nearly said aloud, seeing the shooter. *Way to go, kid.*

When he grabbed that quick look the second time, he liked what he saw. The rifleman was laying there with his forehead missing and frontal lobe half gone.

Welcome to the game, Blake.

Blake yelled over at Haliday, "I can't see them! I can't see where they are! I can't really see the other two!"

They had two men left, both with pistols. One only had one hand, but that was all he needed. Haliday grabbed another quick peek. Both of the guys were ducking down now at the back of the boat. All Haliday could see was the slightest profile of one, his ass, and his back. Haliday fired another burst, causing the man to fall backwards into the water.

"Rick, help me! I can't move my legs! Help me, Rick!" the man said.

Haliday could hear the guy splashing around in the water and Blake firing, but he couldn't see any hits.

"Rick, man, help me! It's cold! Come on, man, I need your help! You gotta help me, Rick!" the man said.

"Hold on, man, I'm coming for you! Hang on, Gary!" the second militia man said.

Haliday watched the back of the boat and saw an arm extend toward the water. He heard Blake fire.

The guy pulled his arm back in and began screaming.

"Rick, I can't stay in here! It's cold! It's cold, Rick! I need help! I'm hit bad!" The sounds of the splashing became less and less.

"I'm sorry, Gary, I'm sorry! I can't get to you!"

"Rick, it's cold in here! Get me out!" Gary reached out once more and the boards on the dock near him shredded from Blake's rifle fire. He pulled his hand back.

The sounds from the water had almost stopped now.

"You sons of bitches, I'll kill you all!" the man by the boat promised. "You guys ain't got the right to come up here and do this! You hear me, you sons of bitches!" The splashes from the water had stopped now.

"Gary, you still there? Gary, come on man, tell me you're still there."

There was no answer.

"God damn you sons of bitches! God damn you! What gives you the right to come up here? Who the hell do you think you are?"

Haliday actually answered him back. "I'll tell you! I was born and raised in this state. This state is part of this country. I worked my ass off and paid taxes like everyone else. I bought my land up here just like the rest of you, with my own damn money. I have every right to be here, you self-righteous prick! What gives you guys the right to rule this place?"

"There ain't any law now, asshole!" came the reply. "It's survival of the fittest now! If we don't control the people around here, they're gonna drag us down, too. We *are* the law around here now! It's up to us to decide who can help us rebuild our community. It's our choice! You hear me, you f-ing bastard? It's our choice!"

Haliday responded, "And what choice do the people have?"

"If they don't like it, they can leave if they want!"

"And you take their food, their weapons, and you beat and torture them?" Haliday was up and moving toward the dock now, rifle slung on his back, pistol drawn. "Answer me, asshole. I said answer me!"

The guy behind the boat stood up and looked at him.

Haliday kept walking toward him.

The man said, "You don't understand survival, dickhead. It's all about surviving."

Haliday saw blood dripping from both his hands. This man was the radio operator.

"Maybe I don't understand survival according the definition you and the other assholes in your group think it means," Haliday told him stoutly, "but I do understand freedom."

The man fumbled to get his pistol reloaded. As the man started raising his pistol Haliday pointed his .40 at him and fired twice into the man's chest and once into his head. The man fell backwards unto the dock.

Haliday turned around and saw Blake standing there with his rifle pointed at the man's body.

Haliday pivoted and walked past him. "He's dead, Blake, trust me. Darwin there, Mr. Survival-of-the-Fittest, is no longer fit." He patted Blake on the shoulder. "Come on, let's go. We have work to do. We aren't out of the woods yet."

They walked over to the deuce. Haliday climbed up into the cab and started looking around. He picked up a small book and flipped through it. Frequencies and codes were all written down along with what looked like a duty roster. He tucked it in his jacket. Two rifles were cradled inside the cab.

"Blake, go crank that wheel and get that boat out of the water a couple of feet just to keep it out of the ice when the lake freezes," he said. "I don't know if those folks will ever get here, but if they do, at least the boat should be okay." He could see a few bullet holes in the hull, but they were above the water level.

Haliday continued looking through the cab. They had some basics in there, just a couple days' worth of MREs, water, and some ammo. Nothing else he could see of value. He was thinking about whether or not to take the deuce.

Spoils of war or theft?

Could be looked upon either way. He would have to think about this one. He got out of the cab and walked around to the back. In the back was a box, likely locked.

He climbed up into the back of the truck and yelled over to Blake. "Check those two bodies for keys! If they don't have any, see if you can reach the bodies in the water and check them! If not, don't worry about it!"

Blake started to check the bodies.

Haliday was at the back of the deuce when he heard the first shot. He practically felt the heat of the round.

He dropped down in the back of the deuce. He hadn't heard the Jeep pull in, but saw it as he dropped. He looked around and saw the bed was armored, but he didn't know to what extent. The sides of the bed slightly bubbled when rounds hit. He lay there, unable to move. The side rails barely covered him. He heard shouts from the Jeep.

"Put your hands up! Put your hands up and stay where you are!"

Haliday wasn't going to do it. No way in hell was he going out this easy.

"Put your hands up and stand up now!"

Haliday lay there longer. "Go screw your cousins, you redneck bastards!"

A ripple of gunfire lined along the bed of the truck. He heard a loud hiss and knew they'd gotten one of the tires. They seemed to care less about their own deuce.

"Gary, Rick, you guys okay? John, Andy? Where you guys at? Can you hear us?" a voice said.

Haliday answered. "I think they're hiding somewhere dick-sucking just like you guys are known for. I saw the billboard that said so."

That brought about a hellacious lead storm.

Haliday covered his ears; they were ringing like mad from all of the noise. He had a splitting headache now. The foam earplug wasn't working that well in the one ear and he had the earpiece for the radio in the other. He keyed his radio and whispered, "Blake, you out there?"

Black answered quietly, "Yeah, I'm hiding behind one of the boats."

"Can you see them?"

"Not really. As soon as I heard them fire I hid behind one of the boats on the racks. I didn't hear them drive up."

"Can you find some better cover?"

"Not really, not without being seen."

"Look around again and check," Haliday directed. "Maybe a quick run for a few feet or something."

"Look, you need to raise your hands and then get up!" one of the men called. "We are not going to warn you again!"

Haliday answered them back. "You guys have an arrest warrant?"

"We don't need one, smartass! We're operating under the authority of the Bad Axe Minute Men!"

"Is that a division of the 4H or something? Never heard of them! You guys hold goat milking contests and stuff?" Haliday couldn't resist being his smart ass self.

"I've had enough of this asshole." One of the guys opened fire and emptied his magazine at the deuce.

"Hey, I want to really thank you for providing me with some great cover here. Your buddies could have used something like this about ten minutes ago!"

"That's it, you prick!" The guy reloaded his rifle and started toward the deuce.

He got about 10 steps away from the Jeep when Blake opened up on him. He tumbled forward into a heap on the ground, his body bouncing around on the gravel as Blake emptied the whole 30-round magazine into him. The other guy fired at Blake's position then stopped; likely a magazine change or something.

"Looks like we have us a little problem here, Mr. Minute Man! You are now outgunned!" Haliday whispered again, "Blake are you all right?"

"Yeah, I ran behind another boat when you pissed the guy off earlier. This one gave me a better view and I thought it would be safer. It has two engines and I'm kind of protected by it. I can't see the other guy though. He's hiding on the other side of the Jeep." Blake answered.

"Okay, look, here's what I'm going to do. I'm going to give him the option to get the hell out of here. If he takes it, let him go." Roger said.

"Are you serious?" Blake asked.

Haliday said, "Yes I am. Chances are they called this in and have more help coming. We gotta get the hell out of here."

"Okay, if you say so. Sounds a little crazy to me, but that seems to be your style," said Blake.

Haliday tuned in to listen to the militia frequency and then called out to the remaining guy. "Look, we want to make a deal! We can let you go if you leave now! We'll leave the truck here along with anything else that's yours. You probably have about five minutes or less before our group comes riding in to help us out. You got that? You leave now and we won't have a problem!"

Over the radio, on the militia frequency he heard: "We won't be there for about ten minutes or so, you copy?"

The militia man in the boat yard said, "Yeah, I copy, I'm gonna get the hell out of here and meet up with you guys. Maybe we can ambush them when they come out."

"Okay," the second voice said over the frequency. "Any idea on the rest of the guys?"

"No idea, but Ron is down for sure. I think the rest are, too. I'm getting the hell out of here. Okay, I'm leaving. I'm getting in the Jeep and taking off."

The guy who'd been on the radio got in the Jeep, started it, and backed up then headed toward the entrance that was about 150 yards away.

Haliday got down from the truck and started running through a gravel parking area that he had to get through before reaching the nearby woods.

He sprinted about 40 yards through the trees and came out behind the Jeep, which was moving down the road at about 50 miles per hour. He emptied a clip into the back of it, quickly changed magazines, and emptied another one at it.

The Jeep swerved side to side, then ran into the ditch, came back up onto the pavement, and then rolled a few times. The driver was ejected and the Jeep rolled right over him.

Haliday ran back through the woods shouting at Blake. "Get your bike! Get moving! Don't worry about taking anything!"

Haliday got on his bike and rode up next to the deuce. He put a couple of rounds into the other tires to flatten them, then shifted into gear and met Blake at the entrance.

As they pulled out of the exit, they heard the vehicles coming down the road barely less than a half mile away. Haliday took off with Blake behind him. The approaching vehicles came up fast. One stopped momentarily by the rolled Jeep and another took the shoulder of the road to go around it. They kept heading straight after the two motorcycles.

Haliday and Blake had a little more than half a mile before they reached the road they needed. One of the vehicles pursuing them turned into the marina, but the other kept up the pursuit. Haliday couldn't make out anything on the ham; his earpiece had fallen out. He was just hell-bent on getting out of there.

They reached a little river which was more like a creek in spots and alternated riding in the water and on the bank. The vehicle following only made it in about 100 feet before it got stuck. The occupants jumped out and fired, but it was hard to zero in on their targets due to the twisting of the waterway.

Haliday and Blake rode on for almost six more miles, cutting through multiple farms and across roads before they found a spot to stop. If they continued, it would practically take them right to the militia compound. They wouldn't be very welcome there, that was for sure. Haliday sat there for a brief moment and tried to listen on the ham, but it was silent.

"Blake, call the group and tell them to use the hams to start searching the frequencies," he said. "Tell them they need to find out what these guys are talking about. Here's their operations book. Tell them to start with these frequencies. If those don't work tell them to do it the old-fashioned way and have the ham scan for them."

All hell had broken loose now. They were in the center of the fury.

Chapter 21

Blake and Haliday were still in their hiding place when Haliday got up to go to relieve himself and heard a voice came from the woods.

"Don't you guys move or so help me I'll put a bullet in both of you!"

Haliday looked at the guy. Mid-forties, medium build, brown hair, dressed in RealTree camo. Basically your average guy off the street around these parts. He was holding a rifle on them.

Haliday looked over at Blake. "Don't move, just stay still, and do what he says."

Blake nodded. "I plan to, trust me."

The man asked, "Who are you guys?"

Haliday answered, "I can explain that. You mind lowering that rifle first?"

"Yes I do," the man said. "It's staying right here."

"Okay, we have some land just south of Cass City. We were just out and about checking out the area. Seeing what else is going on around here," Haliday told him.

The guy looked at them. "You expect me to believe that crap when you're hiding in the woods?"

Haliday said, "I guess not. May I ask who you are, sir?"

"That's not important right now. You want to answer my question?"

Haliday figured, why not? "Sir, I don't think you would believe me." He was going to carefully word his answers and statements to try and figure this guy out.

"Go ahead and try me out," the man said.

"If I don't answer," Haliday said, "what do you intend to do then?"

There was a long pause. "I have a few ideas; probably shoot you, too, so don't worry," the man said.

Haliday asked him, "Why don't you take us back to your camp and we'll talk there?"

Here came the response that set Haliday at ease a bit. "I don't know you or what you're up to, but I sure ain't taking you back to my house."

Next question from Haliday was, "What about your boss, the one that runs things?"

The next answer came, "I'll tell you the same thing I tell her—I wear the pants in the family, now enough bullshit."

"Okay, listen. We came out here to go to our cabin and get away from the city. It's pure madness down there. We figured we might be safe up here. We went into town looking for food and gas and ran into some trouble with your cohorts," Haliday told him.

"What cohorts would those be?"

"Your militia members."

The man nearly spit. "I ain't a part of those assholes."

Haliday looked past the guy when he heard a noise and then a voice.

"Hey, Dad, everything okay?" Two boys in their mid-teens walked up.

The man with the rifle didn't turn. "Stay back, sons; these guys might be trouble."

Haliday looked at the boys and spoke. "You guys save some of that food you got from your aunt's house?"

The father spoke, "How did you know about that?"

Haliday went on to explain the encounter the other night.

The father looked at them. "Why were you guys hiding?"

"Like I said, it's hard to explain."

"You the guys that have been causing the militia problems around here?"

Haliday wasn't sure how to answer. "Look, all we want to do is get the hell out of here and get home."

"You avoiding the answers for a reason?"

"Look, I'm taking a guess here. You were out hunting, and we happened upon this area here and you watched us come in. You got us cold. These are your boys here and you want to protect them and your family, right?" Haliday said. "Let me ask you a question. Has the militia done anything for you and your family? I mean, are they taking care of you guys or are you fending for yourselves?"

"We're on our own, I guess," was the answer.

"Then isn't it a good thing someone is pissing in their Wheaties?" Roger asked.

The guy lowered his rifle and everyone breathed a sigh of relief. "I'm sorry, man; I have the feeling I should be thanking you guys instead of pointing a rifle at you. It's been hell around here. A lot has happened and a lot of it because of those militia. They didn't waste any time when the power went out. No one really saw it coming. Even the sheriff is one of them."

"You mind if we sit and talk?" Haliday asked.

"I'll tell you what; my house is a few hundred yards that way. The blue vinyl-sided one over there. We can go there if you want."

Haliday replied, "No offense, but that's not a good idea. If we're seen, you end up in deep trouble and no telling what they would do to you. Give me a few minutes and I'll heat up some coffee."

He put some water on to boil and made some coffee in a canteen cup and handed it to the man. He made another with hot cocoa in it and gave it to the boys to share. A little more at ease, Haliday told him, "Tell Blake here and me what you know."

The man relayed his story. "Okay, the power went out and at first everyone thought it was just the power. I was working down the street at the general store my brother and I own. After a couple hours, I locked up and walked home. In the morning when everything was still out, I figured it was bad. I went down to the store.

"When I got there I saw a guy standing outside the door with a rifle dressed in camo. I asked him who he was and he told me he was militia. I asked him to move and he told me no. He told me the store was being appropriated by the Bad Axe Minute Men.

I asked him to produce some legal documents and he told me to leave. I told him I would contact the police and he told me the sheriff was a Minute Man and had given his okay on everything.

"They wouldn't let me in my own store," the man continued, drinking his coffee. "When I looked up and down the street I saw quite a few of them standing by some of the stores and the gas station. Not every store, though. Just the stores that sold food.

I went back home and told my wife, and then I took one of my rifles and went back. When I got there they had a couple extra guys walking around the area so I hid my rifle. They had taped up some kind of flyer on the windows.

"I read the flyer; it said the area was under control of the Minute Men, and they had confiscated merchandise for the good of the community. They had some old army trucks and they were emptying the stores. The big supermarkets they chained up and had them guarded. It ain't a big town. Not many stores, but they got them all anyway.

"They said they would be posting information in town and on certain buildings. The flyers were all printed. Not sure if they can print or what," the man said suspiciously, raising an eyebrow. "But it was really odd. I felt like it was some kind of movie or something. I couldn't believe it.

They said no one could walk around or travel with firearms. Curfew was dusk until dawn. Few more rules; looters would be dealt with and all that crap. I guess they got some looters and they keep them at the airport with all of the loot they took. They have it locked up in hangars is what we were told. They have tanks and everything."

Haliday interrupted him, "I'll fill you in later on what they do and do not have; please go on."

The man continued. "They caught people on the roads leaving and going to stay with family. If the people leaving had guns, they took them. Sometimes they beat the people, too. People around here are pretty frightened of them, but they keep telling us it's for our own good. Then you guys showed up. Man, they have it out for you guys."

Blake said, "Oh yeah, wait until you hear the latest from them."

The man said. "They call you guys terrorists. They put out a flyer yesterday. They said in one more week they would open the trade store up. It said you would have to trade jewelry, coins, or valuables for food or gas. I don't know how they can do that. It's not right. It was our stuff to begin with. My store could have fed us for a long time until the government help came in."

Haliday rolled his eyes at that statement. *Why do people insist the government will always rescue them?* he thought. "Listen," he said, "these guys are not legitimate according to Constitutional Law. Even the damn sheriff is wrong. They are rogue thugs in my eyes. You people need to band together and take back what is yours, otherwise you guys are going to die. You have anything at all from the store? Anything stored anywhere else?"

"Not really. I mean I have some item's in my pole barn, but not any food," the man admitted. "It's all toilet paper, paper towels, and things like that, which are bulky. I stored them there to save space at the store."

"Keep it all, you can trade it for what you need. You'd be surprised how valuable a roll of toilet paper will be. Speaking of, now that we've made acquaintances, I really have to go squirt." Haliday left for a minute, then returned.

"Now, back to business. Where's your brother?" Haliday asked.

"They go to Arizona for a couple months each winter," was the response.

It was Haliday's turn to talk a bit. "Now let me tell you what they have and what *they* are all about." He told the guy everything he knew about the BAMM. The guy was awestruck.

"They will be searching for us with a vengeance," Haliday told him. "We killed six of them this morning—somebody's brother, son, husband, father, whatever. But they got what they deserved. They got what they were giving out. But we can't do it all. We just want to get back to our own family as well."

The man asked them, "Where are you guys going to go?"

"We are going to go find a place to camp until it's safe for us to move out. We are going to connect with our family and try and wait it out until we can go home. Not sure when that will be. Hopefully soon."

"Do you guys have food or anything?"

Haliday lied when he answered. "Yeah, we have about two cases of MREs, a few more days' worth of food for us, so we can hang out up here for about one week before we're hunting like you guys."

The guy thanked them for the coffee and cocoa.

Haliday told him again, "This is still your country, your state and your home. These guys don't have the right to do what they are doing. There should be enough people out there to make a difference. Before they summarily start executing people, I'd get an alliance together and do something."

"Can you guys help?" The man asked.

"We did enough; right now we can't do anymore. There's nothing here for us now, we're just fighting to live now, just like you. I'll try to check back before we head back to the 'burbs. I wish you guys luck."

265

Haliday and Blake took off and headed straight south. Haliday told Blake they had to start being more careful to avoid encounters like that again.

They went south, hoping the militia would stick to the north where they were causing all of the trouble. They eventually found a large patch of woodland near a small city named Freidberger.

Blake said, "Friedburger."

Haliday thought that sounded good at the moment. Even though he had given up red meat, a nice juicy burger with bacon and cheese on it sounded real good right then.

Haliday called in to his group. "This is Roger, checking in."

"Roger, it's Dad," came Rich's voice. "We found the new frequency for the militia. It's the fifth one you gave us."

"Hold on, Dad." Haliday had Blake tune in to the militia. "Okay, go ahead."

"You guys are in deep trouble. They are on the hunt for you big time. They know you guys are staying in the spots of woods. It's not safe anymore," Rich emphasized. "Did you guys really do what they've been saying?"

"Dad, I have no idea. We haven't heard their claims. They could be full of it. We're going to find another place to hide. I'll call you guys later."

"Wait a minute, Roger; something else. Some guys from the militia snooped around a bit, checked out the place with binoculars. They know someone is here—smoke from the fireplace I guess. They left a letter in the mailbox with yellow caution tape tied around it to get our attention. We went and got it when it was safe.

"It states who they are and what their mission is. It says that all people in the district they control must abide by the mandates they have in place. It's a whole list of crap; curfew, travel, all that garbage you said it was. They have a form they want filled out and put back in the mailbox."

Haliday asked, "What's the form for? What info do they want?"

Rich responded. "They want to know the names, ages, and sex of everyone staying here. They want to know if we have running vehicles, what kind, how much food and water we have and what kind of guns and ammunition are here. It asks about generators, fire wood—"

"Stop, Dad, I've heard enough. When do they want the form back?"

Rich said, "It's written down that they will pick it up the day after tomorrow."

Haliday thought for a moment, then spoke. "Okay, listen up. It's not that safe outside right now. I'm not sure if they do or not, but assume you have someone watching you. It might be the militia or might be someone else close by that they have watching you. They are probably taking notes on your every move. Do not answer any questions, do not talk to anyone, OK?"

Rich said, "Yes. Anything else?"

Haliday told him, "Yeah, as hard as it's going to be, you need to add a third person to the security watch. Talk to you later Dad"

He looked over at Blake, who was shaking his head.

"Not good," Haliday said.

Haliday dialed in his radio to the militia frequency. "Keep listening, Blake." He pulled out his maps. "Gotta find some place to hide." He kept looking around and referencing his notes. "Let's see, okay, got it. This is the best chance we have right now." He put the map away. "Let's go, Blake. Time to go to school, the old Freidberger School to be exact. This place is very old, very unoccupied. No one has probably been there for years. It's as rundown as you can get and we can hide there for now. I once read it was left to rot out and crumble because of no money to restore it. We just need to get out of the woods if that's where they're looking for us."

They would wait it out until it was dark, and then they would make the move to the old schoolhouse.

In the meantime they ate. Their food was getting very low. They each had an MRE left. Haliday had a couple bags of soup mix and a few other small items. They could get through the night and tomorrow, but after that they were going to start to get hungry. He wished he would have taken a .22lr so he could hunt a squirrel or rabbit, but he hadn't counted on being out long at all.

They sat there and listened to the radio. The BAMM guys had pretty much pulled out all of the stops. Haliday figured that they had about 12 vehicles on the road looking for them. If their area was roughly 35-by-50 miles, that was 1,750 square miles. That was one big area to cover. The only problem was that only about 10 percent was wooded. The rest was flat barren land for crops. The BAMM had to have extra eyes out there as well. They were probably giving food to people in exchange for them watching the area.

The group in control was definitely pissed for sure. They wanted Haliday and Blake badly. They didn't have any idea who they were looking for, other than guys on bikes. Even though the description of the bikes varied, the BAMM would be gunning for anyone found on one. Haliday and Blake had gotten into quite the pickle here.

It was only 1800 hours, but already completely dark out.

"Blake, I hate to say this," Haliday began, "but we only have about a mile to go, if that far, and I think it's going to be in our best interest to push the bikes."

Blake wasn't happy about that but he agreed.

They pushed the bikes along through the woods and across an open field. Haliday worked his way up to the road, then looked around and returned to Blake.

"We have a little problem, Blake. Someone must have bought the land," he said. "The school is still there, but so is a house. I'm going to go back and check out the house."

He ripped out some long weeds and covered up Blake and the bikes. "Wait here, don't move at all, keep watch."

Haliday went back and watched the house for a while. It looked empty. These were smaller farm plots and he wasn't sure if any neighbors banded together to help each other out. He crossed the road and got a better look. The garage door was slightly open and he peeked inside. Nothing inside.

He went in and walked up to the house door. He collapsed the stock on his AR and got ready to enter when he noticed the door here had been opened as well. He felt along the jamb and sure enough, it had been forced open. He turned his flashlight on and placed his thumb on the activation switch, ready to light it up. He slowly opened the door and went inside.

It was a small mudroom. You came in from the field, took your boots and gear off here before entering the main house. He entered the main house and listened. He didn't hear anything at all. He activated his flashlight and swept it around quickly. He had been in the funnel of death; when you stand in a doorway you were at the small end of a funnel. Anyone in the room could concentrate fire to that point easily. It made you feel uneasy.

The place had been ransacked.

Blake called on the radio; it was hard to hear him. "We have company."

Haliday flipped the light off and ducked into a nearby closet, but left the door half open just like it had been. He heard a vehicle pull into the drive. A couple of car doors opened and closed. He noticed a flashlight shine through the windows.

He heard the doors to the house open and saw the light bouncing off the walls and then heard male voices talking.

"Looks like this place hasn't been touched since the last time we checked it. Call it in."

"Let's check the schoolhouse first."

"Forget it. It'll probably fall in on us."

The men left and Haliday just stood there. He heard the vehicle start and then leave. He switched to the militia freq.

Haliday heard, "Papa Four Bravo, we checked Delta Thirty and both were empty. Doesn't look like anyone has been in there since it was last looted. We're heading out to Delta Thirty."

It was just a matter of about three minutes when Haliday heard them again. "Papa Four Bravo, we're out at Delta Thirty."

Haliday waited. It must be the house next door, just about an eighth of a mile away. It was the same routine for the next half hour. The men were moving along the main road, checking it along the way.

He switched frequencies again. "Blake, you there?"

There wasn't any answer.

"Blake, you out there?"

No answer.

Haliday went outside and made his way over to where Blake was. "Why didn't you answer me?"

"My radio went dead," Blake told him, "I forgot to change the battery."

Haliday only had two batteries for each radio; he put them on a small charger connected to his bike with an inverter. It worked, but the past two days had burned through the batteries and needed a good charging. They hadn't really had the time for that. He called the group and said they would be off radio for a while.

"We'll check in every two hours for a minute and that's it," he said. "We have to charge the batteries."

He swapped the batteries around and both radios worked. He turned them off. "We can't listen in, Blake. We need to save the batteries for when we need them. Without starting the bike I can't charge them. Now let's get over there and get some sleep."

They rolled the bikes over the road and put them behind the schoolhouse. They covered them up carefully to hide them, but still made the place look untouched. A few handfuls of dirt and garbage helped with that.

They went inside the school, found a decent hiding place, and got some rest.

Chapter 22

Early the next morning Haliday and Blake were both hungry, so they ate their last MRE apiece. Each had gotten quite a bit of rest. Haliday was still fairly sore from the bruise on his abdomen from the airport shooting, not to mention pushing the bike around. He opened a bottle of Tylenol and popped a couple in his mouth. Blake asked for a couple and he handed him the bottle.

Blake took the cotton out and looked at Haliday. "I didn't think they put cotton in these anymore."

"They don't; I do it so the bottle doesn't rattle," Haliday said. "Just in case I have it on me, it's not rattling around. Same with water; your canteen should be full or empty so it doesn't slosh around. No noise at all if possible. We haven't quite adhered to that discipline, but we should start before we get too lax. How are you holding up, Blake?"

"I'm doing okay."

"You sure?"

"Yeah. I mean, I got sick while you were sleeping," Blake admitted. "I was thinking about the shootings and everything."

"Normal response, Blake. Here's some gum."

"That'll help my stomach?"

"No, it'll help your breath. Take two or three sticks. Please."

They both laughed a bit.

Blake flipped the radio on and called the group.

Kayla answered. "Hey, Blake, you guys all right?"

"Yeah, we're fine. I mean, everything considered and all I guess. Your dad wants to know what's going on there."

"Okay, we had four patrols drive by last night. One actually sat on the road for almost half an hour. They were watching the house. We just burned candles and didn't use the generator at all. We've only had my Uncle David and Dawn go outside.. This way they don't know how many people are here."

"Hey," she added, "tell my dad we heard from my Uncle Alan and his family. They are all okay and at a friend's house right now and they are all okay. They have a radio in the neighborhood that the owner has been letting people use."

"Your dad heard you, Kayla," Blake said. "He's listening in, too. Here he is now."

Haliday got on the radio. "That was good news, kiddo. Anybody else?" He was wondering about his sister and her family in Texas and his brother and his family in Missouri.

"No, that's it."

Haliday had given his sister the frequency, but who knows if she still had it or was able to get to a radio. "Kayla, how's the group holding up?"

She answered, "Everyone is okay. Bobby is okay, and his head looks good. Sarah is just really quiet, kind of in her own world, and everyone else is okay. We have been eating limited rations since we are not real active, but everyone is making sure they get a good balance of protein, carbs, and vitamins."

"Anything on the militia?" he asked next.

"Well, they still don't know how many of you there really are, but they are changing the estimate to about four guys on bikes. They don't believe the trucks are moving with you at all. They think the trucks are hidden and camped out or do not exist. They still think the plan is to raid their camp with all of the stuff you guys are doing."

"Okay, listen," he said. "This is what I want you guys to do. Forget about the form. Don't bother doing anything with it at all. They might try to come up to the house. Remember; be ready to shoot the bastards. I'm sure they know people are there, just not how many yet. I don't want to risk bringing the bikes in yet; that would draw a shit storm for sure. But, we need a care package."

Blake looked over at Haliday. "A care package?"

"Yeah, Blake, we have to avoid drawing any attention to the group right now. We have to give it a few days to settle down if we can. But, we'll need a few more things in order to make it. Food for one; few more toys, too. Kayla," he said, shifting his attention, "write this down, then I'll tell you guys when and where to meet us. Couple of you will have to leave the house for about an hour or so."

Haliday gave her a complete list of resupply items. He would be swapping out his AR for one with a 37mm launcher attached to it. He'd also be picking up his M24 Remington, some more rounds, food, of course, and a couple of other things along with some fresh underclothing. They'd make the exchange and then get back to business.

It would be easier to just head in and try to hold the fort, but with the plane or planes bound to take flight eventually, the tracked vehicle and the way the BAMM group was running the area like they owned it all, Haliday couldn't let things happen like that. They would have to even out the odds a bit more. Not just for them, but the community as well.

If the self-appointed forces at work got a tighter grip on the whole community even more than they already had, the whole area would be a wasteland. Haliday's group had too much invested in their house and land to have to move.

If they did try and move again, who knows what would happen. It was just getting worse out there day by day. Haliday wondered how he'd gotten tied up in such a mess.

As they were sitting in the school they heard a vehicle pull in by the house and stop. They heard a couple of voices. Militia again. They waited and listened. Same old cursory check but this one didn't last long.

He heard one guy say it was a waste checking a house located right off the road. "Better safe than sorry," the other man replied. They checked quickly and then drove off.

After about 15 minutes Haliday looked at his watch, called the group, and asked them if they were ready. The Cherokee from the group was heading out. Haliday and Blake would wait about another 15 minutes and then leave themselves. It was a long wait. They dug the bikes out and headed to the meeting place.

As they pulled up to the meeting spot, they saw the Cherokee off to the side of the road. Kayla and David were out there, pacing back and forth. The signal was simple, if there was a trap, they would just be standing still next to the car. Haliday and Blake pulled up by the Cherokee and got off the bikes. A quick round of hugs and some frantic hand off of the resupply equipment ensued. They didn't want to be seen. The spot was blocked by trees and no one could see them unless they were on the road and close by.

Last but not least, fresh batteries for the radios, three for each of them. David handed them each a cup of hot coffee.

Blake looked at it and said, "What the hell, I'll drink it; not a coffee fan though."

Kayla said, "I added sugar and French vanilla creamer to yours, Blake, so it tastes better."

Haliday said, "Gee, thanks for looking out for me."

Kayla said, "Dad, I made yours the same way."

David brought over a couple of five-gallon gas cans and topped off their tanks and cans.

Haliday asked, "You hearing anything about troops or feds?"

"Nothing Dad, people are complaining about being left out to dry. They say they see activity at bases, but not much and nothing off base," Kayla told him.

"Okay, thank you, sweetie. Keep listening for anything important. Here's a list of what to do and when to do it."

Another quick hug, the list passed off, and it was goodbye.

They all took off. David and Kayla went back to the house and Haliday and Blake down the road and into a small farm by some round hay bales.

Haliday wished he had the map memorized. He actually did, except for the areas where they could easily hide. It was mid-morning and they needed a place to go study the map and come up with some plans.

"Screw it," he said. "This is today's plan."

They headed out and went east back to the old school. They hid the bikes and walked inside. Haliday took a bunch of rags and soaked them with a little gas. He laid a mound of debris around the area as well. Blake went into the house and did the same thing. Both used the cigarette ignition with paper clip assembly, lit them and left.

So much for the house and old schoolhouse. It was another *screw you* to the Militia.

Next up was a visit to a familiar face. They went back to try and connect with the guy who had been out hunting. Haliday stayed out in the woods while Blake snuck out to the street and just walked up the guy's house. He had changed quickly and had on blue jean pants and a grey hoodie, pulled up. Normal kid off the street attire. He walked up and knocked on the door.

The guy came to the door and said, "Can I help you?"

Blake lowered his hoodie and said, "It's me from the woods; I need to talk to you."

The guy opened the door right away and let Blake in.

"What's going on?" the guy asked.

"We need some help. We can help you guys, but we need some help, too," Blake said.

The guy said, "Sure, no problem. Where's your dad?"

"Oh, he's not my dad; he's my friend's dad. He's out in the wood line."

"Well, okay, but go tell him I'll open the back door of the pole barn; you can hide your bikes there. Then we can talk."

Blake said, "Okay; wait until seven though so it's dark."

Blake went back to meet Haliday.

Seven came around and Haliday and Blake pushed the bikes through the dirt field and into the back of the man's pole barn. Haliday went back out and fluffed up the foliage and dragged the rows of the field they used to bring the bikes in and then walked back into the barn.

The man was waiting and holding a flashlight on them. "My name is Rob. We weren't formally introduced."

"I'm Roger and that's Blake," Haliday said. "Can you turn the flashlight off, please?"

"Oh sure, sorry," Rob said.

Haliday asked, "Anywhere in here we can turn on a light and not be seen from the outside?"

Rob said, "I have a small room I keep things locked up in over in the corner. Let's go over there."

They made their way to the corner room and went inside.

Haliday turned on a small LED flashlight with red lights. "Rob, thank you very much. Listen, I'm not going to beat around the bush. We can help you, but we are partly doing so because it will help us, too. You game?"

"Yes I am," Rob said. "Let's hear what you have."

Haliday said, "First things first. What's the latest you've heard?"

Rob pretty much told him what Haliday already knew, but with a different twist; the militia made them out to be terrorists killing people in cold blood for no reason at all. They claimed these "terrorists" were going to come in and take over the community, robbing people, raping women, and things like that.

Haliday chuckled at that and asked, "What do the other people think?"

Rob answered, "They don't know what to think. Some believe them, but a bunch know what the militia is really doing. The rest are just kind of here. They don't seem to care."

"Rob, I won't lie to you. Here's how everything went down." Haliday told him exactly what happened, minus a few small details in order to avoid looking like cold-blooded killers. He wasn't sure Rob would understand the justification to kill. "Now, Rob, if you are still okay, this is what we have planned." He covered a few details and looked at Rob.

Rob said, "That sounds fairly dangerous."

"Well, Rob, it does, but with safety in numbers, it'll be okay."

Rob then thought for a moment and agreed.

They would take the night off and use the whole day tomorrow to prepare. Right now they imagined the militia was running around again, completely upset because they torched the house and the old school. These were areas they knew the militia was checking. They really just wanted to let them know they were still in the area.

The radio was abuzz with the school and house burning, and Haliday, Blake, and Rob listened in. The militia didn't quite send as many patrols as Haliday thought they would, but that was okay. They listened to the transmission on the radio.

Mike started his ruse, he said, "Hey, is anybody there? Anybody out there?"

The militia responded. "This is the Bad Axe Minute Men. You are on a frequency designated for militia operations. Cease your radio traffic and stay off this frequency."

"Hey, man, listen, we need some help. There's a bunch of guys on motorcycles who have been causing trouble around here. The police are long gone and we don't know what to do."

The militia asked them, "Where are you guys located?"

"We're south of Sandusky; they just firebombed a store and then torched a car, too. Can you guys help?" Mike asked.

"That's a negative. You are not located in our control district," the militia answered back.

"Come on, man, help us out," Mike pleaded.

"Negative. Now please clear this frequency and try and contact the government on the civil defense frequency. Do not take the law into your own hands. Let the authorities for your area do it. Locate another frequency."

They went back to their own transmissions. Haliday expected them to change frequencies next shift change. He would have to remember to tell Mike "Good job." The militia might now be thinking they were heading back south after causing trouble up north. The school and house and now the Sandusky area pointed that way.

They discussed with Rob what he would have to do. After a couple more hours, they would be done for the night. Rob offered to let them stay in the house, but they politely declined. They asked him to make sure his wife and boys didn't leave the house and that they remain quiet. Rob assured them it would not be a problem.

As Rob was about to leave, Haliday said, "Hold on one second, Rob."

Haliday looked around the little room. There was a good amount of alcohol in boxes on shelves, evidently for the store. Haliday told Rob to keep this secret, maybe even put some in smaller containers to use as trade items down the road. Rob said he hadn't thought of that. Haliday himself had purchased liquor and empty pint bottles for the same reason.

Haliday went over to his bike. He pulled out four small size Mylar bags and handed them to Rob. "Boil eight cups of water, empty one packet in, and let it simmer for about twenty to twenty-five minutes.

You'll have a complete meal for the four of you. It's like a cross of red beans and rice and dirty rice." He handed him a square of Datrex bars and a baggy full of Tang. "This will feed you guys for four full days and give you what you need. Save what you have in the house for now."

Rob protested, but Haliday wouldn't hear it. Rob thanked them.

After Rob left, Haliday told Blake that they would stay there for the night and rotate sleep again. "Can't be too sure we are in safe hands just yet. Peace offering or not, you never know. We'll get to work on the toys and plans in the morning. Things will be busy soon enough."

Haliday woke up and looked outside the next morning. There was a heavy frost outside. If they didn't get this done soon, it would become increasingly more difficult to move around and not leave tracks. There weren't any tracks around the building in the frost. No one had checked on them last night. Rob had stayed away like he promised.

Haliday and Blake were busy organizing their gear more efficiently when Rob came into the barn.

"You guys can fire up that wood burner if you want to," he said.

"No thank you," Haliday said. "Two stovepipes from two different buildings might attract attention. We'll be fine. You heading out, Rob?"

"Yeah, I'm going to use the kids' scooter to make my rounds."

"Good luck, let us know how it goes."

After Rob left, Haliday and Blake got busy working on their little toys. If it hadn't been for eBay and all the China-marts online, he wouldn't have acquired the things he needed in bulk. The little alarm clocks were a steal. He bought them by the dozen for about two bucks a clock. They were perfect little timers. They only needed a few of these this time around.

Haliday pulled out the homemade chart of the airport and studied it. He looked it over and made some more notes and consulted the map as well. Time for a quick break, he called the group.

Bev answered. "We're all okay," she told him. "Everyone is busy getting ready. We should be all set. How about you guys?"

"Yeah, same here," said Haliday. "Anything more on the patrols?"

"Hold on a minute," she said.

Kevin came on the radio now. "Uncle Roger, I went out to get some firewood to load up in the rack and while I was out there, one of the trucks pulled up on the road. They sat there for a few minutes and then yelled over to me. I asked them what they wanted and they said they wanted the form. I told them we didn't have any form for them, it wasn't any of their business, and to just leave us alone. They talked back and forth to each other a few minutes and then left.

"A couple hours later they came back and had another truck with them," Kevin continued. "They called out on a bullhorn, but we didn't answer. One of the guys started coming up to the house. Uncle David and Dawn went outside and told him to leave. He put another letter in the mailbox and told us we had seventy-two hours to fill it out or they would come onto the property and check personally, said they wouldn't be nice about it next time. They stopped at the neighbor's house, too."

"Well, in seventy-two hours the game will hopefully change. Talk to you guys later." Haliday hung up and looked out the window. He saw a quad coming down the tree line.

The quad was only going about five miles an hour and the rider was looking into the woods as he rode along. He passed the barn without stopping. Haliday went to the other side of the barn and watched the guy continue along. These guys were persistent, that's for sure.

It was late afternoon when Haliday and Blake heard Rob on the scooter. Haliday watched him pull up. It looked comical, almost like a clown in a parade, seeing the big guy on this little scooter. Rob went into his house, then came out about 15 minutes later and came into the barn.

"Okay, I have some help," he told Haliday and Blake. "I talked to only the guys I could trust and they talked to a few family members as well. We have about thirty people."

"That's great news," Haliday said. "That's more than I expected."

Rob said they could double that if they used the older kids. He said he left it up to the others to decide.

Haliday said, "That's your decision. The risk is there, but in a sense it's not. I can't put you or your family in any danger. You are volunteers and if that's what you decide, then I'm with you. Everyone understands the ground rules right?"

Rob said, "Yes."

"Any other news?"

"A little bit. They have a couple motorcycles now and a few quads. Some of the militia are using them to check the woods and property lines. If you are using those areas, you might be in trouble."

Haliday said, "Yeah, I saw one pass by earlier. That won't be a problem. They won't find anything. We covered our tracks enough. Rob, go inside and spend the evening with your family. We'll be fine out here. I'll talk to you again in the morning."

"Goodnight, Roger," Rob said. "Goodnight, Blake. Again, I can't thank you guys enough."

"Rob, thank us if this works, and don't downplay your role. It's just as dangerous and just as important. Tomorrow night is the big night."

They parted ways for the evening.

Haliday noted that the patrol quad drove by twice more during the night.

It was past dinner time when Blake and Haliday ate. They whipped up a package of chili and ate, then turned the radio on and listened.

Just a few more minutes to wait, then it would be time.

Finally they got news on the radio. "This is the St. Clair Tridents trying to raise the Bad Axe Minute Men, over."

There was no response.

"St. Clair Tridents calling the Bad Axe Minute men, over."

BAMM responded. "Who are you?"

"This is Colonel David Howe from the St. Clair Tridents."

"We never heard of you," the BAMM man said.

"Well, we never heard of you either until this morning. Let's cut to the chase," Howe responded. "I don't care if you know me or not, but all we are looking for is some info. We had a citizen give us this frequency after they said they called for help and you answered."

"Go ahead; what do you want?" the Minute Man asked.

Howe continued. "We had some problems last night and this evening. We have some kind of gang causing problems. Lighting fires and shooting at people to scare them. We had a few trucks come through yesterday afternoon, but we lost track of them. The worst part though is they have some motorcycles causing troubles. You guys have any information on them at all?"

"No we don't. We haven't had any problems at all up here except for some local people looting," BAMM stated. "But the police are handling it. If we have any other information, we'll call you on this frequency. We monitor it, but that's all. We wish you luck."

Haliday shook his head. These guys were some cool players. *Protecting their little country, lying through their teeth; they really are something else,* he thought.

Tomorrow night they'd be put to the test.

Haliday called the group before they settled in for the night. "Make sure you guys go over everything again and again. I can't tell you guys enough how important it is. There are going to be a lot of people depending on us, but what you have to consider before anything else is your safety and the safety of everyone around you. Okay," he said, closing the evening, "we're getting some sleep. Talk to you in the morning."

Chapter 23

The morning was a busy one. Rob had taken the scooter and made his rounds to make sure everyone was going to be ready. Haliday and Blake double-checked everything and loaded up the bikes.

Rich, Bev, David, Dawn, and Randy got the Cherokee and Tahoe ready. They, too, were packed and waiting. Kayla helped them go over everything and then made sure the cabin was ready. She would be staying with Sarah, Kevin, Bobby, Karen, Diana, and Elizabeth at the house.

Rich was to drive the Cherokee and David the Tahoe. They headed out, northwest toward the western shoreline of the Thumb. They had with them quite a few little packages. Their main area of operation was going to be the Caseville area and along the shoreline there. As they approached the area, they occasionally stopped—timed surprises to help keep the militia on edge.

It was early afternoon. Over at the airport, a crowd started to gather near the front gate. The militia warned the crowd to leave and they did.

The crowd went about a quarter of a mile down to a feed store. They lit up a couple of burn barrels and stood around. The crowd increased in size, drawing the attention of the militia.

A patrol drove by the congregated peopled at the feed store about every 10 minutes.

*****

Over in the Caseville area, two vehicles pulled into the parking lot of a small grocery store. A militia patrol pulled in behind them. The men got out and approached the Tahoe and Cherokee with their weapons at the ready.

A few minutes later another patrol pulled in to assist the first. They ordered the people out of the vehicles.

David and Dawn got out first. Randy got out of the Cherokee and walked over to the driver's door. He opened it and Rich got out. Rich leaned up against the fender, playing the role of a feeble old man. Randy went and opened Bev's door and helped her get out. He pulled out a small stool and she sat down. The militia approached them.

"Who are you people?" one of the militia men asked.

David explained that it was his wife and son, and his parents. He said they lived in Warren and came up here to bug out.

"Where are you planning on going exactly?" the BAMM member asked.

"We have a small cabin on Rose Island. That's where we are heading to," David answered.

"You guys have ID?" asked the militia man.

Rich walked over slowly and gave him his driver's license. The address was in Warren.

The man from the militia looked over at Randy and the rest. "You guys have ID?"

Dawn said no; David pulled his out.

The guy looked at David's ID and said, "This says Roseville."

David spoke. "Yeah, my parents live in Warren. We live in Roseville and Randy lives in St. Clair Shores. We all made it to my parents' house where we stayed until it started getting bad with riots and looters. Look at my truck," he said, nodding to the vehicle. "They were shooting at everything just to shoot; it's loaded with bullet holes. We decided to head to the cabin."

Over by the airport, the crowd that had previously gathered at the feed store had grown to almost 50 people. They started walking back toward the airport's main gate. When they got there, the militia doubled up the manpower at the gate and told the crowd to go away.

From within the crowd, Rob demanded that he talk to the militia's leader. The crowd called the militia Nazis, criminals, thugs, crooks, and a few other choice words. All were men, women, and a few older teenagers.

Back in the parking lot of the grocery store, the militia told David and his group that they were the authority for the Thumb Region. They insisted on searching the vehicles.

David and the group protested, but the militia convinced them by raising their rifles. The militia ordered them to sit. The militia pulled everything out of the vehicles, just tossing it all on the ground with abandon.

Sleeping bags, camp stove fuel, clothing, food, and some odds and ends—all carelessly tossed on the parking lot. One of the militia opened up a blanket and laid it on the ground. He placed a small .22 rifle on it along with a couple of Mosin Nagants rifles and an older 12 gauge shotgun. Another guy put down two ammo cans filled with various ammo for the guns and opened it.

"I see boxes of 9mm," he said. "You guys have any pistols on you?"

David said, "Yes, I have a 9mm under my coat."

One of them told him to raise his hands, which he did.

One of the guys took the gun from him and then patted him down. He told everyone else to stand up as well. The militia completed the search and didn't find anything else.

"Here's a list of rules for the area," the one in charge told them briskly. "I suggest you go to your cabin and stay there. Check in once in a while in case we have information for you. We post bulletins regularly. You damn vacationers think you can just come up here and do whatever you want and it makes me sick. If I had it my way, we'd be shooting all of you useless assholes.

"We're keeping the guns," he added. "That's our law. You might want to think seriously about how long you plan on staying. Spring would be a great time to move the hell back to wherever you guys came from."

A third patrol had approached and watched the activity. David saw them talking on the radio. He heard one man say that they didn't find any truck tracks at the marina; just the bike tracks. They got another call and the third patrol left.

The other two patrols stayed behind, but David could tell they were getting anxious about something.

*****

Haliday and Blake started to head toward the airport. They were following the path they'd previously taken. Haliday would be taking a different path and he split off from Blake at the juncture. Blake continued on for about half a mile and then stopped and waited. As he was sitting there the patrol's quad came up along the wood line. Blake took off to try to avoid them.

The quad followed Blake as he tried to lose it and it soon closed the distance between the quad and the bike. Blake tried to get into the woods, but he couldn't find an opening.

He looked back, seeing that the quad was even closer. He laid on the throttle, but the bike became unstable on the terrain and bounced around too much, so he slowed back down.

He spotted an opening in the woods and shot toward it. Just after he entered, he hit a patch of leaves and dumped the bike down sideways, sliding along with it. He got up and ran down the path with the quad in pursuit. The quad gunned it and blasted into the woods.

The quad's rider was suddenly whipped backward and a sharp pressure on his chest tore him from the quad. He landed on his back and rolled around in pain from the unseen trap. Haliday had wrapped a piece of small, coated wire cable around one tree and anchored it, then fed the end through an eye bolt anchored to another tree. As soon as Blake had laid down the bike, Haliday, hidden, pulled the cable and wrapped the end around the eyebolt for strength. It had knocked the rider of the quad off.

Haliday walked up and stepped on the writhing man's arm as Blake ran up. He pointed his .40 at him. "You guys don't learn, do you? Still out here playing army and trying to run your own little country?"

286

The guy just looked up at him. He had to be only 18 or 19 years old. Haliday bent down, flipped him over, and applied some flex cuffs.

He searched the kid and pulled off a pistol, a couple of magazines, and a knife. "Blake, gather up the rest of his gear, his rifle, and everything. Take the quad and run it back to where we came from. I'll be right there after I finish with this kid."

Blake did as he was asked. He put everything in the pole barn at Rob's place and threw an old tarp over it. Haliday swung by and picked him up and took him back to his bike.

The kid was sitting up, tied against a tree there. He wouldn't be going anywhere at all. The kid was probably patrolling the wood line and east side of the airport where they would need to be, Haliday figured.

He looked at the kid. "I'm going to let you sit here and then I'll have someone come get you later. Find Jesus while we're gone. Find Allah, for all I care. But get right with your Maker."

Blake asked, "You aren't going to shoot him?"

"No, he can stand trial with the rest of them or they can do whatever they want with him, but I'm not going to do it. I should, but he didn't fire on us or try, at least not yet; rules of engagement, in a sense, a twisted sense though. I did talk to him for a few minutes though.

"The kid basically told me to screw off. He told me they were the new government in the area and they applied new laws to the area. That's about all he said. Kept repeating it over and over along with saying how we were going to get what we had coming to us. Not a very smart kid, either. No understanding of what the law really is.

"Let's go," Haliday said. "We've got to be in place very soon."

They made their way back to the northeast corner of the airport where they had been before. It was completely dark out by this time. They got busy getting ready, knowing this would be more interesting than just watching what was going on.

The crowd at the airport gate had grown to almost 80 people now. They were still demanding to talk to the militia leader. They were still calling them names and such. Someone dragged over a barrel and lit a fire in it.

The militia had called in half of their patrol units. Everyone in the airport compound was on alert and ready.

*****

David and everyone from the group had started slowly packing up their gear. They tried talking to the militia, but the responses were short and rude.

Randy came over from the Tahoe. "Hey, Uncle David, the Tahoe has a flat. Can you help me change it?"

"Yeah, give me a minute. Mom, Dad, you guys wait in the Cherokee where it's warm," David said. "Dawn, pull it up next to the Tahoe so we can change the tire. I need the jack and lug wrench out of the Cherokee."

David said, "Randy, can you get under there and get that spare loose?"

Randy lay down and worked on the tire.

Off in the distance, they heard a series of small explosions.

Randy sat up. The militia sent one of their trucks down the street to check it out.

One of the two remaining guys yelled at Randy. "Get the damn tire changed already!"

Randy got back under and worked on getting the tire down.

Rich got out of the Cherokee.

The militia man asked him, "Where you going?"

"I have to pee. Can't I go pee?" Rich answered.

The guy told him, "No, you can hold it."

Rich looked at him. "I can't hold it. I'm seventy-five-years-old."

"Piss your pants then, old man," the guy replied. "We ain't letting you piss all over the place."

Dawn got out now. "Let the man go the bathroom, for God's sake."

"Shut up, bitch."

"Don't call me a bitch."

The guy lowered his rifle and flipped her off. "Screw you, bitch."

Dawn said, "All he wants to do is go to the bathroom, okay? What if I take a bucket out for him?"

"I don't give a shit. Like I said, let him piss his pants. Should have put on some Depends, old man," the militia man said.

Dawn called him an asshole.

The guy by the militia truck called him. "Hey, we got a big problem! We have to go!"

Dawn said, "Rich, as soon as they leave you can go."

The militia man walked up and slapped Dawn.

Rich bent down a bit and said, "Don't hurt us."

Dawn cowered down and covered her head with her arms.

The militia man said, "You start to listen to us from now on, you stupid bitch."

"Leave me alone, you bastard," said Dawn.

The other militia man started walking toward them.

The militia man called Dawn a bitch again and raised his hand to hit her.

David squeezed the trigger five times, hitting the first man three times. Randy fired his shotgun once at the second man, pumped it, and then fired again.

David walked up and checked the militia man; he wasn't dead, but just lying there injured. He kicked away the fallen man's rifle and grabbed the pistol from his belt.

Randy yelled over that the second guy was dead. "Uncle Roger, was right. Buckshot is good stuff."

They grabbed all of the gear that they could and tossed it into the vehicles. Randy grabbed a can of compressed air and filled the Tahoe's tire. He walked over to the militia vehicle and, using a knife, flattened all four tires. They took what was in the truck and put it in their own, then took off as soon as they could. They left the injured man just lying there.

The second truck came speeding down the road and saw them pulling away. It tore into the parking lot to check out what had happened. They had had no idea that David had hidden a rifle and a shotgun up under the truck. The flat tire and Rich's bathroom plea had been a diversion. Of course, Dawn hadn't expected to get slapped.

The militia men grabbed some first aid supplies and tended to their injured friend. Once they got him quickly bandaged, they put him in the back of the truck and grabbed the other man's body and placed it in the back of the truck. They sped off, heading toward their compound.

David and company made a few turns, waited, and then headed back to the house. This was all that was expected of them. They made it back and put everything away and then turned the radio on and listened. Everything was boiling over right now and it was chaos at the militia compound.

At the airport, the militia had forced the group aside and opened the gate for the patrol truck to enter with the injured man. They rushed him into the admin building, where a nurse from the militia was working on him.

At this same time, the crowd outside was yelling that they wanted to talk to the militia leader. They were not leaving until that happened.

One of the militia came out and asked them what they wanted.

Rob told him, "We want our food and stuff back. You guys don't have the right to keep it. You didn't have the right to take it."

The man from the militia told him to take it easy, to disperse the crowd, and then he would get the commander and they could talk.

"What do you mean get the commander? Who the hell are you?" Rob asked. "I know you from somewhere. You work at the sheriff's office. Is he in charge?"

"The sheriff is the commander. We are under rule of militia law now."

The crowd was yelling loudly now. More of the militia came around by the gate. They now had a few guys continuously patrolling up and down the fence line.

One man ran inside and spoke to the commander. The commander came out and walked behind a barrier. "What do you people want?"

Rob replied, "We want what's ours. What you took from us, what you stole from the community. That's what we want."

The commander responded, "You got it all wrong."

"Then explain it to us!" yelled Rob.

"We are under militia law now. Everything was commandeered for the good of the community. You'll be able to buy food and supplies in a couple of days."

Rob yelled again. "Why the hell should we buy what belonged to us in the first place?"

The commander tried to explain. "Things are different and we need to maintain order. That's why we are in charge."

Someone in the crowd hollered out, "Who the hell put you in charge?"

The commander didn't answer directly. "I was the sheriff and now I am the commander of the militia. We are doing what is best for us. If you listen to us and follow our laws you will be fine. Now disperse and go home and wait for notice."

A woman asked him, "You mean what's best for you or what's best for all of us?"

Someone in the crowd threw rocks at the militia. The commander ordered them to leave. The crowd threw more. Two members of the militia approached the gate with what looked like flamethrowers, but they were a different type of deterrent. They sprayed the crowd with pepper spray from the tanks.

Some of the crowd started running away. A lot of the people were coughing and tears and mucous were running down their faces. The commander ordered them to disperse once again.

The crowd crossed the street, but was still yelling. People continued to throw rocks, bottles, or whatever they could find. Someone threw a Molotov cocktail.

The militia fired toward the crowd to scare them.

One man went down and some others helped him up. He had been hit in the leg by accident. The crowd started running away now, through the houses across the street and down back toward the feed store. The militia fired only sporadically.

Over on the other side of the airport Blake fired first. The round arced over toward the crowd and exploded in the air, lighting up the scene. It was a simple fireworks cartridge from the 37mm. The militia was caught off-guard. Everyone looked up.

Haliday squeezed the trigger on his M24 and dropped the commander. The shot tore through his upper shoulder near his neck. His comrades grabbed him and rushed him into the command center.

The militia didn't know whether or not to fire on the crowd. Some of the crowd ran and some lay down on the ground.

Haliday placed his next shot into the open hangar where they were working on the planes. He fired a shot into what looked like a small fuel caddy and it started to leak. He fired just one more shot into it.

He handed the rifle to Blake and told him to put it away. Blake stuffed it in the case and used some bungee cords to secure it to Haliday's bike. He wrapped a couple quick pieces of hundred mile an hour tape on it. The rifle was too important to lose. Blake grabbed his AR and fired at the compound and kept an eye out for patrols.

The militia sent a couple guys to the fence line closest to Haliday and Blake. These men fired a few shots at them and Haliday and Blake returned fire. Blake emptied a magazine and loaded another into the rifle.

Haliday crawled over to a tree and rose up behind it. He aimed the 37mm and launched a flare toward the hangar.

The flare fell short.

Haliday loaded another one and fired again at the hangar.

This one hit the tarmac in front of the hangar and bounced in. A man came running out. Haliday watched as a group of guys ran toward the motor pool hangar.

Haliday loaded one more cartridge into the launcher and fired it toward the hangar. Blake continued to fire at the men near the fence line; he'd already gone through three magazines and had loaded his fourth.

The fireworks cartridge landed near the open door of the hangar and exploded, sending colorful sparks everywhere. One landed in a puddle of fuel and sent up a wall of flames. A couple guys grabbed some small extinguishers and tried to put it out.

Haliday was disappointed there was no explosion. "A little Fourth of July celebration for ya, Wright brothers. Fly this. Okay, Blake, cover me while I get into the woods."

Haliday crawled about 30 yards into the woods. He took up position and told Blake to low crawl in while he used suppressing fire to cover him. He went through three magazines himself. "Go get ready, Blake."

Blake went a little deeper into the woods.

Haliday continued to fire although he wasn't hitting anything other than the four-wheeler. A Jeep came out of the compound and pulled up close to the intersection. The men fired blindly into the woods.

Haliday and Blake had a path between the two wooded areas that they were going to use and so crawled their way back there. The Jeep moved up slowly and started heading down the path. Haliday and Blake fired at them and the Jeep backed off.

Haliday heard the guys shouting out instructions.

"I think it's a trap," said one of the guys. "Just hold on; it's coming."

Back at the airport one of the militia women had managed to wheel a large extinguisher to the hangar where she released the chemical into the hangar and on the two Piper Cubs. Her efforts paid off and the flames were put out. The condition of the planes was unknown, but Haliday hoped they wouldn't fly any time soon.

The motor pool hangar door opened and the M113 rolled out. It went out the main gate and made its way toward the wooded area where Haliday and Blake were. The Jeep had backed out of the woods and the guys in it got out and jumped in the back of the track. They raised the back door ramp and started heading toward Blake and Haliday.

The militia had five people in the track, two of which were actually women. Haliday had actually done a good job of ruffling their ranks over the past few days. He hoped that using the women meant that their ranks were not numbered as high as he originally thought. The option was very angry wives out for payback. Still, they had enough to accomplish what they wanted to in the area and the women were good fighters as well.

Haliday's man count would later prove to be wrong.

With the promise of food and shelter the BAMM would be able to recruit some additional people as well. Haliday figured they had to have been promising the gas station owners something. Why else would they be restricting the gas? Who knew what else they were promising people or would promise them? With the country in the crapper and people getting cold, tired, and hungry, they'd jump on board in a minute to protect themselves and family.

The store/barter idea would have allowed the militia to selectively recruit people, preferably singles or couples with no kids. As they came in to trade for food and supplies, they could screen everyone. Haliday had to admit, it wasn't a bad idea. That plan may have been disrupted. If they started recruiting, they would win this game.

The track turned its lights on. It moved forward slowly but effortlessly at a walking pace. The path there was wide enough to drive a truck through and was fairly level, with just some bushes and undergrowth in most spots. The complicating issue was the trees on both sides. Lot of places for people to hide, but the gun ports on each side provided cover and a sense of safety.

The upper turret was manned with one guy and what looked like a .308 of sorts, most likely an AR configuration. The track was accompanied by two people outside, bringing up the rear. They were determined to find these guys and even the score. They searched the area thoroughly as they moved along.

The track reached a pinch point in the path where the trees narrowed. This narrow point left barely a few inches on each side of the track. The driver checked his alignment and let it creep forward. As it crept through the trees, two booby trap simulators went off, startling everyone.

The guys in the rear dove for cover and the guy in the turret ducked down as the driver stopped. They were braced and ready to take fire. The guys in the rear scanned the area and did not see anyone. The turret gunner stood back up, but kept nice and low behind the armored cover.

Overhead there came some light popping sounds. They looked up and didn't see anything, but felt fluid dropping all over the track. The gunner and the driver felt themselves getting wet. The driver tried to scramble to get out of the driver's compartment and knocked the gunner down. The floor had become slippery. In a matter of moments, flares hit the track and ignited it.

The track burst into flames. The driver and gunner flailed around inside, screaming as the flames engulfed them. The people inside the back of the track tried to get out and couldn't locate the hatch control. Everything started to ignite inside the track with everyone moving around and spreading the fuel and flames.

The gunner climbed up out of the turret hatch and over the side of the track where he fell to the ground. The driver was rolling around the floor of the track, trying to smother the flames, but it was futile as there was gas burning on the floor as well. One more person made it through the gunner's hatch. Three people didn't make it out of the track, the driver, a man, and a woman.

The flames licked higher and burst the rest of the balloons overhead that had not popped, dumping more gas on everyone.

Haliday had strung up some balloons filled with air and gas over this area. They were tied up in small bunches with fish hooks taped to the strings supporting them. A couple jerks on the fishing line caused them to burst. The gas dropped and he had then used a flare from the 37mm to ignite it. The rest was the brutal nature of fire and it took its course.

The track had been abandoned now and was completely engulfed in flames. A truck came flying up and two militia tried to help their friends. Three had succumbed to the flames and two were badly burned. Only the two outside the track had avoided the inferno.

The militia grabbed the injured and retreated, leaving the track to burn.

Chapter 24

Back near the airport, another alarm had sounded. Every person in the militia group responded and took up defensive positions. There was sporadic gunfire as they fired into the woods and surrounding buildings. No one knew what they were firing at—shadows, light dancing off windows, or just their imaginations.

Vehicles headed in all directions around the entire perimeter. People were then getting out and either lying prone and watching their area or taking cover behind their vehicles. It was a mix of adults and teens and all wore the same Russian camo.

The crowd had cleared out and was completely out of sight. More than half had gone home. About a dozen of the remaining members stayed behind by the feed store with Rob. About 15 minutes later, Haliday and Blake came up from the other direction on their bikes. They ditched them inside a truck well at the feed store.

Haliday walked up to Rob. "How'd you make out?"

"One guy got hit in the leg and old man Burton got shot in the back while he was running away," Rob reported. "He didn't make it. He owned the Burton Tire Shop. He didn't have any family, but we'll get him taken care of."

Haliday said, "It ain't over yet. I guarantee these guys are going to try and remain in charge; that or they are going to come after you."

They heard a vehicle coming down the street and watched as the truck pulled up to the main gate of the airport. After it entered, the gate stayed open, but four people stood there with rifles ready, sweeping the area. Another vehicle came up less than five minutes later. This continued for about another 30 minutes as all of the patrols had made it back to the HQ.

Haliday pulled out his binoculars and looked over at the compound. "Rob, these guys are bunkering down. There isn't going to be any chance of getting in there any time soon. Blake, take some notes."

Blake went and grabbed the notebook out of the saddle bag and came back.

"I count five quads, four four-wheelers, three motorcycles. I see fifteen trucks or Jeeps, about eight golf carts, and two deuce and halves. They must have fixed the tires on the one. I count over sixty people total. I'll assume if they have any younger kids other than the teens, they are shielded inside somewhere. I have no idea how many prisoners they have, if they are even still alive. Hell, I don't know how many others may be inside. They hid their numbers rather well. More recon is what I should have done," he admitted. "This sucks. I'm not sure what the hell they have altogether. That means they had at least a good sixty to start with if you subtract the ten – or was it eleven or twelve – we killed?"

Rob looked at him. "You guys took out that many?"

Roger continued, "I don't really know. Oh, that reminds me. About a half mile north along your wood line is going to be a kid tied up. He's hurt pretty badly; most likely broken ribs and bruised. You guys do what you want with him. There's a quad and some toys in your pole barn. Keep those. You might need them."

Haliday called the group, who was waiting with anticipation. They filled him in on the activity they encountered and he told them he would let them know what was going on when he and Blake got back. They would be coming in very soon.

He then told Rob about the militia vehicle. "You might want to see if you can go get it. It'll help you as well." He gave Rob a couple of frequencies. "Use the kid's ham; you can run it off the quad."

Rob said, "I can't thank you enough for all of this."

A few of the other guys still present thanked them. They were all huddling around the burn barrel in the parking lot of the feed store.

"If I could give you guy's any advice, this is what I would do." Haliday was just about to give them a little advice when one of the other men pointed down the street.

"I think we have company."

A side by side four-wheeler from the compound was pulling out and heading their way. It had a large white flag waving from it. They stopped out in the street just a short ways from the feed store.

The driver yelled out, "We want to talk to whoever is in charge!"

Haliday and Blake both stepped back and took aim. Haliday was scanning the area; he had that feeling. "Step back, Rob."

Rob stepped back, too.

Three men total were at the four-wheeler there. "Can we speak to who's in charge?" someone yelled.

One of Rob's friends said, "Hell, I'll go."

Haliday said, "No, don't go out there."

The guy went out anyway.

Haliday shook his head. "Rob, who is that guy?"

"His name is Jim; he always wants to be in charge and run things. If it's our fantasy football league or anything else not important, we just let him. He's kind of like Mr. Haney from *Green Acres*, always has a money-making scam going on, the next big business," Rob said. "That sort of thing."

Haliday looked around the whole area and backed up some more. "Back up guys, back up."

Most backed up, but a few just stood there. A couple of guys went over by the dumpster there and grabbed some rifles they had hidden. Haliday had specifically told them not to bring weapons to this rally. He wanted to avoid a massacre.

Jim talked to the men at the four-wheeler for a bit, then returned.

"Hey, Rob, one of them is Ernie," Jim told the group. "You know, the deputy."

"Yeah, I know him; he always hassles my boys about the scooter," Rob said.

"Well, listen here," Jim said. "They wanted to know who the leader was and I told them I was it. Told them I designated you to talk for us when we were at the gate. They want to make a truce. They said if we disband, they won't do anything to us."

"Bullshit," Rob said. "I don't trust them."

Jim spoke again. "They also wanted to know who these two were." He pointed at Haliday and Blake. "I told them they were my cousin and nephew from the suburbs."

Haliday spoke next. "Listen, Jim, I'm not sure you fully understand what's happening here."

Jim pointed at him. "Hey, you ain't from around here; I know these people."

Haliday said, "Oh you do, so you knew what they were prepping for and everything?"

"Well, no, but they are mostly good people," Jim said.

"Look, Jim, I'm telling you this is bad shit going down."

Jim wouldn't listen to reality. He told Haliday, "You don't know that. I think it's a good deal. We might be able to get something else out of it, too."

Another guy piped in. "Jim, I think this guy is legit. I mean he's gotta be Special Forces or something; look at the shit he's pulled."

"No, I'm not, nor would I portray myself to be," Haliday said. "I'm just a guy who took advantage of all the training I ever could. Practiced and honed those skills, read everything I could. Knowledge is key. Operators are a different breed; I know a few. I wish we had some right about now. I'm just a dirty fighter."

He spoke to the group. "Look, these guys are just buying time. They will come after everyone here. They won't stop. I guarantee they will not give up that food and supply stockpile without a fight. You all heard the stories of what they're doing."

Jim spoke. "Oh bullshit, I got this handled."

He walked back out to meet the men. A couple more people told him not to. Haliday looked around and motioned for Blake and Rob to back up a bit more.

Jim met the men at the four-wheeler and said, "Ernie, they don't trust you. But I think we can cut a deal here. Look, we'll all go home, but we gotta have something that shows good faith. Why don't you give us all some food to get by until we work out a deal on issuing the supplies?"

Ernie told him the supplies would be sold or traded, not just given out.

"Look, Ernie," Jim said, "I have to agree with these guys; you can't take this stuff and then sell it back to us. That ain't right. Now if that's going to be your final offer, then we can't accept that, you understand right?"

Ernie said, "I understand, but you don't, Jim. That's not the way it works now. We don't bargain with terrorists either."

"Ernie, we're not terrorists, just people from the community like you. You guys are acting like the terrorists here."

Ernie walked away for a minute and talked on his radio, then came back. "Jim, the only deal is you guys go home and don't pull stunts like this again. You're the leader, right?"

"I sure am, but we can't take that offer."

Haliday saw Ernie shift positions. Haliday yelled, "Everyone down!"

Jim never stood a chance as a bullet ripped through his chest. Haliday and everyone else took cover. Haliday tried to fire at the group, but too many of the towns people ran between him and the four-wheeler. A couple of the guys fired at the militia group and the militia fired back; striking another man who spun around and dropped his weapon as a round pierced his shoulder.

Haliday started yelling, "Get back! Get back!"

The militia had lured some of the guys out into the street and into the direct line of fire for their own sniper hidden from view. Ernie had merely confirmed the order and then set up Jim for the shot. Jim had confirmed he was the leader and they figured an eye for an eye was in order, even though the militia commander was just injured.

The militia ducked down behind their four-wheeler. They raised their rifles and fired some shots toward the crowd. Once in a while they hit a man in the back who was trying to run.

Haliday finally had a clear field of fire and started firing back at the militia group. The rest of Rob's friends who had been supporting him had managed to all get clear of the sniper.

Haliday counted three armed men plus Blake and himself. They hadn't hit any of the militia yet. There were quite a few rounds fired from the militia, but only one or two of the rallied men fired back in response. Two had bolt action hunting rifles and one had a Ruger Mini-14.

"Save your ammo!" Haliday yelled.

He crawled over to Blake. Rob was lying next to him. "Rob, take my rifle. I'm going to signal to Blake when I want you guys to fire."

Haliday crawled over to his bike in the truck well. He grabbed his M24 and went around to the back of the building. He climbed a metal ladder that was attached to the building and hoisted himself up on the roof.

He moved slowly toward the peak of the roof. It was a metal roof and very cold. He reached the peak and loaded his rifle and then quickly scanned the compound. "Where are you, damn it?" he muttered, searching.

Not finding the sniper, he searched some more and then spotted a bunch of sandbags up on the roof of the admin buildings.

He looked over at the gate and saw several people opening it. One of the deuces pulled out slowly. The thing was armored up with thin plate steel on one side and on the cab area, but Haliday couldn't see any gun ports or anything. The deuce pulled up behind the four-wheeler and nudged it a bit. The militia got alongside of the deuce, which started to back up slowly.

It was about halfway back to the airport. Haliday watched. *Damn good idea*, he had to admit. *Just roll up, use it as a shield, and roll back home.* He told Blake to hold fire.

One of the guys ran out toward the four-wheeler and jumped in. He started to drive it toward the feed store when he was hit by the militia fire. It just rolled toward the feed store. The man had been hit just below the base of the neck between his shoulders.

Haliday knew it was the moment. "Fire, Blake, fire!"

Everyone started firing toward the deuce. Haliday aimed at the center of the sandbags and fired a round. He fired again and still nothing. He fired two more shots and nothing. He looked through the scope. All he saw was the side of a shoe and a white Nike swoosh. He aimed at the swoosh and fired one last round. He scrambled down the roof and to the ladder.

He climbed down, wondering whether or not he hit the guy. The first four shots were wasted. The fifth shot was the only one that hit its mark. Whoever it was that was up there sniping them would only need to buy one shoe from now on. The whole lower half of his foot had exploded inside of his shoe. Haliday was surprised the guy didn't have boots on. Seeing the swoosh was pure luck.

Haliday called Blake and everyone over. He told one guy to watch the main street and another to watch the back street. "How many, Rob?"

Rob said, "Two dead and three wounded. You get the guy?"

"I have no idea. Rob, you think you can get that four-wheeler?"

"Are you crazy?" Rob asked.

"Rob, it's out of the kill zone for that sniper now. The rest of us will lay down suppressing fire toward the deuce, the admin building, and the rooftop where the sniper was. You guys need that thing. You really do."

Rob looked at him questionably. "You sure it'll be okay?"

"You want me to lie to you, Rob?"

"Roger, please do."

"It'll be fine, Rob," Haliday told him. "We got ya covered." He turned to the rest of the men. "Everyone make sure you're loaded up. You three fire on the barricades by the admin building," he directed. "Blake, you fire on the deuce. I'll fire on the rooftop where the sniper is. Go on three. One, two, three."

Rob ran over and pushed the guy out of four-wheeler while everyone laid down suppressing fire. He got it started and drove it back to the feed store. There was some return fire, but not much. It was a short 40-foot drive to safety.

Rob was shaking like crazy when he got to where Haliday was. "I never did anything like that before. But like you said, it worked out okay."

"Good thing, too," Haliday said. "I was starting to doubt myself."

Rob just looked at him.

"I'm kidding, Rob. Calculated risks; we take calculated risks. Now you guys have yourselves a four-wheeler."

Haliday walked over to the machine and looked around. He opened the little glove box. "A gas card, too. You get every gas can you guys have and you get them filled as soon as you can. Fill anything that will hold gas. Oh, from now on make sure you take firearms with you. Travel in pairs at a minimum." He opened up a case and there was an AR inside. He handed it to Rob. "Give this to someone who's gonna use it."

"What about me?" Rob asked.

"You have one at your house, from the kid, remember?"

"Oh yeah, the quad too."

"Keep this; give the quad to someone else." Haliday looked down at a metal box mounted in the back. He opened it up. It was loaded with 5.56 rounds. There had to be about 2,000 rounds there on stripper clips with some magazines and spoon loaders. Haliday said, "It looks like a lot, but it's not. Blake and I are going to reload our magazines and you can keep the rest. Again, there are several hundred back at your house, Rob."

Haliday and Blake reloaded their magazines.

Everyone stood around and started to ask a bunch of questions. Haliday stopped them all. "You guys know a doctor around here?"

They all kind of looked at each other.

One guy spoke up. "Yeah, my neighbor, but I don't speak to him. Why?"

"You have three wounded that need attention. Get them loaded in this four-wheeler and take them there. He won't like it, but he'll help, it's in their genetic make-up. Then meet back up with Rob."

They got the injured guys loaded up and the four-wheeler took off.

Rob said, "What if the patrols get them?"

"They are all in the compound right now, Rob. I don't think they are coming back out any time soon. Too many injured and dead to worry about and we just handed them their asses. We took hits, too, but we hit hard with those planes and that track," Haliday said, "Is there a place we can go talk?"

One of the guys named Andy spoke up. "We can go to my tooling shop just down the street."

"Okay, let's go," Haliday said.

They left the burn barrel burning and left to go to the man's tooling shop. The fire in the barrel might lead the militia into believing they were still near the feed store.

As they walked by the feed store, Haliday looked the place over. "We'll grab our bikes and meet you there," he said.

They met at the tooling shop. The guy unlocked the door; Haliday posted someone near the door to keep an eye out. "Before we start, what's in the bins and everything over there at the feed store?"

"Oh, it's corn, wheat, and soy. Same with the trucks in the lot." Rob said.

"Damn, that's a lot of food. I'm surprised they didn't take it."

Rob said, "Well, they tried, but no way to move it in bulk. They were trying to find a truck to tow the trailers."

Haliday was surprised the militia hadn't posted a guard there. "I thought it was a feed store," he said.

Rob said, "No, it's an elevator co-op, too."

"Let me make a quick call." Haliday then called his group.

Kevin came on the radio. "We're all fine. Uncle Roger, are you guys okay? We got worried. We heard them say they took out the leader and thought it was you. Dawn and Grandma are basket cases. Well, they were. Now that they heard your voice, they are okay, I guess."

"Yeah, we're fine," Haliday said. "I'm going to cover a few things with the people here. I want to help them get organized so they can handle the militia themselves now; give them some ideas and plans. We'll be there soon."

"Yeah, you keep saying that," Kevin responded.

"Okay, okay, we'll be there when we get there." Haliday hung up and gathered the guys around. "This shop have any welding tools?"

Andy, the shop owner, answered. "Yeah, we have plenty of tanks and torches. It'll be old school, but we can manage."

"You have sheet metal at all?" Haliday asked.

"Nothing more than quarter-inch."

"What about the other shops in the area?" Haliday asked. "There are a bunch of them I've noticed."

"I'm sure we have quite a bit if we put it all together," Andy said.

Roger looked at him. "That's good to know. Anyway, you guys have seen first-hand how the militia here is operating, right? So you all know first-hand, along with the rest, that those people are not here for the good of the community. You need to spread the word."

"How do we do that?" someone asked.

"Word of mouth, use markers, and write on the militia bulletins, whatever you can think of," Rob told him.

"Use the ham, search for others, pass the word about who they are and what they are about. Let them know you do not recognize their authority. Make sure they understand that. Make sure you tell them you are now in charge." Rob looked concerned. "Not like your pal Jim did; I mean that the community is in charge."

"I recommended to you guys already that you need to be teamed up when you are out. I also said that you need to be armed. That means everyone who can fire a weapon. Power in numbers. Carry as much ammo as you can. Avoid firefights, shoot and run to get the hell out of there. You get out of there as fast as possible. They'll win a straight-up firefight.

"The gas stations are important. You need to lock them all down and let the owners know what's going on. That gas is a precious commodity. You might want to think about treating as much of it as you can. Any stabilizer you can find you should use. Don't let them get that either. Park a car over the tank access and take the wheels off; it's hard to move it that way," he told them.

"Save any canned food for last. Eat what's fresh first. Use that grain. Hit up the library and check for cookbooks. Same with auto repair manuals, electrical repair—hell, anything you think you might need. Conserve your wood; burn it for warmth, not comfort. There's a difference. Only burn enough to keep the edge off the cold. Use clothing and blankets to keep warm.

"Think about teaming up in households. It'll help save wood and the safety factor is worth it alone. Make sure the houses are secured; keep doors locked, windows secured—all that good stuff. I can't tell you enough how important it is. Remember safety and security at all times and in all locations.

"If you guys plan to hunt, try to keep it reasonable. I mean, don't hunt to eat meat every day. You can overhunt. If you all go out and hunt everything in sight, within a few weeks it'll be impossible to find game. Ration control is your friend. You'll be surprised at how little you need to eat. Keep a balance of protein and carbs though. Think about crops next year. That's all you guys do around here is farm and fish, right?

"I could go on and on, but it would take weeks. What I will do is teach you some of the tricks I used here and some new ones as well. You have to think guerilla warfare. If you can't work it out with them and you go on the offensive, you need to go primal on them. You've seen how well it works."

Haliday walked out to his bike and brought in a star jack. "These are also known as caltrops. I'll leave this one with you. If you are being followed by bad guys, you toss a few dozen of these behind you and they'll flatten tires. Make as many as you can. Keep them on every vehicle you use.

"Everyone here knows what stop sticks are, right?"

Everyone nodded.

"The cops use them. Well, here's a poor man's version. You take plate steel and cut it in strips. The longer the better. Make them six inches wide. Use a torch and cut some very sharp Vs into the middle. Three inches on each side. Bend those up and sharpen the edges and point. Hide them under leaves, loose dirt, lay them down as needed, you get the idea.

"Don't try to up-armor your vehicles; the weight will kill them. But you can double up this plate steel and make some firing portals. If you build a plate that's thirty inches wide and eighteen inches tall with a slot cut in it, when you are lying down prone behind it, it'll provide cover—except from snipers who take the high ground. But they can't be moved easily because of the weight, so be careful how you use them.

"You can take some peppers, grind them down, mix in some boiling water and let it cool. Add oil, a touch of gas, and use it in balloons, squirt guns, water extinguishers or whatever will spray or spread it. Improvised pepper spray. The stores around here might have some they usually sell for key chains.

"Bug spray and flammables can make some nice little flame throwers. Light it with a match or lighter and spray away. If you feel giddy enough you can tape a candle to the can and light it. Just move slowly so the flame doesn't go out. You guys have to think outside of the box here on everything. I'll try to make contact and give you more ideas."

Rob walked over to him. He extended his hand. "I don't who the hell you are, but thank you very much. I hope I speak for everyone here."

Everyone thanked Haliday and Blake.

"Any parting words of wisdom?" Rob asked.

"Bury your dead, and honor them with the freedom the Constitution gives us."

Haliday and Blake peered outside. They walked over to their bikes and climbed on. A quick wave goodbye and they were on their way.

The streets were all empty. No one was out. They barely noticed any candles burning anywhere as they rode along.

About 45 minutes later they called on the radio.

"Open the doors," Haliday said. "Stand by. We're home."

They put the bikes in the pole barn and walked by the horses' stalls. Haliday paused to say hello; they knew him well. They locked up the pole barn with the help of Kevin and went to the house. They walked in and were greeted with hugs from everyone; even Blake who had found a new family. A lot of tears of joy streamed down their faces.

Haliday walked over to Blake. He gave him a handshake and a quick shoulder hug. "Damn good job, kid, I'm proud of you." Haliday looked around. "No offense anyone, but we'll have plenty of time for stories in the morning. I'm going to bed. Blake, there's a bunk up there for you, too."

Blake opted to stay downstairs for a while.

Haliday went upstairs and passed out. He slept for 12 hours straight.

Chapter 25

When Haliday woke up he felt the surface beside him and looked around, half expecting to be in the woods. He swung his feet off the bed and went to stand up and hit his head on the ceiling. He would have to get used to this. The bunk area of the house was basically a big loft that skirted the perimeter of the house. He looked down and saw Max and Romeo looking at him. "What's going on, furballs?"

He walked down the spiral steps into the common area of the house. "I need coffee."

Dawn brought him a cup, which was unusual. She hated the stuff; even the smell was disgusting to her.

He took a long sip. "Oh man, nice hot coffee and nice warm house."

She looked at him. "You stink."

He raised an armpit and whiffed. "Just a little sweet aroma to this hunk of man-candy. That's all," he said.

"Oh boy. Okay," she said, "coffee then shower."

He sat at the large table and looked around. He'd never really expected to use this place for what his group built it for. It was really just a large cabin they had built and used occasionally in the summers to get out of the city. It was close enough to take a long drive into the cities for shopping and entertainment, but far enough away to avoid crowds of people.

The cabin was built according to plans, which he had had a small firm draw up; had to submit plans to the county for approval or he wouldn't have bothered. Of course they had no idea of the modifications he would make during the entire construction process. Lack of inspectors and the distances they traveled made it easy. They would come out and inspect prior to any particular phase, and then again after it was done. They never showed up unannounced.

The land was roughly 60 acres and just less than half backed up to a large creek and woods. Plenty of water and enough wooded land for hunting. The rest was all flat land for crops. He leased the farming rights out to a farmer who planted crops and harvested them. This helped to pay the taxes and to build the new cabin. During the year they were building the cabin, they hadn't let anyone plant on the land.

There was nothing wrong with the old house that was there except it was just not suitable for what they wanted. They tore it down and left up a pole barn and another smaller outbuilding. They built the cabin to the specs outlined and did a lot of the work themselves. They used a wide variety of different contractors for other parts. The locals just figured he was cheap and looking to save a buck. Security was the reason. No single one contractor knew too much about the place. The locals would know very little about the place.

Four large shipping containers of building materials had been brought in. They sat there during the construction process and disappeared during the process. First up was a new foundation. The foundation would accommodate the cabin which was 30-by-40 feet. A complete, extra deep basement was put under the cabin. Each window was ported to be used as a firing position if needed, armored with quarter-inch steel plate around the small windows.

On two sides of the foundation he had put down one of the containers. The cinderblock walls had been constructed so that he could use a concrete saw and cut access into them after the final inspection was made. He had steel framework hidden in the walls for door jambs. The containers had been reinforced with I-beam steel inside and only buried a foot under the ground. They had been completely rubberized outside for waterproofing. He then built the doors to mate-up properly.

The cabin itself had an open floor plan. Toward the back was a large bathroom and toiletry closet on one side and a large laundry room and linen storage on the other. In front of that was a large kitchen area and massive dining table with bench seats on one side and chairs around the other sides. In between was a spiral staircase with a good old-fashioned fireman pole next to it.

For the bathroom, outside of the cabin he had a rain catch for a large 250-gallon water tank that was elevated, and it supplied water strictly for the toilet. The tank was black to attract sunlight and he used small solar-powered bubblers to prevent freezing in the winter time.

The front of the cabin was completely open as well. They had chairs, couches, and coffee tables spread around for seating and there was a fireplace. There hadn't been any sense in wasting the space on bedrooms. If they had to, they could use the basement to create space for privacy.

When you looked up at the second floor, it was almost completely open. With the cabin being 30-by-40 and an A-frame style roof, the sides had high pitches. You could walk around the entire upstairs close to the opening, which was railed off for safety. The opening was almost 10-by-30. This loft space had bunks galore spread out with under-bed storage and small dressers. There were thin panel walls between bunk areas and curtains toward the fronts. It looked like a large hunting lodge.

The basement was left open as a recreation area, complete with pool table, dart board, card table, bubble hockey, couch and chairs, small library, and games. They even had a space for a TV and entertainment system if it worked. He wouldn't know yet. It was buried underground in a Faraday Cage along with a few other items, with a grounding rod pounded deep into the ground.

Everything they would need was there. They would be able to farm the land, hunt if the game population wasn't decimated, and not too far from the lake's shores to put a small boat in and do some fishing. They had plenty of firewood stored already and access to as much as they needed. It had been a labor of love and now a labor of sustaining their lives.

They had compiled enough food stores to sustain 20 people for two and a half years on normal diets. They could ration and extend this if they needed to. This didn't include any farming, hunting or fishing or what they'd brought with them. That would all be extra. They'd had the other two containers buried as well. One served as a hidden cache and the other as a storage unit for gas, kerosene, diesel, and whatever else they put in there.

The cabin was built using eight-inch logs and they up-armored the bottom 30 inches inside with 3/16th-inch steel plate. It would stop all 5.56 rounds and most 7.62. The areas around the windows were even more heavily armored to provide more protection as gun ports. This was all covered with wood paneling. The doors were all steel and there were only two of them. Haliday hadn't had the money to put ballistic glass in.

The doors to the pole barn and outbuilding had all been re-enforced to keep them as secure as possible. Tools, the trucks, trailers and an old tractor were all kept out there with the two horse stalls. They would move the trailers out shortly to make more space. Around the property he had a few more upgrades to help keep them safe.

The shower felt good on Haliday's weary body. The water wasn't hot, but was warm enough. He had plumbed a coil around the wood burner that ran the course of the hot water pipes normally supplied by the hot water heater, which no longer worked. The coil worked just fine and made it easier to boil water. The cabin was on a well pump and septic system which operated okay, too.

Kayla had worked up a watch schedule which was posted on a big dry erase board near the kitchen. It was the same with chores, wood retrieval, cleaning, laundry, cooking, and whatever else needed to be done.

Haliday walked out after getting dressed. "Can I have more coffee, please?"

Bev put the percolator on.

Haliday walked over to the desk with the radio. He checked in with Mike and Linda. "How you guys doing?"

Mike said, "We're doing fine, Rambo."

That struck a bad chord with Haliday. "Not in the mood, Mike. Just doing what I hope any other American would do—that which was necessary to keep order in a place that didn't have any. You guys going to be set for a while?"

"Yeah, we'll be fine, sorry. I got a deer and we plan to use that up first."

"Okay, talk to you later," Haliday said. He changed the frequency and called Rob. There wasn't any answer. He decided he would call back later. He looked down at a note on the desk. "Oh yeah. Alan." He called on the frequency that Kayla had written down.

There came an answer. It was typical of a ham operator. Call sign and professional.

Haliday apologized for not knowing the proper protocol and such.

The man said, "No problem, I understand."

"If you have a chance, and Alan Haliday asks, can you get him on for me?" Haliday asked.

"Sure, I'll leave a note up for him. I put a message board up for folks," replied the ham operator.

"Hey, my name is Roger by the way; can I ask a few questions?"

"Yes, sir, how can I help you?" came the response.

"You hear anything about the military or feds doing anything?"

"I only know what you've heard," the man said. "They are locked down on the bases, they have had a lot of deserters, and they don't plan on doing anything."

"What do you mean?" Haliday asked.

"Just like I said, they don't plan on doing anything any time soon. That's the rumor."

While it didn't surprise him, Haliday still thought it was odd. "What's going on around you?" Haliday asked.

"Detroit."

Haliday asked, "What do you mean, *Detroit?*"

The guy said, "The city itself is pretty much a wasteland and the suburbs have become like Detroit itself. Looters, robberies, people shooting each other...it's really bad. You can't leave your house and you have to be careful. Hearing that some gangs are on the move. People aren't putting up with a lot though."

"I appreciate the info. Mind if I add you to my friends list or whatever it's called?"

The man laughed. "Yeah, go ahead. I'm Adam, by the way."

"Thank you again, Adam; it's been a pleasure. I'll be talking to you again soon." Haliday sat back and tried Rob again. Still no answer at all. He flipped to the militia freq. This was interesting indeed.

It sounded like they were just attacked by Al Qaida themselves. "This is the Bad Axe Minute Men. Last night we were provoked by a group of terrorists. These terrorists have turned members of our community against us. They attacked us when we were openly attempting a ceasefire."

"Bullshit," Haliday mumbled under his breath, along with some more choice words. *Our community? Oh, that was good. These guys are playing the psychological warfare game quite well.* He couldn't wait to hear what else they were saying. *These guys are playing the victim role really well, too.*

He heard a familiar voice.

"These are all lies people. We united to save our community. The militia stole food, fuel, and supplies from us. They want to sell it back to us while they keep what they want for themselves. They murdered Jim Simmons last night in cold blood; he was unarmed."

Haliday smiled; a propaganda war. The sad thing was this could lead to a civil war here within this little part of the state.

"We had a kid who belonged to them. When we contacted them to turn him over, they set up an ambush and killed the two guys who were taking him back to their compound."

Haliday was taken aback at this. He wished he would have told them how to handle the turnover. *How the hell did that happen?* he wondered.

The barbed bantering continued , back and forth every so often.

Haliday flipped over to Rob's frequency. "Rob, you there?"

"Yeah, I'm here. They shot two more guys."

"I heard. Sorry to hear that. You didn't offer to trade the kid for supplies did you?"

"No, we told them it was a straight up return," Rob said. "We just wanted him out of our hair. The guys were walking him down the street toward the compound and the militia came out from the bushes and shot them."

"I'm sorry to hear that. Listen, you guys need to get busy with what we talked about. You get everyone you can on board. You'll get those who will be on your side, those who will join you if they think you are winning, and those who will care less. You'll also have some against you. I know it's only been a little more than half a day, but time is important.

"Rob, listen up. Someone needs to move into that feed store or co-op, whatever you call it. Fortify the hell out of it. Don't let those guys get it. See if the guy with the tooling shop can build some boxes to cover the pintle's on those trailers so they can't be towed away. I'll check in on you later this evening, but you call if anything major goes down. I suspect they're still licking their wounds."

In another couple of hours, it would be getting dark again. He needed to get out and check a few things. He went into the pole barn and got into the Ranger. He and Kevin took a quick ride around the property boundary. It was simple fencing in most places. He drove toward the west property line and checked the woods, scribbling some notes on some paper as they went.

He followed the property line around and kept making notes. When he got up to the front of the lot he looked across the street at the neighbors. He had noticed the curtains pulled aside in one of the windows. He looked around some more not to make it obvious he saw them, but he made a mental note.

Someone was watching them.

They drove back up to the pole barn. Haliday checked the vehicles. He walked over and looked at his old Jeep. He jumped in and started it up—just like Kayla said; ran like a champ. He looked up and saw Dawn and Diana bringing the horses in for the night. They put some hay in the stalls for them. Each fall they had a large round bale delivered just as a prep.

Haliday checked the small 12 foot aluminum row boat hanging over the Jeep. That should be fine; oars were EMP-proof. He walked over to an old outboard motor from the '70s. It was a simple engine, so it, too, should work okay, and if not, no big deal.

Last but not least, the tractor. If it didn't work, the horses would. They secured everything and went back to the house.

Haliday could smell the cooking. "What are we having for dinner?"

Sarah said, "Burritos."

Karen and Bev were sitting there making tortillas and Sarah was making the beans and the beef.

"Sounds good to me." He raised his voice slightly. "Everyone else please gather around; we have some things we need to do in the next couple of days, and we may have a problem."

Everyone gathered around, sitting at the table or standing nearby.

"We need to get the concertina wire put in place. We also need to put out the foot spikes," he said. These were much like the stop sticks he had described, only they were just a couple inches wide and had slivers from the edge cut and bent upwards, then sharpened. These also had barbs cut into them to tear flesh as they were pulled out. They were easier to hide in tall grass and bury under loose dirt. You'd spot them in the daylight, but not at night.

"We also need to make sure we clean out the holes and have them ready to go." Near the front of the house by the corners he had built some decorative plantings; small, curved landscape walls, but when you took the grass off and removed the cover, there was a concrete culvert pipe sunk into the ground.

These were just like the ones he had remembered using multiple times in basic training at the rifle range; pea gravel on the bottom and sandbags in each to adjust the height of the shooter.

These would let two gunners provide much needed coverage to the front of the house and the sides as well. He had installed planters around the whole area made of double rows of landscape bricks stacked two and three high in places. A few spots of fieldstone were built up and holding garden sculptures.

The holes near the back of the house need to be cleaned out and readied as well. These appeared to be old tractor tires used as sandboxes. Those four holes would provide coverage for all four sides of the house.

Haliday continued on with a few other tasks to increase the security and make it a more formidable structure to defend.

At the top of the house was a large decorative square with a weather vane on top. This was actually a six-by-six fortified hide. One man with a rifle was protected by two rows of wooden beams with 3/16-inch sheet metal sandwiched between them. The roof was sloped, but under the shingles were some quarter-inch sheet metal. Might not be perfect, but it would work. He called it the crow's nest.

He looked at everyone. "The militia might have a spotter across the road. You guys didn't notice?"

"No, not really. Just thought it was a nosy neighbor," David said.

"That's what I thought, too." Nobody gave it much thought except him. He told them what he thought. "After watching them peek out through the window, I was turning around when I spotted a whip antenna on the chimney. Not sure how long it's been there, but with the extra patrols around here it makes sense now. With you guys staying put inside, I don't blame anyone for missing it; hell, I almost did myself. I'm not sure if they heard or saw the bikes come in last night.

"I'm going to go over there tomorrow with a couple of you and we'll introduce ourselves. See what they are up to. Plant a little propaganda ourselves. However, we need to prepare for a fight, just in case. I would say we have three or four days before that happens. It might not. I might be grasping at straws. But, I doubt it. If they know where to find me, they will come on strong."

Everyone just kind of looked at each other.

Rich asked him, "Are you sure?"

"Yeah, Dad, I'm sure."

Dinner was served up soon afterwards, but not a lot of people were really hungry. Almost half of the food was put away for later. Normally it would have all been gone. They were good at guessing how much to make so nothing went to waste.

Haliday walked over and grabbed a glass and tossed some ice in it. The idea of not having gas for the generator one day or a cold fridge really ticked him off. He had a solar array and battery bank, but that would push it even if operating nothing but the fridge and a few lights. He poured himself a couple fingers of Jack Daniels, sat at the desk, and listened to the radio and took more notes. He told Mike what was going on, then checked in with Rob.

Rob told him he had recruited a few more families. Once word spread, they knew who to believe. There were still doubters, and there were still those believing the militia, but the tide was turning. Not bad for a day's work. Rob told him they got the truck from the parking lot fiasco and put tires on it. He also said they managed to round up some quads and a couple of bikes. They were working on a couple other vehicles, but weren't sure.

The kicker was Brady's Hunting Center. Brady had taken everything and locked it up tight. He had steel bars over his windows and no one was getting in. His house was attached to the back of the store. He was willing to fork over anything he had which would be of use.

Bows, crossbows, a lot of bolt action rifles, but he also had close to 12 semi-autos, AR and AK variants. Years ago he had bought a couple dozen SKSs and still had almost 20. They weren't big sellers in the area. To round it off, he had about a dozen shotguns and plenty of ammunition for everything.

"Rob," Haliday said, "you need to make him your best friend. Talk to you tomorrow."

Haliday pulled his shift on watch that evening. It was 0200 hours when he stepped outside for a minute. It was colder outside tonight. He had his balaclava folded up into a watch cap configuration and pulled it down. He had told Diana that he'd be back in a few minutes.

He walked over to the small outbuilding, which was really just an old hand-built shed maybe 10-by-12. He checked it out and found that the single door was secure.

He started to walk over by the pole barn and paused. He bent down to tie his shoe and mumbled aloud. "Damn shoestring; had to break on me now, huh?"

He rose to his feet and walked back to the house and went inside. He told Diana they had a guest outside. Whoever it was had tried to hide behind the pole barn. He noticed their cloud of breath in the cold air. He'd used the shoestring excuse to go back in the house.

He went over to the laundry room and walked inside. Next to the window was a homemade periscope. He had found plans online, but he didn't like them, so he had made his own. He took a six-inch PVC pipe, notched out the top and bottom, then played with mirror angles until he got them set at 45 degrees and glued them in place with Gorilla Glue. He used it to look out through the window.

The person was by the pole barn.

He saw a single figure, small in stature. He wasn't professional, nor was he very careful about his movements.

Haliday watched him try and peek in the pole barn windows, but he had to strain to reach them. He moved off toward the woods. Haliday went to another window and glanced out.

Diana asked him if he wanted her to sound the alarm.

"No, that's okay. It's just one person. The neighbor across the street. I just watched him go back over there."

He walked over to the radio and flipped frequencies. There it was. He sat there and listened.

The speaker said, "I couldn't stay long. Someone came outside but he didn't see me. I thought he would be coming back so I left. I'm sure it's the people you are looking for. I think I saw some vehicles but I'm sure I saw the motorcycles, too." It was a woman's voice.

"Okay," said a man. "Can you try and confirm, then let us know?"

"Okay, I'll go back tonight."

"Thank you," the man said.

Haliday wanted to go across the street and slit her throat, but knew better. They needed a little more time to prepare. In the morning he'd go over there and pump her for information. He knew she was married, but couldn't remember if she was happily married or not. Might have to play spouse against spouse.

When 0300 hours came Haliday woke their reliefs and briefed them. "Wake me at 0800 hours," Haliday said. "I want an early breakfast and a trip across the street."

Chapter 26

After breakfast, Haliday put on some jeans and a polo shirt and grabbed a regular winter jacket. He took Rich and Kayla with him across the street. Psyops—family was always a good bet in order to humanize a situation. Just the nice neighbors coming over to say hello. He still took his .40 and Kayla and Rich had 9mms.

They walked up to the house across the road. Haliday did a quick survey of the property. He kept a hand in the pocket of his jacket with his finger on the gun's trigger guard.

None of their vehicles that he saw seemed to be running. Firewood stacked up in the back, but that was normal out there. Pretty plain; nothing really stood out at all. The only thing was some tire tracks in the driveway that looked a couple days old and the antenna on the chimney. They walked up on the porch and knocked on the door.

A man, early forties, 6'2, 180 pounds with short brown hair came to the door. "Can I help you?"

"Hi, my name is Roger, this is my dad, Rich, and my daughter Kayla. We have the place across the street."

"What is it I can help you with, Roger?" the man asked.

"We just wanted to introduce ourselves. We never really met; just waved across the fields once in a while. We're here for a while and I wanted you to know it was just us."

The man's wife came to the door. She looked tired and was dressed, but looked like she'd slept in her clothes. She was a short woman, 5' tall, weighing 100 pounds, with shoulder length brown hair. "Who you talking to, honey?" she asked.

"Oh, the folks from across the street," her husband said.

She looked the three of them up and down and just said one word. "Hi."

"Hello, ma'am, nice to meet you," Haliday said.

She just stood there.

Haliday repeated the introductions.

There was an awkward pause and Haliday was about to just say goodbye and leave.

The woman said, "Where you guys from? How long you staying? Who else do you have up here?" It was three quick questions.

Haliday recognized her voice from the radio. He answered her questions, but fairly generically in nature. "The suburbs. A few weeks until things settle down in the city, I suppose. Couple others with us," he answered curtly.

"You have a lot of people over there," she said.

"Well, my family is all. They want to be safe, too," Haliday replied.

"Yeah, I guess family being safe is important," she said.

It was Haliday's turn to ask some questions. "Is it just you two here? Don't you have a daughter?"

"She's at her boyfriend's for a while," she said.

Haliday played coy, "Oh, okay, just remembered seeing her around before. Well, anyway, we're going to get going. Nice meeting you. We're across the street, and if you need anything, let us know."

"You, too. We're fine." Her answers were just as quick and almost rude. She walked away.

Her husband looked at Haliday and shrugged his shoulders. He then opened the door some more and extended his hand. "I'm sorry, I'm Lance." He shook everyone's hands. "Take it easy."

Haliday nodded. "See ya around, Lance."

Haliday's group turned and walked back to their house.

"That was weird, Dad," Kayla said.

"I agree with Kayla, Roger," Rich added. "That lady is a little bit off."

"I would expect so," Haliday said.

Rich said, "Why is that?"

Haliday said, "When the husband opened the door to shake hands, there was a picture on the end table."

"Of what, or of whom?" asked Rich.

Haliday said, "Her daughter and her daughter's boyfriend."

"So what's that mean?"

"They were standing next to a quad, wearing Russian camo. I believe I met him the other night," said Haliday.

As soon as they walked into the house Haliday called another meeting. "The lady across the street is watching our every move. I don't know what the husband is all about. I don't think he cares. I'm not sure he even knows what's really going on. But she is definitely buying into the BS the militia offers because Blakey-boy here tried to kill her daughter's boyfriend the other night."

Blake said, "Huh?"

"Yeah, the kid on the quad," Haliday said. Everyone looked at Blake with a curious look. Haliday ended the meeting and went over to the ham radio. He sat down at the radio and called Rob. "Rob, has there been any movement from the militia?"

"No, none at all that we've seen. They haven't left the airport at all," Rob said.

"Can we meet?"

"Sure, when and where?"

"Your house. I'm on my way. Don't panic; I'm bringing friends."

Haliday called Blake, Randy, and Dawn over. "Get your gear together—firearms only. Dress warm, too. Grab me a welfare bucket, meet me in the pole barn please."

The three met Haliday in the pole barn. He went over to his Jeep and started it up. This was a 1982 CJ7 with soft top. He had redone the tub on it and fixed the rust. Instead of going with a lift kit, he actually lowered it an inch. He added 200 pounds of skid plating underneath for added weight. This was to lower the center of gravity and help prevent rollovers in fast or tight turns.

He added roll cage protection and hand holds. The rear seat was a special touch. It could flip over and face backwards. The vehicle was painted flat black; everything on it, bumpers, rims, everything. He didn't have the top and didn't care to worry about that. Canvas was useless for anything but wind and water protection. He folded the windshield down.

They pulled out onto the road and headed south. Haliday went east at the next road and then north at the next one after that. He did this to throw off the neighbor who was most likely watching them. They were at Rob's place in 35 minutes.

They pulled in and he angled the Jeep for a quick, easy escape, but he didn't expect this to be the case. He walked up to Rob, who was waiting. They shook hands and went into his pole barn where he had set up an office.

Randy stood guard with one of Rob's sons. The kid was 16 actually and his younger brother was 15. Randy called the younger son over. He pulled the bucket out of the Jeep.

"Go put this in your house. Do not tell anyone about it."

"Is it going to blow up?" the kid asked.

Randy looked at him funny. The kid had a point. Haliday's little surprises had become well known. "No, it's not. It's for you guys after we leave, but do not tell anyone except your mom and dad."

In a bid to keep Rob on his side, Haliday had brought him a welfare bucket. He didn't like the idea, but it was a needed evil. Feed the animals and they won't go away is what he always said. He needed a couple of friends right now however and Rob was footing the bill nicely.

Rob had the wood burner going. It was nice and warm. He had a map of the area up as well. Haliday noticed another man sitting at the table with Rob. Haliday walked over to them.

"Nice map, Rob," Haliday said. "Where'd ya get it?"

"My store. I used to sell them to the tourists. Want to buy one?"

Haliday flipped him off.

"Nice to see you, too," Rob said. They both laughed.

"Well, we're here on business." He looked at a guy next to Rob. "I don't think we met. I'm Roger."

"Everyone calls me Brad," the man said.

"Brad?"

"Yeah, it's Bradley Brady."

"Ah, the hunting shop owner," Haliday said.

"Yes, sir. I'm helping Rob out with planning and everything."

"You have any info on the militia? Anything at all?"

"We have a couple guys watching them at the compound. Writing down everything they do, how many people we think they have, vehicles, the same thing you did basically," Brad relayed. "The most accurate info we have is a body count. They have thirty-one adult males, twenty-five adult females, ten male teenagers, twelve female teenagers, around eight younger boys, and maybe five younger girls. Give or take a few people, I think."

"Damn, seventy-eight to eighty fight-capable people? That sucks, I underestimated their troop strength," Haliday said. "One of them is my neighbor's daughter; the girlfriend of the kid you guys cut loose."

Rob looked down at the table.

"Sorry, sore subject, huh?" Haliday said.

"Yeah, we should have hung that kid," Rob replied.

"We had that talk, Rob," Haliday reminded. "Rules of engagement, the law; but it's a thin line here and hard to interpret. Any more people signed up with you?"

Rob said, "We have a good sixty we can count on. Not enough though. Not yet. I promised my wife the boys wouldn't leave the house, though."

"Fair enough Rob, keep making your rounds and recruiting. Spread the word. What about the prisoners?" Haliday asked.

Rob looked at him and said, "What do you mean?"

Then Rob remembered, he said, "Oh yeah, the people in the building next to their barracks or housing units or whatever the hell they call them. We haven't seen anyone go in there at all. I'll double-check but I'm pretty certain."

"Rob, they have prisoners in there," Haliday said. "If no one is going in there they are either dead or they aren't feeding them."

Rob asked him what he was supposed to do about the prisoners.

Haliday said, "Nothing right now. They'll have to wait it out until you guys get in there."

"What do you mean *get in there?*" asked Rob.

"Rob, you guys will have to go in there," said Haliday.

Rob said, "We don't have the people for that. There are just too many."

Haliday looked at him squarely. "You can take half. That's all you'll have to do. The other half are going to come gunning for me. So, let's lay down the plan. It'll have to be activated at a moment's notice. You will have to be ready at all times."

Rob and Brad both looked at him. Brad said, "You're kidding, right?"

Haliday said, "No, not at all. Listen, you guys have the advantage."

Rob asked him, "How the hell do we have the advantage? You're defending your house; we have to attack an airport."

Haliday spoke calmly and almost condescending. "Exactly my point, guys. We are pinned down and you guys have the whole town to run away to. Not to mention, you have that same town to use to your advantage."

"I just don't know about this," said Rob.

Haliday leaned back in his chair. "Hell, guys, what do you want me to say here? You want me to tell you that this is all going to be hugs and bunnies? We invite them out for s'mores and hot cocoa? It isn't going to work that way. Rob, you have to know after watching them gun down Jim that they are going to do whatever they want.

"That propaganda they are spitting out is a ruse to buy them some time. They need time so that they can counterattack. That means me and my group, and you guys too. Don't think for a minute that they are going to let you all walk away like it was a bad family reunion and they'll see you next year hoping things changed. They can't have you guys out there rebelling against them. You want ten of them knocking on your door?"

"Roger is right, Rob," Brad said. "We need to get this handled now before winter sets in or we ain't gonna make it." *Finally*, Haliday thought, *someone is getting it.*

Brad said, "We have about five to six weeks before it's too cold to really move around, and plus we have to think about food and water."

Haliday told him, "That's my point exactly, and they know that too. They'll let you wait and they'll let you waste away while you're waiting."

Haliday stood up and stretched. They had been there for almost four hours, but they covered a lot of information and it was time to go. He had to get back and make sure things were getting done at the house. They all shook hands and wished each other luck.

Haliday and his group went back to the house and Rob and Brad started making their rounds and getting their plans in order.

When they got back to the house, they saw that everyone was working. Haliday noticed that someone was in the crow's nest. It looked like it was Kayla. Next to him, she was the best shot out of the group. *Ahh, best to get that done quickly, too,* he thought. He would be setting up a small range and conducting some rapid courses on marksmanship, fields of fire, and such.

Kevin walked over to Haliday in the yard. "Uncle Roger, the wicked witch of the south came out by the road. She leaned up against her fence and sat there and watched us while she drank coffee. She had to have been out here for a good three hours total. What we would do, though, is block areas with the ranger and smaller utility trailer to hide what we were doing."

No sooner had he finished telling him that when Haliday thought he noticed her standing in the window of her house. Haliday said, "She knows we're on to her."

The grass was long and hid the foot spikes quite well. The group had placed them strategically around each of the firing positions. They had used them in areas around the wood line as well, anywhere there was a path. The group knew that if they ran to the woods not to use the paths. They also knew that once they got out of the firing positions, there was a specific route to take. These were meant for close proximity deterrents.

They had constructed it by unrolling concertina wire and placing it around the entryways and windows of all the buildings. The firing positions had been cleared out and prepped as well. Ammo loads were placed in each one. Each position had a person assigned to it with a chart for firing, and, more importantly, a final protective fire. If everyone fired at their designated final protective line, in theory the area could not be breached.

It was possible that they could actually get everyone inside and fight from inside if it came down to that. It was not optimal to do that was only considered a last resort. That was why the concertina was placed around the window areas and entryways, to keep people in the line of sight and within firing reach.

Kayla came down from the crow's nest and joined Haliday in the yard. "How did it go, Dad?"

"As well as it could have gone. I just hope they come through on their end if it comes down to that," Haliday answered.

"You mean when, Dad, *when*."

"Yeah, when. Kayla, we need to get four five-gallon buckets of water into the crow's nest. We can dump them on the roof in case of fire. I also want small buckets of water spread out in the house as well as the fire extinguishers."

Everyone outside turned toward the road. They heard a vehicle approaching. Kayla raised her rifle up. Kevin came running with his as well. Randy already had his shotgun ready.

Haliday dropped to one knee, raised his rifle up and watched through the scope. The dust pile on the road was growing closer. "Take cover, everyone, take cover."

Haliday watched as everyone scrambled. He peered through the scope and then stood up. "Open the gates; open the front gate."

Diana and Dawn ran over and opened up the gate. A beat up old green Datsun pickup truck turned into the drive.

"Go get Grandma and Grandpa, quick!" Haliday said.

Kayla ran inside to get them.

Haliday walked over to the truck. Bev and Rich came out and headed toward the old truck, too. David came over as well. He recognized the faces inside the truck. Bev hugged her son Alan and his family.

"Damn, Brother, I never thought I'd see you guys again," said Alan.

Haliday said, "I'm glad you're here."

"Me, too. How is everything?" Alan asked.

"Well, ugly-ass truck or not, we need the extra trigger men. We have a world of hurt coming down on us soon. That's what we're getting ready for. Come inside and rest. I'll explain it all," Haliday told him. "Randy, please have everyone empty this truck out and get the gear inside. Put the truck in the pole barn." Haliday asked Alan, "Where did you find that green turd?"

Alan told him the story as they went inside the house. "Nancy traded her wedding ring for it. We went over to the auction yard and the owner was there with his son selling all kinds of parts from old cars. This was sitting there with a few other older cars.

I asked him how much he wanted for it. I offered him my Breitling watch, but he said no. He said he'd take Nancy's ring in trade. She took it off and said 'If it starts, it's yours.' With a little starting fluid it started right up.

"We went back to the house and grabbed what we could. I opened the safe and grabbed what was in there and then dug out my shotgun and .308. They didn't find that."

"Who didn't find it?" Haliday asked.

"The house was broken into and trashed," Alan said. "They even took the Harleys. They didn't find the safe or guns though, only things we had hidden the right way. I traded for some gas cans and gas and we drove straight here."

"How bad is it down there, Alan?"

"The place is out of control. People have realized the power isn't coming on anytime soon and the government isn't coming to help anytime soon either. There are gangs trying to form, but people aren't putting up with that and shooting them cold as they go around trying to loot and things. On the other hand, I heard some areas are gang controlled, with the likes of the existing city of Detroit gangs."

Haliday had to take the shot at the city. "Oh, the city council is in session?"

Alan laughed.

"You're here. You're safe. That's what counts. We have a gang of our own we are dealing with. They call themselves a militia, but that's not the case. They intend to run the area." Haliday asked Sarah to get some coffee and snacks ready. She and Karen took care of this.

Haliday filled them in on what has been happening. "We have eyes on their compound; we have about an hour after we're told they are moving out before they get here."

"What can I do to help?"

"Tonight I'm holding a weapons handling crash course. Tomorrow it's range time and we finish prepping the house and property. The kids will stay in the house, ready to dump water on fires or run for ammo. If it gets too bad, they'll be able to hit the basement with Mom, Dad, Karen, and Elizabeth. Everyone else will have to fight. You'll be in the crow's nest with your rifle. You hunt a lot, so you'll be hunting from up there."

Throughout the evening they ate dinner and made some more preparations around the property. Haliday went over the firearms with everyone. He made sure they all knew how they functioned and how to use the stripper clips and everything else. He then walked outside to take a breather and looked over at the neighbors.

There she was.

He waved.

She flipped him off.

He yelled out, "I guess I'm not on your Christmas list this year, huh?"

She yelled over at him, "You're a bastard, you know that?"

"Well, you got to meet my father earlier. How can you say that?"

"You're a son of a bitch."

"You met my mom, too?"

"Oh, you're a real funny man, aren't you? You think I don't know what you're doing over there?"

"I don't care, lady. I really don't," he called. "You're a sellout. You are a sellout to your family, to this community, and to this country. You're pathetic."

She yelled again. "Well, just you wait, smartass! In a couple of days, you'll get yours!"

Haliday walked away and went back inside.

Chapter 27

A few minutes had passed by since Haliday had encountered the neighbor lady. Haliday said, "I expect we'll get hit tomorrow night or the night after. They'll be stupid if they launch an offensive during the day. The bitch across the street said I'll get mine in a couple days, so I figure tomorrow night or the night after.

Everything is pretty much ready to go. We should put three people on security watch. One outside on patrol, one in the crow's nest, and one in the house listening to the ham."

He walked over to the desk and called Rob. "Anything new going on over there?"

"Yes sir, they are loading up a deuce and getting some vehicles lined up," Rob told him. "They keep checking everything and loading up some equipment and what looks like ammo cans. They have a guard on the convoy now, but doesn't look like they are moving any time soon; not enough activity, maybe tomorrow."

Haliday said, "Okay, you guys ready?"

"We lost four guys who backed out, but everyone else is ready."

"Okay, thanks again, Rob."

Haliday looked around at everyone. Even though they had been through a hell of a lot the past week and a half, they were still very nervous. Even the kids knew something was coming. He could try and give them a pep talk, but decided to just let them be for now. No sense in reminding them of what is coming and what could happen.

He flipped the frequency over and called Mike.

"Hey, it's Bill here."

"Hi Bill," Haliday said. "Let me talk to Mike. I have a few things to tell him."

"Okay, let me get him."

A moment later, Mike's voice came on. "Roger, it's Mike. What's going on?"

Haliday answered, "Listen, tomorrow night we expect a fight here at my place. If it comes down to it and these guys need to run, I'm sending them your way. I don't really have a choice. We have a couple of caches around and enough food to get everyone by for quite a while. I'll have a contingency plan in place and then buy them time to get out if it gets to be that bad. I'll have Kayla and the older folks grab the kids and get. Take care of them for me if it comes to that, okay?"

"Roger, listen you sound like you've giving up."

Haliday said, "No, just making sure I have things covered. I'm going to get some rest. Talk to you in the morning."

Haliday stood up and called everyone over. "Okay people, we're going over the plans again." He covered the plans and explained where everyone would be and what was expected of them. He covered the bug-out if it came down to that. "I screwed up the endgame here," he admitted with a bit of remorse. "We might not be in this position if it went down differently. I think I could have done a few things differently. I'm sorry, guys."

Rich spoke up. "Listen, Roger, you have nothing to be sorry about. This all came together because of you. We wouldn't have made it this far without what you've done. There's nothing to be sorry about. Whatever happened to the country happened, and whoever caused that, well, it's their fault, not yours. Those thugs would have made it here in due time and you just reduced the amount of people who could have shown up. We're all proud of you." Haliday thanked him and ended the meeting.

Everyone took their turns pulling security. Some slept; some stayed up longer and kept going over the plans. Haliday just kept checking everything and trying to figure out what he could do that would be better. He came up with a few more ideas. He went out into the small storage building and did some work, and then worked through the night.

The rest he would finish later, he needed a rest.

He walked back into the house where everyone was getting ready to eat breakfast. "You hungry, Dad?" Kayla asked.

"No, sweetie, I'm going to take a nap for a couple of hours. Okay?" he said.

She said, "Okay, we'll wake you up if anything happens or we need you."

He wandered up the steps and lay down for a bit. He slept away for a couple of hours.

Later Kayla woke him up. "Dad, can you come downstairs?"

"Sure." He went to move his legs, but they were heavy. He had a cat and the mutant dog Max lying on them. "Okay, time to get up," he said.

They just rolled over and went back to sleep as he got up. *Must be nice*, he thought, *just stay in bed all day.*

He walked downstairs and looked over at the table and smiled. "Damn, you guys didn't have to."

Mike and Linda were sitting there.

Mike said, "We couldn't let you guys have all the fun now, could we? We even brought a couple of friends."

Haliday looked over at the common area and saw a young couple sitting there.

Mike said, "That's Bill's son Mark and his wife, Lisa."

Haliday walked over and shook their hands. "Nice to meet you, but you guys didn't have to do this."

"Mike thought we might come in handy. Lisa here married me after I proposed to her at Ft. Campbell," Mark said. "I did three years active duty and I am currently inactive reserve. Eleven Bravo, sir," said Mark. He was around 185 pounds, 5'11", and had jet black hair. Lisa was 5'4", weighed 120 pounds and had long blonde hair. Both were in their early twenties.

"It's Roger, and I was an NCO. Drop the 'sir' stuff."

Mark went on. "I did two tours in the sandbox. Lisa here was our unit admin clerk; still knows how to fire a rifle. We even brought our own. They even have a special feature, full auto. We can go if you want."

"No, glad to have you here," Haliday replied.

Mark said, "Let's see what you have."

Haliday went over the entire plan with everyone again. Mark offered a couple of ideas which made sense now that they had extra manpower. They went over the changes and then Haliday walked everyone around the property.

"Listen, we expect this to go down tonight." Haliday said.

"Okay, we'll all be ready," the group answered in unison.

Haliday had everyone double checking everything, adding extra ammo to the stockpiles, placing thermoses of hot tea by them, plus canteens of water and hand warmers as well. They also helped him set the rest of the defenses up.

Dawn and Diana moved the horses over to another neighbor's property. The neighbors were snow birds and were already down in Florida, so Haliday didn't think they would care. He staged the vehicles for a quick departure.

He had Mark hold the range session and get everyone checked out on the weapons.

He looked over at the neighbor lady who was standing there. He made contact first, showed her she was number one. He held that finger high.

Randy called him in. "Hey, Uncle Roger, come in here quick."

Haliday jogged over to the house to see what Randy wanted.

"What's going on, Randy?"

"Rob is on the radio for you."

"Okay, thanks," he said. "Rob, what's the word?"

Rob answered, "You're getting hit tonight. These guys are finalizing the vehicle loads and gear and double-checking everything. I guarantee they are moving out soon. As soon as they move out, I'll be calling you. We are all in position here near the airport and ready to go ourselves. Good luck, Roger."

"Good luck to you, too, Rob."

This was the calm before the storm. Haliday walked around and hugged everyone and thanked them. Everyone was dressed and ready. They were finding themselves idle things to do in and out of the house.

Haliday sat there with his eyes closed and prayed a bit. The ham crackled and he listened.

He ran outside and cranked an old-fashioned air raid siren attached to the porch railing, which sent everyone running to their positions.

He wasn't worried about the neighbor calling it in. She already knew what was coming and he'd had Kevin sneak over there earlier. Kevin had unplugged her whip antenna and connected some power leads to it and had triggered a stun gun which popped a chip in her handheld. He then snipped the antenna to double up the effort. The militia relying on her to relay info for the attack was out of the question now.

The group had placed all the radios they had outside. If there was a need for a retreat, a flag would be raised at the crow's nest and it would be lit up. Haliday would also fire a couple of red flares up into the sky.

He took off for his position. Everyone's blood was pumping and it would be less than an hour now. Anticipation coursed through their veins.

Haliday said into the radio, "Rob, what do we have coming our way?"

"Roger, you have one motorcycle and no ATVs of any sort,.. Scratch that; you have two quads in the back of the deuce. There are four people in the back of it. There are three pickup trucks, and each has two people up front and two in the back. Two Jeeps and a Bronco with four people in each. Thirty-one people total.

"They all have ARs; they look pretty standard except for a few oddballs here and there," Rob said. "Lights attached, lasers, scopes, magazines taped together, the works. It looks like some have some 308s in the same configuration. One guy has some big badass rifle or something, it looks like a small cannon.

"The other night they loaded up all the ammo cans and a lot of other gear. Tonight they threw some packs and boxes in the trucks. A couple of guys look like they have night-vision goggles. Those old ones you see in the movies, nothing new like you see soldiers wearing today. The cases looked pretty old as well."

"Wonderful news there, Rob," Haliday said. "I expected about half. Any idea of the make-up of their ranks, as far as males and females?"

Rob gave him a quick rundown of what he thought there was. "Looked like twenty-four men and seven women. A couple of them were teenagers."

Haliday figured these were the neighbor's daughter and her boyfriend. They were most likely familiar with the area since she lived across the street. Plus, he couldn't forget two fighters across the street as well if both of them were in on it, but he was thinking it was just the woman. "How about you guys, Rob?"

"Oh, we're ready. We just need to know when to start."

"I figure about forty-five minutes or so. Rob, this is the only chance you have. You guys do what it takes. You won't have another chance like this again. I hope to be talking to you very soon," Haliday said.

"You, too, Roger."

Mark and everyone else were listening and heard the news as Rob spoke.

The militia slowly made their way toward Haliday's. They knew Haliday was expecting them, but they also knew the layout of his land, the buildings on it and the intel on who was there. They also enjoyed a two-to-one advantage for troop strength with Haliday having some older folks in the group and also having to worry about younger children.

The convoy moved along slowly, expecting an ambush or traps. They would pause at intersections and blind spots to check the areas out thoroughly before they resumed speed.

Haliday had hoped the bike would be up in the front of the convoy and had set up a catch wire for it.

The deuce led the convoy with an anti-decap bar on the front. It snapped the wire easily.

The next wire was simpler. It pulled out a piece of cardboard between a clothes pin and made a connection which ignited a rocket engine fuse. The fuse burned for a couple of seconds and then sent up a hailstorm of fireworks. It was fully dark now, and Haliday saw the convoy through his spotting scope he had set up. The militia convoy was now about two miles out.

The BAMM pulled over and dismounted their vehicles. They put up some ramps on the deuce and off-loaded the quads.

Everyone rallied around the deuce and went over the plans for their offensive. They realized with the fireworks warning that their attack was expected. The bike and quads moved out first and crept along. They were making sure they did not get caught up in any more wire strung across the roads. They headed off into the woods. The rest of the vehicles split up and went in different directions. The goal was to surround the house and test the defenses for weak points.

The militia man leading the attack spoke. He spit out the usual crap about safety, watching out for your fellow man, and all that garbage, but he also told them something else that put things in more perspective as to what they planned and what they were all about. If Haliday had heard this, it would have made a lot more sense.

The man said, "We are about to try and stop these people from ruining our plans to make this area a better place to live. They want to ruin our chance to let nature weed out those who are weak. Those who can not contribute to our society. Those who will bring us down. We need to make sure we can conquer anyone who will stop us from prospering."

It was almost like a miniature Bilderberg conspiracy.

They again moved in slowly. These guys had made some major mistakes, but this time they were going about it like true professionals. They were moving in slowly, they were spread out, and they had communications amongst everyone; they weren't taking stupid chances, and they simply had it together so far.

Even if Haliday's group wanted to leave right then, there was not a single road they could have taken without running into some of the militia. There wasn't a single side of the house that wasn't covered by at least five people. There was a fair amount of open land around the property, except for the west side which was heavily wooded and it was a little too close for comfort. Haliday had always wanted to cut it back some, but never did.

The militia carefully moved in closer and then took cover.

Haliday's group was lying in wait. Their breathing was rapid. Their heartbeats were quick and adrenaline was flowing. The temperature was around 40, but most of them were sweating. They waited, and then waited some more. The militia was making them sweat it out.

Out in the tree line, a strobe light started to flash.

Haliday called Rob; he didn't waste a lot of breath on words of wisdom or anything. He simply told him, "Start your offensive."

The strobe light flashed about 45 times a minute. It was a small strobe head about the size of a quarter mounted in a small housing running off a small 12-volt tractor battery. It was anchored to a tree about 10 feet off the ground. The type of strobe was normally mounted in fog light areas, back up lights on police cars, car grills or almost anywhere. They were pure white light and worked well. Each pulse was like a flash of lightning.

Tree bark splintered, followed by the rifle's report. The bark splintered yet again and then the report. The third shot hit the battery and exploded it. The strobe light fell to the ground with power being cut to it. The militia sniper had taken it out.

It was hard to hone in on due to the flashing light, but eventually he got it. He was happy there would be no more light to blind the militias' night-vision goggles.

The tree line started to blink randomly. These were all angled away from the house to avoid interfering with the sight of Haliday's group. Pretty soon there were almost 20 of these blinking around the perimeter of the property. If one was taken out they would know where at least one militia member would be or at least the general area. These were meant to interfere with the night-vision.

A white flare erupted and sailed into the air.

Haliday's group spotted movement, but only shadows on the ground. They were able to locate a couple of the militia vehicles, but these were too far away to accurately see what was going on. The flare drifted slowly to the ground. A couple of the strobe lights went out.

The militia sniper was surveying the area. His original thought was to take out the blinking lights, but there were simply too many of them. He would expose his position, which he did not want to do. When the flare went off, he spotted Alan up in the crow's nest. He made his calculations and hugged the Barrett close. He heard a rustling behind him and reached for his pistol.

Haliday had come out of his hide. He would have chosen this spot for his own hide; he counted on this sniper doing the same. He was only 15 feet away from the man.

The sniper rolled over in an attempt to protect himself and fired his pistol.

Haliday leapt forward and came down on the man's upper arm with one knee and accidently knocked the Barrett over with his other. He grabbed at the pistol and managed to move the slide back about a quarter of an inch. It didn't fire. Haliday increased his grip and snapped the pistol around toward the man, nearly tearing the man's trigger finger off.

The man reached up and grabbed Haliday's throat and tried to choke him. One of the first things Haliday taught people in his self-defense classes was how to avoid being choked. If you can stop yourself from breathing, you can stop the choking. Haliday did this with an exaggerated cough and stopped breathing. He managed to free the pistol from the man's grip and tossed it aside.

The man let go of Haliday's throat and punched him in the side of the ribcage. The area was tender and the previously broken ribs had not yet mended.

Haliday gasped for air. He had given Kayla his vest so he had no protection. There came another punch and Haliday went over. Haliday grabbed his knife from the sheath on his tactical vest. The man rolled over and moved to choke him again. Haliday pulled him in close in a bear hug and then brought his right arm up, quickly sinking the knife he held into the base of the man's neck, severing his spine.

Haliday blacked out for a brief minute. He opened his eyes to the sound of gunfire.

Chapter 28

Over at the airport during Haliday's battle, the townspeople had their own fight. The townspeople were going to take back what was rightfully theirs; the food and supplies the militia stole.

The security at the airport was heavier than normal. Rob had spread the word and they did what they could to coordinate the strike. The hunters within the group had taken up residence on the rooftops of the neighboring buildings as far away as they dared to go, depending on their skill. Some of them found other places to hide. Haliday had also warned them about the sniper on the roof.

Down toward the south end of the airport, one townsman crawled up to the fence. He had previously spotted the end of a fence section and started clipping the wire that held it to the pole. He finished clipping by the pole, then started working along the top when he spotted a militia quad heading his way.

The militia rider fired awkwardly with one hand toward the man as the man ran back to the tree line.

Once he reached the tree line, the man grabbed his rifle and fired toward the quad. The rider skidded to a stop and jumped off. He leaned over the seat and fired a couple of bursts. Before he knew it, the rider was facing the return fire from two shotguns and an SKS. He was using the quad as a shield. Two of the tires went flat and the gas tank was ruptured.

The quad rider reached up and tried to start it, but didn't have any luck. He called for help on his radio. He aimed his rifle over the seat and fired a few bursts in the direction of the woods. He looked back toward the compound and saw a side-by-side four-wheeler coming up. One guy was standing in the back and firing a rifle. He had rigged up a harness to keep himself steady.

The militia man heard his partners yelling at him.

"Get in! Get in!"

He leaped up and ran over to the four-wheeler and jumped in; it took off before he actually landed in the seat. The man in the back spun around as it left and laid down some more suppressing fire. The four-wheeler darted to the other side of the compound to get away from the hidden townsmen and their fire.

They were passing a small wooded area when a blaze of rounds opened up from their left. The man in the back went down and dangled from his harness as the driver swerved to avoid the gunfire. The driver took a hit to the arm and floored the gas. The passenger they'd picked up was able to avoid getting hit. The four-wheeler made its way quickly back toward the admin building.

Once at the compound, the militia men cut the harness and lowered the man that was trapped in it. He was already dead, hit four times total. One shot pierced a lung, one his spleen, one his stomach, and the final round severed his femoral artery. He had passed out, and then bled out, all within two minutes. The driver had a shattered forearm. He was taken inside by his friends to an empty hangar where they had set up a morgue of sorts until they could bury the men from the marina and the track fire.

The two townsmen ran back out to finish cutting the fence open. They had started to snip the wires again when another shot rang out. One of the men fell backwards and the other one grabbed his arms and started to pull him back toward the woods. Another shot rang out and the injured man was hit again.

The militia sniper had made it up to his rooftop perch and went to work.

The townsman was already dead when his friend dragged him into the woods.

The sniper had them scared. After Haliday had blown the guy's foot off earlier they'd gone onto the roof and fortified the position with more sandbags. Nobody could really see the sniper now and no one would quite have the range to effectively reach him anyway. The man up there now wasn't one of the two snipers the militia originally had, but he had been training to become their third. He was still a damn good shot.

Across from the airport's main gate there was a small car repair shop. To the west of that were a couple of small houses and a clump of trees by the road. Rob and a couple of other guys rigged up a huge redneck style slingshot behind the trees using rubber tubing. They filled a bunch of quart jars with gas and shot them toward the front gate and then sent over flaming bottles.

The militia had set up two U-shaped sandbag emplacements on each side of the gate. As soon as the gas started to hit the militia ran toward the row of cars behind them to use the defensive positions they had set up there. The sandbags were burning and causing the walls to falter as sand fell out of them.

The two guys had about 50 feet to make it to the row of cars. They had both run for fear of catching fire and burning like the people in the track had done.

From the darkened window of the repair shop came an unnoticeable twang of a bow. The arrow hit one man right in the back and he stumbled forward, fell, and then crawled to safety. His partner just left him there to make it back on his own.

The sniper looked around. He had concentrated on trying to find the guys firing the Molotov cocktails and without a muzzle flash he didn't know where the shot came from. He assumed it was a suppressed weapon. It was too dark for him to see the arrow in his friends back.

The man hit by the arrow made it to the row of cars and crawled behind them.

The sniper continued to scan the area, but could not find the archer. The fires were still burning and had turned the emplacements into piles of sand. The plastic type of surplus sandbags weren't such a good deal after all. The militia would be foolish to try and use these barricades again.

The archer inside the auto shop pulled out an arrow. The arrow had a cardboard tube on the shaft which was filled with black powder and finishing nails. The fuse was taken off some fireworks he had lying around. He drew back and another man with him lit the fuse. He released the arrow and sent it over the cars. They heard the arrow explode but it sounded like an M80 more than it did a bomb.

This gave away the men's position and they headed toward the back of the shop.

The sniper put a couple rounds through the front windows just for the sake of doing so.

The arrow was not effective enough to do any damage, just a few small nicks from the nails. The men had hoped it would have a more profound effect than it did. No such luck. It was a wasted effort. They felt stupid for trying it instead of just using regular arrows and firing from the dark window.

Rob had taken a plastic ball that his wife had used in the washer for fabric softener and packed it with BBs and gun powder. The hole was sealed with wax and a fuse was attached. They lit this and used the slingshot to launch it toward the building. It landed just behind the cars out front and exploded, sending BBs everywhere. This was far more effective than the arrow. The two front windows of the building shattered and one of the militia got hit in the face, losing an eye and embedding another BB in his chin. People always looked too long at objects thrown at them instead of taking cover and this guy found that out the hard way.

The lower windows had been covered with wood on the inside, but a smaller upper window shattered and glass fell inside of the building. Not much building damage, but at least the townsmen had made a statement. They concentrated coverage at the front of the building. The main problem was the sniper on the roof. They couldn't really advance while that guy was up there. They would have to figure out how to get him down.

A woman came out of the back door of the admin building with two men. The men fired wildly toward the street, providing cover fire as she ran toward the motor pool. She had her rifle slung on her back and keys in her hand. From a distance of 150 yards away and from another small building across the street came another shot, dropping one of the men.

346

The round struck him at the base of his nose and his AR fired as he fell. Blood trickled out of his ears and nose as he lay motionless on the ground. The remaining man fired toward the building on full auto, burning through magazines.

The sniper looked, but didn't see anything; he had a lot of ground to try and cover. They were calling the attack in to their patrol group at Haliday's, who were engaged in their own assault.

Both militia groups were on their own.

The townsmen were slow and methodical in their gunfire. They didn't want to waste the only ammo they had and didn't want to give away their positions to the militia. The wide open spaces around the airport made it hard to get close. They were also playing it as safe as they could. They knew this was serious, but didn't know how serious it really was.

They heard a truck start in the motor pool.

*****

Haliday shook it off and rolled over. He looked over toward the house. From within the property and the surrounding area he could see occasional patches of muzzle flashes. He quickly tried to get a fix on where most of the action was taking place. It was sporadic; there was no sustained attack on any one part of the property.

He checked the militia man and found his radio. He unplugged the man's earpiece and listened for a few seconds. It was all static and he could hardly make anything out. During the struggle, the antenna had been broken near its base and the reception was poor at best. Haliday kept it close, regardless. Anything he heard would be better than nothing.

He looked over at the Barrett, grabbed it, and set it back up on the bi-pod. He looked through the scope for a target. Off in the woods he spotted one of the quads. He took aim and readied himself for the shot. He squeezed the trigger and watched the round. *Aw crap*, he thought. He missed it and was mad at himself. He had wanted to check the zero on the scope and the quad was the only readily visible target.

He looked at the scope; it had to be off just a bit. He had knocked it pretty good with his knee and it was just enough to take it off zero. The rifle setup this guy had was probably 12, maybe 15 grand when he purchased it and he couldn't believe how the scope reacted to the hit it took. He didn't have time to play with it. What was maybe a sixteenth of an inch on the scope base could equate to a couple of feet at 700 to 800 yards where the round would impact.

He couldn't afford to use it. He needed accuracy and reliability of the system that he knew well. He ran about 20 feet away and brushed aside a pile of leaves and some loose branches and pulled out his M24. He ran back to the Barrett's location and set up his own rifle and then scanned the area for another target.

Over by the woods they would need the most help. He listened on his radio, but didn't hear much traffic. The militia was still probing. They would advance or fire and then watch where the return fire came from. Haliday kept scanning the area because someone would have to show themselves eventually.

A little more than half of the strobes were still working. He concentrated near the darker spots. He caught a glimpse of muzzle flash and started working on finding the person behind the gun. He'd have killed for a night-vision scope. The illuminated reticle on his scope at night was only good for making sure you were centered over your target, but that was only if you could clearly see your target.

Up in the crow's nest, Alan wasn't having any luck either. He was staying low and using one of Haliday's homemade periscopes to try and find some movement. Once he was able to locate someone, he would then try and fire on them. To just sit there exposed while he hunted for a shot was asking for more trouble than he wanted.

Alan looked down the street and spotted movement along the ditch. It was about 250 yards out. He took a deep breath and lifted his rifle placing it into the notch in the wall, and then also used the wall as his bipod. A figure started to cross over from one side of the road to the other. He fired the round and ducked back down.

The round dropped more than he expected and entered a woman's left shoulder. The round caught her off-guard and she dropped to the asphalt and started to work her way to the ditch. Another militia member ran over and provided suppressing fire toward the crow's nest.

Haliday changed his own angle of aim.

The lady was near the edge of the asphalt at the gravel shoulder of the road. The man with her continued to cover her by firing three and four round bursts. The muzzle flashes lit him up perfectly.

Haliday fired and the round went through the man's left chest area and came out through his right rear shoulder blade, hitting his aorta as well.

The woman sat up slightly and called toward the downed man. She crawled back over to him to check his injuries. Once she realized he was dead, she tried to crawl back toward the ditch.

Alan watched this and popped back up to put another round into her, hitting her leg. The woman now laid there. She had been hit twice and called on her radio for help.

Haliday just heard the crackle of the radio and a word or two. "Road" and "help" was all he could make out. He called Alan on the radio. "Be careful, but keep an eye on that woman. They might be coming to get her. You let me know if you see anything. We might be able to coordinate something."

"Okay, Roger," Alan said. "What about the woods though?"

"I'll watch those for right now."

Haliday called Mark next. "Mark, we have them moving in closer over by the wood line. You near there at all?"

"Yeah, I have a spot next to Lisa and Kayla, who are in their fighting positions. We can't really see anyone yet. They are holding off at quite a distance. All we're getting are probing shots. I only have half our guys here firing back to help keep up a level of surprise."

Haliday heard a light thump followed by four more. He looked over at the street and saw smoke rising around the downed woman. The militia used their own launchers to put smoke down on the road to attempt a retrieval. They had a Jeep speeding in toward the location of the wounded woman.

The crow's nest started to take more suppressing fire and Alan dropped down to the loft floor. He ran over to the middle of the cabin. Earlier he had removed a Velcro cover and piece of insulation. This revealed a one-foot-by-one-foot tin roof vent that he raised up. He would be able to avoid the shots fired at the crow's nest, but still be able to help by firing along this side of the house. He picked up an AR that was set there.

Out past the wounded woman on the road, two rifles had started the barrage in order to provide cover for the Jeep. It was coming in completely dark, not a single light on.

Mike was on that side of the house and he launched a flare into the sky above the road. The smoke was illuminated and looked eerie. The Jeep laid on the brakes momentarily, then it continued on.

NVGs, Haliday thought. The flare ruined their vision. The driver had to stop and take them off.

The suppressing fire continued. They alternated fire between the crow's nest and Mike's fighting position. Mike couldn't get his head up to take any shots. Suddenly the wood line on the other side of the house erupted in gunfire. Mark ordered the group to return fire. Shots were being fired from both Haliday's group and the militia frequently now.

Across the road from the neighbor's house came even more fire. Kevin, Dawn, and Diana returned fired back, striking the house and surrounding landscaping. Kevin swept the shrubs and trees from side to side anywhere from six inches to a foot off the ground. Dawn swept the areas from two to three feet off the ground and Diana sprayed the house and took aim at areas where she saw muzzle flashes.

Haliday was ready to fight and sought out the targets. He had taken over the militia sniper's hide in order to utilize it against the aggressors. None of the BAMM really knew what happened and with all the action they thought their own man was still in it covering their movement. Haliday put an occasional shot into a safe zone for just that effect.

*****

Back at the airport compound the woman reached the motor pool area and ran inside. She opened the door and started the deuce that had the armored side. She drove it out and her first stop was by the downed militia member who had given her cover. The other militia man ducked beside the deuce and it inched its way toward the admin building as he dragged the downed man over there.

He laid the body along the side of the admin building. A few more people came out of the center and climbed up into the back of the deuce, then hunkered down low behind the plate metal. The deuce headed off toward the other buildings. It would pause so someone could get down and into a defensive position before moving on.

The positions the militia had set up had included sandbag emplacements, some were short metal walls angled at 45 degree angles and placed near the corner of buildings, and some were cinderblocks that had been stacked two deep and filled with sand. They had used whatever was found at the airport prior to the EMP strike.

The deuce made another trip and loaded up some more people.

The townspeople could only take an occasional pot shot, and didn't hit anyone.

The group at the airport was definitely the safest. The townspeople would have to regroup and figure out another plan of attack.

The deuce delivered more militia to their positions. They had twenty people dedicated to the fighting positions around the buildings. The sniper on the roof would help extend their reach. The rest of the militia was there to respond where needed and to help coordinate.

Rob spoke with Brad. They had to get this under control. Right now it was simply a standstill with both sides waiting for the other to make a move. Rob asked Brad what he thought.

Brad said, "We're screwed with that man on top of that admin building. We have to flush him out somehow. The distance we're fighting at is killing us."

One of Rob's group had positioned himself up on the feed store's roof where he had seen Haliday fire from a couple of days earlier. He took aim at the militia sniper's position and fired a shot. The shot dropped low as the man's rifle was underpowered. He raised his rifle to adjust the aiming point and fired again to try and flush the man out.

The militia sniper was aware of this position and dialed in his scope. He had invested in an ATN Gen3 scope and looking at the man on the feed store roof was easy. He fired his round and struck the man on the feed store roof in the top of the shoulder. The round traveled through his upper body cavity and he tumbled off the roof and fell to the pavement.

Brad asked Rob who the best shot was. Rob told him it was Tom; the guy had a knack for hunting.

Rob jumped in the four-wheeler and went and got Tom. When he got back, Brad pointed to the map.

He said, "Tom, you think you can climb a tree over in this clump here and get the bastard on the roof of their HQ?"

Tom looked over the map and looked at its scale. "It'll be hard. I won't lie, I might be able to do it."

Brad looked at Rob. "Can we get him there?"

Rob said, "Sure, give us about twenty minutes."

"Okay, you get there, and then get Tom up in that tree." He told Tom to wait for the signal.

"What is the signal going to be?" Tom asked.

"It's going to be like the Fourth of July. When the fireworks start, you try and get that guy."

Brad said, "Rob, after you take Tom there, go around and get these guys ready. Tell them to launch on my signal. I'll pop a flare, and once they start, it's Tom's ball game. Anyone else who can get a shot in should take it."

Rob and Tom got back on the four-wheeler. Rob drove down a ways and cut back up through the same path Haliday had used to ambush the track.

They came across the track and both Rob and Tom just looked at it. It gave them shivers to think about the people sitting in that thing burning alive. The stench of burnt, rotting flesh was pungent. The militia had not been able to get the bodies out of the track. They both looked at each other, then looked up at the trees as panic set in, but nothing was there.

Rob had to back up the four-wheeler and find another route. The track blocked the path and he couldn't get past the trees in the woods. They hurried up, and they were cutting it close. They had to make sure Brad didn't start early. Rob skirted the woods and passed along a brick and block company. *Those would have been useful to build some blockades,* he thought.

He turned the lights off on the four-wheeler and they crossed the road. They parked and got out and headed toward a clump of trees. As they passed a house, Rob saw people looking out the windows. He told them to get in the basement.

The people in the house just watched.

Rob told Tom, "Some people think this is a game, and they just want to watch. Like it's a giant Xbox or Playstation."

Rob gave Tom a boost and he started climbing the tree. He kept looking over at the roof, half expecting to get hit. He climbed as high as he could get and braced himself. He could barely make out the militia sniper from his vantage point. He watched and waited for movement. This was not going to be easy.

The militia was talking back and forth on radios as they tried to identify where the aggressors were. The flare went off and arced over the airport building, then came down without incident. In a matter of minutes, several large fireworks started going. Michigan had just come around to allowing the good ones to be sold, and as with any state that sells them, they were abundant in tourist traps.

As the fireworks danced in the sky, several more flares were launched at the buildings, mainly toward the admin building. Numerous fireworks tubes were aimed directly at the buildings as well. The militia almost laughed at the attack; however, the admin building was getting pelted consistently. One lucky shot made it into the militia sniper's position and he moved to avoid it.

Tom took this opportunity, along with two more townspeople, and started firing. Fifteen shots fired rapidly toward the sniper.

He lay up on the roof as blood ran down from the rooftop.

The militia positions returned fire on the riflemen, but were taking hits themselves from almost 30 different people. The sniper threat had been removed but at the cost of one more of Rob's group dying and two more people injured.

Tom scrambled down the tree amidst the fire. He fell the last seven feet and came down on his ankle, snapping it. Two townspeople assigned to regular posts there provided enough fire so Rob could get Tom out of there. He took Tom back to the four-wheeler and drove him over to the tooling shop they had started to use as their meeting area.

They had a nurse there to help treat injuries. They hadn't been able to convince any doctors to get involved yet.

Rob went back and met with Brad again. With the sniper gone, they could get closer. They thought of every possible contingency. Getting into the compound would be vital to eliminating as many of the militia as they could. Rob wondered how Haliday was doing.

Chapter 29

Near Haliday's cabin the Jeep stopped about 10 feet from the wounded woman. Two guys jumped out and ran over to her. They grabbed her and got her to her feet and took her to the Jeep. She couldn't move well and they struggled moving her. She insisted they take the man's body with them. The dead man turned out to be her husband.

The driver of the Jeep yelled at them to hurry. They had to get out of there quickly and the smoke was practically gone. He put it in reverse and continued to yell at them to rush. As he waited for them, he fired his own rifle into Haliday's cabin and at the landscaping areas around it. He was panicking; this rescue was taking far too long.

The driver fired only toward the house, thinking people were at the windows.

Blake, Mike, and Kevin returned fire along with Alan, who was firing from the second floor portal. There were three more militia groups firing at the house from that side.

The Jeep driver stopped firing and popped a can of smoke and tossed it in front of him, hoping this would help continue to blind them.

Alan was taking aim into the center of the smoke when a round came in, grazing his cheek and splintering the wood next to him, causing bits of wood to fly. He backed away and put the rifle down. He grabbed a pouch from his pocket and tore it open and held it to the massive gash that went almost completely through his cheek. He called downstairs for help.

Bev came up the steps with a bag. She took the quick-clot off his cheek and squeezed the gash together. She placed quite a few butterfly bandages over it and then taped another bandage over those. It was the best he was going to get at the moment.

Haliday fired, striking the Jeep's driver in the back of his head and then the round went on to penetrate the windshield as well. The driver fell limp and the Jeep slowly rolled in reverse as the militia members tried to get the woman into the side. They all dropped down and crawled toward the Jeep in the ditch. They weren't sure where the round had come from.

The woman started to crawl that way, too, but was having a hard time. She was pleading for help. There wasn't going to be any. The men who attempted her rescue were concerned with getting out of the area and getting to a safer location, so they let her lie there. They actually considered whether or not to try to get in the Jeep.

Across the street by an empty house, Kayla saw some movement and called it out. Mark, David, and Lisa along with Kayla kept an eye out over there from her position. The angle was difficult for Kayla and she was trying to keep an eye on the woods, too. She yelled over to Mark and told him they needed help on the west side wood line.

Mark called Alan, who went over to the other side of the house and opened the portal there. His cheek was still stinging like crazy. He eyed the woods, looking for the militia who had really started shooting down the strobes now.

Only a couple of them had NVGs, but even that gave them an advantage. The depth perception and detail was severely lacking because they were early Generation 1 NVGs and so they were mostly for movement or observation.

Mark called out more movement by the empty house Kayla had pointed out earlier and confirmed it was militia. He fired single shots in that direction. Lisa and David waited as he fired and as soon as they saw the first flash, they opened up on that location.

They each fired about 15 rounds. Around 15 feet away from that area, another militia member returned fire, emptying a full clip toward them. Now they knew there were at least two militia members by the house.

The woods to the west were getting fairly packed with militia members as they shifted people to this area. This was the most vulnerable side of the house. Kayla, Linda, and Nancy had their work cut out for them. It was very dark and they couldn't make out anybody. They saw an occasional muzzle flash, but nothing in the same spot twice. Alan couldn't find anyone either. He called Roger and told him the problem.

Karen had Elizabeth and Theresa down in the basement of the house along with the cats and mutant dog. Karen's job was to keep them as safe as possible. She had a pistol and five magazines with her. If they called on her, she could respond if she needed to. She was also ready to usher her young charges to a vehicle in case of a bug-out situation.

Rich had Matthew and Bobby ready to douse any fires in the house and Bev was ready with first aid supplies for whoever could make it back to the house. Trying to use the house as their sole cover wasn't exactly tactically sound, but it had been set up for a strong defense. They did have a few more tricks ready, though, and when the time came, they would use them.

The Jeep from the rescue had stalled out and was now just sitting in reverse in the ditch so the militia men decided to make their way to their sniper. They called him so he could cover their retreat.

Haliday heard the radio static and picked out a few words: hide, cover, retreat. He clicked the transmit button, but didn't speak. All the militia men heard back would be crackling.

The militia headed out at a crawl toward Haliday.

Haliday could not see them well, but knew they were heading his way. He shot over their heads and into a safe zone. He fired almost 10 rounds providing "cover" for them.

Not knowing, Randy, Sarah, and Blake had returned fire toward him.

Haliday called, "Mike, tell them to stop. It's me. I'm not firing at them."

Mike called over to Blake and told him to pass the word.

They couldn't quite reach Haliday, but he didn't care. Now that they stopped firing, it truly appeared that he was safely covering the militia.

Randy, Sarah and Blake understood now, but they didn't know any better when they had fired. They now focused on other militia firing toward them.

The two men from the Jeep kept up their retreat. They were about 150 yards away from Haliday now.

Haliday watched them carefully. *Come and get your cheese, you rats,* he thought.

Lisa called over to Mark about the two people by the empty house. "I think they're coming over the road."

Mark scanned back and forth.

Lisa told him, "By the ditch. By the ditch."

One of the militia got up and sprinted toward the ditch. He dove down into it under a hail of gunfire. He raised his rifle and fired while the other person ran to the ditch as well.

There was one more militia at the house now who had moved there to help provide cover. He fired and the woods on the west side lit up at the same time. The two militia men made it across the street into the ditch on the other side of the road during the diversion. They were now closer to the cabin and a mere 100 feet from Lisa and Mark.

They lay in the ditch, waiting to make their move.

*****

Rob and Brad were in a wooded area near the airport. Rob looked over at Brad. "Brad, we need to get into that compound. We need to get through that fence."

Brad said, "I agree, but it's not like we can just plow our way in there."

"Actually we can," said Rob. "Over by the brick and block company is an old front loader; let's go see if it runs."

They took off to check it out.

The militia had them outgunned as far as type of rifle, but neither group had an edge. The townspeople would fire a shot or two from their rifles and the militia response was usually two or three rounds or a short burst if they had a full auto rifle. Fewer than half had converted their rifles to full auto. For a group that broke so many laws, it was odd they didn't all have full autos.

Word had spread that the sniper had been taken out and some of the guys now sought higher ground. A few used tree stands, but had them on the back sides of the trees in order to use the tree as cover. A couple used the closer rooftops in hopes of being able to get a better line of sight.

A few of the guys got bored and they commenced shooting out every piece of glass they could on the admin building, regardless of the windows being boarded up. The upper windows weren't boarded and they shot these out as well. Since heat rises, it would make it colder inside and harder to heat.

Rob and Brad made it to the brick company. They climbed up on the old front loader into the cab. They searched for a key but couldn't find it.

They went over to the office nearby and tried the door, but it was locked. Rob went around and tried the back door, but it too was locked.

Brad said, "Now what?"

Rob picked up a brick and broke the window out of the back door. They went inside to look for the key.

Hanging on a wall by the shop door was a bunch of keys. Rob looked at their tags and found one that was marked 'loader.' He grabbed it and they went back outside to the front loader. He climbed back up into the cab and put the key in the ignition and turned the switch. The engine cranked, but very slowly.

Brad told him the batteries must be low. They went back into the shop and looked around, but couldn't find any jumper cables. Brad grabbed a fire ax and walked over to a piece of conduit and chopped at it. He followed it along the base of the wall about 10 feet and then swung again. He had Rob hold the pipe as he pulled the wire out. Homemade jumper cables.

They connected pieces of this to the battery of the four-wheeler and then to the battery on the front loader. Rob climbed up into the cab once again and tried. The motor turned over, but still didn't start. Brad revved the engine on the four-wheeler and Rob tried to start it. The engine finally caught and a plume of black smoke came out of the muffler. Brad gave Rob a thumbs-up and then took the wires off the batteries.

Over toward the southwest corner inside of the airport perimeter, one of the militia called for a status check. He was told everyone was in position defending the compound. He asked how the other group was doing and he was told that know one knew yet. The only information they had exchanged so far was that they were engaged in firefights.

This BAMM was a younger man in his early 20s. His parents had volunteered to go on the assault mission and he'd been asked to stay. Now he was wondering if he shouldn't have gone on the mission, too. He started to get antsy, moving back and forth. It had been a few hours now and his mind wandered. The HQ asked everyone over the radio if anyone needed any ammo. One guy asked for something to drink and HQ told them critical runs only would be made.

Brad and Rob didn't know if the fuel gauge worked or not, so they found a can and transferred some diesel from a large 500-gallon fuel tank and over to the loader. When they had it filled, Rob went over and picked up a pallet of bricks. The company had taken the bucket off and had been using large pallet forks. Brad placed a loose board on top of the forks behind the pallet of bricks.

Rob headed for the south end of the airport. When they got near the fence line, he paused and Brad ducked over to the woods, where two more townsmen were waiting. He asked them if they were okay with taking a ride and entering the compound. Both agreed and they all ran back to the loader. Rob plowed over the fence where it was hanging low from being clipped earlier and got as close as he could to the buildings.

The militia fired on the loader.

Rob knew that as soon as he put the pallet of bricks down he would have to take off. Brad jumped up next to the cab and Rob lowered the pallet and backed off. The two guys behind the pallet along with Brad all fired as Rob retreated. A few rounds hit the cab but no one got hit. The two guys that stayed with the bricks started hollowing out a small area of the pallet. They piled up the brick's they removed and placed them on the sides of the pallet to widen their fortification.

Rob and Brad went to the brick company and picked up another pallet of bricks. Rob told Brad to meet him near the west side of the airport with the four-wheeler. Rob drove the bricks through the gap in the fence once again and headed to the west fence. As soon as he dropped the load he drove to the west fence line. Even with cover fire, the loader took hits. It started to slow down as Rob headed straight for the west fence.

The loader stalled out as he rammed through one of the poles and barely made it across the fence. It had overheated and shut down; the cooling system was damaged. Rob's group had two men inside the perimeter, two positions of cover, and two breaches of the fence now. They would need to get more people in. If they could control at minimum the south side, they could start chipping away at the opposition more heavily.

At the southwest corner the younger militia guy had been one to help provide fire on Rob. The breaches got him to thinking some more; this was very serious and they had run into some real opposition. He kept wondering about his parents. He asked the HQ to call for an update. He was told no, there was too much going on. He felt something was wrong. Fifteen minutes later, he called for ammunition and told them he was low and had used a lot during the last breach.

Rob made it over to Brad and they met up with a few fellow guys in the woods who had taken out the gunner earlier. They sat there and watched the deuce come creeping up. The deuce stopped by the guy who had called in for ammo. Rob and the guys watched closely. The deuce's armored side was facing them. They spread out and tried to get a better look.

The young guy was arguing with the driver; he wanted to go back to the admin building and was told that he could not. He pushed his way past the driver and told the driver to stay there in his place. The driver reached out and grabbed him, trying to tell him he had to stay. The guy pushed him off and the driver stumbled from behind the deuce, where he was met with multiple rounds of fire from the townspeople.

The kid watched the driver die and he panicked. He got behind the wheel of the deuce and tried to take off. He wasn't used to the clutch and it was hard for him. The townspeople opened up on the back of the deuce. The guy jammed it in gear and took off. He drove right over to the admin building and climbed out, he took several hits from Rob's men across the street. In his haste he had left the area between the deuce and the admin building wide open—right where he was. He died slowly.

Rob's group had now started taking a toll on the militia, but not fast enough.

Rob called Haliday and Haliday told him he was busy and needed a few minutes. He would have to call him back. He told him to hold on for a few minutes if possible.

Rob let it go at that; he knew Haliday was deep in a fight.

Near the cabin. Haliday waited where he was. Just a few more moments was all he needed. Just a few more moments. He watched carefully. He heard the militia's radio crackle again and just laid there and watched.

The two approaching militia stopped and dropped.

Haliday knew they were calling their sniper and the lack of an answer a second time clued them in to a problem. They were at a loss as to what to do. They thought they were moving toward safety.

Before they had time to run, Roger fired the first round into one of the militia men, striking him through his left eye. His patrol cap came off along with some bits of brain matter. The second man rolled over a couple of times and then fired at Haliday.

Haliday fired rapidly with the remaining four rounds in his rifle. He struck the militia man's rifle in the upper receiver, rendering it useless, and managed to hit the man in the ass as well, but it was not bad enough to render the man neutral. The man was struggling with something that Haliday couldn't see, but he wasn't going to wait; his location and deception had been discovered.

Haliday drew his pistol and initiated slow sustained fire as he rose up and then moved for cover deeper into the woods. He heard shots and ducked down. He crawled over to where he had set his AR. He slung his M24 on his back and grabbed the AR. He heard rounds striking the trees around him. He called for help and tried to explain his location so he wouldn't be hit by friendly fire.

Kayla, Linda, Alan, and Nancy were trying to cover the woods. It was dark and the militia were well protected by the trees and lack of light, giving them the advantage. They were using this advantage to keep the women in their fighting positions. The militia in the woods, over at the neighbor's and the other house across the street all started to fire at once.

Kevin, Diana, and Dawn returned fire as best they could. Dirt was flying all around them and they kept having to duck debris as the militia fire searched them out. Apparently the neighbor had pretty much filled the militia in on everything they needed to know. Kevin was convinced she used to walk the property when Haliday wasn't up here. Who knows what information she had.

The people in the woods crept closer yet. Alan frantically searched for a target. He didn't want to fire until he had acquired a target in order to his location being pinpointed. Kayla, Linda, and Nancy would fire three round bursts and duck. They were starting to lose ground.

The militia member by the empty neighbor's house continued to fire. All of a sudden two cans of smoke were tossed toward David, Lisa, and Mark.

Alan swung his rifle that direction. It was dark and the smoke clouded the area heavily. He scanned back and forth over a distance almost 50 yards wide.

Kevin yelled over to Diana to hit the west corner of the empty house, then told Dawn to do the same thing. As soon as they saw a muzzle flash, they each burned through their magazines. The man hiding behind the corner of the house was shredded. With almost 70 rounds striking within a seven-by-seven-foot area and piercing the vinyl siding and insulation, it was almost like a Claymore had gone off. He was struck eight times by 5.56 armor-piercing rounds.

Randy, Sarah, Mike, and Blake fired toward the activity in the woods near Haliday.

Haliday started crawling like crazy to get deeper into the woods.

The militia man firing on him now had more than just Haliday to worry about.

Haliday managed to use that edge and gained some more ground. He rolled over and put a smoke grenade in the 37mm and fired it toward the man. He popped one more and fired it behind him.

Inside the cabin they could hear the stray rounds hitting the sides. Rich had everyone hiding low so the armored lower half would keep them safe. He sent Bobby and Matthew downstairs to stay and told them to send Karen up.

He called Bev over. "The woods are a big problem. We need to see about helping out."

One of the side windows had been broken out. He grabbed a broom and knocked the glass out, then tossed a folded wool blanket over the broken glass on the floor.

Karen came up the stairs. "What do you need me to do?"

"You and Bev go open that window. You'll have to fire into the woods. I'll use this window."

Alan caught movement toward his left. The first man appeared through the smoke with the second man coming into view, about 25 feet to the right of the first one, both running like crazy. They were heading straight for Mark and Lisa's positions. They were within 50 feet and firing blindly.

Alan opened up on the second man who was actually closer to him. Mark fired on him as well and then spun to fire at the first man who was almost on top of Lisa's position. Lisa had been reloading her rifle and couldn't aim it in time. David had raised himself to one knee so he could fire on the man.

The man continued forward and stepped on one of the foot traps. The three inch spike pierced his heel and went deep inside his ankle. He tried to shake the spike strip off, stumbled, and tripped. The rubber sole of his boot kept the spike strip attached. David hit him once and the guy half fell into Lisa's hide hole. The man's momentum had overcome his ability to stop and control his fire. Lisa couldn't get out and felt the man flailing. Now he was struggling to free himself from the hole.

Haliday called Mike and told him to fire into the smoke only.

Randy, Sarah, Blake, and Mike did as they were instructed.

The militia man hugged the ground and took cover.

Haliday crawled another 20 feet and then stood up and ran into the woods. He angled his direction and headed northwest, then stopped for a moment to catch his breath. *That was very close,* he thought.

He had a problem now. He was literally behind enemy lines. He took a moment to gather his wits and surveyed the scene from his location. He saw the firefight between the woods and the house, but had no idea if anyone had gotten injured or killed or what the count was on the militia side either. He had about a second to make a decision.

As David had fired on the man, the last militia member by the empty house fired toward David, who was partially in the haze of the dissipating smoke; the militia member saw David.

David took a hit to his thigh. He lay down prone and dragged himself back to his landscape wall for cover.

Mark fired on the struggling man in Lisa's hole and the man went limp.

"Lisa, are you okay?" Mark called.

Lisa answered back that she was.

"I'll try to help you," Mark said.

"No, don't move. I think they got David. You might get hit, too," she said. "I'll be okay. I can handle this." The dead man was about 210 pounds and halfway in her hole. She struggled, but was able to get the rest of his body out of the hole.

The militia on the south side of the property was still firing, but not as heavily as before. David wrapped a bandage around his thigh and tied it snuggly. He couldn't crawl back to the house; he would expose himself doing so. He'd ride it out and provide as much support as he could.

Kevin, Diana, and Dawn kept them at bay. It was now pretty much a stalemate on their end.

The east was so wide open that the militia didn't dare try to use it. Early on, they learned that lesson with their casualties and the Jeep. The north side was still a problem, but the biggest problem was the woods to the west side of the house.

Mark, Kayla, Alan, and Nancy needed help. Mark called in to Alan. "Alan, can you get up into the crow's nest?"

Alan said "Yeah, I'll let you know when I get up there. You want me to use the .308?"

"No," Mark said. "Take the AR and as much ammo as you can."

"Okay, I'm on my way." Alan made his way to the crow's nest.

Haliday decided he would try to get to the west to help. He started slowly working his way there. He called Mark and told him his plan. Mark told him it would work with only the right execution.

"Listen, Mark," he said, "it's going to be your call, on your command. I won't be close enough to decide."

"I'll have Randy, Sarah and Blake cover the north," Mark said. "Maybe Mike can get over there."

Haliday made another call. "Rob, this is Roger."

"Go ahead, Roger," came Rob's voice.

"Look, Rob, we're deep in this. We have casualties on both sides and we are getting ready to get hammered with a big offensive. How you guys doing?"

"It's a stalemate over here, Roger. Any suggestions?"

"Yeah, when they get done here and return, ambush them," Haliday said. "Make sure they don't make it back into the compound. I gotta go."

Chapter 30

Haliday heard an increase in the rate of fire. The west woods were heavy with militia. He called into the house. "You guys ready in there?"

Rich said, "Yeah, just tell us when."

"No, Mark has to do it. I'm in the woods and can't see what's happening well enough. Mark is going to make the call and everyone needs to move when he says go. You guys give it everything you have, OK?"

"Roger, we got it; we're ready."

Haliday continued making his way toward the heavy fighting. He was now northwest of his property. He moved in as close as he could and checked his gear. He took his mags and made sure they were all loaded and took out all of his 37mm rounds and checked to see what he had. He placed the rounds he would use in his left cargo pocket of his pants and dumped the rest.

He laid his M24 down and covered it up with some leaves and branches, then piled everything else up by another tree and loosely covered it up. It was more obvious than the rifle, but that's what he wanted. He preferred this to be found instead of his rifle. He had to lighten his load as much as he could and only took what was immediately needed for this part of the assault.

Over by the south side of the house, the militia was firing randomly. The north side was pretty much the same. Mike had Dawn, Diana, and Kevin lay down some cover fire and he jumped from position to position until he made it over to David.

David was laying there looking south to where the man who shot him had been.

"You okay, David?" Mike asked.

David said, "Not really. This thing hurts like hell. I think the bleeding has stopped though."

"David, you stay down. I'll stay here and help out."

"Sounds good," David said.

The two of them waited.

Mark called on the radio. "Hang tight, everyone. Conserve your ammo if you can. You'll need it. Keep your heads low. This is going to get dicey."

Haliday thought through the fight step by step. They had done a hell of a job fending off the militia. He knew they took some heavy fire, but his group was fairly well concealed and had great cover. A rush would end that though. The BAMM had almost succeeded and David had gotten hit, and Lisa almost got it, too. They were almost overrun. One last chance to even this fight out.

Alan was up in the crow's nest working like mad. He had everything he needed laid out and was fixing a little issue with the main component of their next defensive move when the militia rush on the west side came. He grabbed the wires and twisted them together and then double-checked them. It was ready to go now.

The militia on the north started first. They fired at the house, the crow's nest, and the previous positions where they knew Randy, Sarah, and Blake were located. The shots came roughly one every two seconds. The south side started up next, with those guys doing the same thing. It was almost methodical, a slow rhythm of shots.

Diana stepped down from a sandbag she was using to adjust her height. She stepped back near the rear of the hole and was struck in her right upper shoulder area which she had accidentally exposed. She dropped her rifle and tried to pick it up, but her right arm wasn't strong enough. She grabbed it with her left and rested it in position. She would have to fire as best she could.

The west side started up, but far more rapidly and sporadically. The majority of the militia was located over in this area now and they moved a little closer, tripling the rate of fire from that side. In a matter of about 30 seconds the north and south tripled their rates of fire and the west increased yet again. It was a full on assault now.

The entire compound was under heavy fire now. Mark saw movement very close and called everyone. "Now, now, now!"

Alan grabbed a metal spoon and slowly dragged it across a wooden board with terminals on the top. The terminals were connected to a large 12-volt battery wired to Haliday's favorite rocket engine igniters. Throughout the west side of the woods, the trees lit up brightly.

The flares were originally parachute flares that were stripped down, altered, and set in the trees. Burn time was about 45 to 55 seconds. Haliday had installed two sets of them and these couldn't be shot and extinguished. Ten locations spaced along the wood line would constantly burn bright white until they burned out. This was the last of the tricks Haliday had in his bag.

As soon as Haliday heard Mark tell Alan to ignite the flares he started launching his 37mm rounds. These were CS tear gas shells and would cause some serious discomfort to people running for cover and trying to save themselves. He had seven and he launched all of them in about 30 seconds. He took off toward the west wood area to see if he could now help repel the militia.

The militia stopped in their tracks. They were not only completely illuminated now, but they could not see the house or fighting positions very well. They had no sooner started to back off or take cover when the tear gas shells reined down around them. They beat a hasty retreat to get out of the light and tear gas.

Everyone in Haliday's group on that side of the house lit them up. Alan up in the crow's nest fired down into the woods. He kept his eyes on the first flare that went off and as soon as it burned out, he would ignite the second set. This would give them about a total of a minute and a half of light to help even out the odds.

Inside the house, Rich fired a 12 gauge shotgun full of double aught buck into the retreating militia line. He pumped seven rounds as fast as he could, moving from left to right. He dropped down and reloaded the shotgun to fire again.

Over by the other window Bev and Karen were firing 22lrs, and had plenty of magazines and kept the rounds flying. They started at opposite ends and worked toward the middle and then back again.

The group on the ground could hear the shots flying over their heads as they also fired.

Lisa, Mark, Kayla, and Linda all kept firing at the militia. If they saw someone dive to the ground or behind a tree, they concentrated their aim on that location.

The first flare sputtered out and Alan dropped down and started the second set. Everyone else continued the heavy sustained fire.

When the militia had moved forward they didn't expect the flares and barrage of gunfire. As they retreated from this they incurred their heaviest losses yet. They had eight members advancing. Of the eight, only three had escaped unharmed. Two were injured and three were dead. This devastated their ranks.

One man had stopped to aim at a flare that he thought he could shoot and put out. A couple of shots and it didn't go out; however, Mark put a couple of five rounds bursts in that direction, making the man the first militia casualty.

Another militia member moved laterally, not knowing more flares were being ignited, and Rich had hit him with the shotgun twice.

Off on the other side, Karen and Bev had gotten lucky with the 22lrs and hit a woman in the back of her neck as she retreated. She lay there, paralyzed, unable to do anything. One of the other members reached down to grab her and Alan fired his bursts into him. The amount of carnage in such a short period of time was horrific.

The rest of the injured suffered arm, leg, and torso hits, but were able to escape the area. The tear gas had them coughing, with tears and mucous running down their faces. They either didn't don masks or didn't have any. As the flares all died out, so did the firing from the militia. The militia was now just trying to get the hell out of there and handle their injured and dead.

During this, the south end and north ends of the property endured their own battles.

The militia assault on the west side of the house had actually placed all of the militia into action. On the south side, David, Mike, Kevin, Diana, and Dawn were firing on one militia member still by the empty neighbor's house and then across the street at the nosy neighbors. Militia were located there as well.

Diana was having a real hard time and had to stop. Her arm was too weak now and she could not load the rifle anymore. She had a pistol and saved it in case of closer activity.

The shots went back and forth between Haliday's group and the militia, but there was no rush, no forward movement toward the Haliday house—just sustaining fire to keep everyone pinned down. The dirt and shrubs around them were torn to pieces now. If it hadn't been for the fighting positions setup to provide cover and take the inbound rounds, it would have been far worse.

On the north end, Randy, Sarah, and Blake only had a couple of people to contend with. They were using sustained fire to keep the militia in place. No advancement was being made and neither side was hitting anything. This only lasted a few minutes.

The man Haliday had hit in the ass had made his way to a friend's location. The militia fire was constant enough to keep everyone in place so they could not help out on the west.

Haliday's group at the south side thought they had seen someone sneaking up to the road in the ditches. They fired over to that location, but couldn't tell if anyone was there or not. They, too, were only being fired on in order to keep them busy. It was just a ruse to keep everyone away from the west, but it worked. The firing died down almost to a complete stop.

Everyone waited, unsure what to expect, and prepared themselves for another rush.

Almost on cue, the militia started firing methodically again around the entire perimeter. It sounded much different.

Mark listened to their firing and thought it was a ploy and called Haliday. He explained his thoughts. "What do you think, Roger?"

"I'm with you, Mark," Haliday answered. "Pass the word; very light fire to let them know we are still dug in here. We'll let them do it."

They both knew now that the militia was firing to keep them in check while the BAMM pulled out of the area. The group wouldn't pursue the militia. They didn't have the troop strength to both leave the house guarded and track down the escaping militia. They wanted to, but had to maintain their positions at the house.

The militia was still firing, but only received a few shots in return. They used this time to gather their wounded and retreat. They left their dead where they had fallen, something nobody knew. Had Mark or Roger known, they would have continued to assault the group. This went against everything they had ever learned and was ingrained in them during their time in the military.

Haliday had not been able to get in the assault on the west side and do anything. It had happened so quickly he didn't have time to get there. Now he moved in closer and watched as the militia continued the retreat. He didn't engage for one reason; he was far outnumbered and still behind their lines. He would wait it out. He called everyone and told them to cease fire unless they were being attacked. The militia was out of effective range now.

The group sat there at the ready. It was a surreal scene; light smoke drifted in some areas, muted light from clouds and a small sliver of moon, dark bodies moving in the night dragging people away. A group of very unique people were scattered about the property waiting for another fight.

Almost an hour passed after the last round had been fired. Haliday sat still. He had not heard any of the vehicles move out yet. He was worried they might launch an assault on one single location and he knew if they did it would be costly. He closed his eyes and prayed. He heard an engine start—the damn deuce and a half. Then he heard another engine start.

He warned the group. "If they come in vehicles, get the hell out of there."

That wouldn't be the case though; they wouldn't have to.

The engine noises got quiet as the vehicles left the area. Haliday called Rob on the radio.

Rob answered. "Roger, you okay, man?"

"Rob, we took some serious shit with the fan on high and I have to tell you, this family and friends of ours put up a hell of a fight. We all made it through; some injuries, but I'm not sure how bad yet."

"Look, Roger, I can probably get a nurse to you guys if you can hold on six hours or so."

"That would be great," Haliday answered back. "Look, Rob, these guys are now heading back. I can't tell you how many or what shape they are in. I can tell you this much; if they are stopped from reaching that damn airport, then that would be the best thing for everyone."

"What do you suggest, Roger?"

"You fight dirty, Rob, dirtier than you have been. They have to come through that main gate. There are only two ways to get to it, from the east or from the west. You need to put as much of your firepower on those areas as you can. Put them on the roofs, put them in the windows, put people wherever you can.

"Make sure they have cover and make sure they hit them hard and fast. No heroes. No storming the convoy. Don't use anyone as bait," Haliday said. "Once you get these guys taken care of, the compound can be dealt with at another time. Once they realize they are on their own, things will change. You have thirty to forty-five minutes, tops. Good luck; we'll be thinking about you."

"Ok, thanks, Roger."

Haliday waited a bit. He listened for signs of movement. He called in for a situation report from everyone and found that everyone was still alive. The news was incredible. Haliday sat down against a tree, his eyes welling up. They had beaten the odds and did so without losing a single life in his group.

He made his way back to pick up his M24 and the rest of the gear he had left behind. He called the group and told them he would be using the edge of the woods to reach the house.

He reached the west side and called them and told them he was coming out of the woods and to hold their fire. He jogged in and made it to Mark's position. He lay down beside him. "Mark, can you get the injured into the house? See about getting them stabilized and I'll take over your position for you."

Mark said, "Roger, I'm good out here; get your people inside and taken care of."

"Mark, listen, you're a part of this family now, too. No way in hell could this have worked without your help. Do me a favor, get our injured in there for me."

"You got it, sir."

"It ain't, sir. It's Roger."

Mark called Alan, "You keep your eyes peeled three-hundred-sixty degrees. Let us know if you see anything." He told Blake to meet him over by Diana's cover hole.

They met up with Diana and pulled her up out of the hole. She moaned in pain and they ran her over to the house.

Rich was keeping an eye out on the woods as Karen and Bev tended to Diana.

Mark and Blake ran out and helped David up and got him over to the house as well. Mark asked Alan how he was doing and Alan said he was fine for now.

Haliday left his position where he had relieved Mark and crawled over to Kayla. "How you doing, kiddo?"

Kayla was a little shaken. Her voice trembled a bit. "Holy shit, Dad. I mean, what the hell just happened here?"

He patted her on her back. "You did good, kiddo. You did good. What happened was you fought for your life and ours."

He crawled over to Lisa's position next. "You doing all right?" he asked.

She responded, but he didn't understand her. Her words were scrambled.

She said, "I guess so. I feel dizzy a dizzy...a little dizzy, but might just hungry be."

"Nothing to eat in that hole?" he asked.

"I forgot that, I guess I do...I think maybe...I can eat it." She didn't really make any sense.

He put his hand on her shoulder to ask her again if she was okay. He pulled his hand back. It was wet with blood.

"Mark, get your ass over here," Haliday called to him.

Mark came running with Blake.

"She's hit or something," Haliday said. "Get her in the house." Lisa had lost consciousness at this point.

Mark lifted up Lisa and quickly ran to the house. Once inside, he yelled for some help.

Haliday told Blake to get down and stay there. Blake asked if he could move the body of the militia man.

"Yeah, go ahead," Haliday said.

Blake went to grab the body and yanked his hand back. "Damn, I cut my finger," he said.

Haliday said, "Don't move, Blake."

Haliday grabbed his flashlight, took a chance and turned it on. "Damn it," he said. He reached over and grabbed the foot trap that was still stuck in the dead mans body. He tossed it to the front of the hole. "You gonna live, Blake?" he asked.

Blake said, "Yeah, it's just a small cut."

"Grab your first aid kit and clean it out. Put a bandage on it. I'll be right back."

Haliday ran into the house. They had Lisa on the floor, lying on her stomach.

Haliday dropped down and pulled out his knife. "Get her jacket off."

After they took her jacket off, Haliday cut her shirt open. He looked at Mark. "No offense man." He cut her bra away and they all looked at the wound. Haliday barked out some orders.

When the man half fell into her fighting position, the spike strip caught her in the back. She had thought it was just him falling on her. After she got him out of the hole, she thought the pain was just a torn muscle or something. One of the spikes had actually caught her shoulder blade and hit a vein.

Bev and Karen put some gloves on and then grabbed a large syringe and irrigated the wound. They opened a sponge with an antiseptic agent on it and scrubbed the whole area. Bev used some quick-clot on it and waited until the blood stopped oozing out. She put a bandage on it and taped it up.

Haliday said tersely, "Put her by the wood burner and cover her up." He then looked at Mark. "I'm sorry, man, I didn't know."

"I didn't either. I don't think she knew herself," Mark said. "She's supposed to eat every few hours, too. I think we just got caught up in everything."

"Mark, you stay in here. I got the outside covered."

Mark started to follow Haliday outside. Haliday turned around. "Get the hell back in there," her told Mark.

"Roger, she's in good hands. We might still have problems."

He looked at Mark again. "Get in there. You come out before I tell you to and I'll shoot you my damn self."

Mark went back in the house to Lisa.

Chapter 31

Haliday did a check of everyone outside of the cabin. They were all sitting tight and waiting. No one knew if they any more action would ensue. Haliday made sure he talked to them individually as people, keeping things as personal as possible. He had to make sure they hung on to their humanity. They'd fight their own demons over time, but he knew how to help them with that. Starting now would help in the long run.

"Hey, Blake, just think; two weeks ago you were asking people if they wanted fries with their order."

Blake's response was quick. "You mean pick up or delivery?"

Haliday thought, *Good, he has that contact with the past.* "Of course I did, Blake. Get used to my screwing with you on a regular basis, pizza boy."

Kayla was his next target. "Hey, Kayla?"

"Yeah, Dad?"

"You mind running out to Starbucks for me?"

"Oh, you're a riot, Dad," she returned. "But I *am* craving some coffee."

Roger spoke to everyone. "Go ahead and bust open those thermoses. Crack open the hand warmers, too. I'll see if I can't order up some hot food, but stay alert. Weapons checks, too, and let me know if you need ammo."

Mark was sitting next to Lisa, holding her hand. She was very weak, but doing fairly well. The past couple of days they had had little food, expended a lot of energy traveling, and the stress from the assault and everything else combined with the injury had worn her down.

She looked up at him. "I'm fine, honey. I love you."

"I love you, too," he said.

She said, "Go help the others. I'll be fine."

Mark called on the radio to Haliday. "Anything going on out there?"

Haliday told him, "No, just some cold, hungry troops."

Mark said, "Lisa is doing great. She wanted me to help you out. You mind if I come outside?"

Haliday thought about it a second. "Sure, come on out. I'll go in and see about getting these guys some hot drinks and food."

"I have an idea as well," Mark replied. Mark put a stack of wool blankets over by the wood burner. Mark then went outside and relieved Haliday, who went inside to check on everyone.

He walked over to David who was being worked on by Rich and Bev. She had managed to flush his wound and get everything cleaned out. She even managed to get the bullet out which had stuck in his bone.

She packed it and bandaged it. Haliday thought he might need to pay that doctor a visit or get the nurse sooner. He had pain killers and antibiotics and some other meds stashed for occasions like this, but he had limited medical knowledge. He had taken some first responder training and that was it.

Karen had put some water on to boil so she could make hot coffee and cocoa for everyone and had started a big pot of stew. She cooked the meat separately so that Dawn, Diana, and she could have some as well. Haliday could hear Diana telling her to make sure she left it meatless; she was actually a full-blown vegan.

He walked over to Diana to check her injury. "How bad is it?" he asked.

Karen joined them and said, "It went through and broke her collar bone. We got it cleaned up and she'll be fine."

Haliday reached into his cargo pocket, fished around, and pulled his hand out and offered it to Diana.

"You're an ass," she said.

He chuckled, took a big bite of the jerky he held and then blew his breath in her face.

"You're disgusting," she offered.

He grabbed a milk crate, put the pot of stew inside, and stuffed some rolls and plastic spoons and bowls on the side. He carried it outside along with an empty milk crate and made his rounds dishing out the meal and a couple of words of encouragement and thanks. He collected the thermoses and took drink orders. After his rounds, he went back inside and set to filling the orders.

He filled half the thermoses with coffee and half with hot cocoa. He grabbed an armful of the blankets, which were nice and toasty now, and delivered them outside.

After making sure everyone was good to go, he went back over to Mark. "What do you think, Mark?"

"It's your call, Roger. We have about two hours until dawn."

Haliday told him they would be waiting it out until then. He did have a little thing he needed to take care of. He went in the house and changed out his gear load. He took just a few items he would need, and he would be gone no more than 30 minutes he hoped.

Rich asked him, "Where you going, Roger?"

"I'm going to pay the neighbor a visit."

After he walked back outside, he touched base with Mark.

Mark looked at him. "Where are you going?"

"I'm going across the street for some tea and biscuits. I'll be back very soon. Take charge here and make sure they don't shoot me on my way back in."

Mark promised, "Won't happen."

Haliday took off and made his way across the street.

He went around to the back porch of the house. He stopped and listened, he did not hear anything. He pulled out a small telescoping mirror and raised it up and glanced through the window. He didn't see anything; just a couple small candles glowing. He slowly reached up and twisted the handle of the door and it opened.

He entered the house and moved at a snail's pace, his .40 ready. He was in the large kitchen and slowly went down the hall, checking the rooms as he went. He found one closed and made a note of it. He got to the front of the house and stopped by the living room. He saw two figures, one in a chair, and one on a couch lying down.

There was a woman on the couch and Lance was sitting in his chair. He had a bottle of whiskey by him. Haliday looked over at the woman, who was motionless. He watched Lance for a couple of minutes.

Finally Haliday spoke. "Lance, what happened?"

Lance didn't turn around. He just spoke. "She's dead."

"Who's dead, Lance?"

He pointed to the couch.

"Is that your daughter, Lance?"

"No, that's my wife. I shot her." He said it with no emotion at all.

"Lance, you don't look like you're tied up in this crap. I mean, it looks like you've been here in that chair all night."

Lance didn't speak.

Haliday moved a bit closer with his pistol still aimed at the back of Lance's head. He spotted the picture in Lance's hand. It was his daughter's graduation picture. On the table in front of Lance was an opened bottle of pills.

Haliday moved over to the couch and dropped one hand down and confirmed the lady was dead. He had moved her hair aside; and exposed her face and a bullet wound to her temple. On the floor in front of Lance he saw a pistol lying. He also saw an empty pill bottle on the floor.

Lance looked at him. "She did it, Roger. I told her to mind her business, to tell Nicole to get the hell out of that cult or whatever the hell it is. She wouldn't listen. Neither of them would. I begged them both. My wife thought it was a good idea, broaden Nicole's horizons she said. I didn't think it would go this far."

"Lance, where's your daughter?"

"She's in the bedroom. I put her to sleep in there." Lance picked up the bottle of pills from the coffee table and emptied them into his mouth and washed them down with whiskey. He drank quite a few more swigs after that. "Roger, can you do me a favor?"

"What's that, Lance?"

"Bury my daughter for me. She deserves it. She didn't know any better. She was young, in love, and caught up in a fantasy. They left her out there laying on the ground. My wife almost didn't seem to care.

"I don't care about my wife, or even me, but you're a father. You understand. She always liked the tree house I built her. That would be nice over there. I'm sorry, Roger, I really am."

Haliday walked up. "I promise, Lance. I'll do that for you." He slowly retreated, keeping his guard up. He heard the whiskey bottle drop and shatter.

He checked the closed room on his way out. He passed through the kitchen and looked closely at the table. There were hand drawn maps of his property and everything surrounding it. He reached down and grabbed them all. This lady had been spying on them since he bought the place. She had the aerial photos from the internet and drawings of the place before the cabin even went up. The pile was a good two inches thick.

He looked at the notes and figured just as much. She had started from the moment the group set foot on the property. She had the days and times written down and everything that happened, everything they did. She had it marked when he and Blake had returned as well. Every move they made. It was like a journal—I saw, I noticed, I think.

Poor Lance was mere labor around there it seemed like. He never knew what was coming.

Haliday walked back to his house slowly and solemnly. Nothing he could have done could have prevented this. She had his number from the beginning and even if he'd had shot her on day one, the militia knew everything already. He would return tomorrow and bury them as promised. He reached the house.

"What happened over there?" Bev asked. "What did you do?"

"I didn't do anything. It was done already," he said.

*****

Back in town the militia convoy was on its way back. Rob and Brad had everyone in position. The plan was put together rather quickly, but since they had learned from Haliday that guerilla fighting was the only option, that's what they decided to do.

As word had spread over the past couple of days about the militia getting whittled away, the townspeople managed to get a few more people to join the cause. This was their fight for their own survival. Nobody else would be riding in like the cavalry and saving the day.

The militia convoy was coming through the small town now. They were tired, worn, had taken severe losses and wanted to get back to the airport. Thirty-one people had left the compound and nine were now dead and six injured.

Three of the injured would most likely die within the next couple of days. This didn't include the observer, who had been Haliday's neighbor.

In order to take the wounded back, they had left behind two of the quads. The Jeep was left in the ditch as well. They were certain Haliday's group would take them as their own.

The Jeep was the biggest loss as far as the vehicles were concerned. The guy who owned it had about 50 grand worth of work done to it. Lift kit, run-flat tire system, radio, extra roll bars, snorkel kit, and more.

When Haliday had seen it he said it looked like a JC Whitney catalog exploded.

The convoy was getting ready to make a right-hand turn down a small street full of houses that would lead them to the main gate of the airport. The lead vehicle made the turn and got about 200 feet down the road when four people on each side of the road pushed some vehicles down the driveways of the houses where they had been waiting.

The vehicles rolled down the drives and met in the street, blocking it. The militia vehicle had hit the brakes as soon as they saw the vehicles move. The convoy only had about 50 feet between the vehicles and three more had made the turn. They all tried to back up now. The man on the lone motorcycle went across the lawns and made a run for the airport's main gate and he made it.

The militia called the airport for help but were told negative. They couldn't put any more members in danger right then. The vehicles started to split up and moved in different directions. They could cut through the surrounding neighborhood and eventually get to the airport provided they didn't run in to problems.

One of the pickup trucks that had not made the right hand turn shot straight ahead instead. Only 150 feet down the road, they ran over two of the stop sticks the townspeople had made and the tires went flat immediately. The truck tried to keep moving, but the shredded tires and rims on the road made it hard.

They stopped the truck and both occupants jumped out and started running south. The airport was about a quarter of a mile away and they would try to get there on foot. They crossed through some yards and then into an open area with homes on both sides and continued moving. They were hesitant and sensed an ambush.

No sooner had they turned to look for cover when eight of the townspeople started firing on them. The townspeople unleashed a volley of over 100 shots fired. The men never stood a chance as the rounds hit them and they fell lifelessly to the ground. The townspeople moved in and took the weapons and ammo from the deceased men.

The deuce had been second in line. After it had backed up, it moved forward again quickly and rammed the two vehicles. It barely made it through them and continued toward the gate. All of their injured were in the back. The driver did not hesitate; he just kept right on going. If the vehicles used to block the road hadn't been in neutral, it would have been a different story.

He made it through the gate and to the back of the admin building where more members helped unload the injured.

One of the townspeople on top of the roof was going to fire but after seeing the wounded people he just let them be. He couldn't find it in himself to shoot any of them. He would seek out another target.

The last vehicle in line had seen all of the activity and locked up their brakes and hit reverse. The vehicle was going almost 45 miles an hour backwards. A few townspeople tossed some of the caltrops into the road. One of the rear tires blew out and the vehicle careened backwards into a party store. People moved to the store area and then took cover. The militia inside the vehicle got out and took cover behind the vehicle inside the store.

One of the militia ran to the back door and tried to open it. It had been padlocked on the outside from one of their own group during the seizure of all the supplies in town. He went back and told the woman with him that the only way out was through the front of the store. They didn't know whether to fight or surrender.

One townsman yelled to them. "Who are you guys? What are your names?"

The militia couple did not answer. They didn't know if it would do them any good. They thought if they could get out of there and no one knew who they were, they could deny being involved. They talked about it for a few minutes and made their decision.

"Listen out there," one said. "We want to surrender. We'll come out and surrender; please don't shoot."

Brad was with this group outside. He didn't honestly know what to do. He called Rob and asked him about taking prisoners. Rob had no idea either.

Rob called him back. "Hey, Brad, take them down the street to the police department and lock them up. Take all their gear though."

Brad yelled in to the store. "Come on out, hands raised, no weapons or we'll shoot!"

The couple came out slowly with their hands in the air. Brad made them lay down on the ground and a couple of others searched the couple.

Brad was looking at them. "I know you guys. Jerry, what the hell are you guys doing?"

Jerry just looked at him.

Brad asked him again but still no answer.

"Jerry, I can't believe you got involved in all of this. Then you went and attacked that guy and his family. How could you do that?"

Jerry and his wife just laid there.

"Get them up and let's go," Brad said. "Put their asses in the police department and in the jail."

They walked them down to the police department which was empty. They placed them in a cell with the blankets they had had in their truck and locked the cell.

Brad walked over to Jerry. "Man, I thought I knew you, Jerry. I had no idea you could do this."

"Do what?" Jerry asked. "Try and survive. Try to live through this shit?"

"No," said Brad, "turn on your community, steal from them, kill innocent people."

"Don't pretend you would do anything different, Brad."

"I did, Jerry, I'm doing what's right," Brad said. He walked away and called Rob.

Rob told Brad that two vehicles were still out there. He wasn't sure how many people were in them; it was Jeep and a Bronco. Everyone was looking out for them. Rob thought the ambush was going to end it all, but the lack of training and the speed at which they had to prepare had made it hard to control the inbound militia convoy.

Rob called a few guys together and they met at the police station. Brad was there as well.

Rob said, "Let's set up shop here. I don't think the police will be back any time soon. We can watch the prisoners then, too. Let's see about getting a duty roster together and see about heating the place somehow."

Brad said he would handle it.

Rob went back to help try in tracking down the remaining two vehicles.

When Rob returned, another man came up to him. "Hey, Rob, we found the Bronco. It was empty and it had two flats. Looks like whoever was in it made a run for it."

Rob told him to let the guys watching the airport know to be on alert in case the people tried to sneak in there. No telling what they would try in order to get back into the compound.

As morning approached, nothing else happened. They never found the Jeep or the people inside. Everyone was tired and Rob and Brad sat down and wrote down some notes. They would post four people there around the clock for now. Everyone would take turns. Brad went through the militia gear they had captured and distributed it. They would get the vehicles repaired and use those as well.

Rob called Haliday on the radio. "Roger, how did you make out over there?"

"Hi, Rob, we did all right. We have some injured, nothing major, but we'll need that nurse or preferably a doctor if you have one. I'm surprised we didn't lose anyone. We came close, that's for sure. Our neighbor across the road is no longer with us. Weird circumstances," Haliday said. "I'll have to tell you about it later. How about you guys?"

"We lost a few, some injuries here, too, but that was expected. We have a couple of prisoners, but we aren't going to turn them over; not sure what we're going to do with them. We injured a few and killed a few, but they managed to get back into the compound for the most part. We picked up some vehicles and guns too. I'll give you a call later today. I have a bunch of questions for ya."

"Okay, Rob, talk to you later."

Haliday had a feeling that it wasn't over yet.

Chapter 32

Haliday was still outside keeping watch after the battle. He had just checked in on the ham with Rob. They exchanged brief details about what had happened in their locations. Haliday had said he would talk to Rob later and said goodbye. Morning was approaching.

Haliday walked over to Mark. "Mark, I want you to go in the house and get some sleep for a few hours. One of us will have to be up at all times for a little while here. I don't expect any trouble any time soon, but we can't rest now. We need to see it through until we know for sure we're good to go."

Mark went inside and went to sleep next to Lisa.

After a few hours of sleep, Mark got up and grabbed some coffee. He checked on everyone in the house before he went outside.

Haliday was still out there keeping an eye on things and making the rounds.

Mark approached him. "What do you think, Roger?"

"Let's pull everyone off except for a security detail. One in the crow's nest and two outside. Everyone else needs sleep; rotate them through."

Mark took over and Haliday went in to get some sleep. Mark started getting everyone back inside and everything in order. He extended his patrol to cover as much of the surrounding area as he dared. He was amazed at what he saw.

The militia bodies left in place, blood sprayed all over the place. It wasn't that he had never experienced this before; it was the fact that it was here on U.S. soil, Americans against Americans.

Haliday woke up, grabbed his gear and a coffee and went outside.

Mark was standing there. "Good thing it's quiet."

"Yeah, that's for sure," Haliday replied. "You take a look around at all, Mark?"

Mark said, "I sure did. Let's take a ride; I'll show you."

They climbed into the Ranger and took off. An hour later they were back at the house.

Haliday was sickened, much like Mark was and for the same reason.

They walked back in the house. Breakfast was being cooked. It smelled good. Scrambled eggs, bacon, pancakes, oatmeal and hash browns, plus orange juice, coffee, tea, cocoa—it was a hell of a meal. There was plenty to go around and everyone ate more than they had in weeks.

It was well-deserved. Dinner would be a feast as well.

"Okay, everyone," Haliday said. "I need three volunteers. Kevin, Randy, Blake, let's go. Grab your gear, jump in the Ranger."

They all went across the street to the neighbors. Haliday cleared the house and then went and cleared the barn. There was an older Kubota inside and luckily it started when Haliday tried it. He drove it out and over to the back of the yard. There was the tree with the tree house, with dull, faded, pink paint peeling off.

"You guys go grab all of the bigger rocks that you can. Load them in the back of the Ranger," he said. "Keep bringing them until we have around 60. You'll find plenty along the creek bed."

They took off and Haliday used the small back hoe and dug a large square pit about four feet deep. While he was digging, the rock pile had grown large enough and he told them they had enough.

Next they went back up to the neighbor's house. "You guys grab the two in the living room," Haliday said. "I'll grab the other."

He looked through the closets and grabbed a bunch of sheets and blankets. "You can wrap them up in these," he said.

He went into the bedroom. The young girl was lying there, tucked in bed like she was sleeping. Haliday wrapped her blankets around her and took her outside.

"You need a hand, Uncle Roger?" Randy said.

Haliday answered, "No, I got this. I promised him."

He placed them all into the pit with the daughter in the middle, all wrapped up. He covered them up with dirt and tamped it down gently. They used the rocks and formed a crude large cross formation over the grave. Haliday wasn't overly religious, but he looked down at the grave and spoke.

"Lord, we have forgiven them for their sins and we ask that You forgive them for their sins and take them into Your kingdom. They were lost, but we pray in the end that they found You in their hearts and souls. May they rest in peace. Amen." He couldn't leave without at least a few simple words.

Next they dragged out the couch, chair, and mattress and set them on fire. No sense in having them sit there and become a contaminant. They walked out and he locked the house behind them.

They went back to their cabin and they showered up.

"Get some more rest guys, and thank you," Haliday told Randy and Kevin. He walked over to the radio and spoke to Rob. "Anything new over at the compound, Rob?"

Rob told him that no one saw anything happening. "Just normal activity and security patrols. They put some positions around the back of the buildings instead of trying to secure the south part of the complex. That was . I did see them take food to the prisoners, too. I tried to call them, but they did not answer. We do have a nurse and a doctor who are going to come by to see you guys shortly. I can bring them if you give me an address."

Haliday answered, "I'd rather meet you guys close by than give my address over the air."

They set up a time and spot to meet. It would just be about an hour so Haliday got ready. He took Mark and Randy in case there of problems.

They met at an intersection close by and then went to Haliday's. The doctor and nurse got busy checking everyone out. Mark and Haliday sat with Rob, who had brought Brad along as well. They talked briefly about what had transpired, but not too much in detail. Haliday said they went through and grabbed the equipment and firearms off the militia's dead.

"What did you do with the bodies?" Brad asked him.

"Brad, I didn't do anything yet. But I'll tell what we are going to do. You are going to get your prisoners, and one of the pickups, and bring them back here and make them pick up each body. You guys know where the sheriff lived by chance?"

Brad said he had the address at his shop on some of the FFL paperwork.

Haliday looked at him. "Make those people bury their dead. Use the sheriff's front yard. That's going to send a hell of a message to those people. Any idea on whether or not he made it?"

Neither Brad or Rob knew.

"Well, either way it'll be a reminder for them. The sooner the better. I'll have the guys wrap them in plastic, try and keep the animals from dining on them."

Brad and Rob exchanged glances a few times.

Haliday noticed this. "What gives, guys? What do you have on your mind?"

Rob spoke. "Roger, we are at a crossroads here and don't know what direction to take. We need some help trying to figure this out. We need some suggestions."

"Ok, I'll give you a few. Mark here can offer some as well."

They spoke for about two hours and wrapped up when the doctor and nurse finished. Haliday walked them out to their vehicle. The doctor filled them in on what was going on and said he left directions with the folks in the house.

Randy and Kevin came walking up with two of Haliday's welfare buckets. He handed one to the nurse and one to the doctor.

Haliday said, "Here's payment. I can't thank you guys enough. With that being said, this is why I keep telling you guys that you need to get into that compound. You need those supplies for everyone. You all need to work together. Keep me up to speed and I'll be talking to you later. Don't forget about the bodies."

Rob said, "They'll come get them before it gets too dark out."

Haliday shook his head. "No, wait until morning."

Dawn went and brought the horses back. She found them in the neighbor's barn, which was a cinderblock-built barn, but it looked like they hadn't had horses in quite some time. Seems the horses didn't want anything to do with the battle and went to hide.

Romeo and Max were still afraid to come upstairs. The kids were kept in the house; they didn't need to see any of the bodies.

The day was about over.

Dinner was cooking and Haliday went back over to the radio. He wrote down some more notes on what he heard. He even asked for other frequencies so he could gather more information. Any frequency he was on he would listen for specific information or he would ask a few questions. He had quite a note pile going now. There was still no word on any government activity.

They sat down for dinner and enjoyed the meal. They had some meatloaf that Bev had canned, canned corn, mashed potatoes, gravy, corn bread muffins, and pudding for dessert. Haliday even told a few corny jokes to lighten the mood.

"Blake, you ever look in the sky and see a flock of geese in their V-formation?"

"Yeah," Blake said.

"You ever notice how one side of the V is always longer than the other?"

"Yeah," Blake said again.

"You know why that is?"

"No, I don't," Blake answered.

Haliday looked at him. "It's because it has more geese in it."

Blake rolled his eyes and said, "It's going to be a long night."

Rich called Haliday over to the radio. "Go get Ma," he said. "Hurry up."

Haliday went and got Bev and they both went over to the radio.

Susan down in Texas had managed to find a ham and finally got through to them. She said they were doing fine and they caught up briefly on how every one was and said they would keep in touch. This was great news. Now they need to find out about Greg in Missouri.

The one thing Haliday had noted and now confirmed was that the lower part of Texas was more functional than the rest of the country; they even had power in some of the southernmost areas. He had heard the same about California, Arizona, and New Mexico. That really struck him as odd.

The next few days were extremely uneventful. The prisoners, while under guard, had picked up the bodies and taken them away. The group cleaned up the area the best they could and replaced the glass in the broken windows with Plexiglas that Haliday had stocked; easier to cut and handle than glass was.

They plugged all of the holes in the sides, and on the roof of the cabin, and checked for leaks. It was pretty much all back in order now.

Haliday had extra shingles, putty, Plexiglas, screws, nails, insulation, wood boards, piping, and all sorts of building materials to maintain the cabin. This was all kept in the storage building and pole barn. They would be able to fix practically anything that had broken or became damaged.

Haliday accessed his underground Faraday Cage. It was quite unique. It was a beast as far as a Faraday Cage was concerned. The effort put into it was extreme in nature. If it worked, great. If not, he had a big tub of modern antiques. He borrowed the back hoe from the neighbors. He felt odd using it, but he would pay whoever laid claim to their property if family ever happened to show up.

He dug down and hit a piece of rotting plywood. It was marine grade and he had treated it six times sealing it up, but it was meant for indication of the cage location and not protection. Once hitting it, he knew he would have to finish digging the cage out by hand. He turned the tractor off and jumped down.

"Grab a shovel, guys; let's get going." Randy, Kevin, Blake, Mark and Mike all pitched in to help dig.

They cleared the dirt off and removed the piece of wood. Sitting there was a big metal box that had been buried five feet under the ground. The box itself was roughly 48-by-48-by-48 inches. It was actually constructed of a couple of boxes nested inside each other. *Redundancy was the key to keeping the contents safe,* Haliday thought. He had looked up info on cages and everyone had a different idea of what would work, so he went with his own.

He built the first box with one-eighth-inch steel and lined it with rubber. The contents were placed inside and the top sealed with a rubber gasket and then metal tape. This was covered in rubber and then a copper shell applied to this. He was able to sweat the lid of the copper on in order to seal it entirely. Next was another thin metal skin and sealed again. They hoisted it out using the tractor and some slings.

Haliday started the slow process of opening the cage. Once it was opened, everyone looked inside. You would have thought it was Christmas with all of the *oohs* and *ahhs*.

"Don't get excited yet," he said. "We might have boat anchors here." He carefully pulled the contents out and the guys took it all inside.

Haliday walked inside and looked at the pile: two 32" flat screen TVs, two small DVD players, two small surround sound setups, a couple of portable radios, a couple of iPads, two laptops, and a massive computer tower filled with hard drives along with some other various electronics. He grabbed one of the laptops and walked over to an outlet.

He plugged it in as everyone stood there and waited. A few lights blinked and then the telltale Microsoft Windows sound came on.

Haliday looked around. "Solitaire anyone?" he asked.

They all cheered.

They set most of it aside and got a TV set up downstairs along with one of the laptops on the desk. The large computer tower was loaded with files—e-books, dictionary, digital encyclopedia, music, and over 5,000 movie files.

They would be okay for entertainment, and this would help keep some of the normalcy of life flowing. That had been the reason behind having backups for the TV and such, in case something broke before the country was back on the grid. They would limit the use of everything in order to avoid burning through it in a short period of time.

Next on the to-do list was to complete an entire inventory of everything they had and to work out some menus in order to maximize the food stores. They were actually much better off than they thought. The small caches around the property were just a bonus. Farming and bartering would allow them to sustain themselves.

Dawn called down to Haliday. "Rob needs to speak to you."

"Okay, tell him I'll be there in a second."

Haliday went up the stairs and sat down by the radio. "Hey, Rob, what's going on?"

"Roger, we had a problem today. We had the fuel truck from the airport come out with six armed guys. They went to one of the gas stations and took the gas. Well, they took a truck load. We didn't have enough people to try and defend it.

"There's more," he said. "They dropped a bunch of flyers on the ground. They said they were going to be taking more gas and other supplies as form of payment for the vehicles and equipment we took from them. There was to be no interference or they would defend themselves. They also said they would consider anybody on the streets armed and hostile."

Haliday replied, "Rob, that means they'll shoot anyone for any reason. They say anything else?"

Rob went on to say that the BAMM wanted their prisoners back, that they expected full cooperation at all times, and most importantly, they would not be setting up any trade or distribution of food or supplies until spring. "Roger, not a lot of people can make it that long."

Haliday told him that was because that's what the BAMM wanted; to cull the population. For some reason Haliday kept thinking about that.

He sat there in disbelief. He couldn't grasp what he was hearing. The militia had at least 25 dead and maybe 12 injured, of which half of those were likely to die. This was almost half of their forces and yet they continued to hang on and keep up their BS. He spoke aloud, "You'd think they were sitting on Fort Knox or something."

Dawn said, "No, you'd need a bigger army for that."

"Hey, Rob, do me a favor."

"What's that?" Rob asked.

Haliday told him to put a lot more intel on the militia compound. "Try and get a complete count of everything and everyone. There has to be something else going on that we don't know about and we might need to figure it out pretty quickly." Haliday said goodnight and looked over his notes.

Dawn asked him what was wrong.

"I think you found the problem," he said.

"What do you mean?" she asked.

"Their numbers are growing. I kept thinking I was screwing up the people count that I had, but that's not it. Unless they have rabbits in there and they are spitting out full grown humans, then people are getting into that compound somehow. Somehow or at some time, more people showed up." He sat back in his chair and mumbled.

"Meeting time!" he yelled after a moment.

Everyone gathered around him.

"I'm getting a little tired of this stuff," he said. "I'm going to go meet with Rob and his crew tomorrow morning. I think the militia has been growing their numbers over the past week. I would venture to say they had people show up from out of town and they expect more."

Mark looked at him. "That would explain why they still have the attitude. They are trying to hold on as long as they can until their entire group comes in. There's no telling how many are on the way or how soon they get here."

"My point exactly," said Haliday.

Everyone looked around at each other. They wanted to ask but knew the answer. The fight wasn't over.

Haliday sat for a minute more. He looked at Mark and asked him if he would join him to go meet with Rob and Brad in the morning.

Mark slowly nodded. "I think I better. If you're thinking about what I'm thinking about, then yeah, I better go, too."

"Okay, it's settled." Haliday called Rob and set up the meeting.

They would have to take that compound and disband the militia before any more militia arrived or they would have to leave the area themselves and that wasn't an option.

Haliday and Mark arrived for the meeting just outside of town at an old abandoned tackle shop. Rob, Brad and two more guys met them there. They sat down to talk about the militia and Haliday mentioned what he thought was happening.

Brad looked at him. "I think you're right. I've seen a couple of cars the past few days in town that I don't really remember being there. Plug wires were missing, so not sure if they run or not, but one had Ohio plates on it. They must have come in, parked, and then snuck in. No one had really been watching the whole compound until last night. We just watched the main gates and admin building. This poses a big problem for us."

Rob shook his head. "We're in deep, real deep."

"And you don't have a paddle," Haliday added. "However, this is what we are going to do. Take notes."

Haliday and Mark spent six hours covering everything they would need to gather as far as equipment went and what the plan was. They got a good count of how many people they had to work with and what types of firearms. They wrapped up the meeting and set the assault plan in motion. They would play it by ear as to when it would begin because everyone had preparations to make.

Haliday and Mark went home and explained it to the group.

Only Haliday and Mark would be involved; everyone else would be staying put.

Chapter 33

Rob had his people keep a closer eye out on the compound. They noticed that same night that there was indeed another group of people who snuck into the compound. It looked like it was two adults and a younger child around 12-years-old. Brad and a few others had taken it upon themselves to check and mark the vehicles in the area so they knew which ones had been there and which ones were new.

Haliday told them to use chalk and mark the inside of a tire so it wasn't obvious. They could double up by placing a small stone just under a tire. If the first number in the license plate was an even number it went under the drivers front tire, if it was odd it went under the passenger front tire.

They had remembered the newer vehicles that popped up and checked them out. With the help of the auto parts store, they were able to get two of the three running and confiscated them. They would use them for now and then return them if they could convince the owners to leave.

Brad and Rob's group spent the next 48 hours on preparing for the assault. Brad had brought out groups of people who were given a crash course on the tactics they would need to employ during the assault—some basics on cover, fire, escape, and evade. Not nearly enough training, but more than any of them had ever had.

The exception was that Brad was able to find five veterans and three police officers in the group to help them out and take on roles as squad leaders. One of the police officers whose name was Chuck had had formal SRT, Special Response Training, and picked a few guys to help with building entry. There would be two teams for building entry.

After the initial assault, Mark would take over the main assault group while Haliday and Chuck split off with the two entry teams to do the building checks. Once they cleared the buildings, another man was assigned to lock them down. It was as simple as locking the door and then breaking a key off in the tumblers. They had a locksmith who could open them later.

They found some more tractors to use and took them over to the metal fabrication shops in the area for armoring. They would armor the driver's front and the buckets or dozer blades. These were only going to be used for the assault; just enough to get some guys in and breach one side of the compound. The south end was fairly accessible, but most of the people and buildings were all at the north end of the airport.

Brad went through again and picked out the best hunters they could find. Each was assigned an area of the compound to cover. The assigned marksmen were also assigned spotters to watch the area for any surprises or attacks from the rear. They had no idea who might try to sneak up behind them.

Brad had a stock full of tannerite targets. He asked Haliday what they should do with them.

"Easy," Haliday said. "You lay a piece of scotch tape down, a line of heavy finishing nails on the tape, and wrap it around the can of tannerite. Use the giant slingshot and launch them into the compound. The hunters will have a target full of flechette's to fire on.

"The militia won't want to touch them or come close after a few go off. Try and launch a bunch simultaneously and have the guys shoot them at the same time as well. That will be a huge psychological kick in the pants. After word gets out, when one lands near someone they'll want to leave."

Brad looked at him. "You're a sick man."

"Guerilla warfare, Brad, that's all it is. The days of taking twenty paces and dueling with pistols ended a while ago," Haliday replied.

They wrangled up as many tires as they could. They placed them around the outside of the compound in stacks.

The militia laughed at them. *Those things wouldn't stop a .22 round*, was what they were thinking.

What they didn't know was that these would be lit on fire to create a smoke screen to help block some of their activities and to smoke out the militia as much as possible.

Haliday had some townspeople gather up bricks from the brickyard and use those to reinforce some of their fighting positions around the compound. He also had them place a good number of spike strips along the roads so any vehicles making a run for it would get flat tires. They would let people go, but would have to make their point so the militia would know it was over and they would be expected to disband completely.

Haliday made sure that the guys that would be entering the compound and buildings had mirrors to use; these were simple contraptions made of compact mirrors from the cosmetic counter of the drug store, shortened broomsticks, and duct tape. Simple, effective, and cheap. Easily tossed aside or thrown away with no bother of how much they had cost.

Haliday covered clothing with the guys. "Make sure you do not wear any camo. We cannot have anyone getting hit by friendly fire. You have all seen that they wear the Russian camo and know what it looks like. Wear plain black or regular clothes. Make sure they are loose enough to give when you move, but tight enough so they do not get caught on anything. Your shoes are important as well. Boots with ankle support are the best option; avoid tennis shoes.

"Everybody gather around me," he said. "I'm going to cover the rules of engagement. No children are to be fired upon unless they are actively firing on you. Anyone else that is armed and engaged is fair game. If they drop their weapons and surrender, you zip tie them behind their backs. We shoot to neutralize the threat."

"What's that mean?" he heard someone yell.

"Kill," Haliday answered back.

He made a quick count of the people involved. There were almost 120 of them total. These people were starting to get hungry and that meant they were ready to fight. They were starting to realize quickly now what was happening and what their future held. It wasn't just them; it was their families as well.

He called everyone close in. "I have a little speech to give here, people. I hope it doesn't change your minds about anything. People are going to die. That is a cold hard fact you all need to come to grips with. The fight is being taken to them because if you don't, they will become stronger and you will become weaker.

"There are no ifs, ands, or buts in this. It's a matter of getting it done the right way, right now. As corny as it sounds, and as often as it is used in the movies, look around you. This is the reason you are fighting. This is who depends on you. This is who you must depend on. With that being said, Depends might not be a bad option; some of you will crap your pants." He got quite a few chuckles at that, even though it was probably true. "Any questions before we leave?"

There weren't any. Just a lot of thank you's, good lucks, and prayers. Haliday shook Rob's hand and Brad's hand. "I'll see you all in the morning."

Haliday and Mark headed back to the house. They walked in and the mood of the group was somber.

"I'm not going over it all again, okay? It's gotta be done, plain and simple," said Roger.

Morning came and Mark and Haliday were ready to go. They went downstairs to find everyone there waiting for them. A lot of hugs and kisses followed.

Kayla walked up and gave Mark a hug.

She went over to Haliday and gave him a big hug with tears in her eyes. "You better be coming home. You promise me that, Dad."

"I can't promise you that, sweetheart. What I can promise you is that I will do everything I can to make it happen," Haliday said. "I want you to know how proud of you I am. I could never have asked for a better daughter who has grown into a fantastic young woman. You can accomplish anything you want in life, kiddo. Never give up. Take care of the family here. You're the boss for now."

Haliday and Mark got into the Jeep and took off. They didn't say a word to one another on the way there. They just went over the assault plans in their heads.

They arrived at the police station and everyone else started to arrive as well. Haliday pulled out a big pot and a bunch of Styrofoam bowls. One of the folks took charge and started doling out the oatmeal with bananas that Haliday had brought.

Haliday also had made some coffee at the police station and handed out some granola bars along with pitchers of Tang. It was a meager meal, but still hit the spot. He put a few bags of chocolate candy on the tables for some more sugar and thus more energy.

Haliday talked with Rob a bit. "You guys are getting one hell of a bill for my consultancy work here."

Rob asked him if he took cash.

"Oh, now you have jokes, huh, Rob?"

Haliday and Mark had their radios with them and they had brought two extra handhelds for Rob and Brad. They had five mobile units from the vehicles they had acquired. They placed one at each corner of the airport compound. From there they should be able to coordinate the assault.

Everyone had made it in and Haliday did another quick count. They had gained about 10 more members. The doctor approached and introduced another doctor and three nurses. They had gathered as many medical supplies as they could and had an area prepared for medical treatment in the conference room of the police station. Any wounded they planned to put in an office building next to the police station for now.

Haliday said, "Move them out, Rob."

Haliday and Mark went and got ready. Haliday had his faithful old Armalite AR180 with him. He chose it over a short-barreled AR15 because of the folding stock and usefulness in close quarters.

Chuck had his own entry weapon of choice, which was an MP5. After the initial assault, they would meet up with their teams and start the building clearing.

Everyone got into position. The daytime assault was a big risk, but they took it because it would help level the field. No night-vision goggles, or night-vision scopes; plain sight, easy to discern friendly from foe, and the daytime conditions would allow the hunters with their scoped rifles to maximize their ability.

The militia compound was ready for the attack. As soon as they had seen the attack mounting, they sounded their alarm and everyone was in position. They sat there and waited.

Haliday's group sat there and waited, too. He called the militia on the ham. "We are going to give you the opportunity to surrender."

The militia response came quickly. "Negative. Disband and go home."

Haliday called them again and explained it all to them. "Listen, this is how it is. You can surrender and we can go from there. If not, it's going to be ugly for both sides. You have women and children in there who don't deserve this. It's the best option for everyone involved, so let's work this out."

A one-word response came. "Negative."

Haliday mumbled to himself. "What was that song from that stupid movie *Small Soldiers*? Some Spice Girls' song; wish I had that right now." *I'll tell you what I want, what I really really want.* "Oh, great," he said. "I'm going to die with that stupid song stuck in my head."

Mark looked at him. "What's wrong?"

"You don't want to know," Haliday replied.

One more try on the radio. Haliday said, "Listen. A lot has happened, a lot will happen, and we don't need to go down that road. Anyone who wants to give up and go home can do so now. We'll give you one hour to decide. After that we may take action. Don't be stupid. Listen to us. Come on, guys. No one wants to die today."

All he heard was, "Screw you."

"Okay," he said. "One hour. Time has started."

Haliday had told everyone to expect what came next.

The militia started firing on the group's positions in order to try and gain an edge during the assault. They fired a lot of rounds into the barricades, toward the tree line and everywhere else. The townspeople didn't fire a single shot back. Not a single person even got hit as they maintained cover.

Haliday had what he wanted—the proof that the militia would not make a deal and firing first meant just that. They'd given the BAMM a chance and they refused it. Haliday had a few guys fire a couple of rounds toward the compound, but not at anyone in particular. This drew another barrage of fire from the militia.

He clicked the radio. "Forty-five minutes left."

Time was counting down; the militia was persistent in not giving up.

Haliday gave them one last warning. "You have five minutes left. Last chance to get out now for anyone wanting to. Come on out with your hands empty, no questions asked, and we will take care of you and get you to safety." He waited the five minutes and switched the channel to his own. "Game on, folks. Good luck. Godspeed. Fire when you have a target."

Haliday had made sure they didn't have a sniper on the roof of the admin building.

This would have been the first man to go. The militia learned their lesson the hard way by taking hits on that position.

Haliday searched the property with his spotting scope and had everyone else looking as well. He had to make sure they didn't have one hidden. Haliday was convinced no one in the compound had higher ground.

Haliday loaded an armor piercing round into the Barrett he had liberated and fired on his first target. This was the lock on the door of the building that held the prisoners. He saw that they had another lock and hasp on the door and he fired on that one, too. He waited patiently, but no one came out. They would check this building out as soon as they could. There was some return fire from the militia, but nothing to worry about. They couldn't reach his position.

From over on the north end of the compound came 30 shots from four different townsmen. These were all concentrated on the militia's prized deuce, or actually its tires. They flattened as many as they could, rendering the up-armored pig useless. All the militia had to rely on now was the regular complement of vehicles that they had.

The militia took aim and returned fire. They fired almost 200 rounds at the townsmen in a matter of seconds. As far as firepower was concerned, they had the advantage over the townspeople. They didn't have the amount of concealment, however, so many of the rounds were wasted with only an occasional hit.

Haliday took aim at target number three. He hated to do it, but he had to. He zeroed in on the front tire of their fuel truck and flattened it. He shifted his aim slightly and flattened the other front tire. Both the fuel truck and deuce were now out of commission. He started to hear some sporadic gunfire from all sides of the airport.

As he searched out some more targets he gave the order to start the tires on fire. They had some small balloons of gas placed in them and the guys tossed some road flares into them. The thick black smoke started to fill the air in those areas as the tires burned. Nobody was sure how long they would burn, but everything helped at this point.

One of the townsmen throwing the flares took a round to the shoulder. This was only the first of many casualties to come. The men around him fired into the compound and allowed him the chance to get to safety so he could be treated. They had one man and a woman nurse dedicated to picking up the injured with a four-wheeler. They'd be busy today.

Haliday scanned the south end of the compound. The stacks of bricks they were able to get in place were still there. The front loader was still sitting where it had stalled out.

Haliday called Rob. "Rob, get some people over to the west breach and see if you can get that front loader started. Get some people into those brick emplacements."

Rob told him that the front loader stalled out.

Haliday asked him what happened.

Rob told him it had overheated.

"Well, try it anyway. If it didn't seize, it may start. You can use it to at least get some guys into those positions."

Rob made the arrangements and got everyone in place. He gave a command and the whole south end started popping as five guys ran to the loader. The militia positions were quiet as they held their heads down.

The group made it to the loader and sure enough it started. The guys just jumped on and the guy driving it went straight to the brick emplacements where he dropped off two guys at each one. He turned around and headed back toward the west breach and almost made it before the engine seized up. The radiator had taken hits the last time and had stalled out, but this time it was dead for sure with the seized engine. The driver jumped down and used it as cover.

Haliday moved to another position so he could fire past the emplacements without worrying about the guys being in the crossfire. He told the men with the hunting rifles to try and take shots at the militia positions. They needed to take out three of the five positions that could cover the south end if they expected to get the building entry teams in there and continue to take some of the compound.

Haliday moved over toward the west breach area himself and took a look. He glanced over at Rob. "Grab your binoculars and look at that position on the west corner of that building. We need to take out that one and the ones on each side of it. Tell them that's what the plan is."

Rob sent a couple of runners out to the town's snipers and word spread. He used some hand signals and eventually got the point across to the guys behind the bricks and front loader.

Over toward the north side of the compound, Mark and Brad got the men ready. They used some probing fire to see where the militia's strong points were. Mark told Brad to go launch some cans at the admin building. These had been pulled out of the hunting shop and were merely cans of gel fuel. They had close to a hundred of them. They partially unscrewed the lids and launched them all toward the admin building. Almost half hit the building and quite a few landed on the roof. The tops popped off and the gel ran everywhere.

One of the townspeople tried to launch a flare onto the roof, but couldn't get the distance he needed with the giant sling shot. After a couple of failed attempts, he resorted to attempting to use some fireworks, but couldn't get the angle. He risked moving in closer and was met with a few rounds into his chest.

Mark had told them to abandon the attempt if it didn't work with the flares, but the guy had insisted. They had to leave him lay where he was.

Haliday concentrated on the center militia position. He saw the muzzle of the rifle above the sandbags. He took aim and fired a shot. It was off, but close enough to let the guy know he was being watched. He saw the muzzle shift and gave it one more shot into the sandbags, but still had no luck. He moved backwards and into the trees where he looked around.

There was a man up in a tree stand nearby with his rifle pointed toward the compound.

Haliday asked him, "Hey, you can't see these guys at all?"

The man said, "Not enough to get a good center mass shot."

Haliday asked him what he could see. The guy told him that once in a while he could see the top half of a head.

"Take the damn shot," Haliday told him. "Forget that center mass bullshit."

The man steadied his rifle and kept aim at the militia position. Haliday crouched down low and looked at his watch. After almost five minutes, he was about to climb the tree himself when he heard the shot. He looked up and jumped to the side just in time as the man threw up. The guy had taken a perfect shot from ear to ear, cutting a channel through the militia member's head.

Haliday yelled up to him, "It's them or you! Get the hell out if you can't hang or get ready to do it again!"

The man said he'd be okay.

Haliday asked him if there was anyone else in the position there and the guy told him no, it looked like just one guy.

"What about the ones to the left and right?" Haliday asked.

"Looks like two in each."

"Okay, keep your rifle on them, take the kill shots. You're doing good," he told the man.

Haliday moved back toward the west breach area.

Chuck was still there. "What do you think, Roger?"

"Chuck, I think we need to get our asses in there as soon as possible. The center position has been taken out, and we need to get the ones on the sides of it. Let's try and work on the one to the right first."

"How are we going to do that?" Chuck asked.

"Give me a minute to think about it, Chuck."

Haliday thought for a few minutes. He called Rob over. "Look, this is what we're going to do. We have to concentrate fire on the southeast side. A light rate of fire. We need these guys to shift in their positions. At the same time, I need the east side to have some men move in a little closer, not try and rush the east side; just make a few good attempts to get in closer."

Rob said he would get it taken care of.

"You wait for my signal, Rob. I'm going to have Mark pop a few rounds of smoke over there."

Rob headed over to the east side in the four-wheeler and told the guys what they were going to do. The men who volunteered got ready, while over on the west side Haliday told the town's snipers what to do.

Haliday himself climbed up into a tree and got ready as well. He could hardly see the guys behind their fighting positions; admittedly it was harder than he thought.

He took aim on the inside of the fighting position and keyed his mic. "Mark, do it now."

Mark launched four rounds of smoke toward the east perimeter and Rob had some of the men fire into the east side positions as four of the men made short advances through the woods to get closer. The advancing men just concentrated on getting closer and fired just a few rounds from the SKSs they had.

Rob was helping them suppress the militia on this side. He spotted the militia shift in their positions to provide more return fire toward the advancing townspeople. One of the militia was able to fire toward the advancing men and struck one in the abdomen. This man went down and crawled behind a tree. Rob and the rest of his men opened up.

Haliday aimed at the sandbag and saw the color change in his scope. He fired the round and watched it penetrate a man's back square between his shoulders. The man went forward and Haliday could only see his arm and hand on his rifle.

Haliday fired another shot and the man's hand came off at the wrist. Haliday knew the guy was dead from the first round, but with Haliday himself going in soon, he was just making sure.

The men firing along with Haliday managed to wound two and kill one more. Out of the three positions, they still had one fully capable militia, two injured, and two dead. Going into the compound directly from the south was their best option. Chuck came over and Haliday explained the change in plans and they moved the two building entry teams to the south.

Back up toward the main gate, Mark ordered them to launch a dozen of the tannerite cans. They made a last minute change and used fluorescent green highlighters to paint the tape so they could be spotted more easily. A few didn't make it over the line of cars the militia was using, but that worked out in Mark's favor.

He had one of the guys fire and the can exploded in front of the cars and they could hear the nails peppering the sheet metal.

The militia just looked at each other.

One more exploded and the nails flew everywhere.

The militia looked around and saw a few of these lying on the ground behind them. They didn't know what to do with them.

Mark had the guys pepper the whole north side of the compound and around the admin building with the remaining tannerite cans they had.

Haliday's and Chuck's teams each had five of their own that they would use. These were turning out to be nice little devices. Haliday was surprised he hadn't thought of it before.

Mark had them blow a few more tannerite cans and the word thoroughly spread throughout the militia what these things were about. The militia all kept a very close eye on them.

A few of the militia had taken their jackets off and tossed them, trying to cover the cans up. One guy managed to cover up the one by him and then he shot it himself. Kind of like the redneck who says, 'Hey, y'all, watch this.' Fortunately the jacket contained the nails, although it was fairly well shredded.

Haliday was ready to move in. He was behind the wheel of his Jeep and he had four other men with him, one in the passenger seat, one on each nerf bar, and one in the backseat.

He had Rob behind the wheel of the four-wheeler and the rest of Chuck's entry team barely hanging on so they could exit quickly. Haliday had secured the Barrett and was ready with his pistol and AR180.

Each team had four men—two with shotguns, two with ARs and everyone had pistols as well. Haliday was the only one carrying a Smith. The rest had Glocks. He never liked Glocks—something about a pistol that was dishwasher safe didn't appeal to him.

That and the fact that once on the range at the police station years ago he had watched a hot reload blow the top of a grip off. The guy ended up with 25 stitches. Haliday had seven magazines for his pistol , so he didn't worry too much about interchanging mags.

The plan was not as suicidal as it sounded. They had the two injured and one full-bodied man to deal with. With any luck these two would already be neutralized before they got there.

Haliday clicked his mic. "Okay, everyone, we are a go."

Haliday and Rob had about 450 yards to go and left one behind the other.

As they approached the southern buildings, they crisscrossed paths a couple of times and widened and narrowed their space between them to try and randomize their approach, throwing off the target acquisition anyone might have on them. The groups on the east and west sides started firing into the militia positions. The snipers looked for targets.

One of the injured militia raised himself up to take aim on the approaching vehicles, but he went down before he could pull the trigger on them. The other militia positions on the east and west sides didn't have enough cover to help out. To shift fire and help out would mean exposing themselves and possibly being overrun. They continued their fight to the east and west.

Of the three positions the townspeople needed to neutralize, the center one was empty. The one to the east only had one injured man left and this was where Rob was heading. The one Haliday was near was the one to worry about. They still had that one guy in there with his injured partner. Haliday kept a steady pace as he approached it.

The west tree line positions opened up with everything they had. As the Jeep came to a stop, the men on the nerf bars hit the ground running and fired into the position as the other two exited the Jeep. The return fire dropped one of the men with a hit to the chest and one to the man's leg. The other three advancing men fired into the position with 10 rounds of buckshot and a full 30-round magazine.

The guy was hit multiple times and the advancing men heard screams from the other man who had been injured and was now lying down on the ground with his hands in the air, pleading to not be shot. One of the advancing members rolled the guy over and placed handcuffs on him and left him there.

Haliday moved the Jeep toward the building as they rushed to the last of the three positions.

Rob's four-wheeler approached, but before it came to a stop the militia member came up firing. Chuck, who was next to Rob, fired back along with the other two. One of the men in the back fell off the four-wheeler and tumbled along the ground, dead.

A sniper from the east side had to fire three shots, but hit the injured militia member, ending his life.

The militia group on the east fired up into the trees when they spotted this man and hit him. The man had only been hit in the leg, but lost his footing on the tree stand and fell to the ground, breaking his arm and some ribs. He laid there unable to move and the militia finished him off as he tried to get behind the tree.

Mark's area was much harder to assault. With most of the buildings and fortifications in place on the north side, it was hard for the men Assigned to Mark to find suitable targets. Mark ordered a ceasefire unless the snipers could definitely get a shot in. They couldn't afford to waste any more ammunition on just trying to suppress fire.

He called over to Brad. "We need to see about getting these people moving and exposed. See if they can fire into any of the tannerite cans and let's see what happens. If we can't get to them, it's a waste of our effort."

414

Brad and Mark both passed the word along. A few of the guys started to take some shots on the tannerite cans, hoping to hit them.

One of the cans near one of the militia's northeast positions exploded, sending its nails flying. The two people in the fighting position were hit, causing multiple cuts on their backs and the backs of their necks. Two nails embedded themselves in one of the men's neck. He reached around and tried to remove them, but his jacket was in the way.

The other man moved over quickly to help him out.

Mark saw this and waited. When the man went back to his side of the fighting position, Mark fired and struck the man in the left arm and shoulder.

The militia called in for aid and this is when they discovered the situation was worse than it actually was; they were on their own with what they had with them.

The deuce couldn't provide cover for delivery or extraction. The militia would have to stand their ground the best they could until the opportunity arose when someone could get more supplies to them. They had plenty of rounds; just no food or first aid capability for those who needed intensive medical treatment.

Mark called a ceasefire again. He told everyone to save their rounds and not to fire on the tannerite anymore until they could plan a new strategy.

Mark called Haliday. "Roger, how's it going down there?"

Haliday responded. "We are in the perimeter. We have most of the south side now. I need you to get some guys down here to help take out the other two positions."

Mark and Brad gathered a few guys together and went around to the south side of the airport. Once there, Mark assigned four guys to move forward to the brick emplacements and then work there way forward to take over the militia emplacements that had been seized. They would have to alter the positions to make them more effective, but right now they would serve them well enough.

Mark would then concentrate on helping Rob and the rest of the guys take the other positions out of service. With Haliday and Chuck's entry teams clearing the three most southern buildings, they would use these to help continue moving the assault closer to the admin and motor pool buildings. In between these buildings and the ones Haliday would take were the food and supply storage buildings.

Over by the northeast corner of the compound, some of the townspeople started to take fire from behind them. They scrambled for cover. They were now caught in a crossfire. The militia had had a couple of members heading toward the airport to join them.

They had stopped to wait out the assault and then come help if they were called in. One of these militia vehicles had come up directly from the east and was now in a position to help out. The people in this vehicle had found an area to hide.

They were now engaging the townspeople in the firefight.

Chapter 34

Haliday adjusted the entry teams. He now had two teams with only three guys each. They decided to go with two shotguns and an AR in order to prevent over-penetrating the buildings. The first building they entered was the large hangar building furthest south. One of the guys went up to the back door and used the shotgun to blow through the lock.

Once open, he swung the door open and he tossed a tannerite can inside, which Haliday then fired on. The can exploded, but instead of nails they had used the small airsoft beads; basically homemade stun grenades because they didn't want to damage what might be inside. Both teams entered the building and conducted the sweep. This building was completely filled with food and they noticed Wal-Mart tags on most of the items.

The next building was very small. This one they could not reach yet because there was no back door. It was the building the militia had used for interrogating people. Haliday went to the back window and pulled out his mirror and took a peek. He waved Chuck over.

Chuck took the mirror and looked in the window as well. There were a couple of chairs and a table, but there was also more.

The BAMM had built a rack to suspend people from. They could keep the person's hands tied over their heads and their feet barely touching the ground. There was blood on one of the chairs and on the floor. The worst part was a man still hanging from one side of the rack. It looked like he had been dead for a few days already.

Chuck looked at Haliday. "I know that guy."

"Who is it, Chuck?"

Chuck looked pissed. "That's the Chief of Police. He went missing the second day of the outage. No one knew what the hell happened to him. We all thought maybe he bugged out. He and the sheriff never got along. I guess we know now what happened to him. Seems like the Chief wasn't going to put up with any BS and they decided he was a liability."

Haliday keyed his mic and told everyone what they had found. This re-ignited the rage that the people had for the militia. They went back into the first building and made their way over to the west side of it. Haliday's team left and provided cover while Chuck's team made it to the back of another building. This was going to be the last easy building to clear.

Mark had heard the shots being fired over at the northeast corner and knew something was wrong. He called and confirmed that there was a problem. "Okay, Brad," he said. "We need to get over there and see what's going on." He called on the radio and told everyone to keep checking their rear. Haliday and Brad took off. Rob stayed to make sure everyone got up to the emplacements.

Haliday got one team at a time moved up toward the three buildings. They got all three militia positions manned without any problems and spent a few minutes arranging them to make it a bit safer. The next piece of the puzzle would be to get the other two positions emptied out. They had a couple of parlor tricks left. Haliday called a couple more guys up to his position. They came up and each brought a couple of large plastic toolboxes.

Over the next 30 minutes they made two more trips with more supplies and ammo. They were almost ready to make the assault on the two positions. They had to wait for Chuck to enter the other building and clear it first.

Chuck was at the back of the building. They blew the door, tossed in and then blew the tannerite can. As soon as they entered the building more shots were fired.

Haliday and his team got down low. They waited until the firing stopped and then Haliday ran over to the building and crouched down. He yelled into the door. "Chuck, what's the status?"

Chuck's voice came back, "We're clear. We have one wounded and we took out one militia."

Haliday entered the building. Inside were a woman lying there dead and Chuck's man who was hit in the hip.

Haliday walked over to him and checked him out. Chuck had put a pressure bandage on his hip.

"How bad?" Haliday asked.

Chuck said he would be okay, but wouldn't be able to move.

"We can't get him out of here for at least another hour," Haliday said. He looked at the injured guy. "Can you make it until then?"

"Yeah, sure, it just hurts."

Haliday grabbed a bottle out of his pocket and handed him a Vicodin. "Take this. It'll help."

Haliday told Chuck they were heading back to the other building to get ready.

Once they got there, they looked out and saw the target. Haliday asked the guys if they were ready and both nodded. They would be launching a small assault from two buildings, his and the one Chuck was in.

Haliday clicked his mic. "We go on my word. Everyone ready; three, two, one, go!"

Mark and Brad had gone slow and came up across the street from the brickyard where they saw a truck.

"I wonder if that's their truck," Mark said.

Brad said, "Yep, that's where we got the tractor and that truck wasn't there before."

They checked the woods around the brickyard. They spotted some people movement and kept their eyes on it.

Mark told Brad he was going to low crawl up into a better position. Brad kept watch as Mark moved forward.

Mark was about 25 yards closer to the people and watched. He heard some shots fired from the compound area and saw these people fire back. They weren't wearing the Russian camo and he wasn't sure who they were. He wondered if they were good guys or bad.

He motioned for Brad to crawl up. Brad moved up slowly. Mark could tell he wasn't used to this. He looked over at Brad and pointed the people out. Brad looked at them and then back at Mark and shook his head no. He was sure these were not part of Rob's group. He told Brad he was moving over to line himself up better.

While he was moving, the pair fired once again toward the compound. He heard the guy say he got one.

"Good job, sweetie," he heard a woman say.

This was a couple, Mark thought. He moved back toward Brad.

"It's a man and a woman. I'm going to go further east and come through the brickyard. You come along to a point and then provide me some cover. We can't get them from here. I need to take a clean shot and can't get one right now."

They moved east and then found a place to cross.

"You stay here, Brad. I'll cross over and check it out. I'll signal you when I want you to cross."

Mark crossed over into the brickyard and made his way toward the couple. He peeked around a pallet of bricks and spotted two small children hunkered down behind them. He looked across at Brad and signaled him to back off a bit.

Toward the main gate, some of the townspeople took shots at the militia. They were not able to hit them, so they tried to light the gel fuel. They tried bows and arrows and aimed high, hoping the arrows would drop on the guys, but nothing worked. One of the townspeople shot at a vehicle and ruptured the gas tank. The rest of the men with him started shooting the vehicles, trying to puncture as many of the fuel tanks as they could.

The militia had pushed the vehicles in place but did not empty the tanks out. Gas was now flowing along the entire line of vehicles that the militia relied on for protection and cover at the front of the admin building.

Once a couple of tanks were punctured and the militia caught on to what was happening, the militia fired toward the townspeople. The militia unleashed over 1,000 rounds to try and stop them.

The militia hit a man and woman who were injured and another man was killed.

The townspeople lit some fireworks and aimed them toward the vehicle barricade. Finally one struck gas and within minutes they all started to burn.

After about 10 minutes, the line of cars was so engulfed in flames you could hardly see through all of the smoke. The militia was able to pull back toward some secondary defensive positions rather safely. Only one militia man sustained a hit while making the move and it was an injury that left him bleeding, but still able to fight. The townspeople took the opportunity to gather up their own wounded and get them to safety.

Haliday's and Chucks teams approached their assigned buildings at the south side of the airport. Haliday's team popped the door open on theirs at the same time Chuck's team did. The team members with the ARs laid down prone while the men with shotguns took different stances. One kneeled and one stood, both using the thin hangar wall along the door jambs as cover. They instantly started firing toward their assigned militia positions.

The folks on the east and west sides fired as well. Haliday watched one man take off toward the center of the building complex and tried to lead his fire on him. Before he could fire on the man, the concrete next to him shattered, causing him to roll for cover. The two men with him continued to fire and eliminated the threat that fired on Haliday. The militia member that was running made it to another position out of their view.

Chuck's team didn't have such good luck. As soon as they opened to fire, they took hits. Chuck fired away, but one of his guys had his shotgun jam on him and as he tried to eject the shell he was hit twice and went down. Chuck continued to fire as his other man pulled the injured guy out of the way and returned to help Chuck. The town's snipers still didn't have any shots on this militia position and couldn't help Chuck's team.

Rob had everyone moved up into the southern positions and now had a couple of guys in the buildings, waiting. He went over to see if he could help Chuck.

Chuck told him the guys were dug in pretty deep and wasn't sure if they would be able to get out of their position. They all backed up and waited and called Haliday for direction.

Haliday told them to send a couple people to his location and he would come over and see what was going on.

Mark took another look around the area. He couldn't spot anyone else so he made his move. He shouldered his AR and pulled out his pistol. He sprang around the corner of the bricks and took aim at two kids; he put his finger to his mouth. He spoke quietly and told them to raise their hands up, which they did.

Mark then had them lay down and zip-tied their hands together. The kids were maybe 10 or 11 years old, a boy and girl. Mark was shocked.

"Here, kids, you hide here behind the bricks while we go play army." It was appalling in every sense. He didn't like what he did next. He stood them up, and he called out to their parents.

The parents were on the west side of the brick yard. The parents froze when they heard Mark's voice. All they heard was, "Drop your weapons and approach your children with your hands raised high!"

They had no idea who had their kids or what the person would do to them.

The husband suggested he sneak over across the street and try and come up behind them.

The wife protested.

The little girl cried out, "Mommy, I'm scared! One of the bad men has us!"

Mark's blood boiled at this. *He* was a bad man?

Haliday walked in to Chuck's building and looked down at the man from Chuck's team who had gotten hit. The man was losing blood and would need help fast. Haliday grabbed his mirror and took a quick glance out of the door. No sooner had he put it in the doorway than the militia fired. The shots were too close for comfort and one came through the thin steel just above his head.

Haliday looked over at Rob. "Listen, get a few more guys up here. Have them take over here in the building. In the meantime, Chuck and I will take our teams and enter that big-ass building they are using to keep all the food and supplies in. If we can get to the west end, we can take them out."

Rob signaled for a couple more guys that were outside to come over and he said he said he would stay as well.

Chuck and Haliday got their teams together. They needed Rob to draw the fire. As soon as they started, Haliday and Chuck bolted for the door to the big building.

They got the door open and entered quickly without any tannerite can. They all kept low and looked around. They were greeted by stacks upon stacks of food piled high.

Over at the main gate, not only had the smoke and fire given the militia a chance to retreat, it also gave a few townspeople the chance to move forward, close to the line of cars. Four had rushed forward and then laid down waiting for the flames to subside. This was as close as anyone had managed to get to the admin building.

Mark was waiting for the kids' parents to approach. He heard the woman say, "Don't hurt them. I'm on my way."

Mark yelled out, "Both of you! I said both of you!"

There was a pause and she said her husband was injured.

Mark couldn't believe these people were playing games with their kids. "Listen lady, I have two guys in the woods! If he ain't injured, he will be! You wanna keep playing games?"

He heard the man, "Okay, we're both coming out! Don't shoot!"

Mark waited and both of them came walking out, hands held high.

Mark called out, "Brad, come on in, but tell your brother to keep his sights on these two!"

Brad came out slowly with his rifle raised.

Mark ordered the couple to the ground with their hands behind their backs. Brad approached and zip-tied them.

The zip ties came in handy. They were cable ties from an electric supply shop, and Haliday had made sure everyone took plenty with them. He told them to tuck them in their boots, their ball caps, waist bands, wherever they felt comfortable putting them. This was the exact reason why.

Haliday and Chuck made it to the west end of the hangar; no one was there. Haliday looked at the wall and saw no doors or windows. Up toward the top, he spotted two large air vents. Against the wall was a rolling ladder. He slowly moved it over about 10 feet and climbed up. He pulled out his Leatherman and used it to pry open one of the louvers.

He looked down. This was going to be the perfect angle for the one position; unfortunately the next position down the line would have clear shots and the lack of protection would be sure death for whoever was up there. He looked at the other vent. Two shooters could do it; just had to figure out how to get someone else up there.

Haliday kept looking around for something to use. "Anybody have any ideas on a platform for a second shooter?" he asked. "We have to be able to get down quickly, too."

Everyone was looking around. Most of the hangar space had been cleared for the food storage. There wasn't a whole lot they could use.

Brad and Mark thoroughly searched the couple and the kids. Mark walked them over to their Chevy K-5 Blazer and opened it up. He looked around a bit and grabbed some rope and tied them up to a pallet of bricks. He walked back over and grabbed a couple of blankets and tossed them over the kids. It was time to head back to the compound.

Mark called in and told Rob about the four prisoners. He then made his way back with Brad.

Rob went over the situation in his head as it currently stood. They had made some good ground, but needed more. Once they fully secured the south end they could close the noose a little more.

Haliday looked at everyone. "It's not that high. Grab some pallets, quickly. Take the goods off of them if you have to. We need five or six."

With the first three ready, Haliday stood them on edge and formed a triangle. He laid one on top to form a platform. They piled up two more and he moved the stairs over and got up on the platform. "You guys keep it steady," Haliday said.

He pried the louvers of this vent open as far as he could. "This will work," he said, "someone else get up here quick. You guys keep this steady."

Chuck got on the stairs and they were both ready. They would look out the vents and fire when Rob did.

Haliday clicked his mic. "Whenever you're ready, Rob."

Rob and a couple others fired out the door of his building and Haliday and Chuck fired on their targets from theirs. After emptying a complete magazine, Haliday scrambled down. Chuck followed not even a second later.

Sure enough, the walls around the vents opened up with a few holes. One second longer for either of them and they would have been hit. They immediately cleared away from the west wall of the hangar building as it took a few more rounds.

Haliday called over to Rob. "How'd we do?"

Rob said he would check, as he wasn't sure.

Rob got down low and took a quick peek out the door. It looked like the position they fired on was neutralized.

"Wait a second," Rob said.

There came another volley of fire. A man in the position Haliday had fired into had run toward the buildings and into another position as other militia laid down cover fire.

Rob came back on. "Looks like the two guys close to us are dead and the other position was vacated, but someone is left in it and they are dead or injured."

Mark and Brad were studying the north end now. Still the same problem. They got a few townspeople closer, but not enough. The only thing they could do would be to keep more militia from going in and to keep any militia from coming out.

Rob called Haliday and told him the situation. Haliday acknowledged and told him to get some guys over on the south end to get the casualties out.

Mark sent the four-wheeler with their makeshift medic team over there along with two more guys. He settled down and continued to watch the area. Brad threw out some different ideas, but nothing would seem to work.

"We wait it out," said Mark. He reached in his pocket and pulled out a small bag of jerky and gave Brad a piece and chewed on one himself.

Rob sent two guys over to the militia position. The first townsmen entered the position. He was shot with a pistol four times. The second of Rob's guys rushing the same position fired his rifle into the militia man who had been laying there waiting. The second man yelled over to Rob that it was now secure, but they had lost a man. Rob sent one more guy over to the position.

The four-wheeler made it in and they evacuated the wounded and the dead using the two four-wheelers. The injured were taken next door to the police station and the dead were placed next door to that one for the time being. The medical staff got busy working on everyone.

The group had managed to take full control of the south end of the airport and some key buildings. They also controlled the main gate entrance now. The next push would be even harder.

Haliday went into the food storage building and came back out with a case of water. He joined the rest of the townspeople on the south side of the compound. He opened a bottle and drank it down. Most of the other guys with him did the same.

He had a few cases of water taken out and a bunch of granola bars and snacks so they could distribute them to the townspeople that were fighting. They had been fighting almost six hours. They started around 0800 and they only had about four hours of daylight left now. Haliday sat down and cracked open a fruit roll-up.

During the lull in activity Mark had a couple of people gather the militia prisoners and take them to the jail. They had rigged up a wood stove, courtesy of the local Tractor Supply Store, and it was nice and warm in there. Mark asked Haliday for more food and Haliday had it sent. They loaded up a bunch and took it over to the police station as well.

Haliday was drinking some more water when he stopped and dropped the bottle. He held his hand up in a fist which indicated everyone should hold and he listened. He called Mark on the radio. "We have a deuce inbound. It sounds like it's coming from the south."

Haliday started shouting out orders. Everyone started running in different directions. "Mark, get over here quick! Everyone, heads up! Inbound bad guys from the south!"

The deuce was barreling down the road.

Everything was quiet and as Haliday stood there he could hear the shifting of the engine. He knelt down behind one of the militia emplacements they had taken when he saw it approach.

There was a small three-vehicle convoy; the deuce along with a pickup and an older van.

The three vehicles entered the south fence line breach and spread out. He called Mark. "Mark, where you at, buddy? Any idea what's going on?"

Mark told him to wait a minute as he was checking out the convoy from his position, then called back. "Okay, I have the info. We have problems."

Mark gave him the rundown of what was going on. "The deuce is in the middle and the other vehicles are left and right of it about twenty yards and it looks like a makeshift spearhead formation. The vehicles look like the drivers are armored up. They make the approach with any foot troops, and you're screwed.

"The deuce has an upper turret. The pickup truck has an armored portal on the back of it as well. I count six people in the van, two in the pickup, and eight in the deuce. All Russian camo and all carrying ARs except for the deuce and pickup turrets. They have 7.62s for sure. Roger, they have a ton of ammo with them. The deuce has armor on the sides of the bed, maybe thirty-six inches tall."

Haliday said, "That's wonderful. The guys in the woods can't take shots until they get closer and once that happens they are close enough to run us out. We're going to lose the ground we have taken and a lot more lives. Mark, coordinate what you can. Do what you can. Let me know. Make sure the north holds their positions and keeps the militia busy."

Haliday told them that anybody on the east and west sides that could take shots at these guys should do it. "Go for the tires, go for the gunners and concentrate on the rest after that."

The snipers had to hit the gunners and drivers. They had to stop the vehicles.

Mark came on the radio again. "Roger, they are finalizing their plans and gear."

Haliday looked at his watch. It had been about 40 minutes from the time he had first heard the deuce. They were toward the end of the runway and only had about 3/4 of a mile before they reached Haliday's position.

The vehicles started moving slowly forward. The deuce was in front with the others thirty-five feet behind and off to the sides. The pickup had a driver and two gunners in it. The deuce had a driver, gunner, and four men in the back. The van just had a driver and one man who had slid the side door open. The other five men moved on foot.

Mark called and told everyone the militia was moving. The pace was slow and the suspense was getting on everyone's nerves. The townsmen in the tree line started to take some shots at the vehicles, but they were still too far away.

The militia accompanying the vehicles was keeping a sharp lookout to the sides and behind them. The anticipation grew.

The convoy was much closer now and the tree line on both sides erupted with fire. The first vehicle to take a hit was the deuce. A back tire was hit but that was like a scratch and didn't phase it. The deuce paused and one of the guys on foot dropped its tailgate and the militia climbed in. They continued to move toward Haliday's hole-up.

The gunners in the deuce lit up the tree line where they spotted a sniper. The man was hit and started to fall out of the tree, but just dangled from his tree stand harness. He was wounded and trying to free himself as he continued to take fire from the militia. After just a few more moments he went limp after sustaining more hits.

The man who had been using the front loader as cover was in a bind now and was exposed no matter where he went. He looked around for a way to get to safety rather than stay in place. He made a run for another position but the pickup truck gunner took aim and hit him twice. He tumbled forward and fell. The gunner put another round into the man.

The men in the tree line fired again and hit the van's front tire. The tire deflated and the rim dug into the grass and dirt, slowing it down. The rear tires started to spin as they lost traction trying to propel the vehicle forward. The van only made it another 25 feet before it wouldn't move anymore. It was now stuck. The militia men inside readied themselves to make a run for it.

The deuce paused so the men from the stopped van could get in. The van driver leapt out and ran for the deuce as the man at the side door of the van jumped down. His feet had barely hit the ground when Mark fired half of a magazine into the guy. The militia returned fire on Mark, who was lying prone behind one of the metal portals the shop had built.

Mark could hear the rounds strike the steel plate and the woods around him. He called out some instructions to keep him covered. He would have to wait it out for a little bit before being able to get to a safer position. The assault from the front, and now the rear, caught them off-guard. They reformed their plans to adjust for the increase in militia members fighting them.

The deuce and pickup started to move forward again. The pickup now moved in a bit closer to the deuce so they could cover each other's vehicles. This was an amateur move and put the militia in greater danger. Concentrating troops in a small area like this would make it easier to take out more troops at once.

They could gun it and rush Haliday's positions and then all jump out near the emplacements, but that was suicide.

Mark called Haliday and told him he was still pinned down.

Haliday was only able to grab a quick peek once in a while. The gunners were a threat and were keeping him and his men down low and unable to fire back. The pickup and deuce made it to about 200 yards away from Haliday and slowed again.

Haliday didn't know what to do. He had to think quickly. They could try and bail over to the buildings and fight inside, but that wasn't any better. They would be pinned inside with no way out. Haliday was ticked off that they didn't have a better grip on their own rear cover, especially since this was how they got in themselves. He heard a voice on the radio.

"We're coming up from the rear, you copy? We have two bikes and the Jeep. Do not fire on us."

Haliday told everyone on the radio to pass the word. "Do not fire on the vehicles behind the trucks; they are good guys. Concentrate your fire on the militia vehicles."

The tree line lit up again as people fired on the militia and the militia then fired back.

Straight up behind the militia roared two motorcycles and the Jeep. Blake was on his bike and Alan on the KLR. They both went for the cover of the van and took up their positions then fired at the advancing militia from the rear. The first two militia to go down were the two guys in the back of the pickup truck.

The driver didn't know where the rounds had come from. He gunned it and took off for one of the emplacements. His goal now was to get out of the open and into the emplacements occupied by Haliday's group. They didn't want to remain targeted any longer.

The truck bounced violently across the open field as it increased speed. He plowed into the emplacement, crushing one of the men underneath the pickup and the sandbags. The other man had jumped out of the way. The driver got out and fired on the man.

Rob was one position over and saw what happened. He fired and dropped the man and then ducked back down.

They were taking heavy fire from the deuce now. One of the militia in the deuce looked back and his eyes widened with horror. There was this Jeep right behind them with two guys at the roll bar firing into the back of the deuce. The Jeep was only 50 yards behind them. Mike was driving and Kevin and Randy had ARs blazing away. They went through three magazines each in a matter of about a minute.

Mike hit the brakes and swung left, then stopped. They now had Alan and Blake by the van and Mike, Randy, and Kevin by the Jeep, and both groups were behind the militia deuce. The fire was concentrated on the deuce. The deuce slowed and the driver gunned the engine trying to get it to move faster. The two front tires and a couple of the rear tires were flat.

One of the men jumped down from the back and raised the tailgate up. They wanted to protect the men in the back from more fire. They were basically like fish in a barrel.

Blake took aim as the man was climbing up and hit him three times in the back. One of the guys in the back of the deuce had tried to help lift the guy in and one of the snipers took him out with a head shot. The man just hung over the tailgate of the deuce with the other man lying on the ground.

Mark got up and headed along the east side and stopped. He popped some tear gas into the 37mm launcher and put three rounds close to the deuce. The men inside scrambled to put on gasmasks. Mark fired into the tank of the deuce multiple times and watched the fuel drain out. He was about to launch a flare when he saw a couple of white flags waving.

He called Haliday on the radio. "I punctured the tank after I fired some tear gas over there. I was about to launch some flares when I saw two white flags. They want to surrender. What do you think?"

Haliday said, "Let them."

Haliday called out a ceasefire. It took about 15 minutes but eventually all of the firing stopped.

Haliday called over to Mike. "How far away from them are you?"

Mike said, "About fifty or sixty yards. What do you want me to do?"

Haliday asked him, "Can you hear them? Can you talk to them?"

"Hold on," Mike said. "I'll check." He yelled over to the deuce. "Can you hear me?"

Someone answered back, "Yeah, we can hear you! We want to surrender!"

Mike told Haliday and asked him what to do next. Haliday told him to repeat a set of directions he gave mike.

Mike did just that. "You are fully surrounded with snipers and gunmen! Do as you are told and no harm will come to you! If you fire we will fire back on everyone! Do you understand?"

The reply was yes.

Mike continued. "Driver, get out first and walk to the rear of the truck! Keep your hands held high!"

The driver got out and did as he was told.

"Gunner, you're next!"

The gunner complied as well.

"Now open the tailgate of the truck!" Mike demanded.

The driver and gunner opened the tailgate. Inside was a mix of dead, wounded, and men who had given up on the fight.

Haliday told Mark, Blake, Alan, Randy, and Kevin to keep their weapons trained on them.

Mike spoke again. "One by one exit the back of the truck! You must remove everyone, including the dead and injured! We want you fifty feet from the back of the truck!"

The militia carried out the orders.

Haliday and Chuck moved in slowly with rifles ready. They approached the deuce and checked the cab with a mirror, then moved toward the back and the bed, which was empty except for some weapons and gear.

Haliday took over from there. "I want all of you not injured to move forward ten yards and stop!"

The men moved forward and Haliday called Blake and Mike over. Haliday told them to check the dead and injured for any weapons of any type. "Take everything off them," Haliday said.

After they did this, they tossed everything in the back of the deuce. Haliday told the other men to spread out 10 feet, lay down, cross their legs, and place their hands on the backs of their heads.

Each one was searched and all of their gear was removed from them. Haliday had them all bound up. He called and asked if any of the nurses or doctors were available.

One of the doctors came by and had another man with him.

"Who's that?" Haliday asked.

The doctor answered, "He's from the fire department. He's a paramedic."

Haliday told them both thank you. "Can you take a look at these men please?"

"Sure thing," the doctor said. They did a quick triage of the men.

Sixteen militia members had assaulted them. Five were still alive, seven were dead, and four wounded. The doctor said that of the wounded, two more would die within hours. The other two were taken to the makeshift hospital under guard. Haliday asked the militia who was in charge.

One of the men spoke up and said he was the leader.

Haliday walked over to him and said, "It's time to end this thing now. You have women and children in there. You have women and children waiting for you guys out there, and many of them are not going to see their family members alive again. If we continue, it's going to be a lot more. You ready to help end this?"

The man looked around at his fellow militia, the dead on the ground, and then the two dying men. "Yes, let's end it."

Chapter 35

Still at the airport compound Haliday called Blake over to him. Blake walked up and they stepped aside. Haliday looked at him. "Who decided to rush in and help?" Haliday asked.

Blake hesitated a bit and answered. "Well, we heard how things were going and we got our gear ready. We headed this way and hung out about halfway between here and the house. When I heard you call in the deuce, I told them we needed to go now and we all headed this way. Everyone agreed that we needed to help."

Haliday said, "Good job, kid. You saved a lot of lives here. That made all the difference."

They walked over to the militia men and Haliday called a few guys in to transport the prisoners. He looked over at the leader and said, "Pick one more man to negotiate and then call in to the compound and tell them to send out two people. They'll be safe, and if it doesn't work out, they can return."

He cut the man's hands loose and looked around. "Brad, you stay with me."

The militia man then called in and spoke to the HQ.

Haliday listened to the conversation.

"You guys in there don't understand. These people just handed us our asses. We have five out sixteen of us left, you hear that? Five of us." The militia was being honest with their HQ. "Our wives and kids aren't coming anywhere near this place. Hell, if they are smart they left already. You understand what's happening out here? Do you guys understand what will happen in there?"

The man continued. "Listen, they control the south end of the compound and that includes the food. You can't get anyone in or out of the main gate because they have that under their control. It's just a matter of time before they continue forward and push everyone into the HQ building, where they'll probably burn it down. Negotiating a ceasefire is the best we can get."

The HQ replied to him. "They can bring their group in and we can talk in here."

Haliday looked at the guy and shook his head no.

The man spoke, "Listen, you're safer out here and they ain't buying that come inside BS."

HQ said, "All right, we're coming out; give us about five minutes."

Haliday put everyone on high alert and they watched as two guys made their way out of the admin building.

They walked up and looked Haliday up and down.

Haliday returned their study and said, "You guys want a date or what? I don't have time for bullshit here. You guys have caused me enough grief to last a lifetime."

Rob looked at them. He knew one of the guys, but wasn't sure about the other.

Haliday said, "This is Brad, Chuck, and Rob; they will negotiate along with me."

One man looked at him. "You're an outsider. What gives you the right?"

Haliday answered, "Listen, shit-head, I'm not going to explain it. If you'd rather we continue to reduce your ranks, we can end the conversation now and go right back at it. Now you can talk nice or you can go in there and explain to everyone why they are going to die. So this is what will happen.

"First, each and every one of you will surrender. You'll be placed in custody until these guys here decide who to try and who to release. They will hold the trials in a public venue with an impartial jury. The sentences will be final. No appeals. There were some serious crimes committed here. That's not negotiable.

"Second," he continued, "any and all food here will remain in the townspeople's custody and that will be distributed according to how they see fit. There is a community here and everyone will come together and share resources. You guys will be included. You will not be leaving with what you think is yours; too many people paid the price for it already. That's not negotiable.

"Third, your firearms will be seized along with all ammunition. Your homes will be searched. These firearms will not be returned until they see fit to return them to you. This prevents you guys from banding together and playing warlords again. That's not negotiable.

"Fourth, you guys are responsible for any women and children from your group who are now left on their own. You'll take them in and you'll take care of them. I don't mean servitude; I mean as part of your family. We will be checking on them. That's not negotiable.

"Fifth, you will provide burial for each and every person that has died here. You will dig their graves, you will bury them with respect and it will be done with the utmost dignity. You will do so at the sheriff's house," he added. "That's not negotiable. You have any questions?"

"I do," one of the militia said as he moved forward a bit. "What exactly do we get to negotiate?"

Haliday smiled at him. "Your life. That's what you get to negotiate. You take the terms and live or you roll the dice and see what comes out of it that way. You look smart enough to understand that. I'll give you guys a few minutes to talk."

Haliday and his group backed off a bit.

There was some arguing going on for a minute, and then three of the militia members walked over. "Okay, we accept."

Haliday pointed over at the fourth man. "What about him? Is he going to be trouble?"

One answered, "No he shouldn't be."

Haliday said, "Okay, he stays here then." He pointed. "You and you go back in and tell them what's happening. Call me when you're ready. We'll walk you through the process."

Haliday moved away and talked to Chuck, Brad, and Rob. "You guys good with that, I assume?"

Rob said, "Yeah, how do we try them though?"

Chuck spoke up. "I'll help with that."

"That's good," Haliday said. "You'll also need to set up some form of government rule to keep things civil."

The radio crackled.

"They're ready," Haliday said.

Haliday started with the fighting positions. He would empty one and bring the people in. He emptied the second and then had Rob's guys move into the first. Eventually all of the positions were manned by Rob's group. He had the people come out of the admin building two at a time and bring the injured with them.

Everyone was outside now and disarmed. Haliday had them all bound and ready for transport. He'd be sending them to the county jail just down from the police department and would use locks and chains on the cells. They would be the community's problem now. An hour later they were all in cells. The injured were tended to by the medical staff who volunteered to help.

Haliday walked over to the building where they had kept the prisoners. They entered it and found almost a dozen people inside. They were all still alive, but some were badly beaten and they were hungry and thirsty. They tended to these people and moved them to safety. Haliday asked them who was captured in the woods with the motorcycle and a man and woman raised their hands.

"You guys can leave when you want; we'll get you to your boat when you're ready," Haliday informed them.

They went through each of the buildings and made sure each was empty and that they had all of the firearms and ammunition gathered up. This was all placed in the admin building. They made sure nothing that could be used as a weapon was left in the buildings at all, especially in the buildings used for housing.

Haliday rounded up all of his people and they stood around and talked for a bit. He told Rob to make sure the people in the jail got food and water and had blankets so they would be warm enough. "I'd get their work detail busy and get the bodies handled right away. Use the chain gang format," Haliday said.

Rob looked at Haliday. "You mentioned this earlier, why the sheriff's house?"

Haliday told him that if the sheriff ever saw freedom again, he would need a reminder every day.

"Rob, keep this area under heavy security at all times, and move everything to a secure location as soon as you can." Haliday looked around. What a hell of a couple weeks it had been. "Rob, good luck, we'll be in touch."

They shook hands and parted ways. Haliday and Mark took the rest of the guys and they all headed home.

They arrived back at the house. They all passed on dinner and opted for showers and fresh clothes instead. Afterwards they settled for soup.

They sat around in silence. Kayla had security set up for the night. It would be Rich, Bev, Karen, Sarah, Dawn, Diana, David, and herself taking turns tonight.

They let the guys sleep through the night.

Chapter 36

It had been three days since the assault on the airport. Haliday sat at the table drinking his coffee and eating his breakfast burrito. Both Max, the mutant dog, and Romeo, the cat, were eyeing his plate.

"I don't think so, animals," he said.

Romeo had his own food and Max was given scraps and leftovers to eat. The byproduct of that, however, was mutant dog farts, which Max seemed to enjoy sharing with Haliday.

Blake was sitting next to him and Alan was across the table with Kevin. Mark was sitting in a chair next to Lisa, who was doing much better now. In a couple more days, she would be okay, and as long as Haliday was certain no infection or issues arose, he would see them head back with Mike and Linda to Mark's parents' farm.

They all reflected on the past couple of weeks.

Kayla walked over and sat down as well. "Hey, Dad," she said, "how much more of this we gonna have to deal with?"

He looked at her. "I hope none, but we still don't know what the hell is going on. I'd really like to know what the hell the government is doing about this, and what the hell even happened. I think the immediate threat is over for now. I don't suspect we'll get a lot of activity during the winter. Not sure that any plow trucks are working these days, so it'll be hard to get around."

He continued on with his thoughts. "We'll have to get a good grip on the inventory of everything we have. One thing will be to hide as much of the food as possible now that people think we are loaded down with stocks of everything. That will be easy enough though. We'll cover the doorways downstairs with the paneling covers to hide them again. We can move some to the other caches and set up some more alarms out there."

This they would do within the next week.

For the most part everyone was in rather good shape as far as health or injuries went. David was a little worse off. He would heal up, but the leg injury would definitely leave him with a limp and the cold winter days would remind him of the injury.

The loss of the leg would have been much worse, so he was lucky. Both he and his son, Bobby, would have the battle scars to go along with their stories. Haliday teased Bobby, saying it was Bobby's lobotomy scar.

Diana was the one who would get mad at Haliday. Her arm was sticking out in a makeshift brace so her collar bone would heal. She had about six weeks of being in the contraption, according to the doctor.

Haliday would walk up and try to hang some of his laundry on it to dry. Everyone but she thought it was funny. Once he taped a piece of jerky on it and she couldn't reach it to take it off. Since she was a vegan, it drove her nuts.

Alan's face had become infected, but the doctor got it cleaned out and he changed the antibiotics. The doctor had cut a little tissue away in the process, which was enough to leave a reminder every day when Alan shaved.

Alan thought they would nickname him Scarface but they called him Gash instead. He insisted on Scarface once, but Haliday had pointed at Alan's pants and said in his best Al Pacino voice, "Is that your little friend?" He emphasized 'little' and Alan never mentioned it again as they all had broken into laughter.

Alan's wife Nancy would set Elizabeth, Bobby, Matthew, and Teresa down and home school them a little bit each day. No one had any idea if or when school would ever be back in session. They could not afford to have the kids not learn the basics and whatever else they could teach them. They would all have chores to do in order to help out.

After a couple of days, Mike, Linda, Mark, and Lisa were packed and ready to go. Haliday made sure they had ammo and sent a couple of welfare buckets along with them even though Mark insisted they had brought some of their own and had enough at his dad's, not to mention what Haliday previously left.

Haliday told them if they needed to that they could come back, bring his parents and they would co-op the house across the street or there at the cabin. Gas would be at a premium and traveling back and forth would be hard, even if it was only about 20 miles.

Karen, Rich, and Bev settled into routines playing solitaire, puzzle books, reading, and doing their share around the cabin. They seemed the least affected by the change so far. They'd miss their Kindles and casino trips and online games, but that was something they hadn't had all their lives and could do without. The kids were the ones who would be suffering technological withdrawals.

Dawn oversaw the horses and their care. When Diana was healed, she would help, too. They did a lot of reading all of the time as it was, so they would pop on the computer and read or play games. The vegan and vegetarian cooking they were used to would help the group out when meat became scarce, and would help extend their current stores.

Sarah took charge of cooking and kitchen duties. Everyone helped and took turns assisting her. Sarah had long been resigned to the fate of Erik, but didn't mention it at all. Elizabeth was told he was still out helping people and she was content with that. Eventually they would plan on placing a marker by an empty grave to put him to rest in their hearts.

Kevin and Randy used the ham to keep in touch with their parents and their other brother in Texas. It was still puzzling that they had electricity, but as time went on things were made clearer as to why that was. They kept busy playing video games, chopping wood, and getting more familiar with the toys Haliday had around. They were also learning new tactics just in case they were needed.

Blake and Kayla always joined Kevin and Randy to keep their skills updated and fresh. Surprisingly, the two friends were still maintaining nothing but a friendship, which was fine with Haliday. He wasn't ready for any crib lizards to be crawling around, as he called them..

It was quite a mix of people in the group, but they all worked together rather well.

Haliday had called Rob to see how everything was going. He asked them about the prisoners and what had happened with the trials. Rob started with the sheriff who was the militia commander. He was still in fairly bad shape and they put him under house arrest.

When they went to check on him the next day, they found him hanging from a rope inside his garage with a note that just said, 'I'm sorry.' He would have been hung anyway.

Chuck had taken over as the chief law enforcement official for the area. He had made sure each and every one of the prisoners was tried. Most were assigned to hard labor on chain gangs performing burials, clearing the roads of cars, chopping wood, and anything else they needed done. If they didn't work one day, they didn't eat. The children and a few of the wives were released.

Some were allowed to leave the area. Presumably they met with the ones who were waiting for their husbands who had launched the last attack on the south end of the airport.

Five people were hung for their involvement with the militia, the torture of the police chief and the other prisoners. It was later found out that several citizens were summarily executed for almost no reason by some of the militia men.

Brad and a few of the veterans in the area were put in charge of forming a regional defense coalition group. Haliday made it clear to them to avoid using the term *militia* at all costs.

They had quite a complement of equipment with what they had seized and what they already had. As word spread they were able to bolster their ranks. Haliday and Mark would be helping them with training.

Rob asked Haliday how they had been so fortunate as to take out the militia like they did. Haliday told him it was one thing to put on a uniform and call yourself something, and it was another thing to gather the people, to educate them, to train them, to keep up their skill sets and *be* something. This incident was proof of that explanation.

"Rob," he said, "you can want in one hand and crap in the other and I can tell you which one will fill up first. You have to not only want it, but do what it takes to make it happen as well."

Rob was heading up the interim governing body and he would see to it that some proper elections were held and people put in place to help transition the area into the new rule. Rob would end up doing a great job getting that in place and the area to work together through the crisis. He was their best bet.

A couple of weeks later Haliday was at the ham again. He had made quite a few contacts across the entire U.S. The urban areas were in full crisis now. Just about everyone was beyond hungry. They were now starving. People were pulling out all the stops and doing what they needed to survive. Looting became scavenging, self-defense bordered murder. It was utter chaos.

He took notes on all of it. His map was just unbelievable to look at. Alaska and Hawaii were fully untouched. Most of California was operational along the coast, as was Oregon and Washington State. The southern border, like he discovered earlier, was intact. The lower third of Florida was intermittent with functionality. It was almost as if those areas had been untouched in order to preserve the border control of the country.

A lot of Canada was fine with the exception of the southern parts of the country bordering the U.S. The U.S. east coast was devastated though as well. It was a weird puzzle to try and figure out. He had heard most of the navy had been fully recalled and had taken station off the coasts. Most of the military overseas remained there, however. The U.S. was the only country really hit by the EMP and nobody could explain why. No country or terror group claimed responsibility.

Still, there was no major military movement from the bases, and no federal mobilization of FEMA, DHS, or any other agency. There was actually very little from the government in the form of communications. Haliday went over his notes again. He made some radio calls across the U.S. and got some more answers. He heard information from some other countries as well. He started piecing more together.

It all made more sense now. He had heard bits and pieces, but it was clearer now. He never thought this would have happened. He called the group together for a meeting.

This is what he said. "We all know the SHTF. I think I know who took the dump and I think I know who turned the fan on high. There's a lot of manure being spread around. I don't think spring is going to be bright and cheerful.

"It seems we have a civil war here in the U.S. Not north versus south, but large groups comprised of the military, the government, and some other group calling themselves the Constitution Restoration Army. Right now with all of the propaganda, we don't know who is with whom, or who is good or bad. Not sure which of them popped the nukes or EMPs over our own country to cripple us, but we'll find out eventually.

"We have a lot of work to do people," he said with finality. "I have a feeling we aren't out of the woods yet."

Afterword:

Although this is a work of fiction, it is meant to demonstrate how easily the world we live in can be impacted by those events which we can not control. This is not to show you what <u>will</u> happen, but instead it is meant to show you what <u>can</u> happen. The trigger event depicted here has become far too real of a threat in today's technological age. There also exists, however, far too many events that could occur with the same basic ending result.

The actions of the characters in this story may seem far reaching to most. What we need to ask ourselves before judging these actions is a simple question: What will you do to ensure the safety, security, and survival of you and your family?

When mass disasters occur it is true that the best in people will shine through. It is unfortunate, however, that others will use the opportunity to show their worst.

Religious faiths around the globe teach preparedness to one extent or another, from a few simple days to a year or more. The government suggests food, water, shelter, and first aid supplies for a minimum of three days for each person in a household; pets included. Disasters of all magnitudes can happen within seconds.

Are you ready?

About the author:

Matthew D. Mark was born and raised in Michigan, is a U.S. Army veteran, former police officer, and has worked in private security. He has instructed in self-defense, chemical deterrent, and force continuum. He enjoys his family, outdoor activities, and firearms as his main hobbies.

Watch for the sequel, "Dark Days, Troubled Times"

www.ingramcontent.com/pod-product-compliance
Lightning Source LLC
Chambersburg PA
CBHW070345260626
47161CB00001B/17